"There is no doubt whatever about the influence of architecture and structure upon human character and action. We make our buildings, and afterwards they make us. They regulate the course of our lives."

—Winston Churchill,
addressing the English Architectural Association, 1924

THE
BLACK
LOCOMOTIVE

A NOVEL, GRAPHIC

RIAN
HUGHES

PICADOR

First published 2021 by Picador
an imprint of Pan Macmillan
The Smithson, 6 Briset Street, London EC1M 5NR
EU representative: 1st Floor, The Liffey Trust Centre
117–126 Sheriff Street, Upper Dublin 1 D01 YC43
Associated companies throughout the world
www.panmacmillan.com

ISBN 978-1-5290-7442-0 HB
ISBN 978-1-5290-7445-1 TPB

Text, design and photography by Rian Hughes
except Chapter 26: 55 Broadway, RIBA Collections
Ultravox! *My Sex* lyrics by John Foxx ©1977, by permission of John Foxx
Some CADs adapted from stock sources
Churchill portrait p389 by Yousuf Karsh, public domain/creative commons
Library and Archives Canada, e010751643

1 3 5 7 9 8 6 4 2

A CIP catalogue record for this book is available from the British Library.

Printed and bound by CPI Group (UK) Ltd, Croydon, CR0 4YY

Visit www.picador.com to read more about all our books
and to buy them. You will also find features, author interviews and
news of any author events, and you can sign up for e-newsletters
so that you're always first to hear about our new releases.

+++

MY SEX

WAITS FOR ME

LIKE A MONGREL WAITS

DOWNWIND ON A TIGHTROPE LEASH

MY SEX

IS A FRAGILE ACROBAT

SOMETIMES I'M A NOVOCAINE SHOT

SOMETIMES I'M AN AUTOMAT

MY SEX

IS OFTEN SOLO

SOMETIMES IT SHORT CIRCUITS THEN

SOMETIMES IT'S A GOLDEN GLOW

MY SEX

IS INVESTED IN

SUBURBAN PHOTOGRAPHS

SKYSCRAPER SHADOWS ON A CAR CRASH OVERPASS

MY SEX

IS SAVAGE, TENDER

IT WEARS NO FUTURE FACES

OWNS JUST RANDOM GENDER

MY SEX

HAS A WANTING WARDROBE

I STILL EXPLORE

OF ALL THE BODIES I KNEW AND THOSE I WANT TO KNOW

MY SEX

IS A SPARK OF ELECTRO-FLESH

LEASED FROM THE TICK OF TIME

AND GEARED FOR SYNCHROMESH

MY SEX

IS AN IMAGE LOST IN FADED FILMS

A NEON OUTLINE

ON A HIGH-RISE OVERSPILL

MY SEX

+++

©1977 CHRISTOPHER THOMAS ALLEN / DENNIS LEIGH / WILLIAM CURRIE / ULTRAVOX! /
UNIVERSAL MUSIC PUBLISHING GROUP

13 SCHEDULE

It had been designated Anomaly 36.

The previous thirty-five anomalies had all been examined, evaluated, excavated and catalogued; then work had continued on the undocumented Crossrail tunnel extension under central London, the one that would never appear on any map.

They had been diverse: Victorian sewers, forgotten telecommunications cables, eighteenth-century churchyards. A plague pit. Orpheus, playing his harp to an audience of animals, on a Roman mosaic floor. That kind of thing.

This one, Austin Arnold sensed from his foreman's agitation, might pose more of a problem. He had disabled the drilling head and was leaning despondently on the control panel. The air in the cramped cab of the Tunnel Boring Machine was stale and humid and tasted of cement. Austin placed a hand on his shoulder. "Tell me what we have this time, Sanjay."

The TBM was a 140-metre-long worm, faced with a six-metre-diameter cutting head, through which protruded a hundred steel-carbide teeth. The control centre, where they now stood, was positioned a short distance back; what was happening up front was displayed as a series of numerical values and coloured bars on a monitor. Overhead, four more screens showed views of the inside surface of the stationary drill head, but Sanjay was pointing at a series of blinking red warning triangles. "No idea. Whatever it is, it stopped the machine dead. It was making one hell of a racket."

"UXB?"

"If it was wartime ordnance, we wouldn't still be standing here."

"How deep are we?"

"Forty metres. Well below the Bedlam burial ground, Moorlands Marshes and the earliest Roman suburbs. At this level, it's mostly undisturbed London clay and Thanet sand. Silt and gravel. The usual. Nothing's been through here since the last Ice Age mammoth."

The boring machine was a hollow frame, an intricate lattice of girders within a cylindrical sheath. It filled the tunnel – three storeys of walkways, ladders, hydraulics and cabling. It was an impressive piece of engineering, and one his foreman knew intimately. Austin followed him forward along its length, ducked under a gantry and stepped around a conveyor loaded with black silt. Usually this would be carrying the debris away from the drill head, still a short distance in front of them, back along the tunnel to a rail wagon, and thence to landfill on the Thames Estuary.

Today it was stationary. The usual grinding of metal on compacted antediluvian dirt was absent. This was not a good sign; it meant that schedules would not be met. If schedules were not met, Georgia Ash would not be happy. If Georgia Ash was not happy, Austin's life would become even more difficult. He exhaled audibly. "Show me."

A string of strip lights hung over their heads but did little to light the confined space, which receded on both sides into darkness. Austin's voice had acquired an edge absent an hour and a half ago, when he'd checked in at the tally hut above ground. Then, he'd been buoyant and jovial, very much in charge. That mood was fast evaporating.

To complicate matters further, Austin had an unexpected guest with him.

In the tally hut, Austin had issued Lloyd Rutherford with a badge, a fluorescent orange jacket and a hard hat. Rutherford had held the jacket out at arm's length, examining it as if it was some bespoke avant-garde suit. The fabric was smeared with grime and smelled of brick dust and sewage.

He had been an unforeseen complication, foisted on Austin from on high by project leader Georgia Ash herself. Unforeseen complications must be part of his job description.

Rutherford, it transpired, was some kind of artist. Austin had heard that major engineering or aerospace projects often had artists in residence — it was a form of public outreach, a friendly humanities façade sometimes worn by the hard sciences. He'd been promised that this one wouldn't need much, if any, supervision, that he'd already been given the requisite safety training, had full security clearance, that he'd been on the job a while and knew how to keep out from under their feet. Ash had told him just to give the man the space he needed to do his thing, answer any questions he might have, and generally facilitate matters while keeping him out of trouble.

Easy, Austin thought.

Austin wasn't quite sure why this interloper had been granted access, especially right now; but he was used to arbitrary instructions from above, so simply acquiesced and worked it around his schedule.

He'd slipped into his best public tour-guide mode as they threaded their way through the temporary village of wire-mesh fencing and painted plywood, past stacked sections of prefabricated tunnel cladding and reels of cable to the lift, an open signal-red metal box. This ran on a gantry down the side of the enormous concrete-clad cylindrical shaft; fifteen metres wide and thirty deep, it was the main access to the lower levels. The lift was capable of carrying a dozen workers. Today, there had just been the two of them.

Rutherford, for his part, seemed to be happy to quietly tag along, asking the occasional question, taking the odd note, nodding at some arcane piece of technical jargon Austin doubted he understood.

The lift came to rest on a small platform. They stepped out. Far above, a circle of slate-grey autumn sky was crossed by the booms of two cranes, almost meeting at the centre like the hands on a giant clock. A plethora of colour-coded pipes and cables ran up to the lip.

Around them was a breaker's yard jumble of diggers on caterpillar tracks, canisters bearing warning triangles, plastic sheeting and scaffold. Two pairs of parallel tunnels, each large enough to drive a truck through, extended from opposite sides of this central hub.

A functional flatbed vehicle, again in bright orange, was parked on a temporary narrow-gauge railway that ran from a central turntable into each of the tunnels. Austin climbed into the cab and gestured for his charge to follow.

Inside, it had the stripped-down aesthetic of a prototype – bare wiring, raw welding and an unupholstered seat – but it worked, and if it broke down, Austin or one of his cohorts could quickly fix it.

A handle was pulled and the machine lurched forward. Rutherford watched as the arch of the tunnel opening passed over his head, then receded behind them. The grey London light grew even dimmer.

Lights placed high on the curved wall at intervals threw up a series of bright ellipses that shrank into the distance and out of sight around a gentle bend ahead. Pipes and cables hung from supports along the right-hand side, below which ran a narrow walkway of perforated sheet steel. The tunnel itself was cased in sections of concrete cladding, each bearing stencilled numbers and letters: a secret Masonic code that made sense only to initiated construction engineers.

They travelled for fifteen minutes, maybe more. The enclosed space offered few landmarks, just an unchanging tessellated surface. In his early days underground, Austin had found it hard to tell how fast he was moving or how far he had travelled. His peculiar companion didn't seem inclined to talk much, so he let the journey pass in silence, the meditative beat of wheels on track filling his mind.

Presently the engine slowed. The gearing went down an octave, and Austin could see a structure ahead. A frame of white-painted girders, mounted on wheels set at an angle to run along the curving sides of the tunnel. It reached up to the roof, where a guard-railed walkway was visible.

This was the rear end of the tunnel-boring machine, decorated with a warpaint of red and white chevrons and flashing warning lights. The small vehicle they were riding passed between its wheels and into its underbelly.

Austin braked, and they came to a halt alongside a small platform. He lifted a barrier and gestured for Rutherford to step out.

He already knew something was amiss. The machine, usually in operation 24/7, was silent.

Transport 1: **Construction**
Not to scale
Subject to amendment

CAD 18

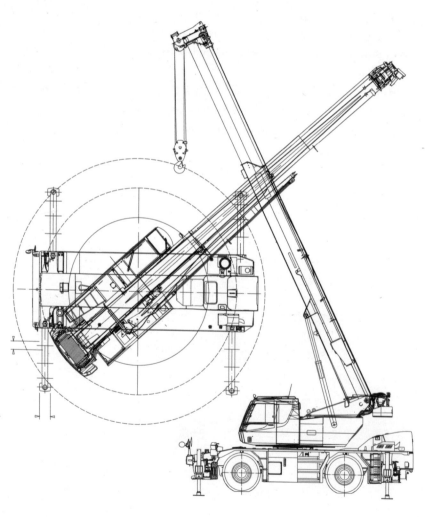

Rutherford stood outside the tally hut in the high-viz jacket and hard hat he had just been issued. He could smell fresh cement: silica, lime, iron ore, fly ash and water. He imagined he could sense the molecular bonds strengthen, the hardening matrix encase the aggregate. It had just rained, and the urban petrichor of airborne particulates and hydrogenated street-food cooking oil thrilled his senses.

This was his first visit to this section of the Crossrail project. Though security was always tight, here it was unlike anything he had encountered before. Airport-style metal detectors. A full-body scan. An expressionless official in a black stab vest with a baton hanging from his belt had gone through his art equipment, flipped through his sketchbook, checked his camera.

His host – Arnold something, Austin? – was waiting on the other side. He gestured for Rutherford to follow him. He was short, clean-shaven, carrying a few pounds; a bead of sweat hung from the end of his nose.

Rutherford looked up, around him. A large space had been cleared between the existing Victorian buildings. The scars of staircases and floors could be seen on the newly revealed sides of what had been tall terraced townhouses. Directly below him, an enormous shaft had been sunk into the cleared ground. Perfectly circular and lined with pristine concrete, he could see its flat bottom tens of metres down, from which smaller tunnels radiated.

The shaft was the negative equivalent of a skyscraper, an absence driven into the ground rather than a presence raised above it. A small lift provided access to the lower levels. Austin Arnold adjusted his hard hat, labelled with a Crossrail logo, and opened the lift's gate.

Austin was giving him the welcome patter. He seemed to have a script. It was mostly a list of achievements, punctuated by statistics: days worked, distance dug, volume of earth excavated. Each was measured not in square metres or tonnes or kilometres, but double-decker buses, blue whales and swimming pools: the SI units of the non-specialist.

He let his attention wander. Austin's voice became a meaningless drone, just another incessant rhythm competing with the activity around them. As they descended, Rutherford scanned the ground below. It was populated by insectile diggers, conveyors and other machines of specialised but obscure function. They had carapaces painted in chevrons of yellow and black, or red and white: the warning aposematism of a subterranean species of mechanical moles. He looked up. The sky was now a grey oculus above them. An occasional large drop of water hit his face.

Machines, and their designers.

Their specificity intrigued him: each had been built for a particular construction role. In this, they were not like human beings. We are built for general purpose use – a brain, connected to a pair of hands with opposable thumbs, with which we can reach out into the world and manipulate it, structure it, remake it in our image. We have evolved to manifest our ideas, make the internal external.

Maybe these mechanical creatures could best be understood as extensions of that human hand: new tools coupled to power sources that can achieve far more than our bare hands and muscle ever could.

We designed them – but did our environment also design *us*?

We came down from the trees to the savannah. In time, we stood taller, we ran faster. We learned tool use, and how to hunt. We wore animal skins, built huts and began to cook our food.

But our self-domestication had unforeseen consequences. Now that we are fully adapted to our urban spaces, in many ways we have devolved, become weaker.

Modern humans cannot survive without clothing, warmth and shelter.

We are still part of nature, but now stand apart from it. The real world is getting ever more inhospitable.

As our food becomes more processed, as our detergents and antibacterial washes get stronger, we become, through lack of exposure, more sensitive to allergens and diseases that would not have fazed our ancestors.

Sometime, long ago, we forgot how to live naked in the world. We have grown soft, and now we need our concrete and glass shelters to protect us from the elements.

In this city, Rutherford rarely heard the mating calls of birds or the breeze threading through branches. Certainly not here, and certainly not today. Instead, he heard the techno-beats of these magnificent machines: the hum of alternators, the hypnotic churning of internal combustion engines, the shush of tyre rubber on tarmac.

It was a life-long, continual background mains hum, like tinnitus.

The symphony of the city.

It was Rutherford's world, and he was in love with it.

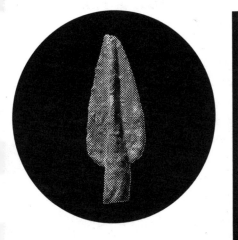

23 FAÇADE

N ow they were up at the business end of the TBM, the massive circular cutting head that the rest of this engineering marvel was designed to support. The ring of hydraulics that pushed the head forwards was visible, and behind that the prefabricated sections of concrete cladding, each transported forwards in turn beneath the frame before being rotated into place and bolted home. Below was an Archimedean screw that lifted the debris up and on to the conveyor. There were perhaps fifteen metres of bare earth visible between the drill head and the completed concrete-clad section behind it.

Rutherford put out his hand and pressed it to the dark dirt. To Austin, despite his background in civil engineering and geology, it had become just a medium to be bored through, something that lay between him and the timely completion of this project. But Rutherford's act gave him small pause: it seemed to be a communion, of sorts. When this stratum was laid down, he reflected, London was not even a crossroads by a riverbank.

Rutherford turned, seemed to focus. He gave Austin his full attention for the first time. Austin was used to dealing with laymen, people for whom the more technical aspects of the job were of little interest, but did he have to be down here, right now? This Anomaly, whatever it was, meant that their jobs had just got a bit more complex.

Sanjay was climbing into the space between the pistons and the head. "Follow me. We pulled the TBM back five metres when we noticed something was up." Austin knew he bore him no ill will; quite the opposite. He would do his assessment as quickly as he could, make his recommendations, and hopefully in a matter of hours the tunnelling machine could continue.

That was not to be.

There was a hatch in the face of the cutting wheel, a black trapezium between the rotating blades. It gave access to the space ahead. Austin knew that beyond lay virgin tunnel, several metres of unclad raw cylinder carved from London's subterranean strata.

Sanjay paused at the threshold. "We knew we'd hit something hard. The hydraulics couldn't move us forwards, and the pressure was building to dangerous levels. We weren't going anywhere. I ordered a shutdown and pullback. At first we assumed it was another granite intrusion. The geology here is pretty thoroughly mapped – we must have sunk over a hundred exploratory boreholes from the surface – but you always miss something."

He jumped through the hatch and dropped out of sight. There was a second or so while he fumbled for his torch, then he shone it back up into Austin's face.

Austin gestured for Rutherford to go through first. "There are rungs below. You can step on the drill head itself, but be careful."

It was a couple of metres to the ground. Sanjay pointed out each foothold with his torch.

In a few moments they were all standing on the bare earth. Sanjay held the torch to his face, cocked his head back. "Over here."

Information 1: **Signage**
Not to scale
Subject to amendment

CAD 26

Flammable

Corrosive

Health hazard

Gas under pressure

Acute toxicity

Serious health hazard

Hazardous to the environment

Explosive

Eye protection must be worn

Safety helmet must be worn

Ear protection must be worn

Respiratory equipment must be worn

Safety boots must be worn

Safety gloves must be worn

Signs for marking obstacles and dangerous locations

Fire alarm

Face protection must be worn

Safety overalls must be worn

Fire extinguisher

Corrosive material

Radioactive material

Overhead load

Flammable material or high temperature

Industrial vehicles

Danger: electricity

General danger

Explosive material

Laser beam

Oxidant material

Non-ionising radiation

Toxic material

Strong magnetic field

Obstacles

Drop

First-aid poster

Biological risk

Low temperature

No access for unauthorised persons

Stretcher

That this section of tunnel even existed was a state secret of the highest order, but by obvious necessity Austin, his crew, and those as far up the immediate chain of command as he was party to were entirely cognizant of its purpose.

It was being built to connect the main west–east Crossrail tunnel to the secret railway station built in the 1930s below Buckingham Palace. This station was connected by a subterranean passage directly to Westminster, accessed via an unassuming door disguised as a closet in a sub-basement below Big Ben itself.

However, like a lot of what went on down here, people had their small areas of expertise, their targets and responsibilities. He had become accustomed to deftly passing over things in conversation that would reveal anything more about this project.

Keep mum, they're not so dumb.

That select group of initiates now seemed to include Rutherford. If he might present security issues, this apparently was not Austin's concern; he was rarely consulted in such matters.

Of course, he'd wanted to record events as they unfolded. As with the photographers who had been documenting the graveyard excavations at Paddington, presumably the higher-ups thought that his presence here might be a way to spin this newest delay. Maybe there would be an exhibition or something after all this was wrapped.

When Rutherford's request had first come through he had casually asked around. Most of the people Austin worked with were not of a particularly philosophical bent, their conversations revolving around the practicalities of the job to hand; they were more comfortable discussing the tensile strength of structural steel than they were the inner motivations of this peculiar man.

Those who had worked alongside him elsewhere in the tunnels and the buildings above ground had said he was pretty self-sufficient. Low maintenance. He asked few questions, and respectfully kept out of their way. He sketched, took photographs with a vintage Rolleiflex, chewed gum incessantly, and seemed to spend much of his time caressing the tunnel wall, pressing his cheek to the concrete cladding, or meditatively sifting fine sand through his fingers.

Austin guessed he was in his mid-thirties. He had the slim, elegant build of someone who did little exercise, but got away with it because they ate far less than they should. His face was angular, clean-shaven, and his short black hair was always immaculately brushed to one side, tapering to the temples. Maybe it was a wig — it reminded Austin of one of those line drawings you could still see in the windows of old-fashioned barbers' shops, a well-groomed man-about-town from another age.

He always wore the same suit. In Austin's limited sartorial judgement, it was a mess. The right sleeve was burned, pocked with charred holes you could poke a finger through, as if he'd pulled it from a house fire; the forearm was missing entirely, the raw edge fraying into a mess of matted threads. The other sleeve was bright fluorescent orange, painted or made from plastic. The back of the jacket and front right-hand side were a brash multicoloured mess of spray paint graffiti and stencilled glyphs, as if he'd fallen asleep one night in an alley and Banksy had accidentally drawn all over him. It was criss-crossed with black and yellow striped warning tape, the kind the police use to circle a crime scene.

This contrasted with his immaculate white slacks and polo neck; these never showed a hint of dirt, a feat in this subterranean industrial environment. They were either freshly laundered each morning or he had an entire wardrobe of them, all identical. Hanging around his neck were a pair of lightweight welding goggles, the right lens criss-crossed with white fractures, the left darker than the darkest sunglasses. His shoes were simple, black laceless slip-ons, always worn over black socks.

He didn't eat with the others in the canteen; he seemed to have some peculiar dietary requirements of his own, and always ate the same meal of sandwiches and tea from a small lunchbox. Some of the staff had tried to engage him in conversation, but his replies had been cryptically monosyllabic. Opinion was divided: Rutherford was either rude, or simply lacked social graces. They left him to do his job, whatever that might be, and he left them to do theirs.

There were other rules that didn't seem to apply to him. Health and safety notwithstanding, he only occasionally tolerated a hard hat, though that peculiar suit of his worked to his advantage, like a kind of high-viz jacket.

More peculiarities came to light: one of the supply team told Austin he'd once walked up behind him, unheard over the din of a pneumatic drill. He was holding a small Moleskine notebook, folded back upon itself at the spine, and was using a page to take a rubbing from the surface of a steel-reinforced foundation block.

Another story had come Austin's way from a quantity surveyor he played Scrabble with on Thursday lunchtimes. He'd noticed Rutherford standing directly behind a diesel generator. He could barely see him, enveloped as he was in black smoke; but he was sure his eyes were shut, he had a beatific smile on his face, and was breathing deeply.

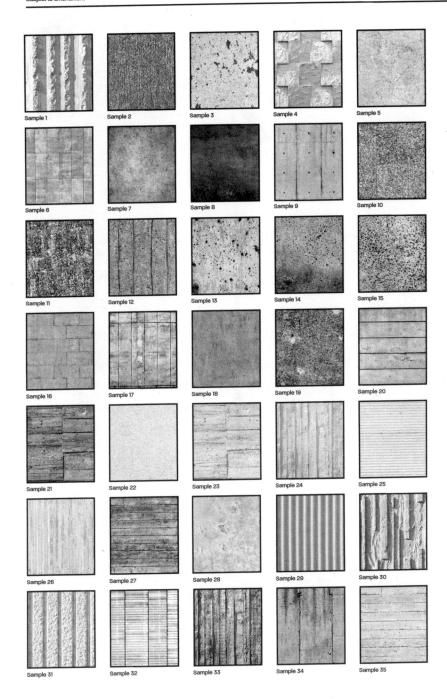

Sample 1

Sample 2

Sample 3

Sample 4

Sample 5

Sample 6

Sample 7

Sample 8

Sample 9

Sample 10

Sample 11

Sample 12

Sample 13

Sample 14

Sample 15

Sample 16

Sample 17

Sample 18

Sample 19

Sample 20

Sample 21

Sample 22

Sample 23

Sample 24

Sample 25

Sample 26

Sample 27

Sample 28

Sample 29

Sample 30

Sample 31

Sample 32

Sample 33

Sample 34

Sample 35

33 SCHEMATIC

Austin held out his hand for the torch, which Sanjay passed him without comment. He shone it on the ground in front of him. A fine slurry of moist particles and gravel glinted back at him. He lifted the beam. Just a few metres ahead, the face of the tunnel was a perfect circle, like a prepared core sample in reverse.

He stepped forwards, running the torch up to the roof, then around the intersection of wall and face. At the five o'clock position, he stopped.

"Ah."

"Not what *I* said, but yes. I've been working with these tunnelling machines for nigh on a decade, and I've not seen anything like this before." Sanjay gestured at the face. It was a cross-section of coloured strata, a layer cake of sediment. "You're well aware that we encounter all manner of undocumented subterranean spaces – medieval crypts, pre-Christian caves, but—"

"But nothing like this."

"Nothing like this. And, this deep – nothing at all."

In the torchlight, it was immediately apparent what the tunnelling machine had run up against. Brutally churned by the drill head, a twisted mass of shredded metal had been pushed up against the face of the tunnel, sharp twisted petals surrounding a jagged opening perhaps a couple of metres across.

Inside was darkness absolute.

They had breached the wall of a chamber of some kind. The exposed surface, scraped and bent, reflected their distorted faces.

Austin experimentally extended his hand. It was cold to the touch. The edges where the drill had bitten looked dangerously sharp, and he didn't try to check his intuition. The path of the tunnel was at a slight angle to the object's surface, so that all told an area of a few square metres or so had been revealed. How much further it extended back into the earth was impossible to guess.

Austin pulled out his phone and took a couple of photos. The flash seemed painfully bright now their eyes had adjusted to the dark. He had been on site when the remains of that Roman villa had been unearthed during the upper level site clearance, and during the sinking of the foundations for the Liverpool Street Station extension, when the Bedlam burial grounds had been unearthed. It was almost impossible to dig anywhere in London and not uncover something of interest. He wondered how many times a potentially important discovery had lost out to looming deadlines and the capitalist march of progress.

"We're way beneath the London Basin here. I assume there's no evidence of an ancient river system, anything that might transport out-of-place objects . . . out of place?"

Sanjay was silent. In fact, they were deeper still: way beneath the Quaternary deposits.

"How old are these strata?"

Sanjay found his voice. "Neolithic. Somewhere between eighteen hundred and three thousand years BC."

"But this looks man-made. Artificial."

He nodded. "So, do we assume it was buried here?"

This hint of a sensible explanation reassured Austin. "Did you see any signs of soil disturbance above?"

"You see what I see. We've not done a more thorough investigation. We hit this last night, around three a.m. Other than the regular crew, you're the first people the boss has allowed down here."

'The boss', of course, was Georgia Ash, with whom he'd had an eventful but fractious professional relationship spanning some twelve years. He could picture her expression of frustration now: *Get in, Austin. Do your thing, and let me know when I can get the crews back to work. Every day we delay costs me more than you'll see in archaeological funding grants in a lifetime.* She'd stand tall in her fitted navy suit, her white mane of hair framing her curt features, her arms folded across her chest. She did not look unfriendly when she smiled, but she rarely smiled.

"Sunshine and fun, your boss."

"Uh-huh."

Rutherford spoke up for the first time. "You've looked inside?"

Sanjay turned and took the measure of him. He had his hard hat on back to front. Surface-dweller, he presumed.

Austin realised he'd forgotten to make introductions. "Ah, this is Lloyd Rutherford. Artist in residence. Access all areas." Sanjay reached out and lifted his lanyard, looking at the photo of Rutherford and back again. "I'm told he's part of the public outreach project. You might have heard that NASA employed artists and photographers to record the Apollo missions? Same thing. Good for PR, apparently." He realised this explanation was of little interest to the technicians at the sharp end:

to them, Rutherford was just another unwelcome intrusion, another responsibility.

Sanjay nodded. "Welcome to the dungeons."

Turning back, he carefully braced himself on the mangled edge of Anomaly 36, hefted the torch and shone it through the opening.

The space somehow managed to swallow the beam whole. "Well . . . this thing isn't powerful enough to show me anything. It must be large."

He shone the beam down. "There's nothing inside to stand on, no floor I can see. It's like . . . like a big empty nothingness."

Austin nodded, and knelt in front of the opening. He could feel a warm exhalation against his face, a faint scent of sulphur and stagnant water. Maybe they'd discovered the entrance to the underworld, and the Styx smelled worse than Mother Thames. He somehow doubted that was possible.

Sanjay passed the torch back and Austin reached in as far as he could, swinging it left and right. He fancied he could see vertical structures, some distance away at the limits of his vision, but was unsure whether they were just after-images on his retinas. He shone the torch down. Again, blackness.

"Can I borrow your jacket?"

Rutherford shrugged. "Sure."

He folded it and laid it over the rough edge of the opening, then, supporting himself, inserted his shoulder and then his head.

The air was indeed warm, and humid. He could hear a metronomic dripping some distance away.

The torch revealed a curved wall, extending out to his left and right and arching up above and below him, undercutting his position.

His eyes were becoming accustomed to the gloom. From the entry point, he judged it was a good twenty-metre drop to where the wall began to sweep back out and become horizontal enough to stand on.

Straight ahead he could definitely see some vertical features – stalactites, perhaps? They sparkled faintly in the torchlight. The reach of wall that he could see below was stained with sediment and limestone, layer upon layer of thin deposits covering the original surface.

Where it was still visible this was ribbed, as if machined with precision; further away he could now see bulb-shaped objects, perhaps the size of footballs, attached to the wall at regular intervals and standing proud of the surface.

The space appeared to be too regular to have formed geologically, even if there was a natural explanation for the metallic shell. Was it artificial? Or could he be inside some gigantic fossilised creature, perhaps? The idea seemed absurd.

If he was careful, he could climb through without catching himself on the sharp edges. It was too far to drop, and if he did there would be no way to climb back up again, but this was not an insurmountable problem – he had engineers on hand who could easily fashion a harness, and liked to take these kinds of challenges in their stride.

Austin pulled himself back out. Sanjay was looking at him expectantly.

"What can you see?"

An energised excitement buzzed in his brain. "A mystery. One we are going to solve. Go and get the rest of the team."

Not to scale
Subject to amendment

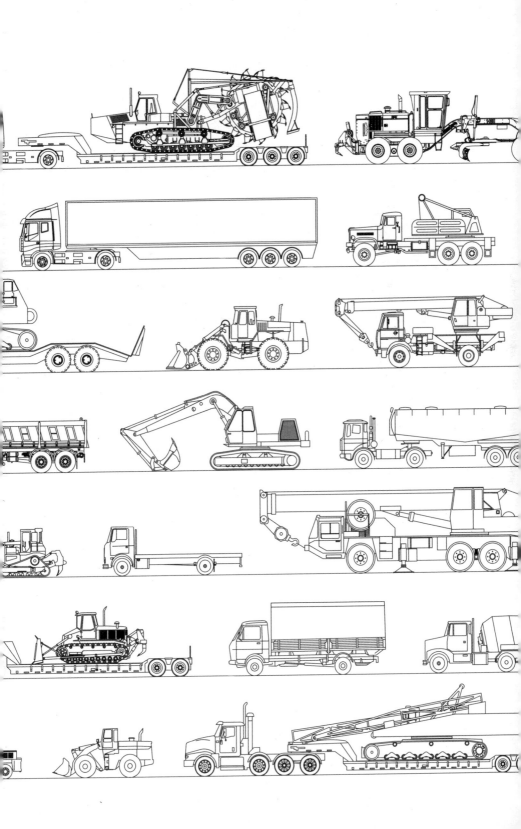

Austin Arnold's foreman had pulled back the TBM and insisted that all non-essential personnel clear the tunnel until the situation could be fully assessed, and if necessary made safe. By mid-afternoon Rutherford, after finally comprehending that this order also included him and that he was currently surplus to requirements, found himself back in his studio.

Here there was always work to be done, and the Anomaly would still be there tomorrow when Arnold and his team reconvened.

Rutherford's studio occupied the top floor of a repurposed pre-war factory in Park Royal, West London. 'Park Royal' was neither royal nor a park – the largest industrial estate in the capital, it covered an area of over 1,200 acres north of the arterial Western Avenue, next to the multi-lane asphalt tangle of the Hanger Lane Gyratory System. In the last few decades, most of the estate's surviving heavy industry had relocated or gone out of business, and many of the large buildings were now empty or derelict. The flat roofs, sweeping balconies and curved corner windows of Rutherford's block, more a sculptural exercise in intersecting planes and solids, still suggested a muscular, optimistic modernism; but one that had become less and less tenable as the 1930s came to a close, and the world had irrevocably changed.

He found his usual focus eluded him. He could not concentrate. The Anomaly was occupying his thoughts to the exclusion of all else.

He absently wandered through the building. If he ignored the rats and foxes, the other floors were now unoccupied; the landlord had managed to prevent the illegal raves that had originally blighted Rutherford's nocturnal working hours by surrounding the whole place with a tall razor-wire fence.

The building's original use was obscure. Down in the basement there were windowless bunker-like rooms, devoid of furniture, whose heavy doors were half a metre thick. Stencilled on the walls were numbers and letters whose meaning, like the abstract glyphs at Lascaux, was lost to time. At the western end, built into the fabric of the building, was what looked like an aircraft's jet intake; it was so large Rutherford could walk right into it. Looking up, it turned ninety degrees through enormous baffles and exited via blackened chimney stacks in the roof. He supposed it had been a wind tunnel or a test bed, though for what he had no way of guessing.

At the eastern end the ceiling of the basement opened up to the ground floor. A staircase set in the wall led up to a garage of sorts, from whose roof swung a heavy-duty chain and winch. A gantry ran around three walls, and a small cabin, from which the winch could be operated, was accessible by a hooped ladder. A large steel shutter, now padlocked shut, took up the entire fourth wall. Tyre marks of a size that suggested heavy haulage ran from the lip of the pit, passing beneath it.

Above a long metal workbench, wrenches, hammers, welding equipment and implements of unknown use hung from numbered brackets. Over everything was an oily residue that barely reflected the dim light that fell through the frosted skylights. Whatever this factory had been used for, it had been abandoned long before Rutherford moved in.

The floor above was offices. A central hallway opened onto rooms either side, some of which were carpeted with loose paperwork that had spilled from files pulled from metal cabinets. The sheets were coloured either blue or pink, and featured sectional drawings of what appeared to be machine parts. Rutherford had picked several at random and laid them out on the floor. A centrifuge, surrounded by electromagnets; a medical instrument with forceps at one end and a drill bit mounted between them; some kind of artificial limb or exoskeleton, attached to which were a series of curved needles; a box the shape of a metronome, with dials and levers mounted at the narrower end. Visible within this was the schematic outline of a figure, with targets placed at limb joints like a crash-test dummy. Was it a pilot, inside an experimental craft of some kind? Or a life-support machine – or even a coffin?

One office contained a large metal desk, and Rutherford had tried its drawers for clues. In one he had found a box of business cards.

Niromad Works West

Conrad Leadbetter, Chairman

1220 Industry Way London NW10

The organisation was not listed on the Companies House database, but as this place had been disused for decades he did not find this surprising.

His studio occupied the entire top floor. It was approached via a set of steps that had once been painted an institutional eau-de-Nil green, but had long since been worn through to the bare concrete beneath. Above, a framework of girders supported a corrugated cast-iron roof. Cables hung down, some ending in electrical sockets, others in hand-sized boxes with coloured buttons. However he pressed them, they seemed to do nothing.

Below the eaves were long narrow windows, through which only sky was visible. They had intentionally been placed higher than eye level, as if the outside world might have distracted the original occupants from whatever important tasks they needed to perform. These, though filthy, gave an even scattered light throughout the interior he found perfect for his work.

At the near end Rutherford had set up a display space, a number of stands on which he had pinned sketches and plans. Currently these were of the Crossrail project: views of the tunnelling machine, the men and women at work, the shafts and the cladding, the textures of self-levelling screed, geotextiles and reinforced aggregate, and the play of light across engine hoods, ribbed polyethylene sheeting and capped deep pilings.

He stood and regarded them. They were a first pass, and still contained pictorial clues to their subject matter. He intended to abstract them further, reduce them to simpler, more elementary forms. The representational record of the project he had been commissioned to make had been superseded by other concerns he couldn't quite yet articulate.

He felt as if he was performing some kind of exploratory surgery on the city itself, mapping its internal spaces, the conduits and arteries that were being built to carry its inhabitants through its interior to their destinations. He did not consider it a post-mortem, as the city was still very much a living thing; more an in vivo dissection.

He walked past the stands. Further down he'd arranged the drawings and paintings that were in a more finished form: a grey canvas, textured like terrazzo and spotted with discarded gum, on which fell the scalloped shadow of a series of balconies; a flyover support, opened to reveal a skeleton of reinforcing steel bars; an aerial view of the corner of a car park, a grid of lines on a black ground, a cross-hatched area and an arrow below pointing to an exit off-frame.

These, however, were not the main event. Dominating the room was a large table, maybe four metres by seven, constructed from Dexion and topped with sheets of marine ply. On this a map was sketched in charcoal: a road plan, divided into streets and city blocks. Into each plot Rutherford had placed a brick, or a chip of stone, or another object – a petrol can, a flattened cigarette packet, a broken car headlight, an abandoned child's pushchair, a bent bicycle wheel, an *Evening Standard* newspaper rack – something that he had found at that precise location in the real world, something that suggested the size and shape of the building that stood there. Lower out towards the periphery, the objects rose higher and became denser towards the centre of the table.

He took something from his pocket.

It was an irregular piece of brick, painted white on the one flat face. He had carefully chosen it that very afternoon from the rubble at the base of the building that had been cleaved to accommodate the Crossrail site. He rotated it in his hand, held it up and considered its profile from different angles.

He looked at the plan laid out before him. There was a small empty space, a pencilled plot between two other blocks. He placed it there, rotated it slightly, then stepped back and regarded it.

He absently pulled a stick of gum from a packet in his breast pocket, unwrapped it, rolled the foil wrapper into a ball and dropped it. It joined hundreds of others, scattered across the floor like ball bearings. He began to chew, absently.

He lifted his gaze from the table, turned and crossed the room. He approached a specific spot, marked by four inward-pointing arrows in masking tape on the floor. He lifted the welding goggles from around his neck and put them on. The unbroken lens winked with reflected light like a Belisha beacon. The goggles cut out most of the ambient light, reducing everything to simplified silhouettes, to their basic geometry.

Visible from this precise point, and this point only, the arrangement on the table formed a familiar backlit skyline.

Each element of its construction taken from the city itself, here in Rutherford's studio was London, in miniature.

Not to scale
Subject to amendment

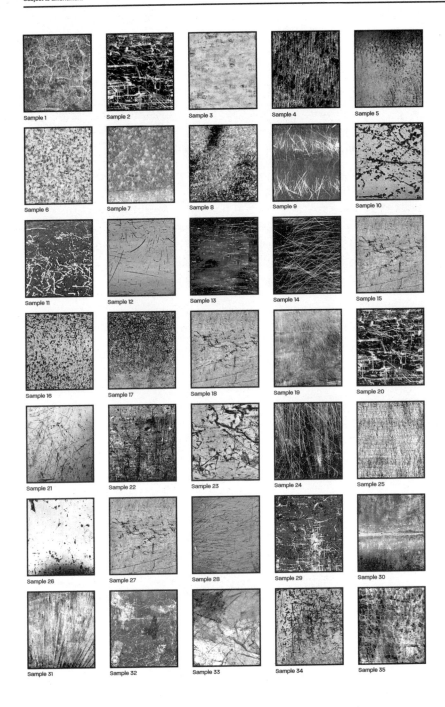

Sample 1

Sample 2

Sample 3

Sample 4

Sample 5

Sample 6

Sample 7

Sample 8

Sample 9

Sample 10

Sample 11

Sample 12

Sample 13

Sample 14

Sample 15

Sample 16

Sample 17

Sample 18

Sample 19

Sample 20

Sample 21

Sample 22

Sample 23

Sample 24

Sample 25

Sample 26

Sample 27

Sample 28

Sample 29

Sample 30

Sample 31

Sample 32

Sample 33

Sample 34

Sample 35

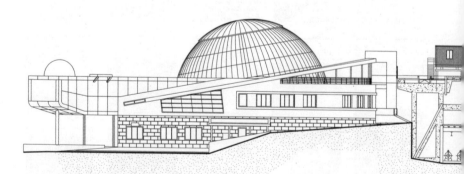

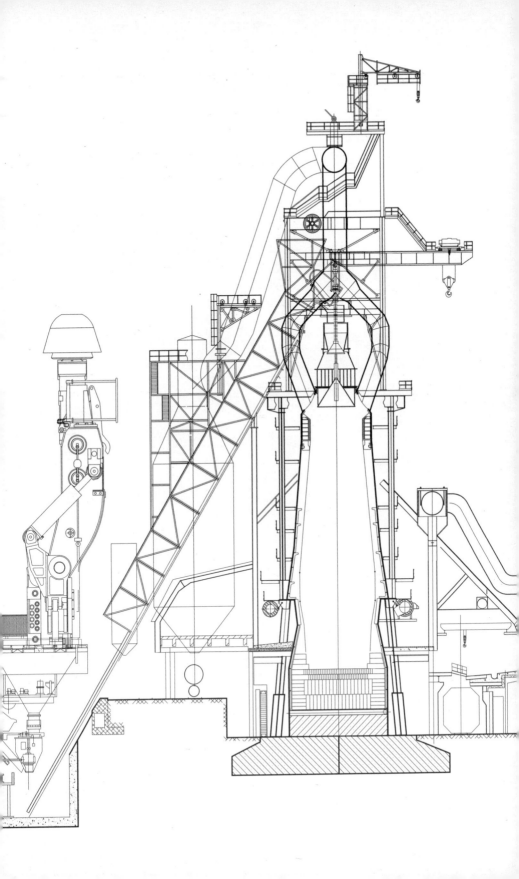

TO THE TRAINS

49 **FOUNDATION**

Austin's team reconvened at Anomaly 36. A mountaineering harness had been acquired from a specialist shop on Tottenham Court Road, and a stout rope had been attached to brackets mounted on the concrete tunnel sheath. Lights had been attached to their standard-issue hard hats. Most of the other equipment and know-how had been close to hand.

He had not thought to inform Rutherford, but he was still here regardless.

Who was to be the first in?

It had to be a qualified engineer. This was not a scheduled event, one they had approved procedures to deal with, and there were too many unknowns. Austin, a stickler for timetables and their punctual application, still felt discomforted by this interruption in the smooth running of the project. But curiosity was getting the better of him. He was the most senior here. He was the most qualified. He would go through first.

He tested the line again. His crew silently stood on the drill head, or looked down through the spaces between the radial arms that held the cutter teeth.

Several of them were filming the proceedings on their iPhones, even though photography was forbidden in the sections of the tunnel governed by the Official Secrets Act.

Rutherford was standing off to the side, drawing.

Temporary floodlights on tripods had been set up around the entrance, and powerful, high-impact heavy-duty torches distributed. The sharp raw edges around the hole had been wrapped in thick duct tape and padding. There was little chance of injury, or the line snagging.

Austin positioned himself, his back towards the entrance. He fed out some slack, and leaned in.

He pushed away, releasing the tension on the line. Dropping maybe a metre and a half, he swung back in to place two booted feet firmly on the wall just below the entrance.

He reached out. The surface in front of him was a deep golden brown; in the light of his helmet-mounted torch it seemed to be coated in oxidised metal, which adhered to his fingertips in moist clumps.

Above, he could see Sanjay and Rutherford looking down at him. Sanjay gave him a thumbs up. "Line's fine. You're good."

He dropped another twenty metres, to the point where the floor was horizontal enough to stand upright. Hanging for a moment, he let himself fall to the ground. His boots slid, found purchase on the uneven surface. He was embarrassed to find he was breathing heavily; though his job was pretty physical, he was not in as good shape as he'd like to imagine.

He braced himself against a rounded limestone pillar that looked like nothing more than the trunk of a felled tree. Where his boots had skidded, a dark reflective surface had been revealed.

With a wave of his hand he signalled up to Sanjay, who was leaning in and checking his line. From this position the opening into the chamber made by the TBM resembled a backlit bullet hole. A trickle of cold water fell from its lower lip, ran down the curved wall and puddled around his feet.

Once he was sure of his balance he looked around him. The torch was powerful, but the space was truly enormous: a cathedral of humid air with an earthy tang of peat.

That it had a regular shape was apparent even from the limited volume now visible. A ribbed torus, but not of equal circumference; it was pinched inwards in several places, possibly deformed by pressure or geological movement. The whole seemed to be canted at an angle – maybe eight degrees, like a listing ship.

The beam of his torch darted around. From what he could dimly make out, the lower parts were filled with a fine silt. Stalactites ran like the tattered sails of beached galleons down to the left, curtailing his view of the darker recesses beyond.

He released the line.

Overhead, the ribbed walls dramatically curved up, then in towards the centre where they gathered to form a pillar. This was studded with globes the size of hot-air balloons, arranged in threes, which reflected his torchlight in fine sparkles. Most of these were an opaque milky white; others were broken, leaving shards attached to their rims like bad teeth. The silt in the lower reaches offered an inviting flat surface, but one that was still some distance away.

Austin was not, by profession or inclination, a caver, but even he knew this place was . . . unusual.

They would need to get the expert archaeologists in. There would be more delays. Georgia Ash would glower like some thwarted autocrat.

He looked out, across the vast space.

He was supposed to be an engineer, not an explorer. How had he come to find himself here?

is looking for new members!

For those interested in all aspects of train lore, we exchange opinions and information in a splendid club newsletter.

FREE enamel pin badge offered to first 200 respondents. Open to all ages.

Please send a stamped self-addressed envelope to:
P. O. Box 42, Westminster, London, SW1.

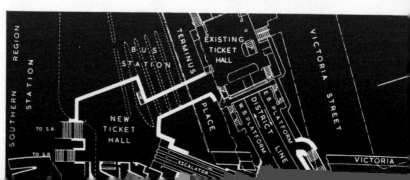

Twelve-year-old Austin Arnold's cultural signifiers were *Look-In*, the *New Musical Express*, the novels of Richard Allen, and listening to Capital Radio on a bright red transistor radio with a single earphone, set at low volume to preserve the batteries. It was the spring of 1975, Disco Tex and the Sex-O-Lettes' 'I Wanna Dance Wit Choo' was moving up the pop charts despite its lack of grammatical rigour, and his older sister was away at her boyfriend's for the week, meaning he had to walk the mile and a half back from school along the Thames towpath alone.

Mr. Yates had not turned up for the double period of chemistry, and apparently the supply teacher was stuck in Hounslow. Austin had once passed through Hounslow on the train, and he pitied him. Usually pupils at St. Stephen's Elementary School for Boys were not allowed their own magazines or comics in class, but if a teacher was absent they were permitted an unscheduled Reading Period.

Ray Langley swung his satchel onto Austin's desk. Out from among the exercise books, boiled sweets stuck to used tissues, dried rugby-boot mud and a seasoning of pencil shavings, he pulled a magazine.

He opened it and slid it across the desk. "Hey hey, A. A. Look at this." Ray had discovered his father's magazine collection, and now ran something of a lending library. For a few pence, he'd loan you a copy of *Mayfair*, *Men Only*, *Spick* or *Span*, or some other vintage pocket-sized journal that featured naked ladies 'artistically' posed in the manner of Greek statues, or cartoons in which a buxom secretary sat on the lap of her portly and monocled boss.

Austin flipped to the cover, back again. This was not that kind of publication – it was a railway enthusiast's magazine. Ray was pointing to an advertisement in the classifieds at the back. They shared some passing interest in trains, though Austin knew nothing about the intricacies of forward bogie placement or *Flying Scotsman* boiler pressure.

Austin read the advert aloud. "'All aboard, chaps! The Smokebox Club is looking for new members!'"

"You want to join? Let's join!"

Austin was not much of a joiner.

Ray was insistent. "There's a free badge!"

"Free badge?" Austin looked more closely. He had a Blue Peter badge, which he kept in a biscuit tin with his marbles, foreign coins and PG Tips cards. His resources were finite, but if there was a nifty enamel badge to be had . . .

"But only for the first two hundred applicants. We have to be quick."

Austin could tell when a deal was in the offing.

"OK. Why not?"

The two of them duly sent off stamped, self-addressed envelopes and waited expectantly for a reply.

A fortnight later, a familiar envelope arrived with his own handwriting on the front. His father placed it on the table beside his cereal bowl. Inside was a single sheet of typewritten paper, a colour postcard of the *Golden Arrow* and a small enamel badge.

The last steam engines had been withdrawn from service almost a decade earlier, to be replaced by utilitarian diesels. For Austin and Ray, steam already evoked the romance of the past, the magic of a more glamorous age; one in which men wore hats, not flares, and women had bright-red lipstick and perfectly coiffured hair, just like those in the old *Spick* and *Spans*.

The smokebox – the round door on the front of a steam engine that gave access to the boiler – always reminded Austin of a clock, the opening mechanism the hands. On the club's badge, the handles were set at the half-past four position; if you held it upside down, it looked like a black Smiley, a *Bash Street* grin on an eyeless face. On the badge's reverse, the legend "Smokebox Club – Official Member" was written around the rim, and in the centre, behind the pin, was stamped a number. Ray's was 127, Austin's was 133. They wondered who the other members were, and who Number 1 might be. It was a bit like *The Prisoner*.

He pinned the badge on the lapel of his school blazer and turned again to the sheet of paper.

```
Welcome to the Smokebox Club!

We are a select group of railway enthusiasts with
members all around the globe.

Wear your badge with pride.
It will help you identify fellow Smokeboxers.

All Aboard!
The Chief Engineer.
```

Chief Engineer. It sounded important. Did the Chief Engineer have Badge Number 1?

He asked his careers master whether an engineer would get to work with steam trains.

"So you want to be an engine driver?" He looked at Austin benignly and pushed his glasses back up his nose. "Steam trains are all but obsolete, but engineering is a broad subject. There are many other jobs that you could do, if you're fascinated by how things work. There's what's called an apprenticeship. When you turn fourteen you can apply for one."

The careers master gave him some leaflets to take home and read. Austin, who had taken his transistor radio apart and not been able to put it back together again, nevertheless felt the future beckoning.

The club's magazine arrived a few weeks later. *The Smokeboxer* was about the size of *Span*; professionally typeset, with a card cover featuring the *Mallard*, the circular Smokebox Club logo and the issue number (Volume 78, No. 2).

Most of the articles were somewhat arcane for Austin's taste, but there was a lively letters section at the back where modelling tips were exchanged, track layouts criticised, and the future of the railways discussed. Each letter was answered by either the Chief Engineer or another correspondent, each of whom also adopted a pseudonym: Signalman Sixsmith, Smoke and Ashes, Choo-Choo McGrew.

Along with the magazine there was a 7-inch single, in a flimsy paper sleeve. On the label, printed in an arch in the manner of a steam engine's nameplate, was the title: *The Smokebox Song.* Austin had to ask permission from his sister to play it on her music centre.

"Hurrah for the Smokebox Crew!
Book a seat! We'll ride with you.
If you're down, or in distress,
We're the Happiness Express!

O'er bridge and through the tunnel,
See the smoke shoot from the funnel!
Like the breath of George's dragon,
Roaring on with coach and wagon.

The Smokebox Crew are just the ticket
If you're on a sticky wicket.
Pull the whistle, hear it scree-eam!
The Crew and you can let off steam.

The signal's green, the line is clear
Let me hear the Smokebox Cheer! (Huzzah!)
All aboard! We leave the station,
Friendship is our destination."

It had the jaunty, overenthusiastic twang of a children's TV show. He played it repeatedly, until his sister hid the record under the rug in the spare bedroom.

Austin decided he had to contribute something to the magazine. But what?

That Sunday he took himself off to the nearby shunting yards at Tattle-combe with the idea that he would interview someone. Who, precisely, he did not know. He stepped into the ticket hall, where a gas stove in the corner lifted the temperature by a couple of degrees, and asked to see the Station Manager.

With the solemnity of a politician being interviewed by *The Times*' top correspondent, he answered Austin's questions on rolling stock, ticket prices, signalling, and the day-to-day responsibilities of a Station Manager. He then allowed him to select one item from the lost property trunk and sent him on his way.

He wrote the answers down in a flip-page reporter's notebook, copied them out again longhand in his neatest handwriting on a sheet of lined paper torn from the back of his French exercise book, and posted it.

In the next issue, there was his letter, with a short but encouraging response from the Chief Engineer himself! Austin ran his fingers over the paper and felt the slight letterpress impression. *His* words, set in metal, inked in lampblack, and printed for others to read! He was now immortal, just like those other greats of English Literature — Shake-speare, Milton, Patrick Moore and Richard Allen.

Thus began an association that, he was later to discover, was being repeated all across the kingdom. Through the magazine there grew a camaraderie, a sense of belonging. Though members, almost by neces-sity, never met — at least, Austin and Ray never met any — they liked to imagine they were part of some mysterious and secretive cabal, an underground network held together by a shared interest. Look around you, at school, in Cinema Club or in the shopping centre. Anyone could be a member.

There was even a secret hand signal.

You held your hand down by your side, index and middle finger form-ing a V, just like the half-past-four position of the handles on the Smoke-box badge. It was just like Churchill's 'V' for Victory sign, but upside down. If another member returned the sign, you could reveal your affil-iation. It was their equivalent of a Masonic handshake.

No one at school ever returned their secret sign, or wore a Smokebox badge — though due to the school's strict policy regarding what was and what was not acceptable uniform, Ray and Austin had taken to wearing theirs *under* their lapels.

Was the Station Master he had interviewed a member? He'd thought it might break some unwritten rule to ask him outright. And if he had, maybe he'd have denied it anyway, as any decent secret agent would have done. What if the ever-absent Mr. Yates was a member too, off on some secret Smokebox mission of extreme import?

That was the thing. Anyone could be a Smokeboxer, and you'd never know.

Austin grew older. He was privileged in many ways society told him he was privileged: bright, studious, from a secure and loving family. But though he had friends, and though he knew they stood by him, he passed the days without any danger of becoming the focus of a young woman's attention. He told himself that might come later, at university.

Without too much effort he left school with three A-grade A-levels and a C in Sociology. Somehow he managed to successfully negotiate four years of Mechanical Engineering at the University of London, passing every test and year-end exam, but without so much as a date. Despite the photographs in the prospectus, the course did not attract equal numbers of men and women, so he had signed himself up for the Chess Club and the Debating Society, not because he was particularly interested in chess or debating, but just because they might pull him out of his comfort zone, which he felt had shrunk to fit like his old school jumper.

He began to think he might be invisible.

True invisibility, though, would have bestowed some advantage. It would have been a superpower. But the ability to pass through social spaces unremarked was not one he cherished.

He had once written a note to Jasmine Schwartz, who also attended his optional computer programming class, asking if she'd like to go and see a double-bill of *Octopussy* and *Moonraker* at the ABC with him on Saturday week. He tucked it under the back cover of her BASIC textbook.

He waited outside in his new jumper until after the film had begun, but she didn't appear. He went in alone and watched Jaws fall in love, Bond outsmart Hugo Drax and attempt re-entry with Holly Goodhead. Austin thought he was just rubbing it in.

He was not to know that Jasmine did not discover his note until twenty-six years later, when she was clearing out the loft after her eldest son had left for university. She showed it to her husband, who was unexpectedly taken by its poetic turn of phrase. Jasmine, with not a little shame, found she could no longer bring Austin's face to mind.

Austin became an apprentice at Acton Depot, rose through the ranks, and through a series of mergers and restructurings found himself head of the tunnelling equipment procurement division. Without much effort on his behalf, at the age of forty-eight he was promoted to the new Crossrail project.

Here, on this project, he felt he was useful.

He had purpose, a part to play.

He was good at his job, and he was content.

If, in his youth, he had been somewhat gauche, in adulthood he had acquired a certain presence, and he liked to think he was a fair-minded and compassionate manager. He was respected, if not loved, and that was reward enough. He wouldn't describe himself as happy, but then neither was he sad – emotion being a dangerously unguarded realm he studiously avoided. Instead, his head was full of schedules and manifests, timetables and rotas.

He had never shared his bed with a woman, and, other than his parents, had never felt another's hand touch him with affection. He rarely masturbated; his imagination seemed to have atrophied through disuse, and sometimes he wondered if he'd allowed it to happen on purpose – he wouldn't miss what he didn't desire.

But there *were* certain things he did understand.

Machines responded to his coaxing, came to life under his touch. He could sense if they were happy by the note of an engine, by the pull on a steering wheel. He could lay a hand on the hood of an earthmover and from the vibration alone diagnose its ills and know how to make it better.

He'd kept his enamel Smokebox badge. Though the magazine that original advertisement appeared in ceased publication sometime in the late '70s, the Smokebox Club newsletter had continued. Eventually it had migrated online, first in the form of a simple messageboard and latterly as a members-only group.

Long-standing contributors might cease posting, gone, Austin assumed, to the great engine shed in the sky, while occasional new voices would appear. As it was a closed group, he had no idea how they found out about it or were vetted.

Was the mysterious Chief Engineer somehow overseeing such matters? Forty-odd years on, he wondered whether the person behind the pseudonym could possibly be the same. Had they passed the cap to some younger apprentice? As far as Austin could divine the style of writing had not changed; by now it was an anachronistic jolly 'what-ho, chocks away' parody.

But that could easily be mimicked.

It was a puzzle.

Austin still occasionally followed the threads, though nowadays he rarely contributed. He'd just dip in, more out of nostalgia. Many of the members had actually worked on the railways back in the heyday of steam, and they loved to share their stories.

This was how he had first heard about the Strategic Steam Reserve.

It was a legend, a myth, a tall tale that had been discussed on and off for as long as Austin could remember. It was even mentioned on the cover of that first *Smokeboxer* issue he and Ray had read.

There were correspondents who swore they'd seen mysterious locomotives running along isolated sections of track late at night, locomotives that bore neither number nor name. Their cabside and smokebox plates had been removed, their bright green or red livery repainted a deep, glossy black.

Some took them to be nostalgic signalmen's fancies, or even ghosts; others proof that there was a fleet of preserved steam engines hidden somewhere under the good green hills of England, waiting patiently in suspension for Albion's hour of need, when they would rise from the earth, breathing smoke like the dragons of old, to save us from the coming apocalypse, whatever that might be.

There was even one account from a member who swore they had broken into a labyrinth of subterranean tunnels somewhere in the West Country near Bristol as a kid, and had actually seen them up close.

Though these stories had once filled his young head with wonder, these days Austin's concerns were of a more practical nature.

It was just a legend. A tall tale.

The history of the railways was full of them.

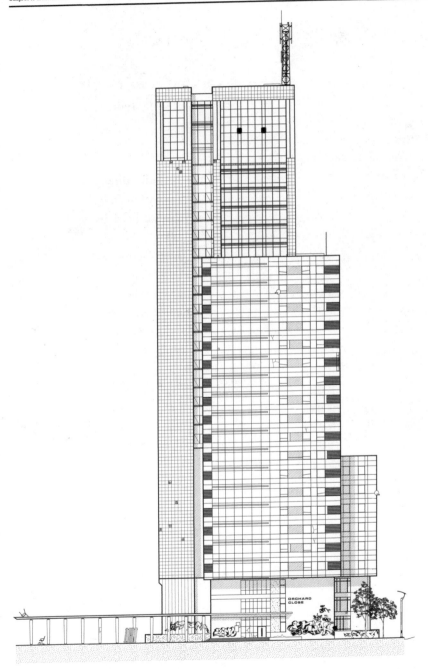

ORCHARD CLOSE

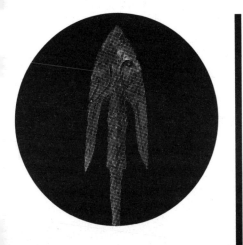

63 **EXCAVATION**

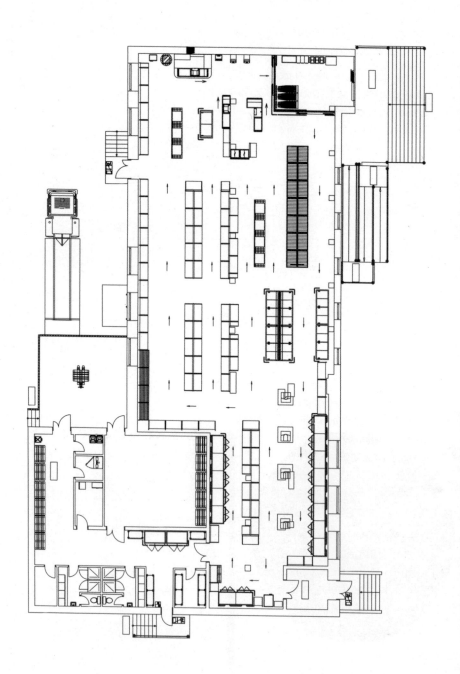

The Crossrail project was not Rutherford's first foray into London's underspaces. For many years he had explored them on foot, whether they were officially open to the public or not. Of particular interest were the labyrinthine subways that connected certain underused East London Tube stations; here, he became entranced by the exit sign diagrams to the city above, the semiotic interface of underworld with overworld.

These corridors were not a destination in and of themselves, they were just thoroughfares, the means to get from A to B. Other than Rutherford, no one came here to contemplate them; they just passed through, head down, earphones in, on their way somewhere else. They were the in-between un-spaces, and they fascinated him.

The walls down here were made from aged and broken tile, encrusted with fly-posters and overpainted with Krylon. They were the public fora, the means of messaging used by London's subcultures, many of whom spoke in tongues none but the initiated could decipher.

They were kept in check by the clean-up crews from the bureaucracy of public amenities. Between them they fought for control of these palimpsests, a guerrilla war of graffiti, stickers and broadsides against jet-powered cleaning guns and whitewash.

He would find unlocked doors giving onto storerooms full of obsolete machinery, or disused offices stripped of their equipment, the walls patched with steel sheet and punctuated with holes where cables once entered and exited. Years ago these had carried information in, to be processed and displayed here; someone or something would then make a decision, push a button or flip a switch, and another signal would exit, carrying a new message elsewhere.

He came across control rooms in which banks of backlit Perspex still displayed the diagrammatic layout of station and track, signal and train, all now dark. A cigarette, its filter stained with dark lipstick, perched on the edge of a console. How long had it been there? Was the smoker still alive?

In a drawer he found a sheaf of old photocopied timetables,

a cross-referenced code of station acronym, arrival and departure times; it was a record of activity once urgent and necessary, but now just a list of numbers on a forgotten sheet of A4. He took a selection to add to his collection.

Rutherford's nocturnal perambulations were not without their dangers.

There were three of them, and they saw him before he saw them. They stood together, side by side, barring the exit ramp, backlit by a humming striplight, silhouettes devoid of race or gender.

The punch came without warning, and he momentarily blacked out. He found he was on the ground, the side of his face pressed against the paving. The terrazzo beneath him was unforgivingly hard, not made for a soft cheek or shoulder or hip, but the sole of a boot.

He wanted to hug it, in the knowledge it couldn't ever reciprocate. Maybe that was the point.

He breathed in the musk of decades of stale urine and vomit. A boot came down on the back of his head, hard. His mouth was full of broken teeth and the metallic tang of blood.

Rutherford imagined he could lie here forever, that this would be his home, that he would become part of the fabric of this city, calcify like a limestone statue until he rotted away inside and only a brittle hollow shell would remain, a Pompeiian sculpture cast from absence that commuters would absently walk around, treat as just another navigation hazard.

He would commune with other statues, the forgotten generals, dukes and politicians that stood on plinths around the city. They did not feel pain. They were above us, above such frailties of the flesh, serene and beneficent. If he was made of bronze or stone or concrete, would he feel anything any more? Would he hear the conversations in the crowd as they passed him by?

A leather-clad hand grabbed him by the collar, pulled him up and threw him over onto his back.

Shapes stood over him, blurred by concussion, but somehow with perfect clarity he could still see a spiderweb of coagulated dust on the ceiling above them, the broken cover of a light fixture. The voices sounded distant, echoing within the walls of this concrete chamber and the internal spaces of his skull, their meaning stripped away, reduced to guttural utterances of ugly intent.

Even in this heightened moment he found himself absorbed by the geometric juxtaposition of anodised trunking above their heads, the way the harsh light fell across the wall, delineating its texture like a mountain range in miniature. Thousands might pass through this place every day, but how many had stopped to observe it from this particular angle before? How many had caught the accidental beauty of the rafters of the Underworld?

He smiled involuntarily, a sign of mammalian subservience, the deep-seated survival mechanism of an evolved ape in the presence of another troop's alpha male. He felt them go through his pockets as the bruising began to swell his cheek and close his right eye.

Then there was just the distant urban lullaby of traffic.

Someone stepped over him, did not pause to help. A minute passed, or maybe an hour. His ruined hearing caught a woman's voice in the distance – or it could have been close by, muffled by trauma – calling an ambulance.

His was a welcome oblivion that was not to be.

Rutherford woke in an emergency room in St Thomas' Hospital with a steel pin in his jaw and a plate in the roof of his mouth. Looking in the mirror, he realised the artificial portion of him was an improvement, that his whiter, more perfectly aligned teeth were a new and necessary refurbishment. One day, and soon, he realised, humans would be able to mould themselves at will, rebuild and redesign their bodies as they now do their built environment.

Finally, at long last, we would all become architects, not just of our city, but of ourselves.

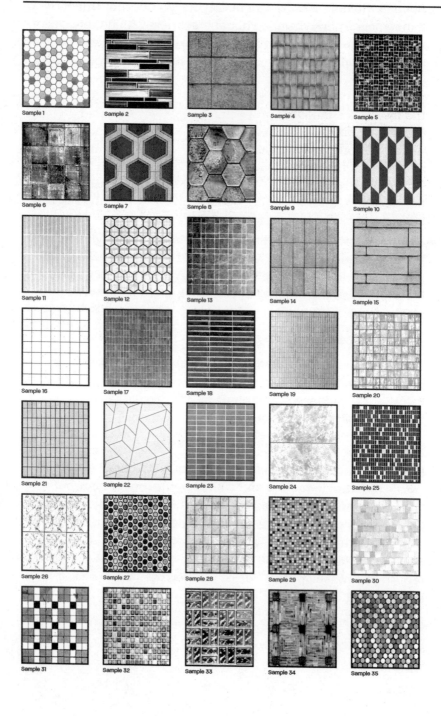

Sample 1

Sample 2

Sample 3

Sample 4

Sample 5

Sample 6

Sample 7

Sample 8

Sample 9

Sample 10

Sample 11

Sample 12

Sample 13

Sample 14

Sample 15

Sample 16

Sample 17

Sample 18

Sample 19

Sample 20

Sample 21

Sample 22

Sample 23

Sample 24

Sample 25

Sample 26

Sample 27

Sample 28

Sample 29

Sample 30

Sample 31

Sample 32

Sample 33

Sample 34

Sample 35

As the Director of Operations at Crossrail, a position that was something of a revolving door in the current parlous state of politics, Georgia Ash wondered if she was taking this all way too personally. Maybe she should just relax – no doubt she'd be promoted sideways again in a year, and then this would all be someone else's problem.

Her remit – to nudge the public away from the use of private vehicles to cleaner and greener forms of transport – was on the face of it a laudable proposition, but she wondered if one of the largest cities in the world really needed more holes drilled under it. If one included all the sub-basement swimming pools and garages, the water mains and sewers, cables and Tube lines, could there be anything left down here to hold it all up? She'd not be surprised if one day London collapsed into the big sinkhole that must now exist beneath it.

While the main east–west tunnel was proceeding on schedule, the archaeology in Anomaly 36 had brought the Palace branch to a halt. Three weeks in, and she suspected the team had barely dug a shallow trench. While she appreciated the need – the *requirement* – to carefully investigate any finds, she also appreciated the pressure placed upon her to complete this project on schedule.

Trains. It was still a boys' game, and the nature of the heavy industrial work down here still required a certain kind of physicality, a willingness to put a shoulder to the wheel and to get grease under your fingernails.

For her, neither of these posed a problem. Though she was interested in how the world *worked*, she was also interested in how she could get the world to work *for her.*

Austin Arnold was efficient, in the obsequious manner of a man who was used to being a passenger rather than the driver of their own destiny. Without real flair or passion, at least as far as she could tell, he was steady, reliable, and reassuringly dull. He rarely met her eye; she realised he found her intimidating, but maybe he found most women intimidating. He listened, he nodded, and then he got things done.

She trusted him implicitly.

They were standing in the tunnel. Austin was explaining the situation. "We're about to enter the, the Anomaly. It appears to be a pinched toroid in shape. Symmetrical. Unnaturally so. Angled at eight degrees to the horizontal. The space is large — more than a hundred and fifty metres across and around eighty high. That's almost as tall as the Statue of Liberty."

He sounded like a tour guide.

Austin gestured for her to step through the opening. Inside, just below the jagged hole made by the tunnelling equipment, a platform had been erected. At one end of this was a small crane, its boom extending out over the edge. Next to it was a prefab hut, much like the ones topside; heavy-duty batteries and other items of specialised equipment Ash was not familiar with were stacked beside it. This platform was at the top of a free-standing fourteen-storey scaffold enclosing a stairway, which spiralled down into darkness. Austin flipped a switch, and lights came on at each landing. She could see that behind her, below the entrance, the wall of the space fell away, reflecting the light like slick dark stone.

The tunnelling machine had penetrated some distance above the midpoint, and the wall arched out dramatically above them, its vertical ribs extending into a complex fractal structure like a filigree hammer-beam cathedral roof; below them it curved out, away from the platform until it hit the vertical, then back in to meet the ridged floor that was just visible below.

She looked out across the immense space. The floods, powerful as they were, could only provide small patches of light. These marked out a trail that dipped down and around stalactites and fallen boulders, finally arriving at the flat grey expanse of silt in the lower portion of the torus far beyond.

Austin led the way down, turning occasionally to check her progress. As they descended, the wall came in to meet them; from the base of the scaffold the stairway turned into a series of switchback ramps, becoming ever shallower as they matched the slope. At the bottom, just to the left, was a store of colour-coded crates containing bagged samples. From here, the walkway finally struck out across the floor of the space.

Smaller lamps hung from posts placed at regular intervals along the way, a zig-zag dotted line that traced a rise in the ground ahead of them only to vanish over its peak. The rest was simply blackness, the true size of the space impossible to judge. She had an impression of a starless plain, without horizon, across which a parade of fairy lights wandered. Down here at the bottom it was sepulchrally cold, and her breath hung as a fine mist in the damp air.

Austin zipped his fur-lined parka a little higher. "The eight-degree angle means that sediment has collected at the far end of the torus, to a depth, we estimate, of around twenty metres. That's where the dig site is." He turned to check she was following him. "Watch your step. The walkway is uneven, and gets slippery with condensation. Best to hold the guard rope."

The planks brought to mind a jetty, reaching out onto a river-bed at low tide. It was wide enough to accommodate the diggers and lifters, which had left dark caterpillar-track marks on the fresh plywood. Either side, she could see the spaces between the exposed ribs were partially filled with silt. Further ahead, they gave way to a flat expanse marked by the occasional larger intrusion: a boulder, a tangle of rusted wire, a more familiar section of London brickwork, or a broken stalactite which the light isolated as if it was a watchful sentinel. What lay further out, beyond the reach of the lanterns, she could only guess.

The walkway rose; here, the shape of the Anomaly provided a kind of saddle, to the left of which was the central pillar. This was also ribbed, and high above their heads hung the spherical objects Austin had glimpsed that first time he'd looked in. They were arranged in triads, spiralling up and around the column. They had a peculiar glassy translucence, and seemed to contain darker shapes, though as yet no one had climbed up to examine them more closely. Natural or artificial, their purpose, if they had one, remained obscure. To Austin they resembled a contemporary lighting arrangement – something you'd see in a corporate lobby, rather than a cave under the capital. They, and the entire space, had been mapped from the air by small drones, the results providing a framework in which the dig was oriented.

They could see the top of the rise just ahead, the line of lamps rising then disappearing over its crest. Here, the base material was again visible, the silt forming pools, like a terraced garden, in its ridged surface.

They paused at the summit. Spread out below them was the dig site itself.

At its centre was a fierce cluster of floodlights, surrounded by the incongruously brash red and yellow livery of the diggers and cranes; the percussive sound of metal on stone came to them through the still air. A small group of single-storey Porta-kabins were visible just beyond; knots of people in yellow hard hats and high-viz jackets were everywhere. The walkway and the trail of lanterns led down towards them.

As they got closer, Ash could see the dig in more detail, a dark rectangular space set into the ground like the foundations of a missing building. Austin was back in tour-guide mode. "The dig is now fifteen metres down. The stuff we excavate is sifted over there – see those frames – and anything we find is tagged and bagged."

"So what have you found?"

"So far? Bones, mostly. Animal." Austin paused. "Some human. The dig leader originally thought they'd been washed down here from above as they were disturbed, incomplete; but she now thinks that may be due to predation, and they might origin-ally have been burials. That this place was used as a, a tomb."

"A tomb." Ash looked out, tried to get an overall impression. The powerful lights rendered everything beyond them invisible. Austin followed her gaze.

This space, whether natural or man-made, had been here a very long time. She was reminded of the interior of a sea urchin shell she'd found on Hastings beach during a school holiday, a fragile, broken thing filled with coarse sand. Were they standing in the fossilised remains of some previously undescribed sea creature? If so, it must have been gargantuan.

A petite figure whose hard hat seemed to engulf her head saw them approaching. She put down her tablet and came to meet them at the outskirts of the tiny temporary village. She extended a hand.

Austin introduced her. "Yumi Lark is the excavation director."

Her dark straight hair framed her face. Ash looked down, then shook the proffered hand. "Yumi."

"Ma'am, thanks for coming down. I hope you'll find what we are doing here of interest. We're all pretty excited. If you have any questions, don't hesitate to ask."

The usual paraphernalia of an archaeological site — the plastic crates of labelled specimens, the sieves, the picks, the Portaloo, the brushes, the spades, the trestle tables — did some-thing to expel the sense of otherness. A Dunkin' Donuts box, a bright red cool bag containing water bottles, and the reflective yellow vests of the crew were brash interventions from the surface world. Lark reached over to a table on which a number of ziplock-bagged items were neatly laid out. She picked one up, proffered it to Ash. "Some finds we can date just by their appearance. Roman potsherds. A Celtic necklace and buckle pin."

Ash took the bag and held it up. "This came from down there?"

"Yes." Lark beckoned for them to follow her over. The dig itself was under a temporary cover of plastic sheeting, protection from the fine drizzle that was always falling from the ceiling. Ash could see a large rectangular section, perhaps twelve metres by fifteen, had been sunk into the silt. She stepped up to the edge.

The pit had been excavated in a series of terraces connected by lightweight ladders, each carefully pegged out and mapped with a grid of string. From their vantage she could see that the floor area shrank with each successive level. Small groups of archaeologists toiled below, engrossed in their work.

Lark continued. "We've been carbon-dating the biological matter as we go. It's finely layered – we think that this area slowly filled over time, and has lain here pretty much undisturbed.

"At least, that's the theory. Here's the thing. In the top levels we found modern remains: plastics, debris that we presume had been carried in here from the surface. A bicycle inner tube. A spanner. Then below that, Victorian glass bottles, spun wire, some ceramic pieces. Next, a medieval coin – a silver Edward III half-groat.

"Then we began to get the animal skeletons, and the worked flints. The stratification here is near-perfect – no geological uplift, no disturbance of the site by ploughing or building work, nothing that would churn the original deposition in this, this chamber, this—"

"Machine?" Austin offered.

There was a short silence. Ash looked over at Lark, but she wasn't going to be drawn. "So. Anyway, we decided to start a second trench. Over there."

Some metres away, another dig was in progress at the point where the floor met the chamber wall. They intersected at around a hundred and twenty degrees; standing there, up close, the space was so large that the curvature was negligible. Ash could not resist stooping to place her hand on the surface.

It was damp and chill to the touch, and when she took her hand away it was coated with a fine residue like rust. Lark passed her a wet wipe. "We're pretty sure the place is sterile, but until we've run all the tests, do be careful. Don't ingest anything."

Ash nodded and wiped her hands. "So what did you discover over here?"

"You may find this . . . interesting." Lark lifted a plastic sheet.

Incised into the wall a metre or so below the surface was a series of petroglyphs. Many were abstract: looping cup-and-ring designs, branching foliate trees. Others resembled animals: horses, or deer, perhaps. There were riders on horseback, holding spears and clubs aloft; men who appeared to sport antlers, or tails. Each was depicted with a simplified economy of line, more a symbol or an elemental evocation than a realistic representation. To an engineer's eye they suggested wiring diagrams, or even Mr. Beck's Underground map.

A Wild Hunt, perhaps?

Ash took in the scene, parts of which were still hidden. To witness the Wild Hunt was said to foretell some coming catastrophe – war, plague, or perhaps the death of the beholder. If you were lucky, the huntsmen would just steal your spirit while you slept and compel you to join the throng, to ride away with them to the Underworld, where you would be forced to remain for an eternity in the company of he-goats, black hounds and Herne the Hunter.

She was beginning to feel as if she'd been abducted into some mythical netherworld already.

"These drawings were covered by layers of silt. We think we're down to the contemporaneous ground level, the one that existed when these were executed. Here, we found stone implements and refashioned metallic points. And there may be more. We're not at the bottom of this chamber yet."

Ash frowned. "Metal points? These are Neolithic, surely?"

"Late Neolithic, early Bronze Age, we suspect. How these points were fashioned – well, that's another mystery. We're assuming the stratigraphic context is reliable, but . . . the carbon-dating and luminescence tests give us ambiguous results. Look." She took another ziplock from a pouch around her waist.

Ash glanced at the object within, but made no move to take it from her. It was a triangular piece of metal, around ten centimetres across. Two sides had been sharpened to form a blade, while a dark encrustation of resin marked the spot where a shaft had once been attached.

"What we can say is that it's been hammered into a point using brute force, probably on a stone anvil. But the metallurgy is sophisticated stuff. We're assuming that they are repurposed pieces of this, this—" Lark looked up at Austin. "This machine."

Ash completed her line of reasoning. "And if that point is Neolithic, then this machine, as you call it, must be older still."

Supplemental 1: **Anomaly 36 (Toroidal antechamber)**   CAD 76
Not to scale
Subject to amendment

Crossrail

postulated continuation of torus wall

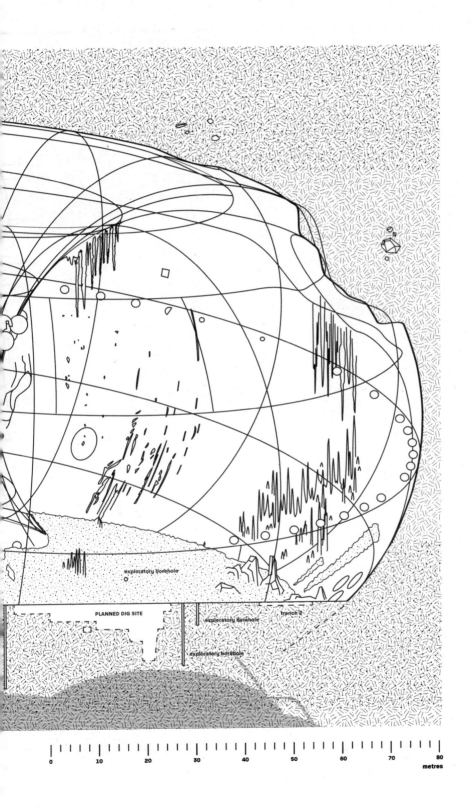

exploratory borehole

PLANNED DIG SITE

exploratory borehole   trench 2

exploratory borehole

0   10   20   30   40   50   60   70   80
                                                 metres

79 **SURVEY**

Rutherford paused in the lock-up garage adjacent to his studio. Just ahead, in its reserved space, was his immaculate metalflake orange Karmann Ghia. It was an indulgence, he knew, but one he justified as necessary transport to and from his place of work.

There was space for sixteen vehicles here, but his was the only one present. He could have parked in any bay, but always chose to park in the one he had been allotted. Force of habit, or simple conformity? He didn't know.

He was struck by the contrast of colour and of shape: the car was all curves, its surroundings all lines.

Angles and lines. The empty parking bays either side bore the dark stains of leaking sumps, set between yellow rules. They were amorphous yet symmetrical, a Rorschach test from which the imagination could conjure shapes.

This one looked like a recumbent man, a Shroud of Turin in engine oil. Just in front, the concrete wall met the tarmac at ninety degrees – there was no pediment, no concession to classical architectural form, just a precise, efficient and undecorated right angle.

A damp stain had made its way half a metre up the wall, and a light fuzz of green mould was following. Looking up, the floor above jutted out overhead. Its underside showed the imprint of the original wooden mould, the poured concrete fingering between the gaps. It was a floorboard in reverse, one material with one set of historical connotations revealing its absence as an imprint in another material with entirely different connotations.

It was a language to be deciphered: the semiotics of materials.

This was not a new idea. Gold means something different from bronze, Formica something different from wood, ivory something different from plastic.

What did concrete mean?

He stepped closer. The wall was cast from a loose aggregate held in a finer matrix, and he involuntarily reached out his hand to caress it. It took a light skim of flesh from his fingers: hard, rough, unforgiving.

What it possessed was an unyielding solidity, the solidity it was possible to build a city upon – but, he already knew, not one that respected the softer, more fragile human forms that inhabited it.

Here, there was a small rebate between two prefabricated concrete sections. It was just wide enough for him to insert his hand, up to the forearm. Could he apply enough pressure to break a bone? Or what if he crouched down on hands and knees, biting the kerb, tooth enamel against stone? What if someone was to apply their boot to the back of his head?

Who would win that battle?

He opened the door and sat in the leather driving seat, breathing deeply. Though the vehicle was vintage, he could faintly detect the aroma of leather, volatile organics, sealants, plasticisers and flame-retardant organobromines.

He declutched, turned the key in the ignition, revved the engine, then let it bite. The car jumped forward as if it had scented the outside world, knew it was being released and was eager to get out. At the top of a short ramp Rutherford wound down the window and presented his electronic pass card. An automatic barrier lifted. He floored the accelerator, swung the wheel round and pulled out into the traffic of the Western Avenue, heading home across London as he had done so many times before.

London sheltered humans, but it did not coddle them. It wasn't a warm and welcoming womb into which its inhabitants could settle, relax and feel cared for. It was the wind-whipped intersection, the six-lane flyover, the office entrance which afforded cover for the rough-sleeper who had to pad its uncompromising brutality with cardboard boxes, sleeping bags and blankets.

London did not love us, but it provided a stage on which our dramas played out.

Behind closed doors, the lighting was softer and the seating cushioned and supportive. Here, in our private spaces, we could escape the buzz and flicker of faulty streetlights, the cacophony of commerce, the civic street furniture designed to be durable enough to withstand the most drunken assaults that mankind and the English weather could throw at it.

These private spaces glowed in the dark. Rutherford could see them as he drove along the Westway: rectangles of warm light filtered through a fine mist that couldn't even work up the strength to become a drizzle. In these spaces, lives were lived, loves were cherished, families were raised.

He passed the new developments alongside the elevated section of the A40, near White City. The apartment blocks were built from a repeated unit, a stack of identical boxes one on top of the other, like a warehouse for storing people. The architectural plan may have only required one floor to be drawn in detail – every other was the same, in precise, production-line perfection.

Step and repeat.

The proclivity for humans to personalise their living spaces, to try and assert some kind of individuality, was revealed through a window box here, a string of drying laundry, a rusting bicycle or a Union Jack flag there.

The architects had found ways to discourage such interventions in their pure and perfect creations; for them, people were just another problem to be solved. If we box them up, curtail their freedom of expression, perhaps they'll learn how to live perfect lives as the perfect citizens of the perfect city.

Rutherford didn't want to personalise his space. That would require having a personality, and that was something he was not sure he'd created for himself, not yet. He found it far easier to accept the guidance of the spaces that contained him, far easier to let them circumscribe his world, his sense of self.

They were inflexible; he was not.

If he was living in a machine, he reasoned, if everything in it was planned to perfection, the issue of free will evaporated. There were no more difficult choices to make in life, because they had all been made for him. He could slot in, retreat into the more welcoming spaces of his own mind, and see his surroundings as an arrangement of surfaces enclosing voids, some lighted, some dark, some interior, some exterior, some containing people with their unfathomable and irrational lives, others the more comprehensible machinery of air conditioning conduit or hot water boiler or electricity substation. He had decided he preferred brick and concrete to flesh and mind – they simply made more sense.

He passed the containing wall of Paddington Basin. Concrete was not a material that aged gracefully; it didn't develop the patina of old wood, or the genteel sun-decked aristocracy of Edwardian brick. It was perfect only when clean and newly cast; from that moment on, it showed every stain, every spatter of bird shit, every graff artist's tag, every damp constellation of mould.

The city abhors a blank canvas.

As such, Rutherford thought, concrete was the ideal modern material: it had no natural grain, no weft, no shape of its own.

It, maybe just like him, needed to be moulded. You built a form, then filled it; then you took the mould away, and the negative shape it described was standing there, solid and inarguable, a three-dimensional void made physical.

It was the perfect material for the perfect city, *his* city.

Sometimes he would pull over to explore a car park, a lay-by or an underpass, inserting himself into the liminal spaces between railway siding, motorway crash barrier and retaining wall. Here, the air was greasy with diesel and he could taste carbon particulates in the back of his throat, the incessant roar of passing vehicles just a short step away. These were the non-spaces of the city, the accidental geometries between buildings, the scraps of landscape left over after the structures with a purpose had staked out their footprints. Rutherford had once cut a series of shapes from a sheet of card, then thrown them away when he found the fragile remains of the sheet far more interesting.

There might be tiles beneath his feet, but no one had stood here since they were laid. Why would they? This was a non-space, a sport of architectural whim. It served no function, it did not provide access, it was not a destination. It was just the result of a plane of paving meeting a plane of wall; if this was part of a natural environment it would become the home of some animal, or provide shelter for some hardy shrub. Here, it didn't even achieve that accidental, unintentional use.

Standing there, or in any one of the many other resonant spaces between or under or around or in the built environment he had discovered in the capital, he was at peace. He watched passers-by on their way to some important meeting, or a date, or a fix, perhaps; and imagined that were they to look his way, he would have taken on the pallor of his surroundings, a chameleon in concrete, and he would be to their uninterested gaze invisible.

He had soon discovered he was not alone. This was also where the forgotten people of the city lived, in the intersection of angles and planes, the platonic geometry of the built environment. Rutherford, crouching in these spaces to gauge their true dimensions, sometimes found others had been there before him, that it might be somewhere someone called home. He'd encounter folded but filthy clothes sporting designer names, stolen from market stalls in Shepherd's Bush, or plastic bags bearing the brand of Tesco or Sainsbury's or Superdrug, the magical sigils of the consumer world, stuffed with the accumulated detritus of an itinerant's life, every worldly good they owned. One contained a collection of stuffed animals; Rutherford understood them as inanimate proxies who could never refuse a hug, never walk out on you in the dead of night.

A twisted and stunted birch tree, hung with plastic bags that whipped like semaphore at sea, gave him a moment's shelter. The birch was an urban survivor – it regularly moulted its skin, sloughing off the dirt with which it became encrusted. It cast a shadow on the overpass stanchion directly behind him. A shadow thrown by the sun would move as the day progressed, but this one was stationary, the same every night, cast by an overhead streetlight. The tree could not sleep, and insomnia had emaciated it. He considered its sculptural qualities: a charcoal sketch on a grey background, a bifurcating construct grown from a seed rather than drawn with straight edge and set square on a drawing board. In so many ways it was also an interloper here, an alien intrusion.

Again and again, it was nature versus the man-made environment. Our victory is a temporary aberration; Rutherford knew if humans vanished tomorrow nature would creep back, and the slow but inevitable regreening of the abandoned urban landscape would proceed with absolute inevitability.

And it would not stop there. We now live on land that was once under the sea, or lay at the poles under kilometres of ice. One day it will do so again. Millennia hence, the slow churning of continental drift will bury flora, fauna and culture alike, and all this architecture will be flattened to another layer in the stratigraphy of geological history. It will become a thin line identifiable only by trace elements of iron, potassium, manganese, steel and rare earths; and that, whatever our pretensions to immortality, that line would be just a ten-thousandth the thickness of the chalk deposits that form the white cliffs of Dover.

Those deposits, built from the skeletons of countless marine creatures, are three to four hundred metres thick, laid down over several million years. If they had possessed a culture or built cities or dreamed of the spaces they lived in, they were now extinct, or had evolved into something else.

All they had now was a fine white powder to show for their ambitions.

Though we try and pave the world, nature plays the long game. It will outlast us all, and in the end it will win.

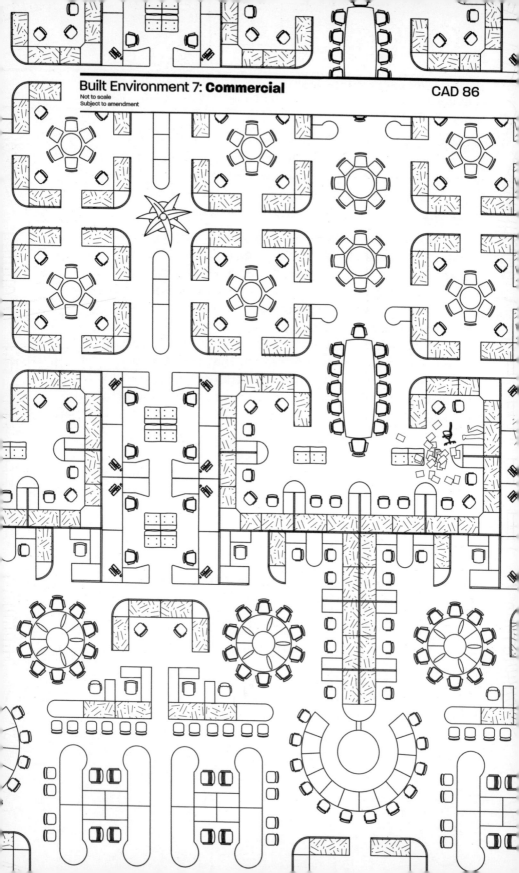

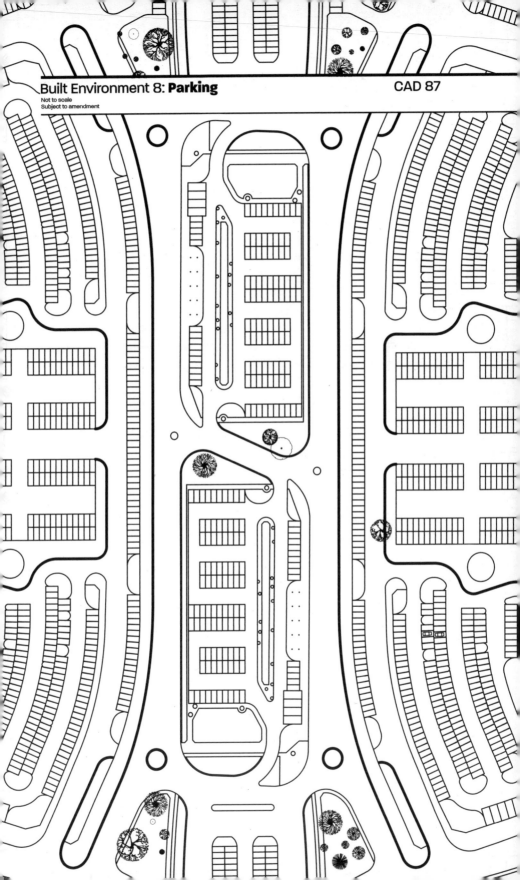

Yumi Lark adjusted her oversized hard hat. "The holographic subsurface radar gave us . . . interesting results."

Project overlord Georgia Ash and her flunky manservant Austin Arnold were down on another of their daily dig site visits. This time they had brought along a tall man in an old suit which he'd worn for a spot of home decorating. Ash had not bothered to introduce him, but he still seemed to be an integral part of their entourage. He had a vintage camera and a large spiral-bound sketchbook in which he occasionally made some indecipherable mark. He looked up, around, but paid very little attention to her, or their conversation.

Georgia had her hand on her hip, in that imperious manner that came so easily to her. "How so?"

"We were trying to map the extent of the, ah, the burials. But it seems that this chamber here might not be all we have."

Behind Ash, the man in the burnt suit with one arm painted a fluorescent orange had taken off his hard hat and placed it on a plastic chair. This, technically, was against site safety regulations.

Austin caught Yumi's look of disapproval. "Ah. Lloyd Rutherford is our artist in residence. He's been, ah, recording events." A pause. "I think that's what he does."

Rutherford spoke in a monotone without looking up from his sketchbook. "Interpreting."

Austin glanced at Rutherford, shook his head. He thought he'd shaken him off, but here he was. "Sorry, 'interpreting'. Show Yumi your work."

Lark thought the drawings bore very little resemblance to what she could see going on here in the dig: a criss-cross of lines and angles, intersecting curves, and lots of small, indecipherable notes. They looked more like circuit diagrams than the realistic, historically accurate site recreations with which she was familiar.

Georgia Ash seemed to notice him for the first time. "We thought it'd be good for public outreach. Deflect bad press over the delays by enthusing people about the archaeology." She seemed to tighten her already thin lips and regard him. Rutherford was oblivious to her presence. "Art in the service of commerce. As it has ever been."

Ash turned back to Lark. "My apologies. You were saying—"

Lark gestured over to another trestle table, where a colleague in another yellow hard hat stood over a laptop, head down between his shoulders, hands on the table. His bottom lip was sticking out and an expression of intense concentration crinkled his face. "Hector – can you show Ms. Ash what we have here?"

Hector looked up, gave her his full attention, then saw the new-comer's lanyard and realised to whom he was being introduced. His gaze seemed to sharpen. "Of course, ma'am." He stood back and indi-cated his laptop screen, which displayed a mottled grey image.

It looked like a medical ultrasound. A ghostly suggestion, rendered in white digital snow. At the top of the image was a large dark space and, towards the bottom, several more could be seen. It was banded horizontally by signal artefacts, and a scale in metres ran down the side.

Hector pointed. "Individual lines of scan data represent a section-al view of the subsurface. We're seeing deposition features, possible archaeological artefacts, and a fair amount of back-scattering." He moved a finger across the trackpad, and the image rotated in three di-mensions. "Multiple scans collected over a larger area allow us to con-struct a tomographic image. We can slice this into plan-view maps at any specific depth." He held his hand out, palm down, to demonstrate. "The patterning this reveals is the most obvious indicator of human activity. The density and saturation of the clay here is not best suited to this technique, but we're still getting a useful picture."

Lark looked sideways at Ash, hoping some of this might be going over her head. She knew it was petty, but she'd like to see her out of her depth, just for once.

She was impassive.

Lark picked up the story. "So, we have several theories. One – this cave, this space, is man-made, and a few hundred years old at most. That most of the artefacts that we are turning up in the dig have been carried here from elsewhere, deposited by the action of water.

"Two: though regular in shape, it is still some unusual sport of na-ture, a bubble formed in the cooling magma of the Carboniferous, the intricate structures the result of entirely natural geological processes.

"Or three: bizarre though it may sound, we are inside the fossilised remains of some gigantic prehistoric creature. The symmetries do sug-gest an organic origin."

There was, of course, another option. It was rarely spoken about, even by the archaeology team.

There was a pregnant pause. Ash broke the silence. "So what does your new data suggest?"

"As I say, the conditions are not ideal, but we're getting a pretty consistent result. The Anomaly, this space—" She gestured up, around.

"This space is dwarfed by what we think lies below."

Ash stepped closer to the laptop screen. "Hector, is it?"

"Yes. Well, we think there may be more chambers, below this one." He indicated the dark areas towards the bottom of the screen. "Many more, in fact, out to the limits of our equipment's sensitivity. This here is just the entrance hall."

"To what?"

"We have no idea. A series of underground caves? A labyrinth?" Hector had Ash's complete attention. Behind her, Rutherford had stopped sketching.

"How extensive do you think this, this labyrinth is?"

Lark drew a deep breath. "Well, no one has used this technology underground before. It's relatively new, and not that portable. But I had a few words with the museum, and arranged to take preliminary soundings — where feasible — at other sites under London. Deep-level Tube stations. The new orbital water main. The Roman amphitheatre under Guildhall Yard.

"Now we know what to look for, we see similar soundings in all the places we've checked so far. Every one. This structure below us, whatever it is — it is *huge*. We have yet to plot its true extent.

"And London is resting right on top of it."

Not to scale
Subject to amendment

93 **COMPONENT**

The late evening sky was a dark desaturated grey, differing from the east elevation of Rutherford's apartment block only in luminosity. It caught the low sun; ominous storm clouds — or perhaps a warehouse fire in the suburbs, he was not sure — provided the backdrop, while in the foreground black birds circled above a ventilation shaft. It was Van Gogh's *Wheatfield with Crows,* transported across three hundred and sixty miles and a hundred years from rural Auvers to urban London.

Rutherford crossed the plaza.

The estate had no centre – it was a miniature town, set out on a crossword grid, but with no uptown, no downtown, no market square. There was no seed from which it had naturally evolved, shaped organically by the needs and desires of its inhabitants.

The wild wood had been tamed, reduced to a sculptural copse artfully planted on a roundabout or a row of brutally coppiced elms along the High Street. The open moors were now rectangles of astroturf in the corporate forecourt, the flower meadow a window box on a tower block windowsill. These concrete cliffs were not populated by nesting terns, but verandahs containing rusting bicycles and plastic patio furniture, their original bright colours weathered to a faded apology.

Across the paved expanse an archipelago of flattened gum seemed to describe a new zodiacal constellation. He wondered if this was the nascent astrology of urban spaces, to be read underfoot rather than overhead. If so, Rutherford assumed it would inevitably convey the same tired messages of due destiny, romance and good fortune for those that could decipher it.

Somewhere a crane ratcheted up, one of the many skeletal towers that populated the landscape like the legs of H. G. Wells' war machines.

Up ahead, an empty rectangular fountain suggested a deserted swimming pool. He doubted summer swimmers had ever thrown themselves into it with abandon – the broken tiles and rusted pipework lining its base were far removed from the sculptural contours of the Trevi Fountain. A shopping trolley had fallen in, and been unable to climb back out. It had become a trap for the unwary.

He passed a bed of bare earth which, on the original plans, might have held shrubs and flowers, but now functioned as an ashtray and rubbish tip. Empty tins of imported beer hid in the corners like shy rats.

Along the main esplanade, streetlights set on poles too tall to usefully light their surroundings were flickering on. As he passed underneath, several fizzled, coughed, went out again. They provided one of the few expressions of unplanned randomness in this place, a reprieve from a purity of purpose.

He passed a short parade of shops. Gulls picked regurgitated chips out of vomit outside a minicab office, while a tame urban fox rummaged in the wheelie bins by the side of the fried-chicken shop. They were adapting to their changing environment, as man had before them. He imagined in a decade or so they'd be playing Texas Hold 'Em in a dive bar with badgers and rats from the suburbs, or carving up the streets in nocturnal turf wars that left flattened carcasses on zebra crossings.

There were ramps and tunnels and sweeping expanses designed solely for cars. These had no pavements, just a narrow crash barrier or kerb that, should you attempt to navigate them on foot, would do nothing to protect you from speeding vehicles. Here, humans were not meant to venture at all – just drive through, insulated in their metal boxes, on their way somewhere else.

Where were they going? To an underground car park, or a designated drop-off point perhaps? And thence to a lobby, an elevator, a long hallway, finally arriving at an apartment in which they might or might not find another human presence with whom they could interact?

These were more non-destinations. Like the departure lounge, the ticket hall, the subway, they were the places we travel through rather than to. Maybe these non-social spaces were the natural result of our desire to isolate ourselves, to obviate the requirement for uncomfortable human interaction and all the messy impracticalities that might entail.

He was passing through an exercise in geometry. Walkways and flights of steps presented themselves in quick succession, with little indication of their destination. Was he inside, or out? Was this or that particular area public or private? Was there even a distinction?

In the space between a wall and a reach of paving, trapped in a miniature whirlwind, was a Sargasso of plastic carrier bags and cellophane wrappers. They circled each other slowly, like dogs before a fight. He paused to watch the dance, and thought of the circuitous routes the wind must take through the estate. Used to bending treetops and caressing grass, there was no give to the surfaces it now moved over and around.

The shops on the ground floor provided the only recreational spaces, a checklist of the tenants' wants and needs: other than the minicab office and fried-chicken shop, there was a launderette, a betting shop, a hairdressing salon, an off-licence, a Thai takeaway, a charity shop, and a small 24-hour supermarket. These were the palaces of entertainment and culture, where, in exchange for cash, diversions and intoxications for mind and body could be found.

Those shops – perhaps the larger proportion – that were boarded up or shuttered with steel blinds provided a gallery space for the graff crews and taggers, their fluorescent Krylon all the more vivid against the colourless substrate.

Rutherford presumed these retail outlets had been another human engineering challenge; he had no doubt that some civic architect had carefully planned the positions of tills, aisles and exits to maximise spending and minimise loitering. As with the public spaces, they did not encourage one to linger – instead, they hurried you from here to there, 'there' always being somewhere else.

The concrete benches that did their best to suggest this was not the case were designed with a central armrest to prevent anyone sleeping on them. This subtle form of social engineering ensured infractions of the by-laws did not need to be policed or punished; they simply didn't occur. The benches were usually empty anyway, positioned as they were where no one would choose to sit — facing a wall, perhaps, or a windswept rectangle of scrubby grass criss-crossed with shortcuts the planners had not thought to provide, their assumption being that the imagined residents' civic pride would mean they'd prefer to walk around instead.

The dimensions of these plazas and concourses, the floor plans of the retail spaces, the speed humps and cameras on the roads — all were designed to govern his movement through them, describe a precise flowchart of his available actions. Certain surfaces were tiled with small pyramids, making them painful to walk on; other routes were indicated with small raised bumps, a guide for the blind, those who couldn't read the embedded visual cues that told them what they should or should not be doing or where they should or should not be going.

Skateboarders and parkour enthusiasts responded to these restricted options in their own inimitable way; the human creative urge can never be fully extinguished, though the unforgiving environment punished them for their infractions with scrapes and bruises, road rash and concussion.

He stopped and tilted his head back, shading his eyes. As a piece of gargantuan physical geometry, his apartment block was uncompromising; the solidity of its presence was as great as a limestone cliff. Above the shops ran open pedestrian walkways, aerial alleys that collected cardboard boxes, unwanted furniture and rancour. Above that, windows and balconies were arranged in a rhythmic repetition whose soundtrack was a pneumatic drill on the nearby arterial slip road.

A clothes line strung from a rusted bracket was a flash of colour against the grey, a small length of bunting that did little to dispel the utilitarian brutalism. These were not the medieval tents of grand families with coats of arms fluttering outside; they were identically laid-out living spaces decorated with T-shirts emblazoned with aspirational brand names that promised lifestyles that were currently unavailable.

These small interventions spoke of messy contingent human existence, of the complex and varied lives that were played out in these identical spaces designed for identical people, unindividuated biological entities without their own personalities, dreams, proclivities or passions. They were meat in a battery farm, but without the endgame that gave farmed meat its purpose.

Even the windows could only be in one of three positions: open, shut, or half-open. The few choices the tenants were permitted had still been circumscribed beforehand, as a matter of design.

Rutherford understood that the flats were an outward representation of an inner conformity, a cowing of individuality in the name of equality. If the tenants, some of whom came from very different countries and cultures, were not all the same, every effort was being made to erase any meaningful distinction.

Rutherford, on the other hand, embraced this conformity. It gave him a sense of depersonalised stillness, a deep inner peace, and made the day-to-day routine of his existence less troubling.

It was a form of self-obfuscation.

Maybe he could take it even further. He wondered if he could dissolve into a wall, become part of it, swap the molecules of his being for the prestressed steel, concrete and Portland cement of this place. He would then become a machine, transcend his biological nature and exist as a set of principles governed by rules rather than an evolved ape with a precocious need for self-expression.

The building knew how to play this game. Here, at the foot of the tower, there was a purposeful flattening of the sense of a grand façade. By contrast, a palace or civic building would present a sequence of anterooms, each more intimate than the last. Progressing through to an inner sanctum, the deepest level reserved for those who have been permitted a private audience, the visitor would reflect on the occupant's status and feel the required awe.

This was not the case here.

And if social class could be articulated or erased through architecture, so, perhaps, could gender: there existed buildings with separate entrances, exits, staircases and spaces for men and women – the architectural expressions of a society in which half the population were confined to the private domestic space, and when allowed outside were still clothed in an extension of that space, one made from fabric instead of brick.

The entrance was a low sweep of reinforced concrete supported by a row of metal columns, above which was a rare act of individuation — the building, at least, was allowed a name:

ROARK TOWER

The awning protected smokers from the rain, while also acting as a wind baffle. It was nothing like a Roman portico, on whose heritage it distantly drew; it was no grand presentation of intent, more a grounding graphical centrepoint from which the rest of the edifice rose.

It must have looked quite impressive on the plans.

The parts required to keep the original revolving entrance in working order were no longer available, so some years ago it had been replaced with sliding aluminium doors. One pane of toughened glass was now a crazed milky-white.

He pushed it open. It emitted a nerve-shredding *screek* as the metal frame scraped across the terrazzo. It was a strange kind of music; in his imagination he looped it, laid the beat of a jackhammer and the *shush* of tyres on the elevated section of the A40 over the top. It sang to him. Not a lullaby, not a fugue, but the heartbeat of this place, the bodily murmurs of these deserted plazas, sunken stairwells and aerial corridors, where a shadowed corner might conceal a neighbour — or an armed assailant.

Sometimes they were one and the same person.

He drew a long, deep breath, held it in. The lobby smelled of wet dog, and put Rutherford in mind of an office block rather than a residential building. Angular parallelograms of daylight fell across the chestnut-brown lino; the area near the doors had been polished by the passage of countless feet, while the recesses were matt with dust. It was like an awkward introduction: it attempted to articulate the language of the threshold, the transition from outside to inside, public to private, but instead this communal space was a no-man's-land, and as such was no one's responsibility. Outside, the council were supposed to sweep pavements and repair light fixtures. In here, a more laissez-faire arrangement held.

The concierge desk was empty, as it always was. An obsolete telephone, no longer connected to any switchboard, was screwed to the Formica. Behind, a tubular steel chair, upholstered in black Naugahyde, spilled yellow foam.

Along the wall were a series of lockers for post, the original cubbyholes having been susceptible to theft. A soiled mattress and an arrangement of black binbags that resembled a baroque sculpture lay under an open staircase to the right, its steel banister the only visible support for the risers hung below it. On the far wall was painted a two-metre-high letter 'G', this motif being repeated on every other floor — there being no other way to tell them apart.

He looked at the lift buttons. One was filled with chewing gum.

He kept his orange Karmann Ghia in the underground car park. He would visit it at night, noting the lines the overhead fluorescents drew across its body. He'd rev the engine in the enclosed space, savouring the scent of internal-combustion by-products. He rarely ventured beyond the M25, and other than the commute to his studio or the Crossrail tunnels, his trips were circular and without destination: they would begin and end, as he thought he himself might, here.

Rutherford's apartment was seven floors up. The lift squealed and scraped, and he absently drummed his fingers on the wall in counterpoint.

He stepped out. The large '7', a relative of the 'G' on the ground floor, had become a noticeboard for marker-pen messages. A corridor ran to the middle distance both left and right. It was lit night and day by fluorescents, and open along one side from shoulder height to the outside world. Through this gap a strip of perfectly featureless grey sky was visible.

He passed a window that gave onto a living space incongruously decorated with William Morris wallpaper. Further down was a replacement door: a faux blown-glass demilune window, plastic wood-textured panelling and a brass handle. Whitewashed cement lions stood either side. The tenants were busy dismantling the architect's original vision, customising, repurposing and perverting it to their own ends.

He stepped over a child's scooter and approached his front door. His neighbours' flats either side did not have curtains. He wondered if this was because they didn't value their privacy, or simply enjoyed the view. Perhaps they just didn't think about curtains.

He could have afforded to live elsewhere, but he chose to live here. In this, he knew, he was an outlier.

Maybe it wasn't that straightforward: he *assumed* he chose, but he suspected the geometry of this place, the peculiar confluences of lines and angles, was beginning to shape his inner thought processes, mute his autonomy. His sense of being a someone had started to fray around the edges.

If the built environment restricted movement, maybe it also restricted thought.

Some of the tenants, in their own inarticulate fashion, seemed to suspect this. They were settlers in a disputed territory, and the lions and the wallpaper and the absence of curtains were a first strike in a guerrilla war of self-expression.

Rutherford, however, felt most at peace when he obeyed the dictates of the building, lived as the idealised compliant automaton the anonymous architect had intended.

Built Environment 5: **Residential**
Not to scale
Subject to amendment

CAD 102

Yumi Lark pushed back onto her haunches and surveyed the site. Her legs were stiff, her hands filthy, and her neck sounded like a bag of gravel when she turned her head.

The dig was progressing. Soon they would hit what the scans suggested was the bottom of the silt-filled lower side of the tilted torus that was Anomaly 36.

Here, if one was inclined to interpret the radar data in such a fashion, was the thinnest part of the floor. Beyond, deeper, lay the other mysterious voids. It was not unknown for the equipment to throw up ambiguous readings; archaeology was rarely an exact science, and these circumstances were certainly unusual.

Still, she had been aware of a palpable excitement growing over the last few days.

Georgia Ash had made regular visits, climbing down the ladders to the base of the dig to inspect the proceedings and up again without much in the way of comment.

She was on her latest visit, still some distance above the lowest level, when she heard a shout.

Lark's spade had hit something solid.

The nearest archaeologists immediately dropped their tools and came over. Everyone else stopped whatever it was they were doing. Lark was on her hands and knees, brushing dirt away.

Ash pushed through the huddle. Hector swung a floodlight around. A section of a convex surface was visible, maybe half a metre across, but growing as the earth was cleared.

In a matter of minutes, an elliptical object had been fully revealed. Lying on, or attached to, the ground, it reminded her of the airtight hatch of a submarine.

Ash voiced Lark's first impression. "A door?"

In its centre was a circular arrangement of bumps. Lark passed her hand across the surface, counting them off: ". . . ten, eleven, twelve." It was made from a similar material to the walls of the chamber, a dark stone with a silken sheen. Around the edges, still holding a residue of dirt, was an incised border design: baroque interlinked ferns, or perhaps an idealised representation of complex molecular bonds. The style matched no historical period of decorative art she could recall.

"It *does* look like a hatch." Her probing seemed to have no effect. She ran her fingers around the rim. There was a small lip; the surrounding surface, or as much of it as they could see, seemed to be made of the same material. She could sense no handle, no release, no hidden mechanism. "Is there a lock?" she wondered aloud.

Ash was now standing directly over her. "A lock requires a key." Lark looked up. Ash pointed. "There, in the middle. What's that?"

At the centre was a triangular depression, the size of a nacho.

Lark traced it out with an index finger. If that was the keyhole, where was the key?

The shape reminded her of something. Something she'd seen recently.

One level up, unseen by the others, Rutherford sketched the new discovery on a fresh sheet of paper.

107 **LOCATION**

Built Environment 6: **Residential**
Not to scale
Subject to amendment

CAD 108

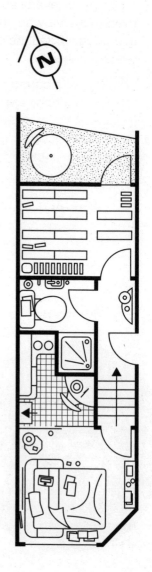

Rutherford stood, feet placed apart to brace himself, on the flat roof of Roark Tower. Rising above him were the winch and gondola used by the window cleaners and maintenance crews, and, above that, a tall mobile-phone mast. Other structures punctuated the scene: a boarded vent, a wooden frame wrapped in chicken wire containing two pigeons, and a clump of obsolete dishes, pointing spaceward at a satellite that may have long ago fallen back to Earth.

There were several sun-bleached deckchairs up here too, even though it was officially off limits. It was another of those everyday infractions of the building's rules and regulations which went unpunished.

He needed to counterbalance his subterranean existence, the long hours he was spending at the dig site. The Anomaly disturbed him in ways he found hard to articulate. The organic curves, the deep sense of history, the growing realisation that if it *had* been designed, it was not for human proportions.

Who had been its architect?

Up here, he had an uninterrupted 360-degree view of the city, the building's ledge mere metres away. The first spots of rain were falling, and he could see a curtain of water moving towards him across the junction of the elevated slip road and the underpass below, turning the asphalt a glossy black. Had he the notion, he could take a long stride, another, then vault the low pediment and out into empty space; there would be three seconds of weightlessness, terminated by an appointment with the pavement below.

His leg twitched, as if it wanted to move forwards of its own volition.

He sat.

He let his mind drift down into the fabric of the leviathan that supported him, and tried to rein in his thoughts.

Below were exactly 270 units, laid out over 31 identical floors: one, two or three bed apartments and maisonettes, each designed to house between two and five people. In many cases they housed seven, ten, a dozen or more; others, like his own, just a single soul.

The tenants were again disobeying the building's rules.

There seemed to be set roles the architecture assumed its residents would fulfil, parts in a play the plot of which had not been revealed to him: Husband. Father. Wife. Mother. Child. Aunt. Uncle.

Lover.

All buildings have a purpose, that for which they are designed. Were these large-scale civic building projects, intended to remake the post-war landscape of the city and usher in the modern metropolis, also intended to refashion their inhabitants? Was the building a three-dimensional exercise in social engineering?

If it was possible to fix the spaces we inhabit, make them rational and functional, then would they in turn fix *us*?

It had a totalitarian appeal. In this perfect machine for living, personal autonomy seemed to have become a dangerous heresy.

It had not originally been this way. Before we had learned how to build, we lived in caves – the shelters nature provided. Then came simple huts, dwellings built by those who lived in them from the materials to hand. The person who laid the stones was the person who dwelt within them: they were expressions of who we were.

As society grew more complex, skills became more compartmentalised. At some point lost to history, the first architect drew the first plan for the first client. Whose identity were they now expressing? The intended occupants', or their own?

In short order it was not just people who needed housing – so did nascent institutions. The meeting hall, the court of elders, the shrine of the forebears – each developed its own language of space and form. Soon these became codified: the dome, pediment and steeple, the architecture of Governance, Justice and Salvation.

Each embodied certain social norms, each endeavoured

to make them more permanent by building them a home. Architecture outlasts people, and thus continuity across the generations would be assured.

Other forms followed: the fort, the theatre, the museum, the gallery, the basilica, the amphitheatre, the mansion, the slum. These buildings, and the concepts that inhabited them, were arranged into towns. On this solid conceptual foundation these towns grew, and eventually became cities.

People were pulled in by the opportunities – social, cultural, sexual and financial – that these places provided. Sprawling suburbs were built to house them, and these soon developed a symbolic language of their own, promising the aspirational middle-management salaryperson an affordable parody of the palaces of old. A ghost of a Corinthian column, a faux turret, a classical pediment cast in concrete, they were styled from the memetic residue of half-remembered history, a new-town built from hand-me-down heritage.

These changes were not all happening at the periphery. As old industries and institutions became obsolete, the shipyard or the warehouse or the church became the harbourside redevelopment or the new-build investment opportunity.

The shopping mall. The cinema complex. The nightclub.

We, or people very much like us, had had these ideas – but now Rutherford suspected the ideas were having us. Power had become embedded in the forms it took, developed beyond the conscious intentions of any individual. We had externalised our internal sense of the world in wattle and daub, adobe, and now concrete, glass and steel in order to preserve it, and now we were living inside our own creation. If this process had begun with those first public buildings that housed the ideas we deemed necessary to run a society smoothly, maybe it inevitably progressed to the likes of Roark Tower.

If Roark Tower was the embodiment of a particular concept, Rutherford was trying to decipher precisely what that concept might be. Whether or not it was the one the original architect had envisaged, he had no way of knowing; what he sensed, however, was that it had a well-defined structure, an expressed form in three dimensions: the layout of its floors, the points of entry and exit, spaces both public and private, the pinches and voids that controlled the degree of social interaction of those who lived in it were not arbitrary.

Whatever the original plan, those planners were long gone. Who was watching now, via the CCTV cameras? Who was in control?

The building *itself*?

Not to scale
Subject to amendment

Sample 1

Sample 2

Sample 3

Sample 4

Sample 5

Sample 6

Sample 7

Sample 8

Sample 9

Sample 10

Sample 11

Sample 12

Sample 13

Sample 14

Sample 15

Sample 16

Sample 17

Sample 18

Sample 19

Sample 20

Sample 21

Sample 22

Sample 23

Sample 24

Sample 25

Sample 26

Sample 27

Sample 28

Sample 29

Sample 30

Sample 31

Sample 32

Sample 33

Sample 34

Sample 35

Yumi Lark strode into the grand hall of the Natural History Museum, past the statue of Darwin, the café and the Mesozoic flora exhibit.

Ever since her first meeting with Dippy the Dinosaur at the entrance, aged six, this place had been a site of pilgrimage; she never ceased to appreciate that this cathedral to science, a monument in its own right, was where she now worked.

Currently the diplodocus was on tour, probably to sell-out audiences who wanted to hear him reminisce about life in the Jurassic and tell anecdotes about how he never suspected those annoying little mammals that got under his feet would ever amount to anything. In Dippy's absence the cavernous main hall now contained the skeleton of a blue whale, a spectral alien presence in the red-brick Victorian space.

The museum was home to specialists in many fields – taxonomy, biodiversity, planetary and evolutionary science and more – but she headed straight to the palaeontology department.

She pushed open the door without knocking. "Martina. That arrowhead."

Martina Martinez looked up from her microscope. Yumi Lark had been bringing her the finds from the dig in Anomaly 36 pretty much on a daily basis, as they were unearthed. They were now arriving at a rate faster than she or her assistant could unpack them.

"Hello. Good morning, Yumi. I'm fine, thanks for asking." Martinez nodded towards a stack of unopened plastic crates. "You want to look through those yourself?"

The third crate contained what she was looking for. A ziplock bag, in which Lark could see an arrowhead still coated in grey silt.

She held it up. "Can you take a look at this now? Please?"

Martinez exhaled audibly, acquiesced. "Pass it over."

Lark did so. Martinez turned it around in her hands, testing the point. "Metal, an alloy of some kind. No particular style of workmanship that I'm familiar with. I'd need to do some tests. X-ray fluorescence. You know the drill."

"How long?"

"Come back after lunch."

After lunch, Martinez's manner had taken a turn. She seemed puzzled.

"This thing is peculiar. It's been worked, quite crudely, into a point. See the marks, here and here, and the abrasions on the rear? But it wasn't originally an arrowhead. Whatever it was *originally*—" She broke

THE BLACK LOCOMOTIVE

off mid-sentence, held it up, shook her head.

"So I did a basic spectrographic analysis. Non-destructive. The results – well, the results make little sense. My first hunch was meteoric iron, which has high levels of nickel and cobalt. That might explain the isotope ratio, which is, um, non-terrestrial."

"Non-terrestrial?" Martinez repeated.

"It's not unusual. Before the smelting of ore had been perfected, Bronze Age iron was almost entirely meteoric in origin. It was extremely rare, as you can imagine, and usually used for high-status items — Tutankhamen's funerary headrest, dagger and bracelet, things like that."

"This doesn't look like a meteorite."

"It wouldn't. It's been forged with a high degree of skill, then later repurposed by someone who only has an elementary grasp of metallurgy. There's a story here, all right. Anyway, I wondered if there was a match in the database, so I did a search."

Though the museum's collection was extensive, the cataloguing system was an unwieldy hybrid of digitised records, ledgers and card indexes, itself a record of changing technologies. Martinez brought up a page on her laptop.

One result. There was no photograph, just a catalogue number and a short description. The identification was provisional: 'arrow point'.

It had been found in the tidal flats on the banks of the Thames, near the Tower of London, by a metal detectorist in 1964. Martinez turned the screen so Lark could read the entry.

"The dating is ambiguous, but probably Mesolithic. Back then the river's banks were marshland. We have evidence that extensive wooden platforms, raised above the high-tide mark, allowed the local inhabitants to move around, hunt and fish."

Whoever had originally catalogued the item had also added a note: OOP/MISCATALOGUED.

"Oop?" Lark had not heard the term.

Martinez clicked a link. *Out of place object.*

The item must be in the museum's older collections, as everything post-1982 had been photographed and the photograph digitised. Martinez cross-referenced the catalogue number. Much of the museum's archive was now stored off-site, and she suspected this might be the case here.

She ran her finger along a line of text. A cabinet number was listed. She punched the air.

"Yes!" Not only was it in the museum, it was actually on permanent display.

They could go and look! "Case number 407. The River Thames collection."

Without another word Lark ran out of the lab, letting the door slam behind her. She sprinted down the corridor, grabbing a doorframe at the end in order to corner at speed, her shoes slipping on the polished floor. Each cabinet had a number, painted in gold on a small elliptical plaque. She jogged past skulls uncovered during the construction of the Blackwall Tunnel, medieval buckles, displays of ornate ceremonial Roman body armour.

"Number 407, 407 . . ."

She came to a halt in front of an iguanodon, frozen mid-roar. It was not going to give her directions. "720. Back . . ."

Lark counted the cases. She must have walked right past it.

"407."

The case contained a variety of early metal items. Wrought iron, bronze . . . a selection of coins. A clasp. A sword hilt, eroded to a tarry black.

Ah. There.

Lark held her hand to the glass to block the reflections. It was listed on the accompanying label as an arrow point, but it was unlike any arrow point she had seen.

This specimen had not been reworked like the others they had unearthed in the Anomaly.

This one was perfect.

Back in the lab, under the lights, she examined it more closely. It was a silken jet black, triangular, with scalloped indentations on each face. The workmanship was exquisite: it had a precise, machined perfection.

She could see why it had been difficult to classify. The arrowheads they had unearthed in the Anomaly had been too mangled for any sensible appraisal, but here, on display in plain sight in a cabinet she must have passed almost daily, was a pristine example, one that had somehow escaped the attention of Bronze Age hunter-gatherers.

If the means of its manufacture were obscure, its style fitted no known Mesolithic culture. There seemed to be no symbolic or decorative aesthetic governing the placement of the markings, though she couldn't shake the impression there must be some logic at work. They were too precise, too even to be arbitrary.

She turned it over in her gloved hands. Like a bog body, it had been preserved by the anaerobic Neolithic peat in which it had been discovered.

She checked the archaeological context in the museum's records. No bones, no scraps of hide or preserved clothing, nothing had been discovered alongside it. Its original owner, whoever they might have been, had left no trace, no clue as to their identity.

Just this.

Had it been lost, perhaps dropped into the reeds along the banks of the river before it could be sharpened, attached to a shaft and turned into an efficient killing machine? Who had stalked their prey, right here in London, on the open marshland that once lay beneath her feet, in an age long before it had been drained, paved, and skyscrapers raised on its foundation?

119 **SITE**

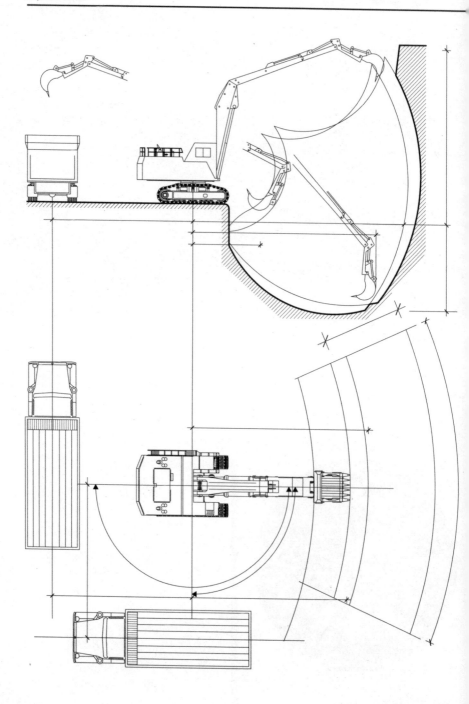

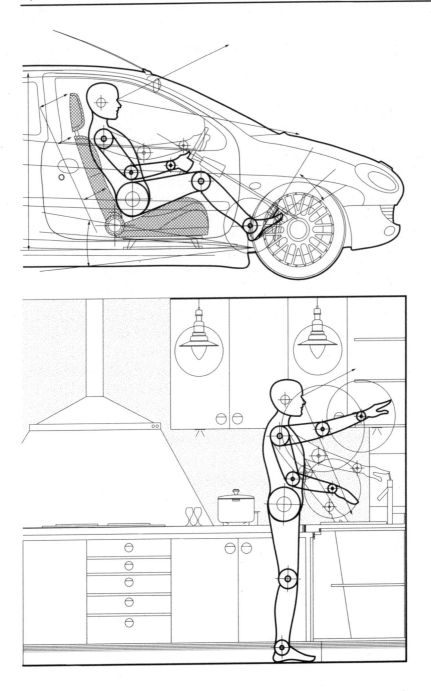

Rutherford's apartment was compact, a precision-engineered and ergonomically designed space for living.

Planned, he guessed, on the drawing board of some idealistic male architect who never intended to live in it himself, it had numerous features of obscure use, some of which he could only guess at. Many of these had been broken, repurposed, ignored, or had not fulfilled their intended function in the first place.

There was a sliding door between the living space and the kitchenette that was jammed in the open position; the handle had come adrift, leaving a raw bullet hole of plywood. At some point before Rutherford had taken up residence, the plumbing had been replaced. As the original pipes were embedded within the concrete itself, the new ones ran up the wall beside the front door, across the ceiling, through a small hole in the intervening wall into the bathroom, and back down to the basin and bath. They had leaked, leaving a large grey stain rimmed with a film of green algae on the rear wall. If he lay in the bath and blurred his vision, it resembled a Madonna and Child – or perhaps a shrouded revenant.

The electrical sockets were also recent, chrome boxes screwed to the skirting in peculiar locations. These had their own network of ducting that could be traced back to a box in the hall to which he did not have a key. In the kitchenette, he imagined studies had been undertaken to find the optimal positions for the washing machine, sink, hob and waste chute, and the number of steps required to perform specific daily tasks – cooking, washing, cleaning – had been tallied and cross-referenced. In this way the required motion of an arm or leg in any direction had been minimised, reduced to a specific set of actions carried out within the constrained space.

He wondered if the living room – or the bedroom – had been subject to a similar analysis, one that measured the movement of the bodies on the bed and plotted some optimum line of least resistance from hip to leg to lip to breast.

The kitchen had fitted units, plastic boxes with rounded corners and orange doors that were attached to the walls with brackets. Several of these had come loose, the plastic having perished, leaving no purchase for replacement screws.

On top of the non-functional gas hob he had placed an electric hotplate; from the grill above he hung his drying shirts. There was a chute that delivered rubbish to a room in the basement that had not been emptied in over a decade.

While yesterday's tomorrows had promised many wondrous innovations, Rutherford reflected, the liberation of women from the domestic space, and primarily the kitchen, had not been one of them. Progress moves in unexpected directions.

In his wardrobe hung his burned and painted suit. It was a uniform, of sorts, one also worn by the buildings he inhabited, the motorways he drove along. It had been decorated with the semiotics of road sign and graffiti tag, the arrows and letters and numbers that named and described the spaces he navigated. He had adopted it as his own, like some kind of urban camouflage.

If the city spoke to him in its own language, much of it had been borrowed from the natural environment it had replaced: the yellow and black warning stripes of the wasp, repurposed as the motorway crash barrier; the multi-hued flowers of the field, the traffic lights reflected in the shopfronts of the high street. The blue of the sky, always out of reach however high we build our skyscrapers, was offered back to us, second hand, in the plate glass of a new-build apartment complex.

In the living room a sofa bed was positioned under the one window; this he always left in the 'bed' position. To the left of this was a wall-mounted long-wave radio that could only receive two stations, one of them Radio 4, and an intercom on which were two unlabelled buttons, one red and one black, that Rutherford had idly pressed several times to no effect soon after moving in. The central heating was on continually, meaning that the windows, even in the middle of winter, were open; he had not located a thermostat.

There were shadows on the wall where objects had been unscrewed and removed, leaving rectangles of lighter or darker magnolia. To the left of the window a section of orange and ochre wallpaper in a large geometric repeat had been revealed; this, he had decided, resembled a framed landscape, a window into the apartment's past. He would lie on the sofa bed at night and watch car headlights project vertical slashes of light across it, populating it with two-dimensional characters from an imagined two-dimensional drama.

He walked into the room which he supposed should have been the bedroom. Here he stored paint swatches and press clippings, his portfolios of drawings and prints. Custom shelving held box files and ring binders of architectural catalogues: tile finishes, paint swatches, small square samples of stone, industrial carpet and non-slip rubber matting. This minor defiance of the interior designer's original intentions gave him a small thrill.

If the place was an exercise in optimisation and function, the efficient systematisation of human need and existence, who they had actually had in mind when they built it remained opaque. The ideal citizen, the worker-drone, the nuclear family? Rutherford considered the shopping trolley in the waterless fountain outside, the lost child he could hear wailing in the off-licence, the dysfunctional family two doors down whose nightly fights he noted with a resigned disinterest.

They had not been part of the original plan.

Maybe they felt their lives, their happiness, were now the building's responsibility rather than their own, that it owed them the ideal life it had been designed to provide.

Rutherford again found this thought comforting. If his existence was simply a codified set of possible moves, like a game of Tetris, it absolved him of the mental effort of recreating it himself. His choices had already been made for him.

He could lie on the floor and let his consciousness float above his still body, a mind freed from the challenges of self-determination. He then had all the time he desired to chart his internal mental spaces, which he suspected more and more had come to resemble those he lived in.

He heard an impact followed by a muffled expletive, and looked at the wall. Just two metres away was another apartment whose interior he would never see, housing people in whose lives he played no part. If this place had been a village from centuries past, the people he was surrounded by would all be known to him since childhood, and perhaps for generations prior to that. Their lives and his would be intimately entwined. They would all be hauling behind them a long family history, and all the social obligations and concerns that that engendered.

He imagined it would be like never leaving school. All the bullies and bastards would follow you through adult life, an entourage you could never give the slip.

But here, in the city, he could be invisible. He was anonymous, and thus he was free.

He reached for his phone. The other innovation the original architects had not foreseen was digital.

There were smartphone apps that allowed him to penetrate these concrete cubicles through which no sound travelled, no hand could reach. They collapsed distance and opened up secret corridors that bypassed the architectural spaces of the plaza or the street, or the predefined social arenas of the bar or club. Rutherford pictured them as an extra-dimensional roadmap, linking not physical destinations with a defined location but *people,* and all their myriad and peculiar needs and requirements. It was an association of common interest rather than geographical proximity.

He'd order food to be delivered before he left the studio, and on cue, a driver who never took his or her helmet off would arrive at his apartment just after he did. It could be the same driver every time, and he'd never know. The app informed him when they were outside the door; he'd open it, press his thumb to a screen, and close it, all without a word being spoken.

His personal relationships, if that's what he should term them, were becoming increasingly similar. He'd swipe and scroll, find someone new, and soon he'd get a reply.

Sometimes they were women, sometimes they were men. Sometimes they were both, or neither.

They would meet somewhere neutral. There would be drinks, or dinner, or an aimless nocturnal perambulation. Rutherford, distant and unengaged, would listen and nod in a manner he thought they might appreciate; then he'd leave, or they'd ask him back, or he would suggest they might continue talking at his apartment.

Sometimes the conversation would be entirely superficial – a negotiation of terms, perhaps. Or he would find he'd delved deep into a subject of some complexity, revealed parts of his character that came as a surprise even to himself. There was a peculiar intimacy in anonymity.

He'd heard confessions of misdemeanours that would have earned the perpetrator life without parole, childhood traumas revealed by way of coded metaphor; seen scars both mental and physical, some accidental, some self-inflicted, others performed in coercive relationships in which the recipient was only now coming to terms with their victimhood.

Some laughed and left with promises to return; occasionally they did. Some thought they should save him from something. Himself, perhaps. Others were racked with guilt over affairs they had conducted years previously or accidental verbal slights Rutherford thought no more than indiscretions, while others would mention in passing that they'd killed a man, or, aged fourteen, had drowned their only child.

These were the true tales of the city, plucked at random from its eight million inhabitants. Highly accomplished or barely functional, privileged or from the underclass, articulate or incoherent, he listened without judgement. If demons still kneaded the stomachs of their victims, if victims they were, their only judge was their own conscience.

But these were diversions. Most of his time was spent on his art. It was a calling, an obsession. Only in his work did he truly lose all sense of himself, feel the borders of his being seep into the angles and planes of his city. He opened a portfolio and spread some of his recent drawings out on the floor.

Curves and triangles.

This was new. In the Anomaly there were no rectilinear walls which met at right angles. No signs that told him where to go and what to think. If this was architecture, it spoke of ideas he could not divine in a language he did not understand.

He felt that dislocating sense of the unfamiliar, the alien, begin to rise again in his gut.

Leisure 1: **People**
Not to scale
Subject to amendment

CAD 127

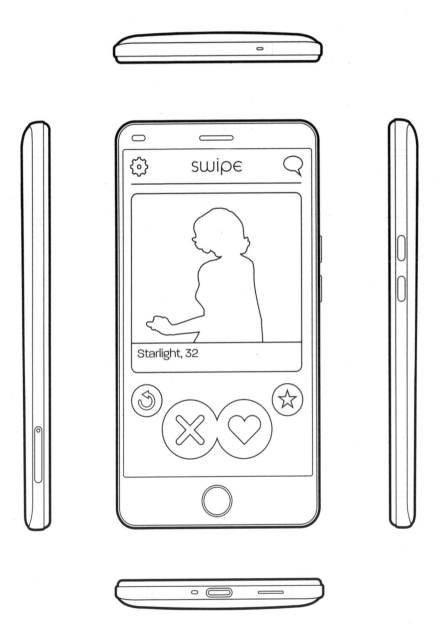

Leisure 2: **People**
Not to scale
Subject to amendment

CAD 128

Yumi Lark was kneeling beside the newly uncovered door early the following day, her hard hat a vivid accent of colour under the floodlights. She was in conversation with Georgia Ash. Rutherford observed them from a short distance. He could not hear what they were saying – their voices didn't carry, even in this enclosed space.

Lark held something dark and triangular just above the door's surface, rotating it left and right. Ash nodded.

Lark climbed up, passing Rutherford without acknowledgement. He reached out and touched her sleeve. She looked down at his hand in surprise, then up at Rutherford, giving him a swift appraisal.

Without preamble he pointed back to the hatch. "What did you find?"

Yumi Lark found Rutherford's intensity disconcerting. Though she had been told he had full access to the site, she still chose to ignore him whenever she could. "Why don't you go and ask her?"

A shadow fell across the ground. Georgia Ash looked up, considered Rutherford's fluorescent sleeve and burned suit. There were charcoal smudges around his nose. Though his hair was still immaculate, there were dark rings under his eyes. He looked like he rarely slept. "You're the artist, right?"
    Rutherford nodded.
    "I assume, if you're down here, you have proper clearance?"
    He appeared to be confused. "I was under the impression it was you that had provided it."
    Ash decided she might like this peculiar man. "Hm. No, it is not my remit to decide who has what level of access. I'm only in charge of the . . . let's say, the more practical side of this project. Your presence here was decided several levels above my pay grade."

This revelation gave Rutherford some pause. His appointment as artist in residence had arrived by email – he had not pitched, there had been no submissions process or shortlist. He had simply been informed, if he wished it, that the job was his. Not for the first time, he wondered if he had been put forward by someone he knew, someone familiar with his oeuvre. Who?

One of his nocturnal visitors? It wasn't beyond the realms of possibility. He rarely asked about or recalled the details of their public lives.

Had Ash been one of them? He'd remember her, he felt sure.

Though he had asked in passing where his recommendation might have come from, no more information had been forthcoming.
He had been sent a form on which to list his head size, chest measurements, dietary requirements, medical history and religious affiliation, if any. This had been followed by a calendar invitation giving a date, a time and a location.

This is how he had found himself in a tally hut with Austin Arnold, who he suspected knew no more than he did.

Austin was now standing to Ash's right, his hard hat pushed back and a rugged iPad in his hand. He pointed at Rutherford with his pen, then at his screen. "Says here he has Q clearance. All access."

Ash nodded slowly. "Q, eh? Right you are."

She gestured vaguely in Lark's direction, now several levels above them. "To answer your question, she's found what she thinks may be a key."

Rutherford glanced down at the hatch. "Has she tried it yet?"

Ash turned to Austin conspiratorially. "He's an eager beaver, isn't he?"

Austin's expression did not change.

Rutherford was insistent. "I want to be there. When you open it."

"*If* we open it." She had already grabbed the ladder leading up to the next level. One foot was on the bottom rung. "Q clearance." She shook her head and began to pull herself up. "You have more right to be here than I do."

A day later the area around the hatch had been cleared to a radius of several metres. No other features had been revealed; just more of the same dark stony material from which the walls of the chamber were made. The floods had been brought down and positioned around it, and a camera set up on a tripod. This was now running. A hush had fallen over the archaeological team, Austin, Rutherford and Ash.

Lark carefully took two bubble-wrapped objects from a ziplock bag and unwrapped them. She wore white gloves, and held the first up between finger and thumb. Rutherford got his first clear look – it was rotationally symmetrical, of a polished sheen like smoky chrome.

Lark addressed all those present. "This is an arrowhead. Well, it was re-fashioned into an a arrowhead. Originally, I think it was something else." She turned it over. "It's badly mangled, completely bent out of shape, but we could still do some metallurgical tests. The alloy is unusual. Not what you'd consider a match for Bronze Age hunter-gatherer technology." She looked up around the ring of faces. "In its current state it's beyond repair. But it turned out we already had another."

She unwrapped the second item. It was the one from the Natural History Museum, perfect and precise. "So, now we have this hatch." She paused. "And perhaps we also have a key." She held the triangle a couple of centimetres above the indentation, turned it around. There was a faint line that ran from one point to the base of the opposite side, and a mirror image in the triangular indentation in the hatch. She lined them up.

She dropped it into the recess. There was an audible *chakk*. It seemed to be held fast, as if by a magnet.

Around it, the circle of raised bumps began to rise from the hatch's surface, a small palisade of rods. Lark jumped back. They rose to a hand's width, then a series of sharp reports was heard. A hidden mechanism had been released. The door, under its own weight, swung inwards.

There was the crump of stone against stone, and a foul grey vapour issued forth, quickly filling the immediate vicinity.

Lark recognised it immediately. "Phenacyl chloride! *Mace!* Get back!"

Those closest to the hatch were in convulsions. The skin on the back of Austin's hands reddened and bubbled, his eyes were burning and his chest was racked with pain.

Ash, without hesitation, took control of the situation. *"Everyone out. Now!"*

Fifteen minutes later they were all topside, sprawled in the tunnel. Stretchers and respirators had been brought down from the first aid station, and medical staff with the requisite clearance were checking vital signs.

Austin lay on his back, his hands covered in petroleum jelly. "My staff, count yourselves off. Names. Are we all here?" There were affirmative shouts from his crew, more from the archaeologists. "Is that everyone? Have we missed anyone?"

Ash's face hove into view. She looked down at him. The concrete panels of the tunnel curved up behind her to form a tessellated arch. The fluorescents created a harsh halo of light around her head. He could not see her face. "One man is missing. And one gas mask."

Austin knew who it was. "Rutherford."

133 CONCEPT

Rutherford hung from the lip of the hatch. The pressure had equalised, and the gas was dissipating. The gas mask obscured his vision, but by the light of his torch he could see a flat surface some three metres below. The torch was a rugged heavy-duty model, clad in yellow impact rubber; without hesitation he let it fall, then lowered himself down after it, swinging for a moment before dropping to the ground.

Turning, he could see the door hanging vertically above him, the rods on its surface still surrounding the arrowhead. He reached up, and it came away easily in his hand.

The door began to swing shut. The floods outside delineated a shrinking ellipse of light, then it closed completely.

The door had moved of its own volition. Rutherford considered this. *Was it counterbalanced somehow, or was there some kind of power source down here?* A shudder seemed to pass through the floor, like a small earthquake.

The torch, a metre or so away, dimmed, flickered. Rutherford could taste a sudden metallic tang in his mouth, as if an electrical field was being pulled through his fillings. The torch light steadied, then grew stronger, in a short while regaining its original strength.

He picked it up. It was warm to the touch, and a faint discharge, like a nerve tremor, passed up his arm. He dropped it. The beam jumped around, throwing jagged shadows across the floor.

Shaking his arm and wrist in an attempt to disperse the unpleasant tingling, he reached for it again. This time he felt nothing. It was just an ordinary torch.

He shone it up, to the underside of the door. There he could see an identical triangular depression to the one on the other side.

He flashed the torch around to get his bearings. He was in a circular room, no larger than his apartment, made from the same dark material as the cavern above. The walls and floor blended into each other, and were canted by the same familiar eight degrees.

There were no flat surfaces. This echoed the chamber above, and suggested a space that was grown rather than built, like the internal organs of some gargantuan creature.

Ahead was an opening that was more of a constriction. Raised linear features like veins weaved across the floor and walls towards and through it.

Rutherford braced himself for another explosive decompression, but it did not come. He had not considered that these internal voids might not contain breathable air; whether the atmosphere here had been preserved since prehistory, containing all manner of poisonous subterranean gases, or was suited to something other than human lungs, he had no way of knowing.

He passed through the opening into a larger space. Here the walls had a gangrenous glow, like the lure of a deep-sea predator.

He had yet to see anything resembling an interface suited to humans — there were no seats, tables, control panels. If this was a machine there was nothing to suggest that it was designed with the human frame in mind, or any other creature's needs or interests for that matter.

Machine or organism — the distinction, he reflected, might not actually be clear-cut.

What this second chamber did resemble was the inside of a pig's stomach. The ground was a patchwork of lacy ribbons a few inches high. He stepped from space to space between them, towards a larger area he could see at the centre. Far above, similar ribbons hung down like shredded plastic curtains in a cleanroom. He wouldn't have been surprised if the place had convulsed, as if to expel him; but it was silent, and the sections of ribbon he could not avoid stepping on turned into dust without complaint as he passed.

He paused. Here he could see the ridged walls curve up to meet above him like the vaulting of a Roman basilica, or the interior of a pepper. At the very centre hung a chandelier of tight convoluted spirals, from which fell thin glossy threads.

Their organic appearance again unsettled him; he was used to the clean geometry of angle and line, the play of sharp midday shadows across cast concrete.

Here, in this subterranean space lit by a sickly glow rather than a sodium streetlight, everything seemed askew. Above, there had been the busy clatter and buzz of the site, the revving of the mechanical diggers and the infrasonic hum of the floods; here, the absence of sound was absolute. The familiar murmur of traffic, the background drone of aeroplanes in a holding pattern over Heathrow, the distant police siren, the living heartbeat of the city — all of this was missing.

He pushed his gas mask up to his forehead, took a shallow breath.

The air was cool and tasteless. He waited a moment with some trepidation.

He was fine.

If the stratigraphy Lark and her team had excavated was reliable, this place must be truly ancient. Had Anomaly 36 been here when the Ice Age embraced northern Europe, and glaciers transported the liths of London down from the north? Had this thing he was now exploring, whatever it was, come down south with them?

Or did its origins lie elsewhere?

Rutherford wondered if any mention survived, in fable if not the archaeological record, of earlier interactions with this place. Gaulish curse-tablets speak of Annwfn, the Otherworld; Ande-dubnos, ruled by Gwyn ap Nudd, the king of the Fair Folk. King Arthur journeyed into Annwfn, and though three ships' complements accompanied him, only seven men returned. The denizens of the Otherworld were said to be bizarre: a wide-mawed beast with a hundred heads who bore a host beneath its tongue; a clawed, black-groined toad; a mottle-ridged serpent containing a thousand souls, tortured by their sins in the folds of its flesh. As with the Deros and Teros of the Shaver mythology, we feared the denizens from below had designs on those of us who live in the light.

Rutherford shook his head to try and dispel such notions. He mustn't let his imagination run off with his sanity. So far, this place appeared to be deserted. But if the old stories were to be believed, it wasn't — those hypogean gnomes and knockers, boggarts and trolls that could sour the milk and cause dogs to go lame would steal away the innocent.

And he had willingly come down here, into their realm.

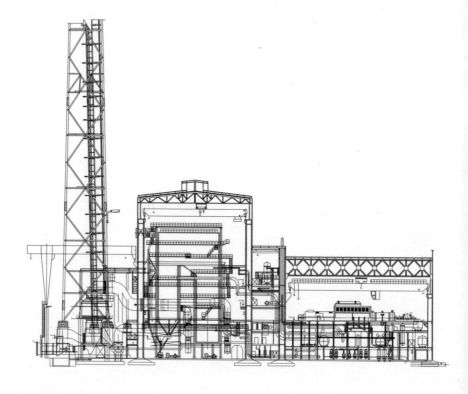

A bove, at the dig site, Austin, Lark and Ash assessed the scene.
The gas had dissipated.

There had been other unexplained effects: the computers had all stopped functioning, and the battery-powered lights had failed. They discovered that the diesel generators were still working, and so the floods positioned around the hatch had been rerouted.

Under their glare, it was now plain to see that the hatch was again closed, and the rods had withdrawn back into its surface.

There was no key, and there was no Rutherford.

No one had seen him emerge into the tunnel. There was only one possibility.

He was now inside.

A feeble but undeniable vitality was returning to the nerves and conduits of a long-buried system, one that traced its origins to a time and
place more distant than Rutherford could imagine.

He was, of course, unaware of events now unfolding above ground,
in the city of London itself. If the effects on Rutherford's torch inside
the Anomaly had been peculiar, or the failure of the electrics at the
dig site had been unexpected, on the surface they were immediate
and widespread.

Triggered by his presence, by the recognition of life by life, a tremor
in the coherent etheric substrate of consensus reality expanded at the
speed of thought from the Anomaly through central London. Invisible
to all human senses, this primary harmonic described a sphere that
encompassed Highgate in the north, Shepherd's Bush in the west,
Canary Wharf in the east and Clapham Common in the south.

Within this a second, smaller but more powerful concentric sphere
coalesced. Here, where the reins of molecular bonds and the usual
chronological imperatives were more pliable, an ion cascade shorted
unhardened computer chips and melted wires.

It was unintentional – the Anomaly's waking systems had no way of
knowing how they would affect the city above – but it was dramatic.

From Marble Arch to the Shard, the British Library to Battersea
Power Station, the lights went out.

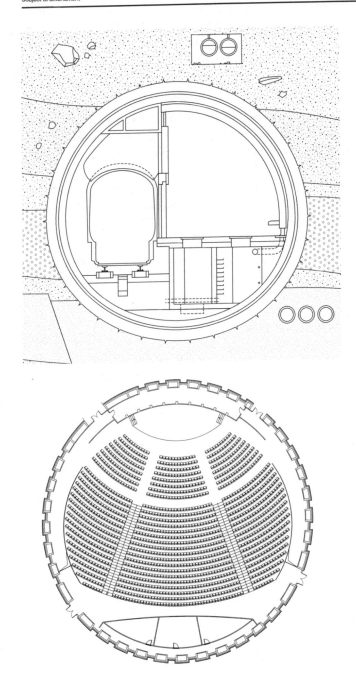

Hospitals, government offices and police stations went dark.

In the operating theatre at St Mary's Hospital, Paddington, a surgeon held a scalpel above an anaesthetised patient's trachea, suddenly unable to see the difference between blood and flesh in the dim red glow of the emergency lighting.

At Prime Minister's Question Time, the microphone suddenly went dead and the lights dimmed and fluttered like gaslight. A silence fell across the chamber for the first time in days, in which the Right Honourable Knights, Citizens and Burgesses of the House of Commons in Parliament Assembled could all hear the *whump* of the petrol generators turn over in the basement like Guy Fawkes' ghost.

Water systems lost pressure, mobile phone networks were downed, and television and radio stations went off the air. The internet was unresponsive.

At the BBC's Television Centre, out near the periphery in White City, newsfeeds stalled, transmitters lost power, and the stage lights on *The Jonathan Ross Show* failed just as Samuel L. Jackson was taking his seat.

Modern cars stalled; their steering seized, their brakes failed, and they rode up pavements, into walls, other vehicles, or coasted to a stop, scattering pedestrians in their wake. Older models without complex computer systems remained drivable, though the roads became obstacle courses. Buses were immobilised. A taxi drove off London Bridge. An articulated lorry blocked the bottom of Southampton Row, making the area around Covent Garden impassable.

Those vehicles that were still operational drove slowly and cautiously; due to the usual heavy traffic in the city, few collided at speed and there were only a dozen or so casualties. The vast majority of vehicles pulled over and were left where they stood, their occupants either continuing on foot or joining the throngs moving across Westminster Bridge and south, or heading towards the centres of Trafalgar and Leicester Squares.

Traffic lights were out; choppers hovered high overhead, not daring to come lower in case their systems were affected. The Tube, Overground and tram routes shut down; many trains were trapped between stations in the dark. Drivers and station staff with kerosene lamps began to evacuate passengers along the tunnels and up the non-functional escalators to the nearest exits.

Trams without power had also been abandoned; the cars that were still operational weaved around them. Gridlock spread; hire bike racks were soon empty.

People fled their offices on foot; the evening streets, byways, bridges and tunnels were crowded with pedestrians leaving the city by any route they could find.

The advertising hoardings at Piccadilly Circus were grey grids of lifeless LEDs. The London Eye stopped turning; dozens were trapped between floors in lifts. Trains into Paddington, Liverpool Street, King's Cross, Waterloo and other major London terminals were cancelled at the point of origin.

London Airport suspended flights, redirecting incoming planes to Stansted as air traffic control was inoperative, while in Docklands the financial markets were suspended. Petrol stations were unable to pump fuel.

Pentonville Prison blacked out, but within minutes had switched to backup generator power. In the few moments of darkness, three gangland vendettas were settled with deadly violence. Phone batteries overheated, causing minor fires and personal injuries.

The Mayor declared a state of emergency, despite there being no means to broadcast the fact.

Communication through Twitter and other forms of social media was impossible; to find out what was going on, people did what Londoners usually think unthinkable and began talking to each other. Bars and pubs quickly became hubs for those who had abandoned the idea of returning home; many decided the best approach to unfolding events would be to enjoy themselves – in basement taverns, by candlelight, it was still possible to pour whiskies and pull pints.

Freezers began to defrost; Amarino's gave out enormous gelatos to bemused passers-by in Covent Garden; Fortnum and Mason's Diamond Jubilee Tea Salon held an impromptu banquet, the cooks serving Scottish Glenarm ribeye and lobster on the house; Bar Italia in Greek Street set up their tables in the road and gave out pastries and cappuccinos to Soho's throng. Lively crowds formed outside McDonald's and Patisserie Valerie as office workers and street cleaners drank prosecco and ate warm cheesecake and Chicken McNuggets.

As afternoon became evening, the cast of *Mamma Mia!* and *The Book of Mormon* performed an impromptu hybrid outside The

Moon Under Water in Leicester Square. A functioning diesel generator was commandeered and soon a street party was coalescing around Nelson's Column. A set of turntables was set up and the vintage record shops in Berwick Street brought down crates of vinyl. The choir from St Martin's in the Fields sang hymns and Beatles songs a capella on the steps of the National Gallery, where Melvyn Bragg and Tracey Emin stood guard against looters armed with a length of scaffold pole, a hunting rifle and strong words.

Portable light towers were set up at unlit intersections. Ten thousand police officers, the Household Cavalry, the Queen's Guard and the entire Fire and Rescue Service voluntarily stayed to maintain order. Police dogs, barking nervously, were kept on a tightrope leash, as unsure as their handlers what might transpire.

Rickshaw riders set up an informal messenger service, ferrying people to and fro, bringing water into the centre, towing generators and diesel fuel to hospitals, and carrying handwritten notes between those trying to coordinate the police response. Thousands who took the opportunity to indulge in a spot of recreational violence and looting were summarily arrested.

A double-decker bus was hijacked, driven into the grounds of Westminster and set alight before police on horseback arrived; tasers didn't work, so they rugby-tackled the perpetrator to the ground. Several people set fire to themselves while trying to light candles. The Turkish and Kurdish shop owners in Edgware Road stood arm in arm with the old-money aristocrats and new money Middle Eastern oil princes of Park Lane to see off organised gangs. Further out, Wembley Stadium went dark with five minutes' play left on the clock of the FA Cup semi-final between Brentford and Manchester City.

Children were conceived in darkened rooms, tourists mugged and beaten in Oxford Street, inebriated office workers raped; prayers were held in Westminster Abbey, songs sung in silent discos; shops were looted, scores settled on sink estates, lives were reassessed and found wanting, and lifelong friendships were forged between complete strangers.

Hotel rooms were soon booked out, but people continued to turn up late into the night. They slept in hallways and foyers, ballrooms and boardrooms. Many had no light or power, except where the establishment had emergency generators. Those who could not find lodgings slept in parks and on the steps of public buildings, many wearing alcohol overcoats that insulated them from the night's chill.

Every person saw their city with new eyes. The familiar public spaces and thoroughfares had, if only for a night, been repurposed; they now served not the lords of high-street commerce and the bustle of business but played host to a new, disruptive, communal sense of belonging.

This was their old familiar metropolis, rendered new and unfamiliar.

Those abroad late into the night felt their eyes drawn up to the heavens; for the first time in any young Londoner's memory, the Milky Way was clearly visible, a tattered banner of stars rising up from the Thames Estuary and the low glow of Thamesmead out east to the zenith above. It was reflected back from the surface of the sullen river, an arc of pale light laid through the dark landscape, interrupted here and there by lightless buildings. Satellites, modern technology's wandering stars, could be seen crossing the sky.

It was a celebration with an undercurrent of desperation; though the vast majority assumed this was a one-off, a power cut due to an entirely explicable technical mishap, many wondered if it might be a harbinger of something more sinister.

A few who had lived here a very long time knew that London had been dark once before. This time there were no flying bombs crossing the Channel from a fascist ideology ravaging the Continent, but a city like London has a long memory, one that far outlasts the fleeting lives of those who inhabit it.

London's birth is lost to Alzheimer's and supposition, and the stories that survive have been polished into myths by the retelling. One tells us Brutus of Troy, descendant of the Trojan hero Aeneas, was founder and first king of Britain; he defeated the giant Gogmagog a thousand years before Christ was nailed to a cross.

Others are more prosaic: growing from a village on the river near Vauxhall Bridge where the River Effra meets the Thames, Troia Nova became Trinovantum; King Lud, who legend has it is buried at Ludgate, renamed it Caer Ludein, from which came London, the name it settled on in its maturity. The Romans called it Londinium, against which Boudicca, the queen of the Celts, rose up in revolt.

London has weathered plague, fire, invasion, civil war, aerial bombardment and terrorism. She has survived two world wars: the shrapnel and unexploded bombs still lie buried in her foundations, lodged too deep in the patient to remove.

Acid rain has eaten her monuments and urban redevelopment car-buncled her skyline, but she is still here, still very much alive.

London without light was an unconscious London, but its inhab-itants, the T-cell antibodies of its immune system, had been tasked with bringing her back to life, as we had done before and would do again.

If she had shut her eyes, just for one night, her inhabitants were keeping theirs open. London had withstood far worse, and she would prevail.

Transport 3: **Automobiles**

Not to scale
Subject to amendment

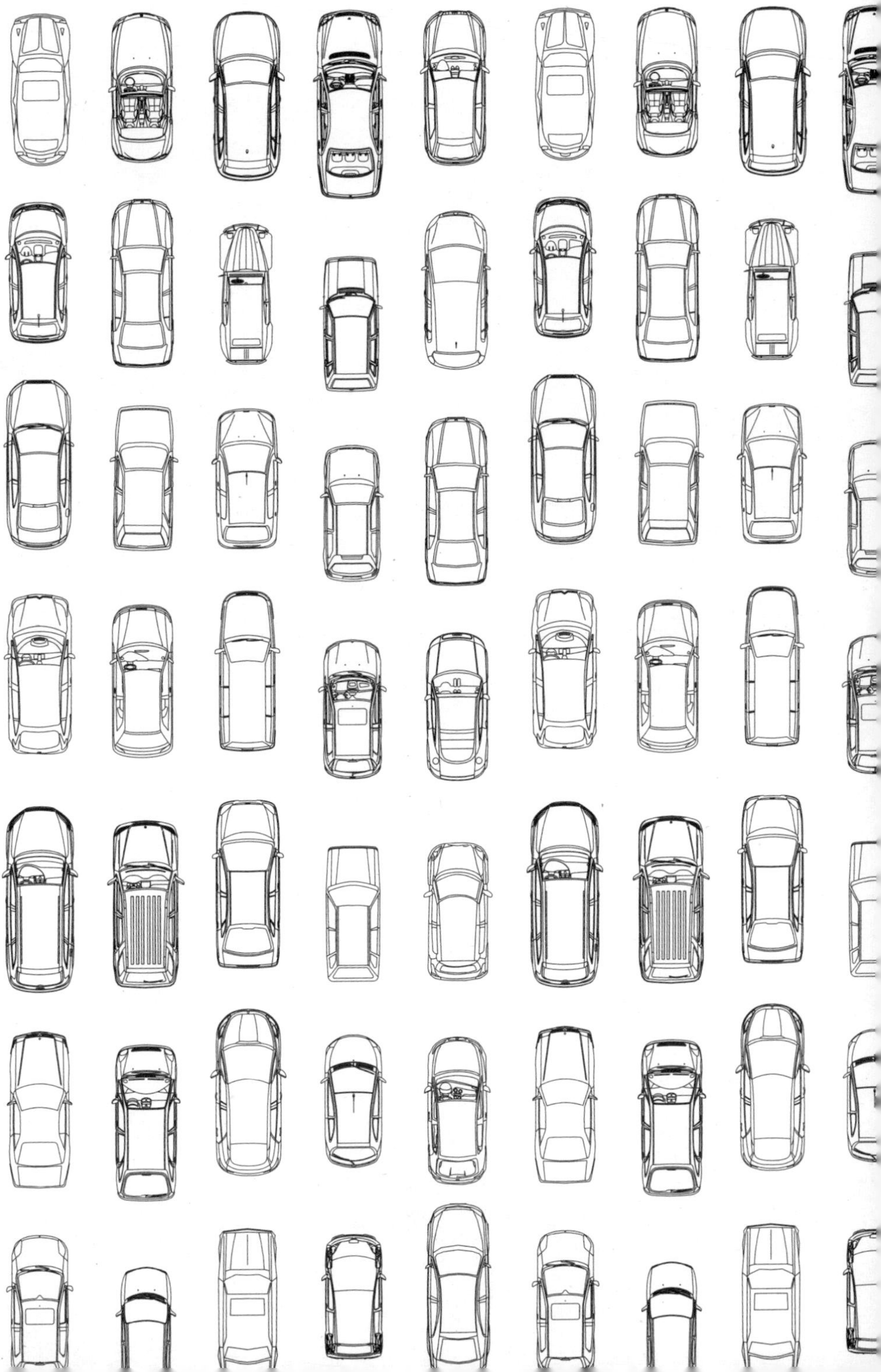

149 **PLAN**

Rutherford could only guess at the extent of the subterranean maze he was exploring. His battery-powered torch, clad in bright yellow impact rubber, had the heft of serious industrial hardware, but he knew it wouldn't last forever. He needed to factor in the return journey; this place would be unnavigable in the dark.

At some stage he would pass the point of no return. Maybe he already had. Used as he was to navigating the interstices of a darkened city in his nocturnal explorations, the thought did not disturb him as much as he suspected it should. He pulled a stick of gum from his pocket, unwrapped it and absently began to chew.

He was beginning to become accustomed, inasmuch as anyone could, to the peculiar collisions of shapes and volumes he was traversing, very few of which seemed to care about human proportions or human modes of locomotion. There were balconies without balustrades that went nowhere, giving onto dark spaces into which a slip of the foot could so easily plunge him; places where the ceiling became so low he had to crawl, only to find the way blocked completely further ahead. There were doors shaped like large portholes he could not open, sections of vertical corridor with no way to climb them.

Some spaces were filled with a delicate filigree, like the skeletons of dry leaves, that crumbled when he touched it. Others had floors sloped at such steep angles as to make crossing them impossible. It was as if the very fabric of the place was attempting to find its proper shape, not knowing or understanding the needs of the residents.

If he found he could go no further he'd retreat, try another direction.

The ground, when flat, was still set at that same disconcerting angle. Whatever this place was, it had been disturbed at some point in the distant past, thrown off its true orientation to rest askew.

Almost everything was made from the same dark material, like burnished fossilised wood; he suspected this was due to age, rather than the interior design tastes of the architects, whoever they might be. It had a silken textured grain, and felt cold under his touch, but not uncomfortably so; like the underside of a pillow.

There were still no signs of the original inhabitants, if indeed there had ever been any.

He passed along a curving passageway lined with marbled jet patterned like fatty meat, and found he was in a cul-de-sac.

Set in the curved wall ahead was another hatch, identical to the first. His torch flitted over its surface and the walls surrounding it. To one side was a raised panel; on this were a series of indentations, each containing a set of raised bumps, like Braille.

He held up a forefinger, hesitated. He'd convinced himself that this place was dormant, without power, but the hatch in the dig . . .

He touched the panel. He felt a shiver in his hippocampus and coloured lights sparked behind his eyes. He jerked away. There was something there, faint, to be sure, but something . . . responsive? Alive?

He tried touching the panel with two fingers. The lights returned, brighter. If there was some PIN code, some password, he had no way of guessing what it might be. Voice operated? He smiled. *As if.*

"Open." His voice sounded even less confident than he felt. Those lights again, as if in response.

Hah. Maybe the builders just didn't speak English. *French? Italian?* He turned his attention back to the door. In the centre was the same circle of raised bumps, with a triangular indentation in the middle. He felt in his pocket for the key.

He held it up. There was that magnetic pull again, and a faint *clakk.* He quickly pulled his hand away. The key was now attached to the door.

Nothing. He again touched the panel, three fingers this time, and pictured the door opening.

There was a pop, and a hiss of air as the pressure inside and outside equalised. He had one hand on the gas mask hanging around his neck, but there were no poisonous clouds issuing forth. He pushed on the door with his foot.

It swung open.

In the light of his torch he could see another space beyond.

It was a small domed vestibule, from which led several corridors like spokes from a hub. At the centre was a tiered object not unlike a fountain; it was the first thing he had encountered that seemed to be in any way familiar. It rose in a series of nested cups, each containing a brackish liquid he did not examine closely. At its top was a stylised flower, though it was not one he recognised. Its petals were folded back, and visible inside was a small homunculus, like the foetus of some humanoid creature. It, too, was made of the same petrified material as the walls.

If it was a fountain it didn't seem to function as one. It looked like a half-formed shade, a sculpture made without comprehension of the subject's purpose or meaning.

But it wasn't the fountain that held his attention. Beside it lay a figure.

It was the first indication of any presence, human or otherwise, he had encountered. He had not even seen a rat, and there were many of those in London's old underground tunnels.

He moved closer. It was wrapped in the remains of a linen shirt or shawl, and its head was hidden behind a Corinthian helmet. That, and the trident that lay beside it, told him this person, whoever they were, was indisputably Roman.

The helmet was full-face, with two small teardrop-shaped eye holes and a nose guard, and was surmounted by a semicircular crest, most of which had long ago turned to black powder. The figure was not statuesque, and Rutherford suspected it might be female. Still, it wore warrior garb: a cuirass, the fragile remains of a woollen undervest, an armoured tunic, sandals and baltea. At the waist was a short sword, the intricate metal chasing of which had tarnished to a dull silver. The figure was lying on its side, as if asleep; one leg was tucked up under it, and the trident looked as if it had been carefully placed alongside, within easy reach.

The other accessory was the shield. This was round, less than a metre across, with a metal rim and a pointed boss at the centre. From this radiated four raised stripes, dividing it into quadrants and coloured a deep burgundy. She – Rutherford was now certain it was female – held it to her breast as if to protect herself from something.

Roman. Two thousand years old. How could the preservation be so complete? The air down here was breathable, he was testament to that. It must be unusually pure, devoid of micro-organisms. He wondered what he might have inadvertently brought in here with him.

Had she been an explorer, like him? Had she lost her way, and paused to rest? He mentally calculated the distance and time it would take to get back to the dig site.

He wondered how she had died. There were no discernible marks on the body, no sign of battle that he could see. It was as if she had lain down here, gone to sleep, and never woken up.

He knelt down. His hand hovered over the helmet, then he changed his mind. Whoever she was, she deserved to rest in peace.

He stood, and was about to move on when the trident again caught his attention. It was long, taller than he was, and surmounted by a central arrow-shaped spike flanked by two smaller half-arrows.

A weapon, if he needed it. He doubted that whatever might have killed this unfortunate could still roam these spaces, if indeed it had ever been physical; but he thought it wise to take precautions.

He wondered if it bore some symbolic significance. He hefted the shaft, found its centre of balance.

It felt right. He stepped away, turned back towards the tunnel.

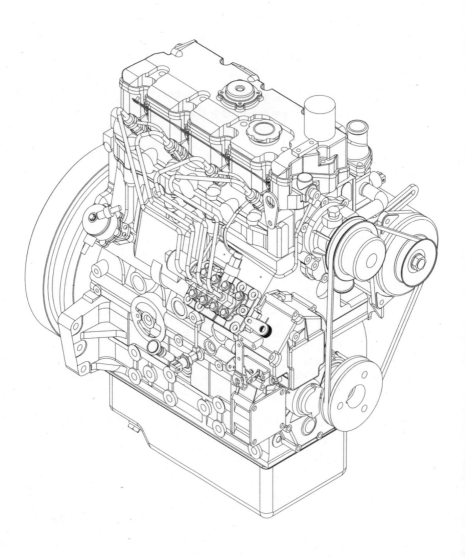

The kerosene lamps around the dig site gave it the appearance of a friendly campfire scouting trip. Whereas the four still-functional floods were a daylight white, these were weak and yellow. Ash had managed to requisition them from somewhere, though Austin thought it more likely that she had just taken them, there being no effective command structure currently in place on the project. The remaining staff informed them that work on Crossrail, and pretty much all non-essential work throughout the capital, had been suspended. They were to make their own way home and await further news. The powers that be had more important things to think about.

Here, in the tunnels below, at least they were safe from the unrest on the surface. Austin knew there were supplies of tinned food in the canteen that would last the better part of a week, and the high razor-wire fences and hoardings would keep out all but the most persistent.

They knew there was no way to communicate inside the zone; cellphone networks were inoperable, and messages had to be carried outside the radius on foot or by bicycle before they could be relayed over patchy satellite links. Through this system Austin had sent messages to family, friends; he assumed Ash had done likewise, though she wore no wedding ring. Somehow he was not surprised.

The hatch remained steadfastly shut. Ash sat back on her haunches. While she might be a formidable manager, Austin sensed that, for him, she now held something between contempt and disdain.

"He was your responsibility. *Yours.*"

Austin held up his hands. "He had Q clearance! He was weird, yes, but I think we all assumed he was trustworthy! Plus, plus my fucking *hands* were melting! What was I *supposed* to do?"

Ash picked up a kerosene lamp. "London is in chaos. What you're *supposed* to do is find a *solution* to this problem of ours."

She climbed up the ladder and out of the dig. Austin watched the lamp go, bobbing like a marsh light on an overcast night.

He followed her up and out, along the wooden walkway. Impotent diggers were parked either side.

"The cranes at the entrance are out of action. The machines we do have down here are useless. Is there no way we can source some kind of, I don't know, welding torch, lower it down here and cut our way in?"

Ash kept walking. "Can you can lift oxyacetylene cylinders the weight of a grown man unaided? I'm guessing you can't."

"Explosives?"

"Explosives need detonators."

"Pick and shovel?"

They had reached the base of the scaffold structure that led up towards the original hole. She stopped and turned. "Tell you what. You go for it."

They ascended in silence. At the top, they stepped through into the Crossrail tunnel. It seemed reassuringly familiar, even lit by the dim lamps. Some of the stretchers were still here, abandoned; those who had not been taken to the infirmary had managed to exit on foot. Austin wondered if they were still somewhere above, in the city, or had taken refuge outside the perimeter of the electrical dampening effect.

By rights that was where they should now be, too.

Austin was losing his patience. "Ash, has anyone ever told you you're a fucking nightmare to work with? I have a good team here. An excellent team. They knock themselves out for you, day after day, and then you come down here and treat them like they're a bad smell. Now half of them are hospitalised. On *my* watch. You think I don't already feel shitty enough about that? So, just for once, why don't you wind in the attitude and try and be just a tad more constructive? Can it *really* be that hard? Who knows, you might even get to like it."

This was new. Ash had not seen this side of Austin before.

She exhaled, shook her head. When she spoke, there was a softer tone to her voice. "The Commons Defence Committee has long suspected that certain countries and proscribed groups – those who are resisting international pressure to curtail their weapons programmes – could build and deliver a non-nuclear, electromagnetic pulse weapon to the heart of the city."

"You think that is what happened here?"

She pointed up, to the surface. "It's what *they* think has happened here."

Austin could sense she was under enormous pressure. "But *we* know that there's a machine beneath—"

"We now have no access to whatever is under that hatch. We have no hard evidence. We just have a confluence of events and a missing artist."

"You think this is all *coincidence?*"

"Listen, Austin. Her Majesty's Government is somewhat preoccupied at the moment. I'm not exactly top of their must-call list. The probability of a high-altitude EMP attack was thought to be minimal, though the potential effects, they admitted, could be quote-unquote 'disruptive'. Just how disruptive, I was not informed – threats of this nature are routinely downplayed, at least at a level where there's a high risk of such discussions becoming public.

"If such a device *has* been detonated above London, it would certainly have knocked out the National Grid. If power is not restored, the city will, in a matter of days, become uninhabitable. *That* is their focus right now. Archaeology can wait."

Austin was used to finding solutions, even if others didn't think the problem needed solving. *Especially* if others didn't think it needed solving. "Look. I'm an engineer. In order to breach that hatch, we'd need an armour-piercing anti-tank round. The kinetic energy of, say, a truck, moving at seventy miles per hour."

Ash looked up and down the tunnel, shading her eyes for theatrical effect. "Trucks, trucks . . . Hm, looks like there are no working trucks in the immediate vicinity." She patted her pockets. "And I'm all out of anti-tank rounds."

She turned and marched off up the tunnel, head low, arms swinging. Austin watched her go.

Almost everything that incorporated electrical components was now non-functional. Even if he did somehow manage to figure out how to get a truck, or a tank, down here, it'd have to be old enough to operate without electrics.

One from the Imperial War Museum? Austin chuckled to himself.

The idea of a WWI Mark V negotiating the tunnels did have a certain appeal. But he'd need to find a driver, gunner, and live ammo, and somehow lower it fifteen metres down a hole in the ground.

Scratch that.

He walked to the main hub, the vast cylindrical shaft from which the rail tunnels branched away. Here, the heavy plant stood immobile, the open cage lift to the surface inoperable. Ash was nowhere to be seen. Above, he could see a perfect circle of blue London sky, artfully framing a delicate fluff of cirrus cloud.

It looked serene. Perfect.

But above ground, London was in crisis.

159 SPECIFICATION

A ustin Arnold locked the site's main gate behind him.
It was the day after the night before. He had slept on the couch in the tally hut. Breakfast had been a can of Irn Bru and a cheese and pickle baguette from a vending machine. A skeleton staff still remained, but Ash had not returned. He had no idea what he should do. Get out of London? He knew many of the roads were blocked with stalled cars; others had turned into impromptu race circuits. Walk?

The street outside was empty. To his left was an enormous 48-sheet billboard on which a model pursed her lips and smouldered at the camera in a manner no woman had ever looked at Austin. She seemed to suggest it was business as usual, that there was nothing amiss, but in the distance he could hear staccato gunfire. He walked in what he hoped was the opposite direction.

Presently he found himself on Charing Cross Road. A '37 Bugatti, viciously scraped down the right flank, shot past at speed. If, as he'd been told, most modern cars were inoperable, older models seemed to be having no such issues. Austin suspected that it must be stolen, as its real owner would surely have taken more care. There were few people about, and those that were did not linger. He walked south.

The streets were full of detritus, the leftovers of last night's party. As he approached the Garrick Theatre a Reliant Robin drove by on the wrong side of the road. It cornered sharply in front of St Martin's in the Fields, barely keeping all three wheels on the ground, and passed out of sight behind the National Portrait Gallery. Turning the corner, he could see a Morris Minor performing handbrake turns around one of the fountains in Trafalgar Square, leaving black arcs of rubber on the pavement.

He heard the crowds before he saw them. Arranged around Nelson's Column like spokes on a wheel was a veritable classic car rally – a vintage Sunbeam in burgundy and pinstripes, its soft top down while the occupants held court; there was a flathead Mercury in lime green, and a rusted Ford Capri, the vinyl roof peeled back like a facepack to reveal the unpainted metal beneath.

Here, for good or ill and despite the dangers, there were numerous people abroad who were determined to make the most of the strange circumstances.

"*Hey, Austin!*"

Austin turned, trying to locate the source of the shout.

"What are you doing out and about?"

An immaculately restored Ford Popular, resprayed a deep purple, was idling along at a walking pace beside him. Every wing mirror and hub plate was chromed to a flawless mirror finish. Austin recognised it immediately.

"Kelvin Neville! Well, I never. How's life?"

Kelvin nodded sagely and rotated one white-gloved hand in a regal fashion. "Hunky-dory, old boy. Just, you know, checking out the scenery. Where are you headed? Can I give you a lift?"

Austin had to admit he had no idea where he was going.

But a vague plan had begun to form in his mind. He needed something with no electronic parts. Something that ran on rails. Something that might double as a battering ram. But without a phone, without any means of communication . . .

He stopped walking, turned to Kelvin. "I'm heading out. Out of the city."

Kelvin leant over and popped open the door. "Hop in."

They sped off down the Mall. Ahead, Austin could see Buckingham Palace, in front of which were a fleet of Green Goddess trucks and an armed military contingent. They gave them a wide berth and turned right, towards the Wellington Arch and Hyde Park Corner. A stalled double-decker bus had blocked the left carriageway at the bottom of Park Lane, so they drove up the opposite side of the road to Marble Arch.

Neville gunned the engine. He seemed to be on something of a high. "Get these empty streets! I just couldn't resist!" Then, more seriously: "You shouldn't be walking around, Austin. The police are out in force, but they can't cover everywhere. It can be dangerous."

"Says you in your purple car. Inconspicuous, you're not."

"So far I've not attracted anything other than admiring glances." Neville was wearing a wing-collar leather jacket and flat cap over his close-cropped afro, a white scarf artfully thrown over one shoulder. Behind his mirror aviators, Austin thought he could see his eyes sparkle. He held the wheel lightly with his white gloves, as if handling a delicate museum specimen. "So, out of town. Closest sensible route is due west, White City way."

"Sounds perfect."

Austin had first met Neville at a specialist garage in Kew four or five years previously. He was there to pick up one of the diggers whose caterpillar track had come loose; Neville was there to have his engine manifold and rear lights chromed. The two had talked fuel tolerances and net torque until the shop owner had pointedly rattled down the shutters.

They raced down the Uxbridge Road at well over the speed limit. Austin thought that the absence of traffic lights meant that some prudence should be shown at junctions, but Neville was an experienced driver and wouldn't risk a dent to his charge.

Plus, the speed cameras were probably out too.

At Notting Hill Gate they rode up the pavement to avoid a scrum of looters outside the Record and Tape Exchange. Some of them paused to look their way, but before they could switch targets, they were gone.

Somewhere along Holland Park Avenue, Austin pulled out his phone. Nothing. The screen was blank. He tried to reboot it.

"Who you trying to call?"

"Not call. Text."

"Who you trying to text?"

"It's a, an old schoolfriend. He belonged to a club. We both did. A group who shared a common interest. I think they may be able to help."

"Help with what? *This?*" Neville drove anticlockwise around the roundabout outside the Westfield Shopping centre. Flames rose from its roof and an acrid pall of smoke was moving away to the north-east, over Ladbroke Grove.

Austin knew he was referring to the current state of affairs. "Yes. I have an idea. I need a very large hammer to crack a very hard nut."

His phone beeped. The home screen appeared.

"Finally."

He typed a short WhatsApp message.

Neville looked at him over the top of his shades. "This something to do with your top-secret underground tunnelling job? You intrigue me, my man. That you do."

Austin couldn't recall mentioning what he did for a living, but he'd evidently not been as discreet as the non-disclosure agreement he'd signed had stipulated. He decided that, all things considered, he didn't give a shit.

"Yes, actually, it is."

He briefly explained what he had in mind. Neville nodded once. "No problem. I'm taking you all the way. In fact, I insist."

He floored the accelerator and they sped out due west, through Acton, Ealing, Southall, the western suburbs, and into the open countryside.

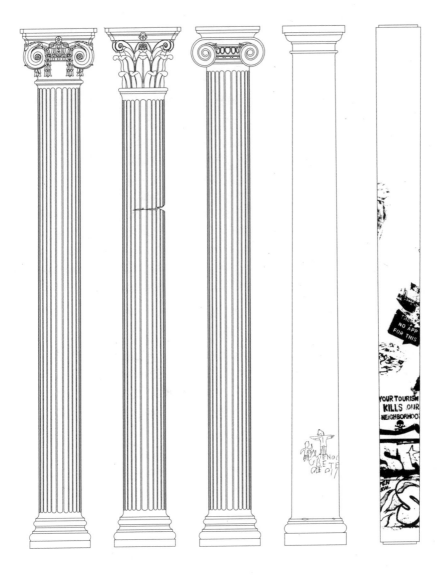

He was heading deeper. If the spaces he passed through resembled the internal organs of some creature, others suggested a great channelling of force – ducts and airways veined with corkscrew ridges, passages with sphincters so narrow he had to push his way through, only to open up again into stadium-sized voids in which his torch barely lit a circle around his feet.

There seemed to be a directionality to the passages he followed, as if whatever lay deeper funnelled its energies up, through these conduits and towards the surface. Sometimes he felt as if he were inside a rocket exhaust, that these imagined energies, passing through a pinch, would then expand to drive the whole forwards. The layout followed no symmetry he could divine, and the ubiquitous eight-degree angle still played like a funhouse on his inner ear.

He stopped again to run his hand over a section of curved wall, as he had done so many times above ground. Down here, he felt not the skin-abrading roughness of concrete or paving, but a smooth polished sheen, without joint or rivet. It reflected the beam of his torch like black glass, sometimes with an opalescent sheen or a subsurface patterning, like the hide of an animal pressed against a window. The materials from which it was made seemed to suggest an advanced technology, though the function of this labyrinth was still entirely opaque.

Yet he also encountered spaces and objects that, like the fountain, had a disconcerting familiarity.

He entered an aircraft-hangar-sized cavern in which his footfalls echoed just a bit too loudly for comfort. Across the ground, as far as the torchlight could reach, were placed structures in what appeared to be different stages of completion.

On a whim he turned off the torch. It took his eyes a few moments to adjust to the darkness, but, as he had suspected, a pale chartreuse glow, as of bioluminescent algae, ringed the walls of the visible portion of the enormous space, providing something like an artificial horizon. Against this were silhouetted numerous geometric shapes, like a skyline blocking the coming dawn.

Some were familiar Platonic solids: cubes, tetrahedra, interlaced solids. Mathematical entities with an idealised purity of form. They ranged in size from very small – barely distinguishable from gravel he accidentally crunched underfoot – to large, maybe two or three times his height. It reminded him of a sculpture park, and he passed cautiously between them, flicking his torch over their immobile forms. There was no machinery, no cables or winches, no sign of a workforce to suggest that this had once been a shopfloor; these shapes seemed to have been extruded from the ground itself, and by their colour and sheen, seemed to be made of much the same material.

The notion came to him that they were experiments, stages in a process of learning how to build something.

But who was doing the learning? Other than the remains of undoubtedly human origin he had found, there was no one here.

He walked through this landscape for what he supposed might be twenty minutes, maybe more. He tucked the trident under one arm and pulled a bag of Quavers from his jacket pocket; the crunching sounded far too loud inside the echo chamber of his skull, so he folded the packet and stowed them again.

The objects became larger, more complex. A grammar of form was beginning to emerge. The shapes had become more rectilinear, ranging in size from a car to a house to an office block. He could imagine he was walking along a road in a small town without a street plan, one in which the buildings had been simplified, like a basic computer game without a texture map.

The circle of light circumscribed by his torch, which he was shining just beyond his feet to avoid tripping over the smallest outcrops, came up against a wall. He stopped, pointed the torch up. It extended into darkness. On either side it was the same.

But it was the texture of the wall he found intriguing. Its very familiarity was its peculiarity: it was made of brick, a perfect, regimented repeat pattern of course upon course, interleaved with cement.

He reached out to touch it. It had the correct texture, and as he took his hand away he could see a dusting of powder on his fingertips. He raised them to his nose.

Definitely brick. But there was something about it that did not ring true. It was too uniform, too perfect. There was no weathering, no imperfections, none of the random variations a real brick wall, however skilfully built, would show.

He shone the torch back the way he had come, to the left and right. He could see other, smaller structures, also constructed from what looked like brick or stone. They still retained the perfection of the geometric solids he had passed earlier, as if produced from an algorithm rather than built by hand.

The generative schema of floor and wall, street and pavement?

A city, in prototype?

He pointed the trident left then right. The polished spikes reflected slashes of pale ambient light across his face. Then, for no particular reason, he turned left.

Small alcoves began to appear, set at regular intervals in the wall. Each was more deeply recessed than the last, until they formed a continuous corridor behind a series of arches, supported on cylindrical columns. These bore the suggestion of Romanesque capitals and maybe a pedestal at the bottom, but again much simplified. He stepped through an opening and found himself in a colonnade.

Through the arches he could see the glow of the false horizon, again at the ubiquitous eight-degree angle. He steadied himself.

He found it hard to gauge distances here. Out across the flat plain, lit from behind, he could see many more large structures. Some suggested elegant tiered bell towers, or low crenellated walls along which ran rows of identical rods like flagpoles. In the middle distance was a tall narrow pyramid with a jagged broken tip, very like the Shard, while closer to hand was an elongated egg reminiscent of 30 St Mary Axe. Others were more organic in appearance, silhouettes resembling headless figures on misshapen long-legged horses atop rectangular plinths. It was a deserted cityscape, a playground of experimental geometry, and it put him in mind of Giorgio de Chirico's metaphysical paintings, or his own diorama, his London made from parts of London, back in his studio.

Were these shapes down here distant reflections of the architecture that had been erected above, on the surface, over two millennia?

Or were they London in potential, the original progenitors of its form, the *idea* of the city? Had they been here before its construction, and was London the resonant echo, built above to fulfil its expression?

He remembered the recumbent figure, the original owner of the trident he now carried. Like these half-formed streets, he wondered if she also had some resonant counterpart above, in the light, a projection of the person she longed to be, filtered and focused through the capabilities of this strange machine.

A Boudicca, a Britannia, an ideal given form.

Rutherford stepped out from under the colonnade and approached the nearest plinth on which one of the strange statues rested. From a distance, just its basic shape was visible: a suggestive form outlined in pale green. As he drew closer, he played his torch over it.

It was . . . unsettling.

Neither fully human or animal, it was like a half-remembered chimera, malformed, simplified. An arrangement of musculature and backbone, a tight interrelation of curved surfaces and spindly extrusions suggestive of legs or arms. It had no features or anything that he could identify as a face, as if it had been made by a blind man who had only the vaguest concept of what a representational sculpture might look like.

It was a loose sketch, a work in progress – nothing more.

Rutherford suddenly felt exposed out in the open amongst these bizarre objects. The nape of his neck prickled, as if he was being watched, though by who or what he could not guess. The silence was still absolute.

He hefted the trident higher for reassurance, then swung the torch around and began tracing his steps back to the colonnaded wall. He was used to nocturnal urban rambles. This place should not disconcert him.

He followed the corridor behind the arches for several minutes more. The gentle curve suggested a circular form many times larger than the volume he had assumed he was passing through.

He realised that the roof of the colonnade just above his head was becoming higher, the detailing more precise. The columns were now fluted, and he noticed that the coloration was more accurate, a clean veined stone unblemished by age or weathering.

An archway unexpectedly opened to his right, giving into a dark interior. He stopped, shone his torch in. Ahead, he could again see a faint glow. He walked towards it.

After ten metres or so, the corridor opened up into another room-sized space. This time the floor was patterned with inlaid stone, laid out in arabesque fractal geometries. From here, he exited onto a semicircular platform.

Above and below him, sweeping up and around in perfect symmetry, were the seats of a grand amphitheatre. Twenty, thirty tiers arranged in an almost complete circle, interrupted halfway up by a praecinctio. Directly ahead was a four-storey classical façade, punctuated by the dark rectangular recesses of a valva regia and hospitalium. These were flanked by rows of columns to either side, with a suggestion of a window or a balcony between them.

For all intents and purposes it was a Roman theatre – but one buried deep under London.

Londinium infernus. London below.

Rutherford guessed that no play had ever been performed here, that the seats had never held cheering crowds. This was more like an architect's model, an unpopulated prototype. But who had built it, and for what purpose?

His torch flickered. By now he knew he'd passed the point of no return.

He climbed down the levels to the open space at the centre. Without pausing to consider his actions, he strode out and across the stage, towards the large door in the middle of the façade and stepped through.

13

171 CROSS-SECTION

They parked in a cul-de-sac off the Bath Road, somewhere east of Chippenham. It was one of those places that could have existed anywhere up and down the country – a small development of 1970s bungalows with no architectural merit whatsoever, populated by, Austin imagined, families whose darkest secret was a weekend flutter on the scratch-cards or a predilection for Center Parcs half-term breaks.

They pulled up alongside a short row of garages. A boy attempting wheelies on a bicycle watched them warily. Austin had the sense that if anything interesting was happening, it was happening elsewhere.

They waited till the cyclist lost interest and rode away, back down the hill. Neville turned the engine off. Austin could tell he now felt more out of place than he had in London.

"This is where I drop you? Next to some garages and allotments in the arse end of nowhere?"

Austin opened the door. It gave the well-oiled clunk of a mechanism lovingly cared for. "All the best adventures begin in the most inauspicious locations."

Neville turned, one arm over the empty passenger seat. "You sure you don't want me to come with you? I can, you know, keep a secret. I'm top spy material, if you give me the opportunity."

Austin stood beside the car. In the midday sun its purple livery almost hurt his eyes. "No, I'll be fine. You've gone far out of your way already. I owe you big time."

Neville pointed a finger at Austin, shaking his head. "Admit it. You love all that NDA shit. Secret tunnels, shadowy goings-on, people in high places—"

"Penthouse to pavement, boardroom to back alley. I secretly control the whole world."

"Yeah, yeah. Rather you than me, Austin. Sounds like a tough job, especially right now. Personally, I'd not want the hassle." Neville checked the rear-view. "Be seeing you." He spun the car back in an arc then drove away, one gloved hand waving as he went.

Austin took one last look around to make sure he was alone, then ducked under a wooden fence and across a series of allotments to the treeline.

He pushed through the brambles and nettles. Hidden on the other side was a steep wooded embankment which dropped down onto a railway line. He knew there were no trains running – services were suspended in and out of London for the duration – but he still looked up and down the line before he stepped out. The ballast crunched under his boots.

It was a clear warm day, and he could feel his mood lift despite the circumstances. He checked the GPS on his phone.

A small dot blinked at his current location. There was a destination marker just up the line. He walked in its direction.

In less than a minute he could see a small two-storey building in the trees by the side of the railway. It was an abandoned signalbox. Its lower portion was brick, the upper decaying wooden slats. Its roof was a skeleton of exposed beams, and ivy clogged its broken windows. A steep external staircase ran directly to the top floor.

There was someone waiting for him.

"Ray flippin' Langley. How long has it been?"

Ray held his arms wide, then enveloped Austin in a bear-hug. "Forty-six years. Too long, Arnold." He held him at arm's length and squinted through his glasses, getting the measure of his old friend, then patted him on the shoulder. "I can just about see the scruffy bowl-haired kid still in there, behind all the wrinkles."

"Thanks."

"No, no, you're looking good. Must be all that physical exercise you get working on Crossrail. Me, I'm working on my gut." He patted his considerable stomach. Ray had the jovial manner of someone who had slid comfortably into middle age. His shirt was casual, his jeans had grease stains.

"You still a mechanic?"

"Yep. After Julie left, me and the kids moved to Bristol. I have a garage. Small, but we get by. You have kids?"

Austin shook his head. "No. Never met anyone who wanted to settle down. To be honest, I just . . . never met anyone."

Ray nodded. "Way it goes . . ."

Austin changed the subject. "I wasn't sure you'd answer. I wasn't sure you were still an active member. I rarely if ever look at the Smokebox Club messageboards these days."

Ray laughed. "It's mostly technical shit, people arguing the toss over livery exceptions, timetable revisions and other minutiae. It's called trainspotting for a reason."

"So, anyway. Thanks. For replying."

"Hey, it's what us members do. *If you're down or in distress—*"

Austin held up his hands in mock-surrender. "Don't sing the song. Please don't sing the song."

Ray chuckled, then became serious. "So, all this shit going down in London. You have a plan?"

Austin shrugged. "If the legends are true, I have a plan."

Ray pulled out his phone and tapped the screen. "Well, we're about to find out. At your suggestion, I put out a few feelers. I have another Smokeboxer contact who says he can help. We're about to meet him."

"Here?"

"Close by. Just waiting for the nod."

"'The nod'. Sounds like the Smokeboxers really *are* some kind of secret cabal."

"If they are, they'll know where their loyalties *really* lie. The Smokebox Club has its sleeper agents." Ray paused, then gave a self-congratulatory laugh. "Sleeper agents. Geddit?"

Austin's face was impassive.

Ray's phone beeped. "Right, we're go." He gestured out of the broken window. "We're to walk up the line, to the . . . the western entrance of Box Tunnel."

Austin was familiar with Brunel's masterpiece of engineering. Tunnel-building technology had come a long way from blasting with dynamite then digging out the rubble with pickaxes, but Box Tunnel was still the forerunner of the kind of engineering projects he was now involved in.

They walked east beside the rails. Ray gestured to the gently rising patchwork of fields and hedgerows that was Box Hill, visible above the treeline. "Take it from me, the Ministry of Defence has something going on up there. It looks just like an out-of-town industrial park from the road, all low-rise and inconspicuous, like it's trying to hide in the bushes. But they've been there since before the Second World War. It's a massive site – parade ground, barracks. But if you go poking around, you'll find there are older buildings. Buildings that aren't what they seem."

It was apparent Ray had done his homework. "Pockeridge House, over to the east of the site, that's been there since the eighteenth century. Coach houses, stables and a walled garden. It was used as the officers' mess. Then there's Sandhurst Block – that looks like an old monastery, if monasteries had clock towers. Built by the War Office in the thirties, when they remodelled the whole site for some reason or other."

"How come you know all this?"

"It's not hard to find out if you do a bit of research. It's still very much operational – currently it's home to the MOD's Global Operations Security Control Centre. This is where they store all that CCTV footage, your browser history, stuff like that." He seemed to remember something. "Well, anyway, it's a big important place. Staff of a couple of thousand people, at least. Home to the British Army's 2nd Signal Brigade and the 81st Signal Squadron."

Austin was beginning to think this might not be such a good idea.

Ray had stopped, and was waving his hands in the air for emphasis. "A chap who brings his car to my garage tells me they even have a cyber unit. Sounds scary, right? Cyber is— well, they're not building killer robots or anything, don't get me wrong. We let the Americans do the heavy lifting with those kinds of projects these days, then just pay through the nose to use them afterwards. Long gone are the days when plucky Brit back-room boffins set the standards for innovation the rest of the world envied."

Austin looked at a smear of fox excrement he'd collected on his heel. He wiped it in the grass on the verge, and they continued walking. "We won the war, but lost the peace."

"*Right.* All that know-how, all that entrepreneurial can-do energy, killed by governmental bureaucracy, a suffocating class system and the Luddite attitude of the unions to new technology. A killer three-pronged pincer movement."

Austin could tell this might be one of Ray's hobby horses. "Box Hill. You were saying."

"Yes, so, here's the interesting bit. If you look carefully on Google Earth, you can see low pyramid-shaped structures that are turfed over to make them inconspicuous from the air. Bunkers? Entrances to something underground? So I ask myself, what if the buildings up top are just window dressing?"

Ray's face was alight. Austin could see the enthusiastic schoolboy was still there, under the patina of four decades of lived life. "See, rumour has it the hill is honeycombed with old quarry tunnels. *Miles* of them.

"So, us in the Smokebox Club, we do a little digging. There are records of a redevelopment programme approved around ten years back. This happens to mention in passing that there are three hundred and forty acres of underground space down there. That's more than two hundred football pitches. You could host the entire football league, every team, all at once, and still have space over for the amateurs."

Sport-related analogies were not Austin's forte.

"So. Big."

"What could they be hiding down there?"

What indeed.

They had rounded a gentle curve. Up ahead was the tunnel entrance.

It was a solid-looking edifice. Austin had to concede that they didn't build tunnels like this any more. Topped with a classical balustrade and flanked by square fluted columns, this was civic engineering by 1830s standards, when grand gestures overruled stark cost/benefit analyses.

Either side, sweeping wooded embankments held back the earth. Beyond rose Box Hill itself. Legend suggests Brunel aligned the tunnel so that the rising sun shone through it on his birthday. Every monument, every building, has its hidden meanings, but though Box Tunnel hid one of the best-kept secrets of modern times, this was not one of them.

There was a smaller entrance in the façade to the right of the tunnel, a low rectangular opening. Unlike the main entrance it was functional, without architectural merit, and did not draw attention to itself. The track forked, the set of rails leading to it rusted through disuse. Ray followed them.

Briar and brambles clogged the approach. Nothing had passed through here in a very long time. Ray pulled up a thread of ivy and ran his boot across the top surface of a rail. It was covered with a thick layer of brown grease, but underneath the steel was bright, clean and reflective.

"Hah. Interesting."

The smaller entrance had been remodelled with reinforced concrete, and had the appearance of a bunker rather than a grand feat of Victorian architecture. Oxidised ducting ran down the vertical face and into the corners of the tunnel like some kind of surgical instrument designed to keep the aperture open. Every surface was stained with rainwater and rust.

Entry was barred by a two-door metal grille backed with corrugated iron that blocked any view of the interior. It was padlocked. Two insets at its base allowed the rails to pass underneath. To Austin it looked like it had been undisturbed for decades.

Ray ignored the lock. Referring to something on his phone, he was fumbling at the side of the arch, where a short wall parallel to the tracks provided a lee hidden from passing trains. He seemed to locate what he was looking for.

They heard a heavy bolt slide back with force, as if pulled into its housing by an electromagnet. Smooth and efficient – not the sound of some rusted wartime mechanism. He pushed the door and it opened as one unit, padlock, frame and all.

Ray was enjoying this immensely. "Do step inside."

"We're not, you know, trespassing?"

Ray laughed and looked up to the sky. "I think our overlords have other things on their minds right now, don't you? And laws . . . well, whether they apply to you or not does depend on whose side you're on."

Inside was a short tunnel, maybe four metres wide and twenty deep. The ground was flooded to a depth of a few centimetres, the rails standing proud of the green slime. Debris, a mix of rotting sleepers and concrete blocks, some sprouting shoots of rusty reinforcing iron, was strewn around. Ahead, the rails were two bright lines that led into darkness.

Bricks had been placed like stepping stones in the water between the rails, and Ray stepped from one to the next. At the far end, their way was barred by a solid wall of breeze blocks.

Ray pointed. "False antechamber. Classic tomb-robber misdirection." There was a small room off to the right. Austin imagined it might once have been a checkpoint, though now the windowpanes were broken and just the metal frames remained. Inside was a rusted desk, its top surface a Pollock painting of flaking Hammerite and animal droppings. Ray felt under the rim, and after a second or two found something.

Somewhere deeper still, they could hear another mechanism click into place.

Ray came out and gestured towards the back wall. "Please stand clear of the doors."

Information 2: **Signage**
Not to scale
Subject to amendment

CAD 178

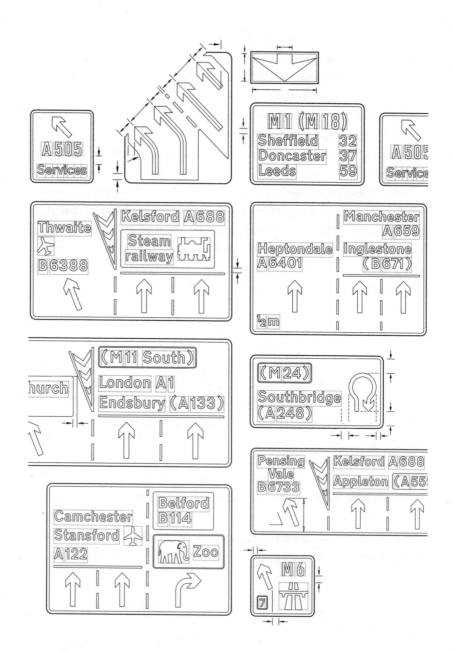

The wall pivoted up and over their heads like a garage door. A fine curtain of dust fell in the light of Austin's mobile-phone screen.

Ray sneezed. "Looks like they don't have many visitors."

Beyond, the tunnel extended into the distance, curving gently away to the right. Striplights in the roof flickered on, held. Apertures could be seen opening either side at regular intervals, but they were unlit. The rails, here shiny and clean, were flush with the floor and ran down the centre of the tunnel ahead of them to the limit of vision. The low hum of a generator could be heard somewhere in the distance.

The ground was clean, the walls free of graffiti. The tunnel was definitely old – the whitewashed brick was bubbled and cratered, and crumbled under Ray's touch, but it was apparent that this facility, whatever it was, was still very much in operation.

There was no one waiting to meet them.

"So where's your contact?"

Ray was looking at his phone. "No signal."

He hit a red button on the wall and the door swung shut behind them.

The two of them stood there in the unflattering light, wondering what they should do next. Austin recalled the Sunday afternoons he and Ray had spent exploring the deserted factories along the Western Avenue as thirteen-year-olds, and found himself savouring a nostalgic mix of elation, curiosity and trepidation. They'd climb under a chain-link fence or wade under a bridge to explore derelict office buildings and abandoned garages in which local gangs had scrawled their footballing allegiances, or skateboard in empty reservoirs that were being reconquered by scrubby grass. On one occasion they'd found a den in the roots of a large tree that had been built by the older boys at school; it was strewn with cigarette butts, beer cans and pornography, and they had not dallied. If they'd been discovered, Austin knew they'd have faced a beating for their incursion into enemy territory – here, he had no idea what the punishment might be. It would be hard to pass off breaking and entering as childhood curiosity when you're two grown men.

Ray interrupted his reverie. "Can you hear something?" A regular squeaking was just audible, becoming louder.

A shape was approaching, alternately lit from above then silhouetted from behind as it passed under the lights. It resolved itself into someone on an old bicycle. Whoever it was waved. "Yo! Ray, right?" The male voice echoed in the enclosed space.

A well-dressed man in his late sixties braked to a stop in front of them, putting one foot on the ground for balance. He wore a white dress shirt with the sleeves rolled up, a tweed waistcoat and a thin-brimmed bowler hat, and had waxed his moustache into two points. His trousers were tucked into his socks, and a greasy rag hung from his belt. He was a peculiar mix of formal and functional, as if he'd turned up for work one day in the wrong outfit and never thought to change.

Ray stuck out his hand. "Yes. Hi. You're Roger Garcia?"

Roger ignored it, and instead gave a theatrical salute. "Reporting for duty!"

Austin had no idea if this place was bugged. He could see no CCTV cameras, but if this was a top-secret government facility he assumed they must have all manner of surveillance equipment in place. He pointed to his eyes, to his mouth. Roger looked confused.

"What? No, no one can hear us down here. Come *on!* The chaps topside are barely aware we exist." He patted Austin on the shoulder. "Welcome." Then to Ray: "Is he—?"

Ray seemed to assume they could speak freely. "Yes, he's a fellow Smokeboxer. He's the reason we're here."

Roger didn't look convinced. "You know the secret hand sign?"

Austin wondered if this was all a game, a childhood club that adults had forgotten was just that – a club for children. "Of course I do."

He held his hand down by his side, two fingers apart, mimicking the Smokebox badge.

Roger clapped his hands together. "*Hah.* For the true enthusiast, as Ray here will testify, the railway is nothing short of a *faith.* We know the true tenets of obsession. We are the original underground network."

Ray looked a bit sheepish, but nodded, acknowledging the point. "Keepers of the firebox flame."

A small boxy vehicle, painted a utilitarian green, was parked at the side of the tunnel. "At CERN they have Segways. Here, we have old bicycles and toy trucks. Take a seat."

Roger lifted his bicycle into the back of the truck then dug into his pocket. He inserted a key in the ignition and pressed a starter. The engine turned over, echoing painfully in the enclosed space. He executed a sharp three-point turn, a deft manoeuvre he'd obviously performed many times before.

The cart picked up speed, its small motor a steady whine. The tunnel forked, and to their left and right numerous smaller passages branched off into blackness. Roger seemed to be following the rails.

He raised his voice over the engine. "What do you know about this place?"

"You know, the rumours. What you can find out online."

"Don't believe everything you read on the internet."

"Or on the messageboards of the Smokebox Club?"

"The Smokebox Club does have— Well, let's put it this way. It does have members who aren't just spouting conspiracy claptrap, and may actually know a thing or two." He pointed at himself and smiled.

"So, what you may know: there are over sixty miles of tunnel down here. Bath limestone, used for construction since Roman times, is still quarried round these parts. This track, the one we're following, was used for decades to transport stone out to the main line, and thence to the rest of the UK – it's been here since at least 1886.

"This place was a working quarry right up until the thirties. When the situation in Europe began to deteriorate, in '36 the tunnels were acquired by the War Office. When Hitler's troops marched into the Rhineland in clear violation of the treaties of Versailles and Locarno, this former mine became Corsham Central Ammunition Depot.

"We're now a hundred feet below Box Hill, a perfect natural refuge. Not only was it a vast ready-made underground storage facility for munitions, it also became a working operations base. These very tunnels were intended to house the Emergency Government War Headquarters. Known as Burlington Bunker, this place was to be the government's top-secret home from home, should London fall."

Austin took all this in. There had been much discussion, all those years ago, in the pages of the Smokebox Club magazine along these very lines.

Now, at last, they were finding out the truth.

Did this place also hide that other rumoured secret, the grail of steam enthusiasts?

The reason he was here?

They passed signs painted directly onto the walls, lit by antique spotlights:

They had the decaying charm of an abandoned Tube station.

"Where does your electricity come from?"

"Two huge diesel generators. Enough to power a small town. We're pretty much self-sufficient. This place has sewerage facilities, a vast underground lake for fresh water. Flood pumps. Stocks of canned food. If the worst came to the worst, the government and essential staff could have lived down here for the duration. There are – were – kitchens, showers, medical facilities, bunk rooms, dining rooms, offices. Churchill had a private suite."

"*Churchill* stayed here?"

"The records, as you can imagine, are patchy or non-existent. This was black ops, off the books. But there are stories the old guys still tell. Maybe they'll tell you themselves.

"Apparently Churchill hated the artificial light down here, and would often be seen up top, hiking to the summit of Box Hill on a Sunday afternoon, or knocking back another Johnny Walker in the King William IV in Dorking. At closing time, the landlord would put him in a taxi and send him back here."

"Hah. 'Keep it dark.'"

"A small contingent of staff was always in readiness. Site 3 was to be kept ticking over, available at a moment's notice to return to full operational status should it be needed.

"In the latter days of the war, an emergency communications centre intended to cover the whole of south-west England was installed in District No. 1, part of the complex that had not been given over to munitions storage.

"Then, in the late fifties, the place was refurbished to house Harold Macmillan, his entire Cabinet Office and all the necessary civil servants and support staff. From here, they would have access to the communications infrastructure and transport links. They had everything they needed for four thousand people. There's even a TV studio, from which he could've addressed the nation."

"Four thousand people," Austin repeated, with not a little awe. He was beginning to appreciate the sheer scale of this underground facility. They had been travelling at some speed for around fifteen minutes, maybe twenty, along a corridor easily tall and wide enough to accommodate two large vehicles side by side. Colour-coded cables, trunking and pipes, some over half a metre in diameter, hung from the ceiling or were mounted along the walls.

More dark openings passed at regular intervals on either side. Some had enormous steel doors so heavy they required wheels; these had been swung open and latched to the walls or padlocked shut. It seemed that the place was laid out on a grid, a criss-cross of tunnels at right angles to each other; a legacy, he supposed, of the original stone quarry. In some sections so much material had been excavated he wondered why the roof didn't fall in. They passed more signs, again hand-painted in black capitals on the uneven whitewashed walls.

NORTH WEST RING ROAD
THIRD AVENUE
THE MAP ROOM

Roger braked sharply. "The Map Room! Here—" He gestured expansively through an open double door the thickness of a safe. "If the government *did* decamp down here, this was where the big decisions would have been made."

He flipped a Bakelite toggle switch. Striplights blinked, then steadied with an audible mains hum. In the middle of the room, two large tables, pushed together as if for a Christmas family lunch, were circled by a dozen or so chairs. A triptych of wartime information posters had been pasted directly to the wall; rust stains had disfigured them, lending the glamorous woman in the 'Keep Mum – she's not so dumb' poster a sinister undead complexion. Dexion shelves on the far wall held dozens of identical bound volumes, each labelled with a stencilled number, while front and centre was a fifties-vintage overhead projector. A rectangle on the rear wall had been painted white to act as a screen, and beside it was a green chalkboard on which someone had drawn a portcullis. The overall effect was of a high-school staff room in a state of dilapidation rather than the mid-century modern nerve centre of a Kubrick movie.

Above the screen, in a simple wooden frame, hung a black and white portrait of the young Queen Elizabeth, and on the wall to the right, a similarly sized photograph of Churchill. This one was unfamiliar – a younger, trimmer, more sprightly man, dressed in some kind of formal regimental attire. From his epaulettes hung tasselled cords, and on his otherwise plain tunic Austin could see a small medal, or perhaps a badge.

He stepped closer.

It was circular, black, about the size of an old sixpence, and he recognised it immediately. Inscribed within a black circle were two hands, like a clockface but of equal length, forming a little V.

"Wait – *Churchill* was a member of the Smokebox Club?"

Roger grinned broadly. "We're not the Masons, but we do go deep." He straightened, faced the portrait, clicked his heels together and held his right hand down by his side, forming the Smokebox sign.

Then he held it up. His index and middle finger formed the familiar Victory V.

"He also stole the club's salute. Apparently the Chief Engineer was furious."

Not to scale
Subject to amendment

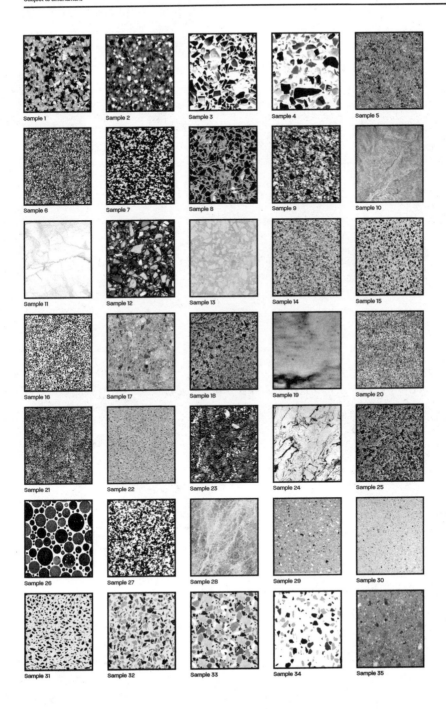

Sample 1

Sample 2

Sample 3

Sample 4

Sample 5

Sample 6

Sample 7

Sample 8

Sample 9

Sample 10

Sample 11

Sample 12

Sample 13

Sample 14

Sample 15

Sample 16

Sample 17

Sample 18

Sample 19

Sample 20

Sample 21

Sample 22

Sample 23

Sample 24

Sample 25

Sample 26

Sample 27

Sample 28

Sample 29

Sample 30

Sample 31

Sample 32

Sample 33

Sample 34

Sample 35

14

187 FABRICATION

Rutherford stepped from the stage of the amphitheatre into a corridor. A series of coloured lines, like an airport wayfinder system, ran along the wall. It was reassuringly human in its proportions, as if designed for the passage of creatures not unlike himself.

He reached out a hand and let his fingertips stroke the wall as he walked. It was cold to his touch, and a faint electrical buzz seemed to travel up his fingers into his forearm. He stopped, and touched the floor. He sensed the same buzz again. His shoes had insulated him from it, but skin contact told him it was there. Was this place alive? Had he somehow woken it? He wondered if it had any idea he was here, exploring its interior.

Set in the walls were dark apertures, windows giving onto unlit rooms perhaps. He stopped at one, shone the torch through. He fancied he could make out some low-hanging objects, a series of looping pipes like a heating element in a boiler. Through another, just darkness. He could see no doors through which he might access these spaces.

Ahead there was a larger opening, barred by an opalescent material like glass. Here the ceiling came low, and the coloured lines on the wall parted to flow over or under the screen. He could see vague shapes through the glass on the other side, unmoving.

He looked around, back the way he had come. In the dimming torchlight he could clearly see his footprints in the light dust that covered the floor. There were no other marks; no creature, however small, had come this way in a very long time.

The walls here were a smooth featureless ivory, occasionally coated with limestone runoff, its oxidised brown tint hinting at some dissolved metal it had carried here from elsewhere. To the left the corridor continued, but a short way ahead it was blocked by stalactites the diameter of his wrist, reaching down like the bars of a cage to touch the floor. They were perfectly vertical, and seen in context against the leaning walls gave him a visual reference that settled his sense of balance.

He stepped closer, his torch casting sharp shadows and throwing back sparkly reflections. Beyond, there seemed to have been some rupture in the ceiling, and centuries of slow geological action had modelled what looked like an ornate faerie grotto. Below finely detailed fluted columns and waved draperies was a series of sinter pools which held perfectly transparent water. Rutherford reached through and scooped a handful up to his lips. It was clean, with a slight metallic aftertaste.

He returned to the opalescent glass threshold. He imagined he must now be many storeys deeper than the entrance in the Crossrail tunnel, perhaps hundreds of metres down. If there was a centre to this maze, a solution, perhaps it lay beyond this door.

In the centre of the glass was another panel, similar to those he had encountered before but without a triangular recess. This one had a dozen indentations, arranged in no patten he could discern. Choosing at random, in five of these he placed the fingers of his left hand.

There was that show of lights behind his eyes again, the faint electrical fizz of a connection. It was as if this place was asleep, but in its dreams had the vaguest awareness of his presence. He wondered if he should show more caution, should step away from this doorway and what might lie beyond, but he remained pinned to the spot, held by a sudden sense of the enormous weight of earth above him.

Open. This time he didn't vocalise the word, just said it to himself. The faintest of hairline cracks appeared down the centre of the door. He inserted the point of the trident, pushed it forcefully to one side.

The door split vertically down the middle and the two halves parted. There was a grinding of glass on metal, and they seemed to jam. Beyond he could see another dark space, from which emanated the faintest scent of decay.

There would still be room to squeeze through. He held the torch aloft, pausing at the threshold. He wondered if he should call out, but caution caught at his vocal cords.

He could sense that just beyond lay the nerve centre of this vast construct, and whatever it might hold. Shining the torch at his feet, perhaps to save himself from some revelation he felt he might not be capable of facing, but more prosaically in case he stumbled and pitched himself into oblivion, he stepped inside.

Not to scale
Subject to amendment

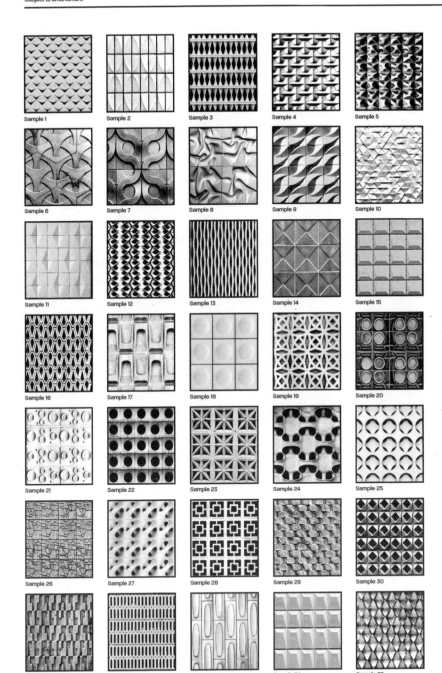

Sample 1

Sample 2

Sample 3

Sample 4

Sample 5

Sample 6

Sample 7

Sample 8

Sample 9

Sample 10

Sample 11

Sample 12

Sample 13

Sample 14

Sample 15

Sample 16

Sample 17

Sample 18

Sample 19

Sample 20

Sample 21

Sample 22

Sample 23

Sample 24

Sample 25

Sample 26

Sample 27

Sample 28

Sample 29

Sample 30

Sample 31

Sample 32

Sample 33

Sample 34

Sample 35

R oger led them from the Map Room out into another windowless hall. "This is the communications centre."

Running the length of the large space were rows of numbered telephone exchanges. They were antiques: banks of numbered sockets, connected by plugs on lengths of cable. Beside each was a rotary telephone dial, set on a small stanchion between sets of colour-coded switches. Above each was a large red clock with unusual eye-shaped icons at the cardinal points. Austin wondered if they originally showed different time zones, or had simply ceased to function at different times. Rows of swivel chairs, their upholstery rotted through to a skeletal frame of springs, listed in front of dust-covered counters. It looked as if no one had sat here for decades.

"This was cutting-edge tech, for its time. Back in the heyday there was a round-the-clock staff of sixty in this section alone. This state of affairs was maintained till the sixties . . . then the staff was reduced, bit by bit over the years, down from a few hundred to just a handful. By the nineties the Cold War was over, we were all supposed to be friends, and these vast military projects simply couldn't justify their price tag any longer."

Roger drew his index finger through the dust on a crimson countertop. "When they decided to cut the staff from fifteen to eight, we knew what was on the cards. But at this point they were down to the hard core, and a few of us refused to go. We'd tended this place for so long, sunk so many hours into keeping it going, that it had become our own passion project. We were an integral part of its history.

"Nowadays there's just four of us in the whole complex. And I'm only here three days a week, setting the rat traps, priming the flood pumps, restocking the drinks cabinet and the cigarette dispenser."

"You can smoke down here?"

"Churchill certainly did. But the damp air will get me *looooong* before the tabs will."

Austin took it all in. "You're *sure* you're not taking a risk, letting us in here?"

Roger snorted. "*Please.* Most of the brass upstairs don't even know these tunnels exist. Need-to-know basis. The low-level grunts are certainly oblivious. The staff turnover is so high these days, it'd be a security nightmare to act otherwise. No, don't you worry. They can eavesdrop on Putin while he's on the shitter, but they don't know what's happening beneath their very feet."

Roger pointed up, to the installations above ground. "When there's a change of personnel in the upper ranks, maybe *then* we might get a visit. We do the usual tour, the show and tell. But other than that, even those with the necessary clearance rarely come down here. I've worked under operational commanders who didn't bother to visit us once in ten years."

"And so you're still here."

"For the moment. We've seen I don't know how many directors come and go, and so far we've outlasted them all."

Ray nodded. "The forgotten minions who live in the sub-basement. You're the Morlocks."

Austin chuckled. "Well, that'd make *them* the Eloi. And instead of eating them, we're trying to save their arses."

Ray put his finger in a dial, turned it and let it spin back. "This place . . . it's incredible."

"Isn't it?" Roger clasped his hands. "But the viability of a place like this is a hard case to make. This communications centre? Obsolete. Even in a state of war, even with whatever is happening in London right now, this kit would never be required. Time and progress have left us all behind.

"But time and progress don't always equal reliability. We now operate in a web of interlinked technologies – the power grid, GPS, radio and cellular communications, the transport infrastructure. This interconnectedness is its vulnerability. Knock out one of those key pillars, and the rest can fall.

"They knew this when they built this place – that's why we have our own generators." He leaned on the wall. "Feel that thrum? Number Two generator, Old Reliable, still gives us all we need. She's been running for over seventy years. My phone is two years old and it's already obsolete."

Roger pulled his rag from his belt and wiped it across the glass face of one of the clocks, leaving a dust-free arc. Underneath it was still bright, as if he'd just turned up the saturation; everything else down here seemed to have been sapped of colour by years of neglect. It had stopped at half-past four, the time Austin always imagined was shown on the Smokebox Club badge.

"But I've not shown you the highlight yet. The national secret this entire place was designed to house."

"The secret government?"

"That. But how do you get a secret government here in the first place? Picture the scene. The bomb has been dropped, nerve gas fills London, the capital is in chaos. You can't hail a cab."

"Plane?"

"You'd need to get out of London to an airfield. Shoreham. Heathrow. Helicopters aren't a practical solution when the staff to be evacuated number in the thousands. And what about the Royal Household? The War Cabinet?"

Austin smiled. "The old tunnels." That there were secret tunnels under London was common knowledge in his line of work – Parliament and Buckingham Palace are linked by passages that run under Green Park to the Piccadilly line, and thence to Heathrow and safety should the Royals need to be evacuated in time of national crisis. The 'Q-Whitehall' tunnel that connects Parliament with Trafalgar Square (now Charing Cross) station had been used as a route between different branches of Whitehall during World War Two. Austin had once concocted a reason to explore them in his early days in the business – the antique cage lift, the cramped spaces hemmed in with shelving, the rusted junction boxes and the bare concrete floors carpeted in Woodbine butts were a time capsule from another era.

Make do and mend.

The Crossrail extension was just the latest in a long line of subterranean escape routes that had begun with the first castle with a back door.

"Exactly. The tunnels, the old network under London that connects Whitehall and Buckingham Palace to the main rail routes out of the city. From there, we just needed suitable transport."

Roger was enjoying himself. A childlike enthusiasm had swept over his features. His eyes seemed to shine from within.

"The prize, the secret, the main event is just through here."

He walked to the far end of the hall. Ray and Austin followed him through a set of double doors and out onto a railed cast-iron balcony.

The subterranean space beyond was unlit, but Austin sensed its vastness. The damp air smelled of turpentine and sulphur.

He couldn't see much by the light seeping from the room behind them – a hint of a soot-black vaulted roof, cut from the raw limestone of Box

Hill, cables mounted in brackets on the walls nearby. The ground, some three or four storeys below, seemed to be an oily black, with work-benches and cranes set at intervals.

Beyond that was just darkness, though somehow he had an almost supernatural sense of dark shapes filling this underground space, crouched beasts made of iron and history.

Roger had his hand on a large circuit breaker mounted on the wall. "Gentlemen, I give you . . ."

With a dramatic flourish he flipped it up, like a ringmaster raising the curtain on the greatest show on Earth – or under it. There was a sharp squeal of metal on metal, a circuit was completed, and fierce arc light filled the chamber.

Ray and Austin covered their eyes, squinting through the glare.

". . . the *Strategic Steam Reserve.*"

15

197 **SCHEME**

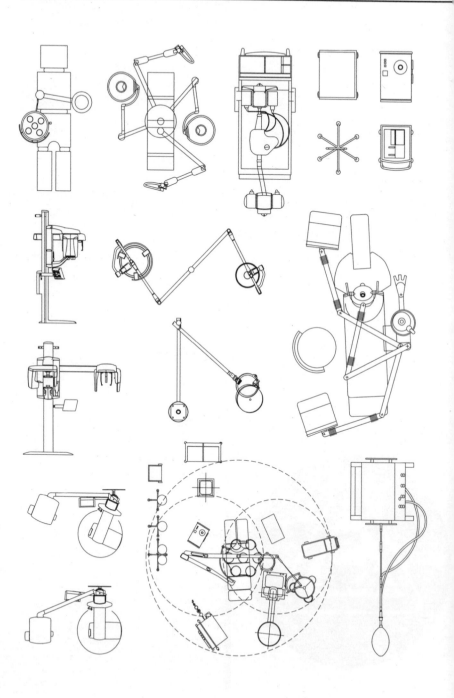

In the fading light of his torch, Rutherford could see a raised dais up ahead on which loomed a dark bulk. It was silhouetted against a vacant opening in the far wall which glowed faintly with a ghostly phosphorescence. It appeared to have its back to him, facing the opening as if in contemplation.

He assumed it was a seat, a pilot's seat, perhaps, or a throne – from behind, it was hard to make out details. It seemed to grow up from the ground, like the exposed roots of a tree, then knot and interweave to form two armrests upon which there was some kind of control interface. The back opened up like a winged armchair, then swept up and around to form a conical hood that was attached to the ceiling by a central shaft. The whole, though perfectly symmetrical, had the organic sculpted form of something that had been grown, or perhaps fashioned by a mathematical algorithm, rather than built.

It had the approximate proportions of an object that might hold a human being.

The torch dimmed again, and he hesitated at the doorway. *Calm yourself,* he thought. He had not encountered any living thing in his explorations, and he did not expect to now.

The floor was a crosshatch of fibres through which he could see another level, some distance below. Again it reminded him more of the internal organ of an animal than a built environment. The ceiling itself was a network of veins or cables, radiating from the central column and out, down the walls. The space was not large, maybe ten or twelve metres across, and it occurred to him that it might have originally been filled with liquid, a marine environment in which the uneven floor would not have been an issue.

Keeping his distance, he walked around to the right. His torch picked out more details. An array of articulated instruments hung from the ceiling, pointing inward to the place where the occupant's head might have been. It put him in mind of an operating theatre, and he had a notion that some medical procedure had taken place here. One armature ended in a succession of finer and finer pincers; another was equipped with a fan of hair-thin needles. Leading away from them – or it could have been into them – were more of the cables that ran like arteries throughout this space.

He felt a sudden cold flush of adrenaline through his extremities. He had assumed the throne was empty – it was not.

Slumped low in the seat was a diminutive figure. It had the dusty skeletal appearance of something long dead, a desiccated bag of brittle bones. Its skull had come loose from its spine and rested in its lap.

It looked human, probably male.

He was old, but the preservation was incredible. The bone mount of his spine held up a tent of dried flesh, the small cranium below still holding onto the occasional tuft of white hair. His nose was aquiline, and a set of blackened teeth protruded below. His lower jaw was loose, hanging by one mummified strip of sinew. One arm rested along the wing of the throne, fingers inserted into cavities in its form; the other lay, palm up, in his lap, cupping his fallen skull.

A covering of tan animal fur was still wrapped around his lower torso and groin. His legs didn't reach the ground; long ago, his feet had disassociated themselves from his calves and now lay at the base of the throne like discarded slippers. A dark fuzz of fungal hair clung to his body in piebald patches.

Rutherford wondered if he had had a spoken language, and if so, if he had had a name.

Still inserted into his head were a half-dozen filaments, like transparent needles, and Rutherford could see that they had originally been attached to one of the instruments surrounding the throne. They seemed to be well preserved: though darkened with the patina of age, he could imagine them still at work in some modern hospital.

What had happened here? The primitive clothing suggested someone from the Neolithic, completely at odds with the technology of this fantastic device. He couldn't imagine that here was the original builder or designer; this place was beyond the capabilities of our ancient ancestors. Beyond us now, perhaps. He was surer than he had ever been that Anomaly 36 must have come from further afield.

Was it a forgotten relic of an advanced but vanished Earthbound race? A Vimana, a Hindu flying machine from the *Mahabharata*? Or some mystical vehicle from Kumari Kandam, Ultima Thule or Atlantis, or even something from our own future, thrown back into the distant past?

Or was it an artefact of entirely alien origin? Though the idea seemed absurd, he was now willing to entertain any and all possibilities.

At the base of the throne lay a small leather knapsack, sewn together with thick twisted reeds. A thin loop hung over the arm of the throne, where it had originally been placed. The clasp had broken, and its contents were scattered across the dais. Rutherford directed his fading torchlight down. He could see a set of bone needles, a polished shell. And an arrowhead.

It was fashioned from metal, like the ones found in the dig above, like the key Yumi Lark had discovered in the Natural History Museum. It had been carefully filed to a sharp edge. This prized possession must have given this hunter-gatherer an advantage like no other – a technological game-changer, a power-multiplier akin to the steam engine.

But it had not been smelted from ore mined here on Earth, by humans or their close precursors; this had been adapted from an object found here, in this place he now occupied. Technology from elsewhere, adapted for use in a different, more primitive context.

He picked up the arrowhead. Was this desiccated body its maker, its arrowsmith?

He ran his finger along its sharpened edge, and it drew a spot of blood. It was still sharp. He sucked his finger.

An arrow is a projectile launched from a bow.

A tool, a weapon.

We have our modern counterparts: the fighter plane and the rocket.

But an arrow is also a *symbol*.

It is an indicator of direction. An arrowpoint *points*.

It shows us where we are going.

Where *are* we going?

Towards something of significance; a desired destination, perhaps?

A future, one yet to be defined?

Rutherford imagined he could feel the spaces around him constrict. He suddenly became viscerally aware of the thousands of years that this tomb had lain undisturbed, of the sheer weight of geology above him, of the layer upon layer of sediment laid down through periods of settlement and cultivation, Roman invasion and Saxon counter-invasion, revolutions both social and industrial, technological and cultural, as London was built, brick by brick and thought by thought, above him.

From the moment the hatch had closed behind him, his presence here had not gone unnoticed. Unbeknownst to him he had introduced a sympathetic vibration of sorts, a recognition of life for life. And though the Anomaly was for all intents and purposes incapable of what we would call full self-consciousness, its being more a coalescence of complex equations than a miracle of biology, within it something akin to life was once again stirring.

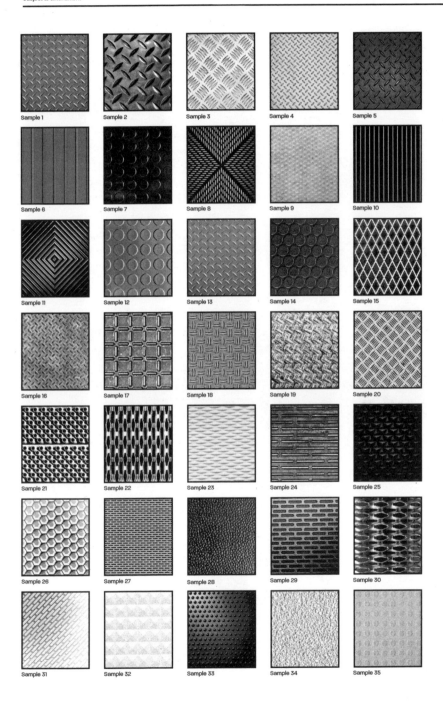

Sample 1 — Sample 2 — Sample 3 — Sample 4 — Sample 5

Sample 6 — Sample 7 — Sample 8 — Sample 9 — Sample 10

Sample 11 — Sample 12 — Sample 13 — Sample 14 — Sample 15

Sample 16 — Sample 17 — Sample 18 — Sample 19 — Sample 20

Sample 21 — Sample 22 — Sample 23 — Sample 24 — Sample 25

Sample 26 — Sample 27 — Sample 28 — Sample 29 — Sample 30

Sample 31 — Sample 32 — Sample 33 — Sample 34 — Sample 35

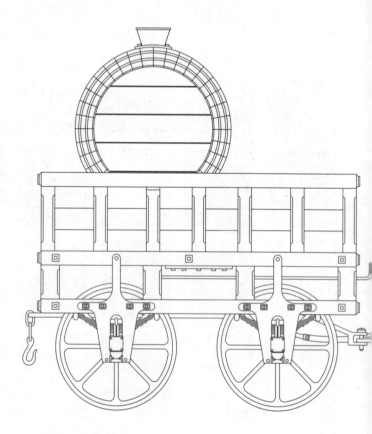

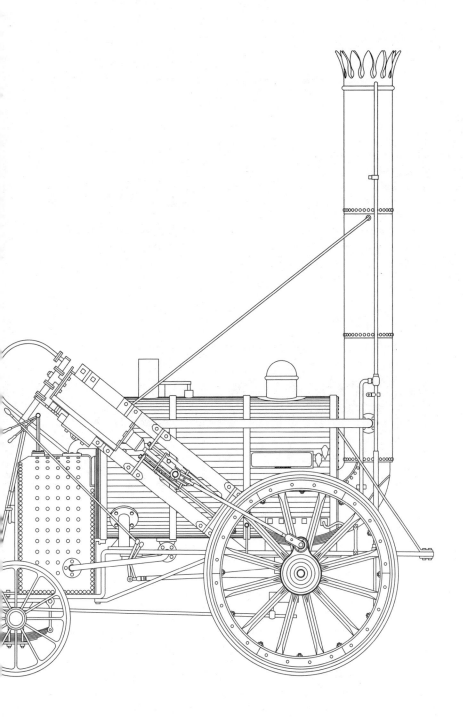

They were *magnificent*.

The true scale of the underground cavern could now be appreciated. Austin guessed it was larger than any London terminus. Cut from the limestone rock, the ceiling was held aloft by stout piers placed at regular intervals and criss-crossed with brick buttresses tied with iron rods. At its highest point it must have arched fifteen metres above their heads, and they were now standing well above the cavern floor.

Set below them and a short way out were twenty or more pairs of buffers, and just beyond them . . .

"How— how many?"

"One hundred and sixty-two locomotives. Eighty-four fully operational. More, if you include the diesel shunters or the ones we use to scavenge parts."

They were lined up head to tail, on parallel sidings, all pointing towards them at their elevated position at the end of the hall. How far back they reached was hard to tell; the lights, though almost painfully bright, were not adequate to illuminate the entire space, and Austin had the impression of further spaces, maybe just as cavernous as this one, lying off to the left and right through connecting arches.

The arc lights reflected from their livery, drew bright reflections down the length of their boilers.

One hundred and sixty-two locomotives, each repainted a deep glossy black over their original Malachite Green. Their funnels were dark circles, their wheels polished silver, their smoke deflectors like blinkers on thoroughbred racehorses.

And these were certainly thoroughbreds: their hides glowed with a healthy sheen, their steam domes were their high withers, their brass fittings glinted gold and their greased buffers were factory-fresh.

Austin followed their lines back into the recesses of the enormous hall. They probably hadn't felt a spot of English rain in decades. Behind each was a tender, the heaped coal sparkling like diamonds. Even if they had once seen lengthy service, each had been immaculately restored. Any one would have been a museum centrepiece.

He realised that each had been stripped of its cabside and smokebox number plate. They were all incognito, nameless black locomotives deep undercover. He wondered where they had originally come from.

If Arthurian legend tells us the once and future king lies slumbering under Glastonbury Tor, waiting to be revived in Albion's hour of need, the steam enthusiast had the Strategic Steam Reserve.

Roger broke their awestruck silence. "These are British Railways Standard Class and ex-Great Western Railway locos. One withdrawn here, one there, discreetly and over time so no one would notice. Then they were sequestered here, kept in storage and ready for use if the bomb was dropped, the power grid went down, the country faced disaster and only the old technology could come to our rescue."

It made sense: large parts of many European railway networks, the UK being no exception, are electrified, this being far cleaner and more efficient than diesel. But in the event of natural disaster, or (it had been whispered darkly by the more conspiratorial on the railway messageboards) another war, the power grid could easily be disrupted. Electric locomotives would be shedbound.

Diesel locomotives, though capable of running under their own power, could also be at risk if supplies of imported fuel were unavailable, or if the solid-state components in their control circuitry were compromised by the electromagnetic pulse caused by a nuclear strike. Ray had read these posts, and their exhortations to stockpile food and weaponry, and taken them to be a peculiar local manifestation of the American survivalists' paranoid world view: the Powers that Be, our secret masters, had plans for such eventualities that they didn't share with the proletariat.

But it had been a persistent rumour. One that, despite an almost complete lack of reliable evidence, had not gone away. Good stories always outlive the dull facts of the matter.

And sometimes, just sometimes, turn out to be true.

Austin felt like he was eleven years old again. His diaphragm constricted with unexpected emotion and he thought he might cry. "The Strategic Steam Reserve. It's *real*."

"It's real. Members of the Smokebox Club have cared for and maintained these slumbering giants since the last V-2 fell, the Allies cornered Hitler in his bunker, and the Yanks spirited away the Third Reich's top scientists and engineers in Operation Paperclip. Wernher von Braun might have taken them to the Moon on kerosene and liquid oxygen, but it was us, *here*, who cared for the old technology, who kept the dream of steam alive."

They had come here under false papers, through the quiet post-war winter nights, one by one over a period of some fifteen years. Panting softly like loyal dogs, they had put their trust in their engineers and drivers and had been saved from an ignominious death by blowtorch as the last days of England's romance with steam gave way to the uninspiring practicalities of diesel and electric. These were the very best of their kind, machines that represented the pinnacle of their craft – the technology of boiler and piston, funnel and furnace, honed to an efficient symphony of moving parts.

"Ah, it was dark *Boy's Own* stuff! The engines were listed for scrap, taken on what was billed as their farewell journey to some depot – Woodhead, perhaps, or Craigendoran – and there the documents were falsified, the books altered. Their identifying numbers were removed, and then they were run back here, to us, in the small hours."

"No one saw *any* of this?"

"Occasionally an enthusiast, out and about at some ungodly hour, would spot an unmarked loco which should not exist – you remember the odd report that used to circulate in the railway magazines? That's how rumours of the elusive, mysterious Black Locomotive arose.

"So we ran counter-intelligence in the newsletters. Every locomotive had been accounted for. The paperwork was a matter of open record. It was just a case of mistaken identity.

"Ghosts, we called them. How those devotees would have rejoiced if they'd known they weren't hallucinating, that they really *had* seen a Pullman, lights out, visible only by the red glow of the furnace and the sparks from the funnel, shooting across the South Downs on a misty November night!

"So that's how they ended up here, waiting patiently to get up a head of steam at a moment's notice one more time to serve Queen and Country. The boilers are certified, the pistons greased, the tenders loaded. Just look at them! Tell me these aren't the most beautiful machines in the whole world!"

"They're beauties, all right." Ray was resting his chin on the hand rail in silent supplication.

"You should have seen this place twenty or thirty years ago – we had Royal Engineers, fitters, metalworkers, machinists. We had drivers with the accumulated knowledge of a lifetime riding the footplate behind them, knowledge just a few of us now try and preserve. Once there were hundreds of us here, but now we're down to just a handful of true believers, fighting the faceless bean counters of Whitehall.

"Since Beeching pruned the network, what use are machines that can't even go where you need them, they said. They weren't supposed to be here in the first place, they said. The money would be better spent elsewhere, they said."

Roger paused, drew a long stuttering breath. His emotions were close to the surface. He lowered his voice to a whisper. "Don't get me wrong. It's important work, the defence of our nation. And I know we've been surplus to requirements for years.

"But now those philistines want us to cut them up, here on site – to turn this place into an abattoir! We can't even pass them over to the heritage railways! They'd look after them for us, they'd give them the retirement they deserve, but no. There'd be too many questions."

He looked out, across the silent locomotives. "Us down here, both man and machine, we know our time is coming to an end."

Austin did not voice the idea aloud: *Maybe not just yet.*

lb/in²

0   40   60   80   100   12

DUPLEX GAUGE

...N RESERVO...

16

...ESTINGH...

211 **PERSPECTIVE**

Rutherford placed the dying torch on the dais, front and centre. He rested the trident upright, against the right arm of the throne. The peculiar articulated instruments, he found, could be moved; he swung them clear, then carefully picked up the mummified head.

It felt dry and brittle. Placing it on the ground, he turned back to the body. Reaching under and around it, he lifted. It sagged in his hands, a fragile bag of dried skin and bone. One arm swung free, but the whole still held together. He laid it out on the ground in front of the throne, beside its head.

The seat now only held a sprinkling of dust and detritus, which he blew away. Was he actually going to do this? Was he going to sit on this throne?

What did he expect would happen?

Possible answers beckoned to him. He wasn't sure, but he knew he couldn't leave here without trying.

He turned and lowered himself down onto it. A chill seeped though his trousers, as if he'd spilled icewater in his lap. It was not built for human proportions, that much was clear; his heels did not touch the ground and the armrests, if that is what they were, extended too far out on either side. He felt his way along their surfaces till he sensed a familiar subsonic buzz, just as he had before. One, two – his fingers located several spots that seemed to respond to his touch.

Lights again danced behind his eyes, stronger this time – ochre, green, a deep orange, other colours he had no names for that fell outside the usual range of human vision. They formed geometric patterns, vibrating chequerboards or zigzags in his peripheral vision.

Then, without warning, a vertiginous rush seemed to render him weightless, as if he was in freefall. His sense of self expanded dramatically, and his body seemed to drop away.

Above, he glimpsed a turbid churning of low cloud, and below – below him were stars. No, not stars – he was above the city, above London, right now, and could see lights laid out along the tangled geometries of the capital's streets. Long streamers met at brighter nodes, sparkling as if refracted through warm air; a darker, looping gap though the midpoint marked the path of the river. For a moment he thought they were streetlights, or cars: but these were the lights of several million individual minds, a riot of life in all its unpredictable, multihued fervour.

The upper extremities of his being felt a rarefied coastal wind from Folkestone, a messenger from the Continent; his south-eastern flank bore the old scars of Dockland's obsolete industrial technologies like a rusted caliper. Around his south-western fringes were open fields where kings once hunted stags and ornamental lakes winked like shallow eyes, while to the north rose hills of brickearth and clay.

Then he was pulled back down to Earth. An immense weight, a billion tonnes of steel and stone, pressed down upon his back. Porcupine quills of pre-stressed concrete and glass rose above him; the River Thames, crossed with the cartilage of bridges carrying rail and road, formed the central spinal fluid of his being. Beneath the surface he could feel a rhythmic pumping: arteries of chlorinated water, and veins of waste on their return journey to the treatment plant.

He could taste a fug of isopentane and sulphur dioxide, a dry precipitation of particulates falling from the troposphere to envelop him like a morning mist. Vehicles powered by primitive combustion engines scurried to and fro like lice across his hide, a toughened skin of tarmac and aggregate.

His vision was a multitude of faceted views, a cubist concatenation of angles piped from every CCTV and cameraphone in the capital. He saw his face reflected back at him from the sides of city skyscrapers, twenty-story-high self-portraits made of shadows and light.

Between granite and asphalt, where the kerb met the road, parallel lines kept his arteries free of the coagulant of cars. He was striped in yellow and white, the semiotic signalling of lane and bus stop, direction indicator and box junction. His saplings were phone masts, his oases public houses, his hunting grounds the nightclubs.

His fingers were the new-build developments of Canary Wharf, grasping at a stale grey sky, his daylight filtered through a fine haze of hydrocarbons. His occipital lobe was the bright sprawl of Leicester Square and Piccadilly Circus, his pineal gland the Roman amphitheatre preserved under Guildhall Yard. His basal ganglia were the walled old City, the original square mile. Out, towards his periphery, he could sense the suburban sprawl of grey matter, the whorls of residential closes and cul-de-sacs branching off from the main highways. His fields were car parks, his cliffs plate glass; his avenues were asphalt, his glades roundabouts. Cranes and transmitter towers formed the canopy overhead.

Nerves of copper cable and fibre optic below ground, electromagnetic waves of radio and WiFi above carried his modulated nerve impulses through silicon synapses. Dividing and subdividing into each and every home, every smartphone, every screen, they connected the countless private and public living spaces of the hive-mind of humanity, each individual a single cell in this city organism, the memetic engine of a unique culture.

Segmented metal worms aerated his bowels, carrying commuters who, looking out through scratched windows, would see only blackness and their own faces reflected back at them.

He was infested – by people. The city had a vast, cohesive intellect all its own, built from the interactions of all the collaborating and competing individuals within it, each seeking their place in the reproductive ecosystem of new company upstarts, takeovers, mergers and bankruptcies; flagship store openings, rental opportunities, blue-collar crime and low-life criminal cartels.

He was a delicate balance of costs and benefits, the unforgiving push and pull of needs and resources. He was the car showrooms of Park Lane, the underground swimming pools of Chelsea, the shop windows where everything was available, for those who could afford it.

He was a harsh taskmaster for those who couldn't: the late-night delivery motorcycle rider, the teenage runaway convulsing in their own vomit as their last fix finally releases them from the pain of life, or the transvestite turning tricks in King's Cross. Here, two thousand years ago when London was a town in size, not just in name, the Iceni beat back the Romans, the interlopers from Europe and beyond who now made up more than half of his population.

He was a fleeting glimpse of pediment against azure through an Uber window, an unexpected proposition in a dimly lit wine bar. He heard the disharmonious hum of a million conversations: pleas, declarations, screams and laughter. He could see them all, every one. Somewhere in Waterloo, a Ukrainian émigré crafted a heart on a head of froth on a macchiato. In Camden Town, a pickpocket threw a stolen wallet into the canal and folded away a hundred pounds in cash. In Amen Corner, a Liverpudlian prostitute agreed a fee for her services with a married stockbroker. On Goldhawk Lane, a child lost a Lego figure down a storm drain, and was inconsolable.

For the winners, he was a kingdom of lights looked down upon from the penthouse highs of privilege, from the desirable riverside residence with concierge and gym and pool.

The ideal city always cast its shadows over the cardboard city; the department-store awnings of Tottenham Court Road and High Street Kensington provided shelter for the transient and the terrified, those without the means or the memes to be a useful functioning part of the whole.

He had once been told that London had no heart, because it couldn't afford one. But he could also sense great love and kindness, the beautiful and brutal in close collusion.

His populace did not fight dragons but train timetables, his nights were no longer populated by wild boars and rutting deer but pub bores and imported beer. He was lit by streetlights instead of campfires, and his highwaymen wore hoodies and carried knives, not tricorns and pistols.

He was a complex agglomeration of discrete parts, each with their own individual volition but obeying certain rules that made coexistence possible. Though he was constantly being pulled in many different directions at once, he still somehow managed to cohere as an organism, as a whole.

Bricks and mortar and flesh and mind.

Sleepwalking through his being, most of his inhabitants were unaware of the sensuous pleasures of the aged underpass or cantilevered flyover, the poise of pre-stressed concrete that supported them in their passage, the roads they passed over a thousand times and never caressed.

Ensconsed in your vehicle where the air is conditioned, your body cushioned, the radio tuned to your favourite station, the city is held at bay. You are safe and secure, the outside world passing by in abstracted stream of colours and lights, too far away to touch, too distant and uninvolving to be anything other than a movie projected on a screen the size of a windshield.

He was a destination for dreamers, and the nightmare to which they awoke. He was everything and anything you want him to be, your darkest desires made manifest; he would test you and try you and quite possibly break you, and you might not be able to tell opportunity from annihilation.

He offered promises, with hidden caveats. Terms and conditions apply.

His one constant was change. A city has no reproductive system, no DNA through which it can replicate. It is singular, but it can grow to accommodate the multitude that live within it. He was the ether-vision of countless anonymous civil engineers, the heir to Betjeman's fields of root and Elliot's unreal city.

His original floorplan was the old leaf-skeleton of Londinium, laid out around mother Thames, who carried the blocks of his being down from Reigate and Maidstone, the raw materials for his royal crescents, the cobbles for his boulevards, the beams and rafters for his medieval roofs. He was the colonnades and porticos of the cities of antiquity to which every later metropolis paid homage, and whose remembered glories they attempted to emulate: the echo of Alexandria or Athens, Carthage or Corinth.

He was the city, and the city was him.

All these patterns were not arbitrary. These thoroughfares and structures reflected a plan already in existence, beneath the streets; the expressed neural net of an ancient buried machine of alien origin and unknown purpose.

While the physiology of the throne's original occupant must have been very different from his own, its sensory range subtly shifted in ways he could only guess at, there was enough of an overlap for the alien mechanism to get a purchase on his biological systems, an inexact match that still afforded him an endorphin rush of exaltation.

He felt out to his periphery and understood the true shape and size of the Anomaly and knew that it had lain here, undisturbed, since the late Neolithic. There were broken systems and rerouted sensory blocks, vast areas long ago given over to darkness and decay. He probed his being in more detail, noting the subterranean rivers that now ran through his person, the pressure of clay and rock and sediment piled upon him, his north-eastern limb long ago flattened and buckled by geological uplift and faulting.

He was filled with a buzzing cacophony of creativity, concentrated into three hundred square kilometres of seething humanity. He somehow understood that the city above owed its very life force to the machine he now occupied; indeed, that the machine's presence had been the catalyst for its creation, that the rich and creative lives of the creatures that called London their home were all a consequence of this alien engine and its ability to shape reality.

Wasn't that the promise London had always offered?

To re-imagine oneself, to become whoever one wishes to be?

Built Environment 13: **Zone extent**

Not to scale
/Subject to amendment

CAD 218

The locomotive's black livery, originally a wartime initiative and then a symbol of their hidden and secret status, reflected the open sky. Overhanging trees drew a curved crosshatch of shadows over the boiler. For the first time in – how long? Fifty years? – this marvel of engineering was standing proudly and unapologetically outside, open to the skies, in the late afternoon sun.

The diesel shunter withdrew into the hidden entrance, the driver waving as he went, leaving the locomotive facing east on the deserted main line into London. Just ahead, the impressive pediment over the entrance to Box Tunnel framed the scene.

Roger and his crew had their favourites, of course, though they tried not to let the engines know. Before they had been stripped of their identities, they all had had numbers – and many of them had had names.

If you have a name, he imagined, maybe you have feelings. For Roger, it was a reciprocal arrangement.

They had chosen a Lord Nelson class locomotive.

The Lord Nelson class had seen service on the Golden Arrow route down to Dover and the Continent; before the Pacific class came into service they were considered the most powerful locomotives in Britain.

Sixteen of them were built, and they were all named after famous admirals. As far as the public was aware, only one – the very first of its class, the Lord Nelson itself – had survived, preserved as part of the National Railway Collection.

But the Strategic Steam Reserve held six more, six that had been saved from the scrapyard:

SIR RICHARD GRENVILLE
SIR WALTER RALEIGH
ROBERT BLAKE
LORD ST VINCENT
LORD DUNCAN

And one more: this one.

Roger walked up to the front, running his fingertips along the boiler. She was a superb specimen. The piston shafts were slick with amber lubricating oil and the wheels shone like burnished two-shilling pieces. Every part of the coachwork was a rich, deep black, even the originally signal-red buffer plate.

The buffers themselves were shiny catseyes, the only reflective surfaces to be seen from the front; they lay low to the ground, the bulk of the engine above suggesting a creature about to pounce.

What was its name? Perhaps there were records in deep storage, but these would have been altered. Its history had been erased.

But Roger Garcia knew. Though it now bore no nameplate over the wheels, this was the

LORD HAWKE

It had seen service throughout the Second World War, surviving a German bomb attack and derailment at St Denys, Hampshire on 14 August 1940. Nursed back to heath and put back to work, it had finally been withdrawn in the early sixties, whereupon the necessary arrangements had been made to bring it here. Sometimes Roger felt he was running a retirement home.

The Nelson class had a low funnel, and the required headroom for what they intended to do.

Roger handed Austin and Ray caps. On each were three letters in a circle, the old logo of the Great Western Railway.

Roger patted Austin on the back. "If we're going to do this, let's do it properly. This beauty has patiently waited here for more than half a century. If this is to be her last outing, we need to dress the part."

Ray pulled on his cap and walked up to the engine, placing his hand on its side. It was warming under the sun. Soon a fire would be lit in her boiler, the heat would cause the dew to evaporate, and the full gloss would return to her black pelt.

He couldn't guess her weight, but her sheer size was something to behold. Once she was up to speed, there was very little that could stop her.

That was the point, after all.

Roger began to shovel coal. "Up here. Give me a hand. This isn't a free ride. We need to work together as a proper crew if this is going to be a success. Don't tell me you two never wanted to be engine drivers?"

Austin grabbed a handrail, swung himself up onto the footplate. "We're the fucking Smokebox Club. Of *course* we want to be engine drivers."

Roger knew every valve, every rivet. He could coax an extra ten miles an hour out of her just by carefully adjusting the boiler pressure. He knew this machine more intimately than he knew his husband, and if truth be told, loved her more.

He tapped the glass of the water gauge. The tank was full. He opened the firebox. He had already loaded the grate with coal, and was holding out a petrol-soaked rag and a lighter. "Want to do the honours?"

Ray held up his hand. "I think you should. She's your baby. I wouldn't want to take this moment from you."

Roger gave a small nod and flicked open the lighter. He dropped the burning rag onto the coal shovel, tossed it into the firebox and shut the doors.

"How long does it take? To get steam up?"

"Usually a few hours, from cold. But we don't have that luxury." Roger pulled a lever. "Let's see what we can manage." He was enjoying himself, Austin could tell, though he assumed he knew there'd be hell to pay later.

If there was going to be a later.

He'd thought that what he had in mind might be a hard sell, but Roger had listened to his plan without interruption. There had been a short pause, during which Austin thought he might laugh at the absurdity of it all, but instead Roger had nodded solemnly, just once. "It's what the Strategic Steam Reserve is *for*," he had said. "If it's going to be scrapped anyway, this may be the last opportunity we have."

And that had been that.

Ray checked his watch, then opened the firebox. A blast of hot air and soot blew back into the confines of the cab. He slammed the doors shut again.

Roger pointed. "You'll be helping me feed that."

The air smelled of iron and sulphur. It reminded Austin of fireworks night, and he felt that same childhood thrill, the promise of drama and bright lights and some grand finale yet to come.

The interior of the cab was a circuitboard of copper piping, the inner workings of an analogue technology. Above was a series of glass-fronted dials in which needles quivered, indicating boiler pressure, temperature, and a half-dozen other variables. It was not a sleek and tidy interface, the mechanisms hidden from view behind a dashboard like a modern vehicle; instead its functionality was on full display, just like the tunnelling machines he was familiar with, and it seduced him.

This was the pure-blooded steed that would take them to London.

Roger rested a gloved hand on the brake. Steam had begun to lift from the funnel. "*Every* kid wants to be an engine driver, right? If only for one day.

"This, my friends, *this is that day*."

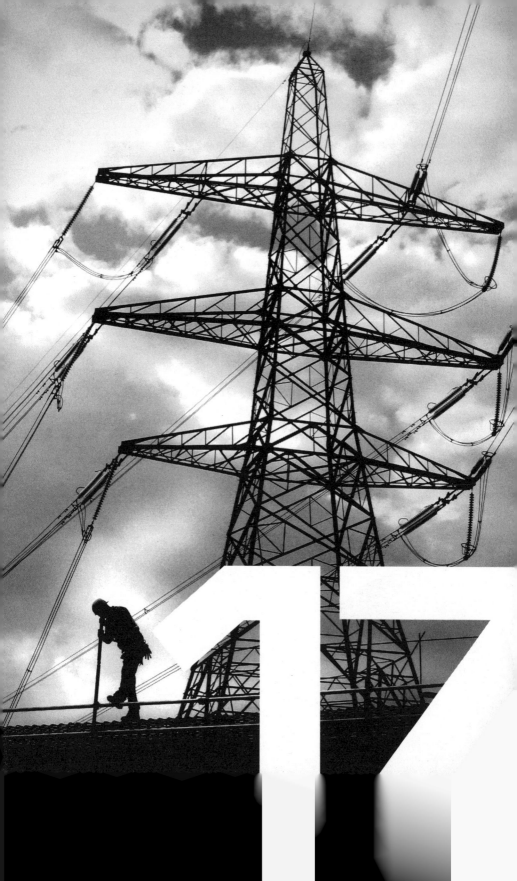

225 **PLOT**

If he was now intimately connected to this machine, the arrangement appeared to work both ways.

It seemed to be exploring the recesses of his mind. He could sense an anxious probing of his inner self, a sifting of his memories for information. Events that he had not brought to mind for many decades were picked up and turned over, examined, analysed. It was disconcerting. Not least because some of them were painful, or embarrassing. Some of them he had buried for a reason.

His first impression was of a faithful animal, one who had waited patiently a very long time, wanting only to serve its absent master. A war horse, perhaps: a hardened steed, trained in the theatres of some distant crusade to perform certain tasks on command and without hesitation. But it was also more than that: a symbiotic relationship, a blending of evolved and manufactured biology into one enhanced unit.

The Anomaly had no higher volitional sense of self, as far as he could tell; the pilot provided that. It was responsive and accommodating under his mental probing, weighing up different potential courses of action, bringing possible scenarios to his attention.

It was a machine designed for conflict, of that he was certain, but he couldn't quite alight on the precise nature of that conflict. It seemed to be existential and ongoing, but also without clear purpose or beginning. More a war of attrition, of survival against poorly understood and overwhelming odds. Rutherford had a sense of a disassembling of entire cultures, the bringing to bear of resources on gargantuan scales.

He now had no doubt that that war involved many races and cultures that were not of this Earth. The stage of life had suddenly become so much larger.

The Anomaly – this ship – had been badly wounded in a minor skirmish of little strategic importance, far from the main arena of this incomprehensible war. While distant – over sixty thousand lifetimes at light speed – the machine's original rider knew that it was still very much a present concern. There was something peculiar about the linear unfolding of time, of the logical ordering of events; Rutherford assumed he must have misunderstood.

Though distances were hard to fathom, there was an event with high emotive importance some 300 light years distant, in the direction of Vulpecula, below Cygnus in the northern sky. Something awful had happened there.

Two millisecond pulsars spun where once a binary system of blue-white stars had warmed a family of planets. Now they were swept with jets of hard radiation as their diseased suns precessed around their axes. This information was tagged with a deep ultramarine sense of loss and the ache of four billion dead.

This was not a natural event. It was unprecedented. What kind of weapon could have caused such devastation?

He framed a question in his mind.

The ship began to tell him its story.

R oger released the brake. The engine seemed to stretch, pull at an invisible leash. It began to slowly move forward, groaning and creaking, smoke belching from the funnel and steam hissing from the pistons like the mutterings of a middle-aged man rousing himself after a long slumber.

He sympathised.

pant   pant   pant pant pantpant

They entered Box Tunnel.

In the dark enclosed space the smoke could not escape. Instead it was forced back, enveloping them. Ray pulled out a handkerchief and pressed it to his nose and mouth. The gruff exhalations of the engine were deep and resonant; it broke from a trot into a canter.

The breaths grew more frequent, accelerated to a heartbeat, then faster still. Austin fancied his own heart was racing to match its pace. The wheels beat out a rhythm on the track.

diddi da diddi da diddi

From the firebox whipped snippets of orange flame, and from the funnel fled vulcanous black smoke that freckled their faces with smuts.

Ray shovelled in more coal and the glow of the fire lit him from below like some teller of fireside tales, and Austin knew that, whatever happened, this was one tale he would tell and retell.

Roger didn't even need to look for the controls. Hand lightly placed on a brass wheel, a finger on a gauge, his was an instinctive relationship with a lover, one in which he anticipated their next requirement, eased them into each curve with a practised hand. The engine was a set of variables he sensed intuitively and adjusted with a consummate skill honed by decades of practice.

"On the test runs we never got to push her to the true limits of her capability. We had to be as inconspicuous as we could. This is our opportunity to see what's she's really capable of."

The panting of the engine accelerated, the rhythm of wheels on track quickened further. Austin felt his chest expand. The dragons that once roamed this land had nothing on this beauty.

Coal rattled out of the tender and onto the floor, and it was all Ray could do to shovel it straight into the firebox. The heat and exertion made him perspire; this was not a job for an ageing man of sedentary habits. The cab was as loud as a nightclub, and as hot as a sauna.

Suddenly they exited the tunnel into daylight.

Roger pulled a cord, held it. The whistle was deafening: the exhalation of the whale, the air-raid siren of the pending apocalypse. It was a shout of sheer exaltation bellowed out across the Downs, through the hamlets and byroads of a rural English landscape that had changed so little since this engine had been built, a landscape that had not seen such a magnificent machine for far too long.

The afternoon light approached the golden hour, throwing long shadows across the track. Crows darted around them, diving in and out of the plume as if they recognised in the locomotive their Lord of the Crows, an earthbound deity that grounded their skybound existence.

Austin's teeth juddered and his legs buzzed, the beat of wheels on rail hammering in his chest like an iron heartbeat. They rode a shadow, one that had by need and circumstance been nocturnal for sixty years, its occasional night-time outing a surreptitious affair noted only by an insomniac hiker or those that should not be abroad at such an hour. For them, it had passed like an apparition, a phantom from another age, a night terror.

The Lord Hawke would hide no more.

Austin shovelled more coal.

Black coal. Black soot. Black livery.

The blackness of the locomotive enthralled him.

It was their Whiteness of the Whale, their leviathan, their Moby Dick.

From an engineer's perspective, black is the absorption of all wavelengths of light. Nothing is reflected – but if black was an absence of illumination, it was not an absence of meaning.

Did it remind him of the black leather jacket of a Hell's Angel, burnished with engine oil? Or the black banner of the religious extremist? In ancient Rome black was the colour worn by craftsmen and artisans, not priests and judges. Which they were had yet to be decided – were they fanatics on a final mission of deliverance, or old fools playing with their toys?

In the capital tonight, the windows would be dark, the streetlights unlit, and the darker measures of mankind would feel free to roam again, for another night, unchecked. There would be no glow ahead on the eastern horizon to guide them in this evening.

Towards that peasoup blackout raced this antique beast, its steel-cold weight coaxed back to life by a new fire in its belly. Its filthy and steadfast crew fed it anthracite forged from the dead wood of the Carboniferous, mined in Black Country towns under the shadow of pit wheels far larger than those that were now turning with great force beneath them. They were riding a chariot hitched to the horsepower of several thousand black bay stallions.

Water, when vaporised at sea level, increases 1,700 times in volume. This extraordinary multiplier allows power to be extracted, and work to be done. This is the accident of physics that drove the Industrial Revolution.

Steam turbines still generate a huge proportion of the world's power; even nuclear plants use their heat to generate steam, and thence electricity. The future, as always, is built on the technology of the past.

Austin looked ahead, up the line. Beneath him he could feel the locomotive's weight and presence through the floor, a sense of an unstoppable mass driving itself ever forward on silver rails towards its destination. Streaks of orange along the low horizon were reflected back from the engine's cylindrical body, lending it the sheen of a nocturnal beetle.

London.

If the bright electrical light of modernity had failed there, perhaps the smoke and steam and thunder of six-foot wheels on track, a jet-black herald of deliverance named Lord Hawke could save the day.

Legend 1: **The Blackness of the Locomotive**   CAD 233
Not to scale
Subject to amendment

Key

Hex: Hexadecimal
RGB: Red, Green, Blue
        (additive)
HSL: Hue, Saturation, Luminosity
CMYK: Cyan Magenta Yellow Black
        (subtractive)

0K
The Page
Hex #FCFCFC
RGB (252, 252, 252)
RGB (100%, 100%, 100%)
HSL (0, 0%, 100%)
CMYK (0%, 0%, 0%, 0%)

10K
Whitewash
Hex #E5E5E5
RGB (229, 229, 229)
RGB (90%, 90%, 90%)
HSL (0, 0%, 90%)
CMYK (0%, 0%, 0%, 10%)

20K
Cement
Hex #CDCDCD
RGB (205, 205, 205)
RGB (80%, 80%, 80%)
HSL (0, 0%, 80%)
CMYK (0%, 0%, 0%, 20%)

30K
Concrete
Hex #B3B3B3
RGB (179, 179, 179)
RGB (70%, 70%, 70%)
HSL (0, 0%, 70%)
CMYK (0%, 0%, 0%, 30%)

40K
Paving
Hex #999999
RGB (153, 153, 153)
RGB (60%, 60%, 60%)
HSL (0, 0%, 60%)
CMYK (0%, 0%, 0%, 40%)

50K
Brick
Hex #7F7F7F
RGB (127, 127, 127)
RGB (50%, 50%, 50%)
HSL (0, 0%, 50%)
CMYK (0%, 0%, 0%, 50%)

60K
Stone
Hex #666666
RGB (102, 102, 102)
RGB (40%, 40%, 40%)
HSL (0, 0%, 40%)
CMYK (0%, 0%, 0%, 60%)

70K
Asphalt
Hex #4D4D4D
RGB (77, 77, 77)
RGB (30%, 30%, 30%)
HSL (0, 0%, 30%)
CMYK (0%, 0%, 0%, 70%)

80K
Soot
Hex #333333
RGB (51, 51, 51)
RGB (20%, 20%, 20%)
HSL (0, 0%, 20%)
CMYK (0%, 0%, 0%, 80%)

90K
Printer's Ink
Hex #1A1A1A
RGB (26, 26, 26)
RGB (10%, 10%, 10%)
HSL (0, 0%, 10%)
CMYK (0%, 0%, 0%, 90%)

100K
The Black Locomotive
Hex #000000
RGB (0, 0, 0)
RGB (0%, 0%, 0%)
HSL (0, 0%, 0%)
CMYK (0%, 0%, 0%, 100%)

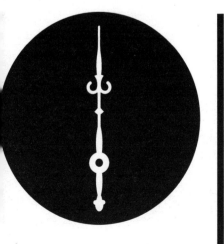

235 **CONVERSION**

Images came.

Sounds, tastes.

Emotions he had no name for.

>

>

>

>
>

>
>

>
>

>
>

>

>

A modulated set of clicks, like wheels on a track.

```
>>>>>>>>>>>>>>>>>>>>>0>>>>>>>>>>>>>>>>>>>>>>>>>>>>>>>>>
>>>>>>>>>><>>>>>>>>>>>>>>>>>>>>>>>>>>>>>>>>>>>>>>>>>>>>
>>>>>>>>>>Ki>>>>>>>>>>>>>>>>>>>>>>>Ma>>>>>>>>>>>>>>>>>
>>>>>>>>>>>>>>>>>>>>>>>>>>>>>>>>>>>>>>>>>>>>>>>>>>>>>>>
>>>>>>>>>0>>>>>>>>>>>>>>>>>>>>>>>>_•>>>>>>>>>>--->>>>>>>>>
```

A rush of digraph phonemes, though not produced by the human vocal tract —

```
>>>->*>>>+>>>>•>>>>+>>>>>>>0>>0>>>>>Ra>>>>>Xi>>>>Ka>Mi
>Ru>Yo>Pa>>>>>Yi>Ki>Ve>Ga>>>>>Ko>Li>>>>>Wo>Xe>Zy>Ny>Qu>Lo>Pe
>Cy>Ol>Fo>Fe>Oh>Og>We>En>Eb>Bo>>>>>>Li>Es>So>Te>Hm>Yq>En>Ji
>Zo>Ne>Gi>Uk>Ko>Le>Fa>Ra>Po>Ir>Ge>Ro>Ep>Hm>Ch>Ta>To>Jo>Uq>Cj
>Pr>Dl>Sw>Sb>Id>>>>>>In>Ec>Hb>Nq>Du>Ab>Lj>Cq>Qf>Rt>Le>Th>Ts>Cy
>Gh>Wz>Ld>Zp>Cv>Rx>>>>>Rj>Su>Uy>Vd>Bz>As>Qa>Uc>We>Oy>Ap>Mn
>Qn>Sy>Zv>Pf>Co>Jg>Kj>Mp>Hq>Qj>Aw>•>Gi>He>Qt>Wz>Qq>Xg>Fg>Eu>Kc
>Fa>Of>Ji>Cw>Ah>By>Ux>Tu>Yk>Zv>>>>>>>Ja>Ae>Wo>Tk>Zt>Gn>Zr>Qc
>Gk>Ue>Xi>>>>Zi>•>Ls>Cu>Ep>Mk>Tx>Hz>Hh>Mz>Mi>Nd>Av>Io>Qx>Rk>Yy
>Xs>Kg>Qc>Ph>Dq>Jx>Fv>Yh>Ni>Jd>Je>Fm>Sk>Sb>Zl>Cc>Ce>Ce>Ml>Fn
>Hj>Gw>Ex>Lq>>>>>Pb>Qy>Xf>•>Cj>Vm>Te>•>Nh>Zb>Xq>Hj>Fv>Zn>Jj>Zh
>Po>Dq>Mw>Ry>Nc>Ef>Xd>Ec>Oz>Og>Vv>>>>>>>n>Uq>Dq>Fn>Wj>Dk>Uf>Et
>Hx>Sd>Ej>Ir>Lq>Jc>Ns>Wx>Kd>Vy>Nf>Fj>Og>Kz>Ci>Kr>Cq>Uc>Ax>Ns>Ca
>At>Qs>Di>•>Wr>Ig>Hf>Jy>Oo>Ql>Qp>Yw>Mq>Bm>St>Ii>Oe>Aj>Yf>Yo>Aw
>Jm>Vd>>>>>>>>Os>Qo>Od>Rh>Hf>Ct>Fy>Nw>Ay>Ft>Pf>Ht>Ke>Yr>Ok>Qm
>Tp>Wo>Od>Ns>Le>Wm>Ly>Jx>Bp>Gz>Eq>Tl>Ck>Bp>Qp>•>Qr>Ey>Sx>Vd
>Tt>Tv>Zh>Cu>Mb>Jm>•>Jy>Vh>Ye>Jk>Jt>Eh>Pl>Dl>Hw>In>Hy>Le>Kl>Ya
>Lo>Zj>Oi>It>Hk>Oo>Lq>Rr>>>>>Yk>Pn>Ai>Px>Kd>Al>Vl>Jx>Vj>Pw>Nm>Cb
>Go>Bq>Ff>Lm>Ip>•>Uj>Uh>Gs>We>Ix>Dt>Na>Of>Iz>Pp>Il>Zo>Xa>Mp>Vn
>Tn>Yl>Vc>Or>Ju>Xh>Mq>Qs>Ed>Oc>He>Se>Gv>Cd>Sr>Ox>Ci>Kr>Om>Bv
>Ob>Bi>Xc>Vl>Ty>Uy>Tt>Zb>Ph>Mc>Ra>Eu>Pv>Iu>•>Qh>Te>Sh>Ux>Yy>Uf
>Mz>Gh>Lj>Ct>Yh>Jr>Ko>Pa>Ri>Ca>Ok>La>By>If>As>Am>Do>So>No>My>Or
>Up>On>Oh>Ex>Go>At>He>Us>Is>To>In>An>We>Of>Me>Be>Zy>By>Ra>Xi
```

Rutherford felt a vertiginous rush building within him. Something overwhelming and desperate was pulling at his mind, and he gave himself over to it.

>Ra
>Ki

Ki? Ra?

>Kikikiki!<

These two sounds, above all others, seemed to vibrate
with significance.

>Kiiiiiiiiiiiiiiiiiiiiiiiiii!

>>>>>ra<<<<<
>
>Ki!

>Ki!

>Ki?

A name?

>

Causality, duration and distance seemed to be pliable concepts.
He assigned them more familiar terms where he could, but there
were many other experiences he could not put into language.

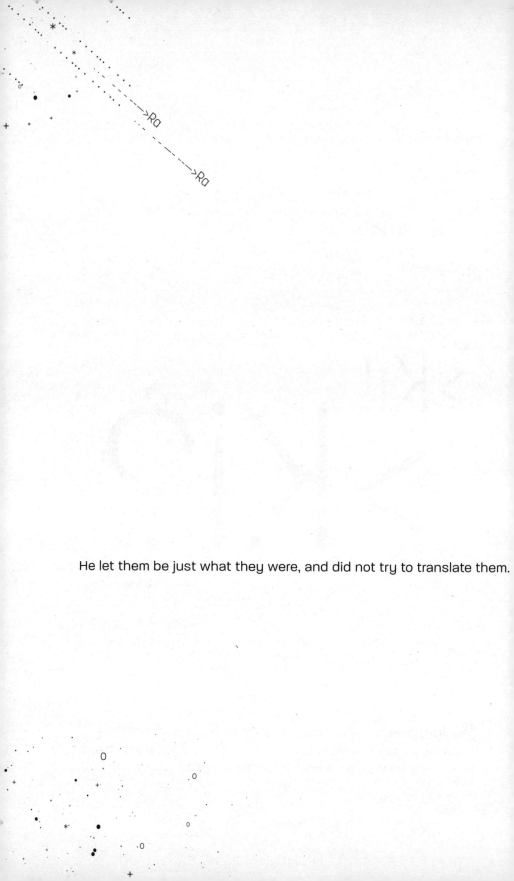

He let them be just what they were, and did not try to translate them.

Though his comprehension was limited, still Rutherford listened.

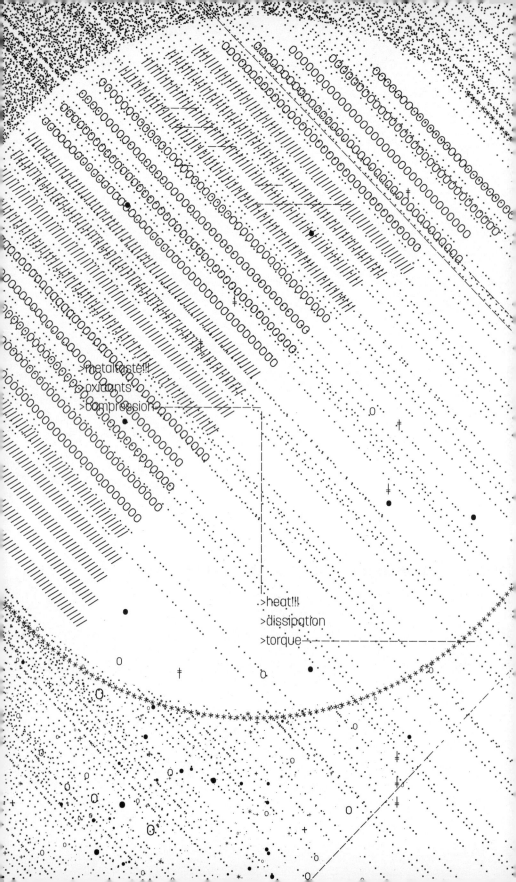

>metaltaste!!!
>oxidants
>compression

>heat!!!
>dissipation
>torque

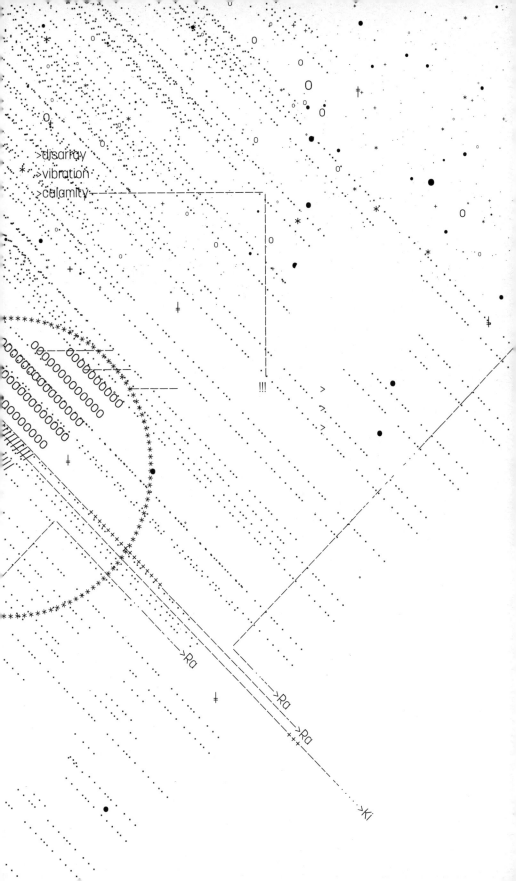

>disarray
>vibration
>calamity

!!!

>Ra
>Ra
>Ra
>Ki

> k

> K

> Ki could feel the upper reaches of the tenuous atmosphere caress the underside of xir vessel. It bucked, though it was hard to tell if this was due to turbulence or just skittishness this far from the Hub, and home. Ki thought calming thoughts, and it steadied under xir.

> This unplanned planetary insertion would not be smooth; xir angle was too steep and xir speed was too fast. Xe pulled in xir extended being, throwing the densest parts, the parts that were not essential to xir higher functions, to the fore. The remaining electromagnetic waveriders shifted to an attenuated ultraviolet as the incoming vector and velocity packets savagely compressed.

> This was a war in which there had been not one victory, however small. Every skirmish had been a massacre, every battle a rout.

> How had xe ended up here, so far from the Hub, trailing a debris cloud over an insignificant small blue planet on the outskirts of the Bar'roshira Sound? That the interlopers had managed to push them back so far, so fast, was testament in itself to their desperate situation.

> They called themselves the Ra. They arrived unheralded, from somewhere beyond the stellar nurseries of the Artemachi Wall, armed with nothing but an unshakeable conviction.

> Their technology was simple, utilitarian. Their primitive barques were barely capable of light speed, and appeared to have no weapons or defences. Reports from the first Mara forescouts, who sent their ethereal forms out in their stead as was their kind's ability, revealed that though they were bipedal, they breathed a mix of xenon and neon poisonous to most other races the Consilience had previously encountered. The folded sails on their backs and their atrophied legs suggested they had evolved in the beltwinds of a gas giant, though even this was supposition. They wore no clothing, never spoke, did not seem to read, write or sign. They came with little, in fact, but their own peculiar faith.

> They held a symbol above their heads at all times, a stylised split sun fashioned from bronze inside which spun a dark core. Though the meaning of this remained obscure, The Recess judged their technology to be no threat, and had extended the formal greeting issued to all newly discovered spacefaring species.

> There had been no reply.

> Fearing that some communication blunder, some unintended misunder-standing had occurred, a delegation was sent in person to meet their fleet. This diplomatic mission returned with a crew of new converts, each holding the split sun above them and professing their faith. They swore there had been no discussion with the newcomers, for they weren't newcomers at all; they claimed that they had always been known to the Consilience, that this is how they had always thought, and seemed confused when presented with evidence to the contrary.

> More alarmingly, the evidence itself, on closer examination, supported their claims.

> There were obvious logical fallacies at work here that were immediately apparent to those of the Recess who were watching from the Hub. How could members of the Consilience profess a long-held belief in a philosophy they had only just become acquainted with, one held by a race that had only just been discovered?

> It was impossible. But there it was. The records kept in the core memories of the Recallers indicated that this was, in fact, the truth, and that it was the recollections of those races who had not come into close proximity with the Ra that were at fault.

> That their faith, so strongly held, could actually warp the course of events, could even reach back in time and reshape history, took the Consilience some time to process. As far as they were concerned, the Universe obeyed inviolable physical and mathematical laws, always, everywhere, and with-out exception. In the five thousand millennia the Consilience had grown from a small group of independent and diverse cultures to a vast trading con-glomerate, there had been no belief, however strongly held, that could not be measured against reality and judged accordingly.

> This, in fact, had been the basis of the very accords that bound them, the one thing that they were all agreed upon. The Consilience encompassed species whose languages were so divergent that some could only commu-nicate in the vaguest and most universal terms, but they had all still lived peaceably within this framework.

> This assumption – that reality would not bend to belief, however fervently held – proved to be the Consilience's weakness. The Hub fell under the Ra's control in under thirty years; as far as those within its sphere of influence were concerned, that is how it had always been.

> At first the resistance had been disorganised, fractured, since a sensi-

ble defence was hard to conceive. What reports the remaining unaffected members of the Recess could rely on suggested that, in close combat, the Ra did not lift a hand in defence; like their ships, they were unarmed. Instead they would emit a low ululation, and a sense of beatific ecstasy would come upon their peculiar features even as they were cut down.

> Despatched to engage them, the first squadrons of needlemen found they no longer hove to their genetic predisposition for unimaginable violence executed with precision; instead, they discovered their epigenetic markers had been rewritten, their carefully bred propensity for destruction edited out.

> This had set the pattern. From here on, every battle had been lost before it had begun, every advance somehow became a retreat.

> After some calculated expenditure of life, something the Consilience regarded with utmost dismay, a captured and neutered Ra had been transported to the Recess-in-exile on Rafortheroh, where it was examined by the most experienced xenosurgeons from the theatres of the Hac. They discovered that the invader's brains seemed to exist in a superposition between this and other, parallel realities, ones where the familiar laws of physics were subtly different, or perhaps did not apply at all.

> The Ra were simply choosing the one reality that most suited their ends, and collapsing the others to zero-dimensional incorporeality. The only defence imaginable was for the remaining members of the Concilience to learn how to do the same.

> Thus a small cadre of carefully chosen and trained warrior-gods had been assembled. Each was equipped with a semi-autonomous, independently conscious craft that could sense its pilot's thoughts and adjust the flow of their surroundings in concert, both temporally and spatially. They were bonded to their riders, both through rigorous training and a shared neural web. The craft increased the rider's sensory range enormously; through them they could feel the more attenuated fields and fluxes of the electromagnetic spectrum, the mass-density depression of the local gravimetric net. The subtle potentials that flowed over the periphery of their combined being were sensitive to the undulations in space-time caused by the merging of distant black holes, or the collapse of a neutron binary a million light years away and a million years ago.

> These craft would serve three functions: first, as personal interstellar transport; second, as protection, both from the vacuum and any unwanted

temporal backwash that might inadvertently rewrite xir motivations; and third and most importantly, they would act as amplifiers, a form of resonant cavity that could affect a large volume of space around them.

> Within this space, they learned to do what they thought was impossible, but the Ra had revealed was not. They learned how to alter the laws of physics, and bend reality to their imagination.

> The pushback could at last begin in earnest.

> Ki remembered being chosen by this ship, when xe was up for auction at the Craven Marches. Xe had felt pride, then, and a flash of relief; xe finally had a ship which wanted xir, a ship xe could call xir own.

> Xir ship had already seen combat in the forward volumes, long before xe had been assigned, and bore with it the scars of the loss of its original pilot. It exhibited self-destructive behaviours xe had coaxed and cajoled into submission, a careful purging and rerouting of synaptic systems that had been the work of half a lifetime. Xe knew xe was inexperienced, but had been so grateful to be offered even this wounded veteran of a ship to work with.

> So Ki had taken xer responsibilities seriously, and soon they had developed a bond of trust. Now, though xe had not behaved capriciously, xe knew xe had let it down, here in the further reaches of the Bar'roshira Sound, so far from the hot heart of battle.

> This waterlogged planet had no name – just a number, an automatic designation assigned by cartographic necessity. Recent skirmishes had been vicious; though Ra barques were easy to sense at some distance as they were unshielded, the very act of sensing them could have unexpected consequences. Xe and xir vessel had avoided non-corporeality twice by spinning out extra, subtler dimensions, then slipping between them and away to quietly reappear yesterday, or next week.

> Working in harmony, they once increased the force of gravity within a sphere ten light seconds across ten-thousandfold, reducing a flotilla of Ra barques to a flush of hard radiation and a ball of disassociated nucleons the size of a virus. Ki imagined they might have even collapsed it to a singularity.

> Ki had found that accelerating the local temporal frame sharpened xir concentration. In this war they needed every advantage they could bring to bear; If truth itself had become malleable, mind was now the universal substrate.

> Using a similar technique, the Recess had learned how to loosen molec-

ular bonds by altering the fine structure constant. Though this manoeuvre had other, hard to calculate ramifications, they imagined they might be able to disassociate an entire planet into a mist of quarks.

> For the first time in a long time, the free races of the Consilience had allowed themselves to feel hope.

> But recently, Ki's contact with the Recess had become patchy, incomplete. Missions of the utmost urgency fell from the agenda, their objectives somehow superseded or forgotten. Ki's orders became briefer, more perfunctory, and sometimes xe suspected they didn't actually know who xe was, or what they had instructed xir to do only a short time ago.

> Ki began to suspect the Ra had found their way into the upper echelons of the Recess itself.

> Communication through the fine tachyon filaments preferred by the Consilience's engineers was not without its issues, to be sure. To reach the Hub, and for the Hub to reach back out here, this far into unsettled space, would take many thousands of years even at light speed. Just to ensure some semblance of simultaneity required that it be temporally backshifted into the past several thousand, maybe tens of thousands of years, but this, Ki knew, could have dire consequences.

> Informational bleed into the past, however well encrypted, risked alerting the Ra to their plans in advance; they suspected this was why they seemed to be able to check every move almost before it was made.

> Then the messages had ceased entirely.

> From this vast distance, a third of the way across the galaxy's disc, it was very hard to directly detect the technosignatures of the Hub at all, but Ki settled into a low-energy elliptical orbit around the system's sun and took a five-month, broad-resolution image in gamma to infrared of the area of space in which the Hub resided.

> Nothing.

> It was as if the Hub, the Recess, and even the Consilience itself had never been. Ki wondered if the Ra had somehow thought them out of existence altogether.

Materials 7: **Concrete**
Not to scale
Subject to amendment

CAD 253

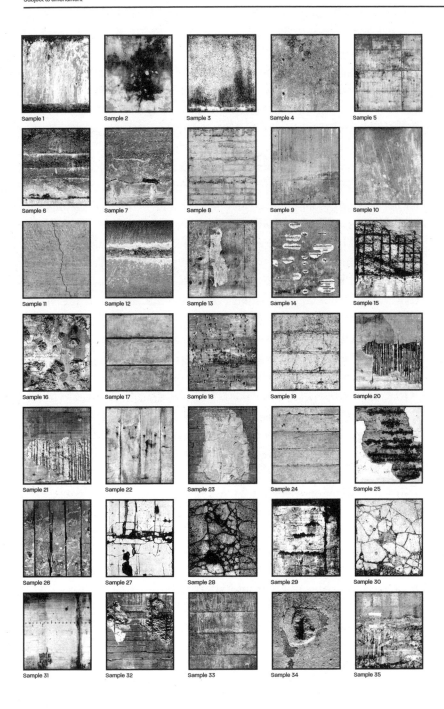

Sample 1

Sample 2

Sample 3

Sample 4

Sample 5

Sample 6

Sample 7

Sample 8

Sample 9

Sample 10

Sample 11

Sample 12

Sample 13

Sample 14

Sample 15

Sample 16

Sample 17

Sample 18

Sample 19

Sample 20

Sample 21

Sample 22

Sample 23

Sample 24

Sample 25

Sample 26

Sample 27

Sample 28

Sample 29

Sample 30

Sample 31

Sample 32

Sample 33

Sample 34

Sample 35

The locomotive was their suit of armour, and they were going into battle.

Leaning out, Austin could see the rails, polished by speed, converge towards the horizon, thin lines of light cut across by the shadows of the trees on the embankment.

Steam rose from the pistons, corkscrewing around the coupling rods. Thin wisps came into the cab, smelling of humidity and engine oil. Above, the enormous plume of smoke hung like an overcast sky, a foggy whiteout. Embers danced around the funnel, pirouetting in the updraught.

The locomotive was getting into its stride, a lean long-distance runner settling in for the haul. Fields raced by, outhouses and corrugated-iron barns, hedgerows and church steeples. Low light strobed through the cab as they passed a long row of elegant beeches.

Austin had been silent for a while. They passed an unlit signal at speed.

"Other trains—"

Ray raised his voice to be heard over the noise. "There are no other trains on the line. Since London's dark, the rail service has been suspended right out to Manchester."

Austin wasn't entirely sure this was the case.

"And how are we going to steer this thing? We can't get out and change the points without stopping."

Ray tapped his head. "You think I've not thought of that?" He was trying to suppress a childlike grin. "The *Club*."

Austin was holding a brass wheel to steady himself. "OK, I know I'm the lapsed Smokeboxer here. But how's the Club going to help us now, exactly?"

Roger adjusted a valve. "I told you before that we went deep. Even before my time, before Beeching decimated the railways, certain Smokeboxers had decided to take a more, ah, active role.

"When plans for the Reserve were being put together after the war, we already had members in very high places. Kids who had built model train sets, kids who were steam enthusiasts in their schooldays – kids just like you and me – were now working on the railways for real, in the Engineer Corps, the RAF, in the companies contracted by the government to lay track and dig cuttings, build platforms, tunnel tunnels, design the rolling stock. The Smokebox Club had – has – members *everywhere.* Almost by accident, we had infiltrated every branch of the government's transport and engineering agencies. If the powers-that-be were intent on scrapping our heritage, we decided it fell to us to save as much of the lore, the engineering know-how, the sheer passion that the Club represented."

Austin realised he'd been a sleeper agent all along, without even knowing it. But by *accident*? "It does all sound like some kind of cunning plan."

Ray cocked his head. "Uhuh. The thought did occur to me. Plant an advertisement in the railway enthusiasts' press. Recruit them young. But—" He shrugged. "It's too contrived, too much like some tin-foil-hat conspiracy theory. To what *ends*?"

Austin couldn't hazard a guess.

He turned to Roger. "Did you have to disclose your membership when signing the Official Secrets Act?"

Roger laughed and pulled on the peak of his cap. "We're not a proscribed organisation, because no one knows we exist. And if they *did*, it'd be like banning the, I don't know, the Dennis and Gnasher Fan Club."

"How many of you are there?"

"How many active members? Who knows. There's no roll-call. There are a few of us at Box Hill, of course. Jon, who drove the diesel shunter, is one. We don't talk about it openly. Just on the online forum. But we do occasionally wear the club badge, under the lapel."

Roger lifted his lapel. Underneath was the black and silver smokebox emblem. "It's like our secret handshake."

"Who else?"

"I know very few members by name. Club rules insisted that everyone used, ah, uses a pseudonym."

"What's yours?"

There was a pause. "Chuffer."

Austin emitted a bark of laughter and slapped the side of the tender. "*Chuffer.* Not, I don't know, Stationmaster, or something sensible?"

"I was nine years old!"

"*Chuffer.* Good grief."

Ray deftly defected. "Who ran the Club? Who was the Chief Engineer?"

Roger looked ahead, down the line, on into the middle distance. He seemed to be recalling something. "That, my friend, has been the subject of speculation for as long as I've been a member. See, if you think about it, the Strategic Steam Reserve has been hard to justify on civil defence grounds for *decades*. Unlike the Green Goddess trucks they used during the fire-fighters' strikes in '77, a train can only go where the rails take it." He adjusted a lever. "We may be facing the chop now, but by rights we should have been shut down in the late '50s, and the Reserve sold for scrap back then. But we weren't. Why do you think that was?"

"I don't know."

Roger gave a 'V for Victory' hand sign.

"Churchill?"

Roger raised his eyebrows. "Churchill was a Smokeboxer. No doubt about that. You've seen the photo. Maybe he appointed certain people who share our long-term vision. That's *my* guess."

There was a pause while Ray and Austin considered this. They passed under a girder bridge over which a lone car passed, engulfing it in smoke. It braked sharply, its headlights lighting up the interior like a Chinese lantern. "Smokeboxer, for sure. But was he the Chief Engineer?"

"No idea. That was the rumour, but there's no real proof, nothing that's not circumstantial. And if he *was*, who is the Chief Engineer *now*? Someone by that name is still active on the forum. If it's an honorary title, it must have been passed down – maybe several times – since the end of the War."

They passed another unlit signal.

"Roger—"

Roger had taken his smartphone from his top pocket. He held up his other hand to reassure Austin. "Relax. As you know, the newsletter is now online. Not like the old days, where there was a month between issues, a month before you got a reply. Now, you don't write in, paper and pen – you log on to the closed messageboard. See, the Smokeboxers are a clever bunch." He waved the phone. "Some of them even understand how to program this new tech. Me, I was always a nuts-and-bolts kind of guy. If I can't see how it works, the actual *mechanics* of it, I can't fix it."

He was holding the phone up so Austin and Ray could see the screen. On it, they could see a black circle with two hands at the half-past four position. The Smokebox Club logo.

"There's an *app?*"

"Of *course* there's an app."

With his forefinger he spun the handles on the logo alternately clockwise and anti-clockwise in a series of precise moves, like the dial of a combination lock. The smokebox door opened, and a list of messages scrolled down.

"Like I said, we're not the Masons, but our loyalties do go deeper than any Official Secrets Act. See, we took a kind of Hippocratic oath, back when we were young. That oath still holds."

"An oath?"

"Well, more of a *song*."

Austin gestured as if to give Roger the permission he knew he didn't require. He was going to sing it anyway.

"Hurrah for the Smokebox Crew!
Book a seat! We'll ride with you.
If you're down, or in distress,
We're the Happiness Express!"

Roger held out his hands, lifting them repeatedly, encouraging the other two to join in. Ray caved first.

"O'er bridge and through the tunnel,
See the smoke shoot from the funnel!
Like the breath of George's dragon,
Roaring on with coach and wagon."

Then Austin, in close harmony.

"The Smokebox Crew are just the ticket
If you're on a sticky wicket.
Pull the whistle, hear it scree-eam!
The Crew and you can let off steam."

The three of them were now singing as loudly as they could, the beat of wheels on track the rhythm section beneath.

"The signal's green, the line is clear
Let me hear the Smokebox Cheer! (Huzzah!)

All aboard! We leave the station,
Friendship is our destination."

The three of them held onto the last note as long as they could. Eventually Austin collapsed into fits of uncontrollable coughing. Ray's voice tailed off like a deflating balloon finally running out of air. Roger held on, his face turning a deep claret, but scant seconds later his voice also hit the buffers. Bent forwards, he held up one hand in surrender, the other supporting himself on his knee.

When they had all regained some composure, Ray looked up at the other two in wonder. "Not bad, for a rank amateur barber's shop trio. And *we remembered all the words!*"

Roger thumped his chest. "*I* had the vinyl 45 that came with the membership pack. The lyrics were printed on the back cover."

"So did *we!*"

Austin pulled out his phone. "*I* need that app."

Roger stood with some effort, prodded his screen a few times. "OK, I've just sent you an invitation. But—" He held up a finger. "We only need the one. Save your batteries. Where we're going, recharging might be difficult."

There was a short silence, punctuated by the *squaw* of a crow caught in the updraught.

"So this, um, this oath — you think it was taken by other people, people in high places who might be in a position to help us out?"

"High places — and low. For our requirements right now, either will do. Every member of the Smokebox Club is honour-bound to help any other in their hour of need. And I think this might just qualify as our hour of need."

Roger was typing something on the screen with his thumbs.

"You asked how we can reset the points between here and London. There are no trains running — well, no *scheduled* trains — because the power, and thus the signals, are out all along the line. This also means that the points can't be switched from any central control room.

"So we need people on the ground, people who can do it *manually*." His fingers paused above the screen for a moment. He looked up, and smiled. "This is where we call in our Smokebox Club sleeper agents."

Information 3: **Platform indicator** CAD 259

Not to scale
Subject to amendment

3
Trains to Londo

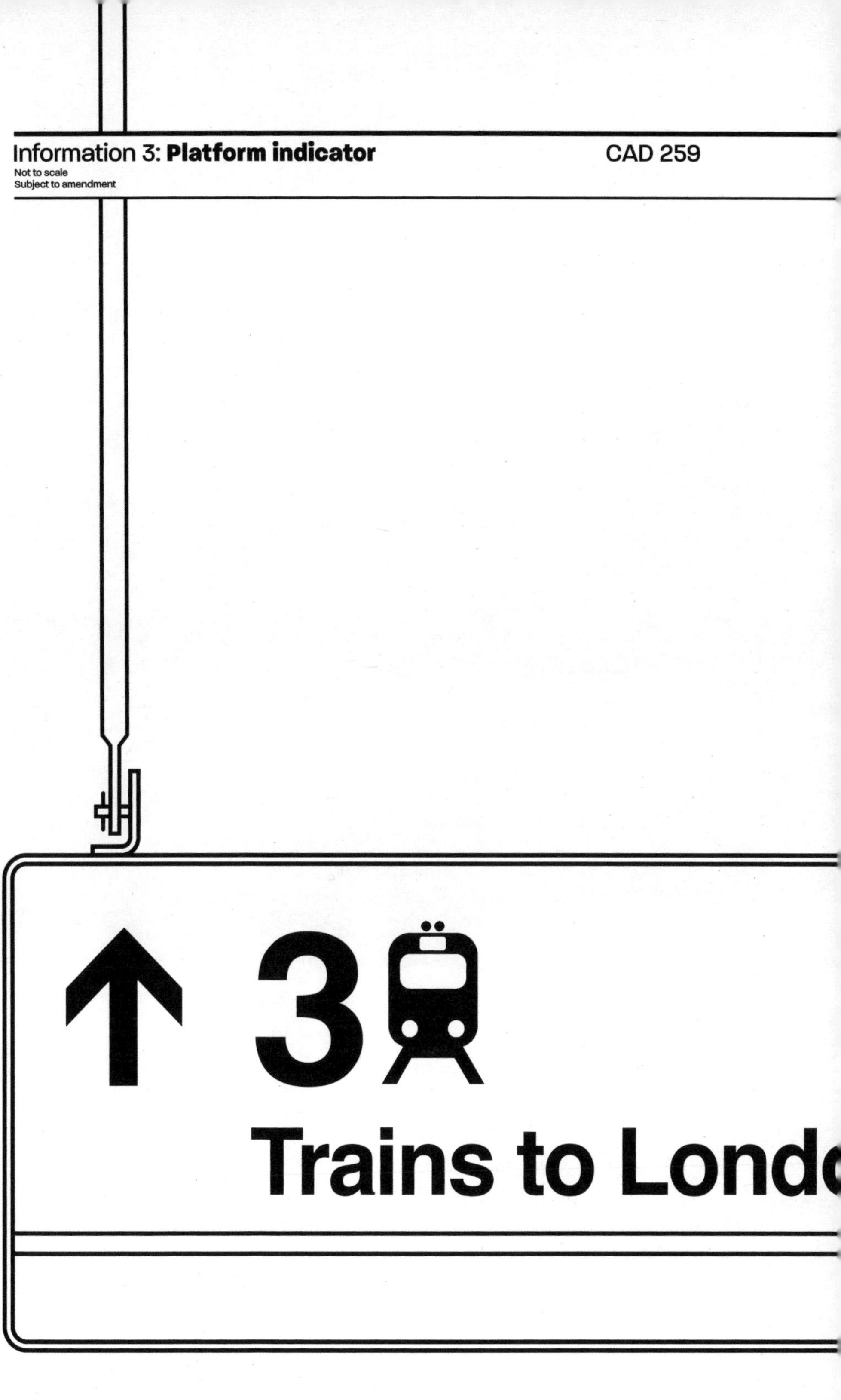

261 **EVALUATION**

Thelma Sharp looked out of the window and across the
car park of the UK Space Agency's offices in Swindon.
Through the trees, she could just see the train station.
It was deserted. Usually at this time in the evening
there'd be a throng of commuters, the impatient honking
of horns, but everything was quiet. She checked the day
on the large office calendar again. It most definitely
was not a Sunday.

The office was running a skeleton staff - the line
from London being suspended, it had fallen to those that
lived locally to come in, though there was precious
little to do today. Everyone in the tech team was
trying to figure out what the problem was with the
electrics in London, and several of her colleagues had
been conscripted into some focus group meeting that was
several levels above her pay grade.

Her phone beeped. The Smokebox logo appeared.

It made her jump, an unexpected intrusion into a day
that already had more than its fair share of unexpected
events.

She scrolled. There was a message. Though it was not
addressed to her in person, she knew immediately that
she was the only person who could answer it.

She swept up her coat and keys and ran down to the
foyer. The entrance looked apologetic, more like a
suburban high school than Cape Canaveral. Instead of
a satellite launch schedule, a pinboard held notices
detailing the crèche opening hours and the next Cards
Against Humanity club meeting.

She ran across the forecourt to the main road, through
the trees and over the footbridge. The platforms below
were wide, almost wide enough to play a game of five-a-
side. There was a temporary barrier, which she vaulted,
and a notice, which she didn't read.

There didn't seem to be anyone about, other than
a lone figure she suspected was a guard at the other
end of the platform, down by the café. The destination
boards were blank. She jumped down onto the rails.

Where?

She jogged up the line, stepping from sleeper to
sleeper, trying to orient herself. The location marker
on the map on her phone moved in the opposite direction.
She spun, ran back the other way. Some yards ahead, a

complex cat's cradle of points criss-crossed the lines. She needed to find three specific sets and ensure they were in the correct position.

She was wondering how she would find the first of the three when the location marker beeped. She looked down. *Aha.* The first set was already in the correct position.

She stepped over to the line running parallel, jogged up to the next junction. This one was in the right position too.

Maybe her luck was in.

She heard a shout behind her. She ignored it.

The third set was a short distance ahead. She could see two branches curving off to her right into sheds and sidings. Behind her, she could hear the crunch of footsteps on ballast.

"Ma'am!"

She checked her phone again. Yes, this was definitely it. And this one was also in the correct position. Three out of three. She dropped to one knee and tapped her screen.

A red-faced man in a Network Rail uniform, panting heavily, came up beside her.

"Ma'am, you are not supposed to be on the railway, even if no trains are running. It may still be dangerous, And, and you're trespassing."

Thelma stooped, pretending to pick something up. She slipped off her wedding ring, then stood, turned to the guard, and held it up triumphantly. She could see him through it, encircled. He was bent over from the exertion, hands on his knees.

"Ma'am—"

"I found it! I thought I'd lost it forever, but *I found it!*"

On Roger's phone screen was a simple diagram, a map of the route from Box Hill to London. On it, a section of line changed from red to green.

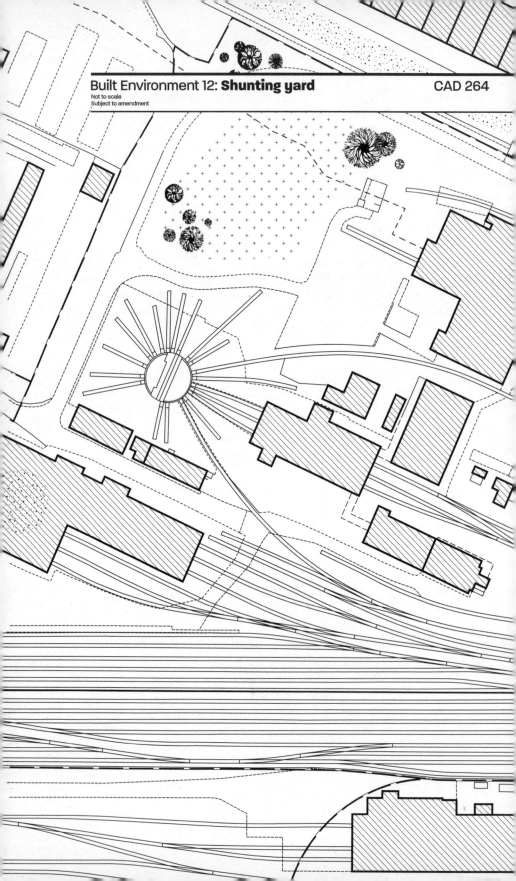

Graham Boyd thought his hearing aid might be on the blink again. "A steam engine? On the Bath to Paddington line?"

George Smith, his fellow Meadowside Care Home inmate and best friend of seventy years, waved for him to keep his voice down. Rashmi, the duty nurse, was over the other side of the sunroom, checking the plastic pill containers. She tapped their lids and wrote something down in her notebook. "Not so loud. You want the whole world to know?"

"I doubt the whole world is within earshot." He looked around at the others seated out on the veranda. John had his head back; his snoring had dislodged his dentures, and his plaid blanket had slipped to the ground. He'd forgotten to wear pants under his dressing gown again. "It's just us, here in God's waiting room."

George dropped his voice to a conspiratorial whisper. "Look, you know Sandy gave me a mobile phone, right? So I can call her?"

Graham tuned up the volume on his hearing aid. "Sure. Though I think she mostly calls you."

"Well, it's one of those fancy ones. Almost like a computer." George pointed to a grid of apps. "That's a calculator. That one is a web browser. You know, Google and all that. That one with the sun and a cloud tells me the weather."

George was confined to a wheelchair. If Graham didn't push him out into the back garden twice a week, he wouldn't know if they were in the midst of an Indian summer or a blizzard.

Graham nodded. "Useful."

"That one is the BBC. Radio. TV, even. I can get TV on this if I want."

"You watch TV on that tiny thing?"

"Well, I would if I could figure out how the app worked. Anyway. See this one here?" George's finger hovered over a circular black icon with a white chevron. It looked like a clock-face, set at the half four position.

Graham pulled an expression of mock astonishment. "A clock? You mean to tell me this modern marvel also tells the *time?*"

George tapped the icon. The Smokebox emblem filled the screen.

He spun the handles and it swung open. A list of messages appeared. Next to each was a green or red light, like a train signal. Some were green, most were red. "I'm part of a club."

Graham, who had known George since the two had been evacuated to the same small village in Kent during the war, knew many things about his old friend – what Kathleen had told him in the treehouse, how his younger brother had lost three of his fingers working in the steelyards – but this was something new. "A club?"

"Yes. For railway enthusiasts, Trains, and all that."

"You didn't tell me."

"Well, it's secret. I'm not supposed to be telling you now."

"What's so secret about a railway club?"

George shrugged. "You know, I don't know." He seemed to be considering something that hadn't occurred to him before. "I never questioned it."

"And they have an app?"

"They do. And a few minutes ago it beeped."

"Beeped?"

"That's the signal."

"The signal? George, just get to the point."

"Sorry. Mind isn't as sharp as it used to be. So, anyway, there was a message. For me." George held up the phone. Graham felt in the top pocket of his dressing gown for his glasses. "Let me see." He scrolled down. "Ah. Mmm-hm. Hmmm." George was watching him intently. He had gone very quiet.

"Did you get to the bit about the steam train? About changing the points?"

Graham looked at him over his glasses. His face was serious, like when he was losing at rummy. "What's the time?"

"It's on the computer."

"What?"

"The phone."

"Ah." Graham pressed the home button and returned to the main screen. "Jeepers. Fifteen minutes."

Graham stood, which took a wee bit longer than it used to, wrapped his gown tight around him and knotted the cord. "Hold on, old chum."

He took the handles of the wheelchair, swung George around and pushed him towards the main doors and the exit beyond. There were several obstacles between them and the outside world, first of which was Rashmi. In the entrance hall was a small hatch that gave onto the nurses' room, from which prescriptions and reprimands were dispensed. Inside, they could now see the back of Rashmi's head. Graham chose a walking stick from the elephant's foot at the bottom of the main stairs and threaded it through her doorhandle.

They were almost at the double doors when she spotted them. She slid the glass on the hatch back. "Graham. George. Where do you think you're going?"

"Well, Rashmi, we thought we'd start with a gin and tonic in the Coach and Horses, then, if the fancy takes us, move on to Peppermint Lace in Maidenhead."

"It's two for one on lapdances," George added, by way of explanation. "Senior's special offer."

She was not smiling. "You two stay right there." She disappeared from the window.

Graham leaned forward, throwing all his eight and a half stone behind the wheelchair. The door to the nurses' quarters rattled.

The stick held.

The front doors were automatic. In a few moments, they were outside in the car park.

Graham looked despairingly up and down the high street. "George, how far is it? Is there a map, or something?"

George was checking his phone. "Over there. That's our Uber. It's like a phone taxi."

A large Mercedes with wheelchair access was parked discreetly over the other side of the road. The pavement sloped down towards the kerb, and Graham was finding it hard to keep up. He was no longer pushing, more hanging on.

As they crossed the road at speed, George stuck his slippered feet out in front for protection, though they would have been next to useless against the minibus that had just rounded the corner then slewed up onto the pavement to avoid them.

The Uber driver had somehow missed this. He had the back door open and the chair hoist down. In a moment they were strapped in and he was back in the driver's seat. He looked at his sat nav. On it, a blue dot marked a spot where the main road ran alongside the railway, just out of town.

He turned to George and Graham, noticing their dressing gowns for the first time. "Is that right? Don't look like there's anything there."

They could hear indistinct shouting behind them.

"A very special train is coming through, in about—" George checked his phone. "Eleven minutes."

"Trust us." Graham gestured at the two of them. "We're train-spotters. Advanced level. Black belt."

The Uber driver shrugged. "Right you are. Please be holding tight!"

He pulled away. In his wing mirror he thought he could see someone in a nurse's outfit run out into the street behind them; but then they turned the corner and she was lost from sight behind St Barnabas' Church Hall.

The Uber driver checked his GPS. "We're here."

They had pulled up on a low verge where a small stone footbridge crossed the railway. Graham and the driver pushed George up to the top. From there, looking east, a single set of points could be seen.

George pointed. "Look, up the line. See that fork?"

The Uber driver disinterestedly followed his finger. "Sure." A pause. "Um, I'm happy to help push you up here, but I—"

"We'll need to get back again afterwards. Just keep the meter running. You have a meter, right?"

The driver looked at these two elderly gents, fired up with the enthusiasm of men half their age. Make that a quarter their age. "You say a train is coming through. There are no trains running, not since that thing in London."

"Then you won't mind running up there and changing those points, will you?"

The driver didn't move. "Look, I can offer you a generous tip."

George fumbled in his pocket. Had he left his wallet back at the home, on his dresser? He tried the other one. He pulled out two vouchers, edged in silver, on which were photographs of pneumatic women beneath an ornate copperplate script.

He waved them triumphantly. "Two-for-one lapdances at Peppermint Lace!"

The driver took them, examined one, the other. George craned his neck from his seated position and pointed. "Though between you and me, Chardonnay doesn't look much like that in real life." He turned the voucher round so he could view it the right way up. "I think she's been retouched. Enhanced. They can do that, these days. Computers."

The driver tucked them into his inside jacket pocket. "The points, you say?"

"Yes. Look." George held up his phone. "Follow the instructions."

The driver squinted, nodded. He swung his feet over the low wall. From here, a set of steps led down to the tracks. He loped up the line to the points. From their vantage, George could see him examining a mechanism attached to the side of the rail.

Graham was looking the other way. A regular puff of white smoke was visible above the treeline, closing in on their position. "I can see it! A *real*, *actual* steam train! Not seen one of those since sixty-nine! And it's getting blinkin' close!"

George saw the Uber driver stand, give a thumbs up. "He's done it!" He tapped the screen, and the icon turned green. Then, as loud as he could manage: "Get back up here! Quick!"

The driver ran towards them, then scrambled up the bank, arms waving for balance.

Moments later the Black Locomotive was upon them.

A fury of smoke and steam, a black bullet fired from a distant gun, it seemed to be the very embodiment of urgent determination. They felt a powerful upthrust of displaced air, and in an instant were engulfed in its sulphurous white breath.

The old stone bridge shook. Visibility dropped to zero, but they could still sense the sheer weight and presence of this magnificent piece of engineering as it thundered through at speed below them.

As it passed the points, it released a high, sharp, hearing aid wrecking whistle.

Graham's eyes were smarting from the smoke. That must be why he was tearing up.

Bouncing up and down in his wheelchair, between deep hacking coughs, George was punching the air and whooping like a ten-year-old at a cup final.

273 **PERFORMANCE**

Fatouma Kaba and Charlotte Potterton were supposed to be in Mr. Hall's social studies class, but you weren't allowed phones in Mr Hall's class, and they were waiting for an important message. If he caught them again, they'd be put in isolation for sure, no joke. They weren't supposed to be in the gym either, but here they could at least hide behind the benches.

Charlotte cupped her hand over her screen, pointing. "See, the others have a green dot next to them. That means they've done their bit, right? Look, there, that's us. We're next on the list."

Fatouma held her hands out, imploring. *"Buuuut..."*

Charlotte put her phone back in her blazer pocket. "Look, we're probably in trouble already. Let's just do this, and we can face the consequences later."

They ran through the changing rooms, out of the side door, across the netball court and ducked under the fence that ran along the railway.

Fatouma looked back, across the expanse of grass to the main block. Charlotte pulled on her skirt.

"Get down, they'll see you."

They shuffled down the embankment on their backsides, then turned left and ran alongside the rails. The loose gravel gave under their feet, and they waved their arms for balance. "No trains. That's why half the teachers aren't in today, see."

"Mr. Hall is!"

"Stop wailing. Look, no trains means we're safe. But, you know, just in case, don't touch any rail." Charlotte stepped over by way of demonstration. To their right, up the line, the platforms of Didcot Parkway station rose either side of the tracks. She hoped they were too far away to be seen. Bottle-green awnings reached over the platforms, and two whitewashed clapboard towers rose beyond. In the far distance, a regiment of electricity pylons were silhouetted against the sky.

She held up her phone. "See, on the map, it says we have to move this thing across – see, like that – so the train will go to London."

"One day, I want to go to London."

Charlotte glanced up at Fatouma. She looked like she wanted to cry. Her blazer, several sizes too big, hung off her thin frame; it'd be a year or so before she grew into it. Her hair was a riot of tight wiry plaits, each ending in a tiny red bow. "Look. Help me with this, then we'll go back to Mr. Hall's social studies class, sit up front, yeah, pay attention, ace our exams, be, like, top of the class, best evah, move to London and be, like, well famous superstars. Kaba-P. You and me. We'll *rock.*"

Fatouma managed a weak smile. Charlotte pressed her advantage. "See this lever, right, it attaches to the points here, and I just need to pull it – like this."

She pulled. It didn't move.

Fatouma looked at her, looked up and down the empty railway, back at the lever.

"*Fatooooo!* We'll be here, like, *forevah* if you don't help me now, fam!"

Fatouma held up her hands in acquiescence, then walked around, grasped the lever, and braced her sensible school shoes against a sleeper. Together they both pulled as hard as they could.

The lever began to move.

Two minutes later, Roger's phone vibrated. He pulled it from his back pocket and glanced at the Smokebox app.

Another two sections of the line ahead had just turned green.

He had no way of knowing who was behind each pseudonym, but without any central organisation, without any further instructions from him, complete strangers connected only by their membership in an obscure club were now working to together to prepare their route.

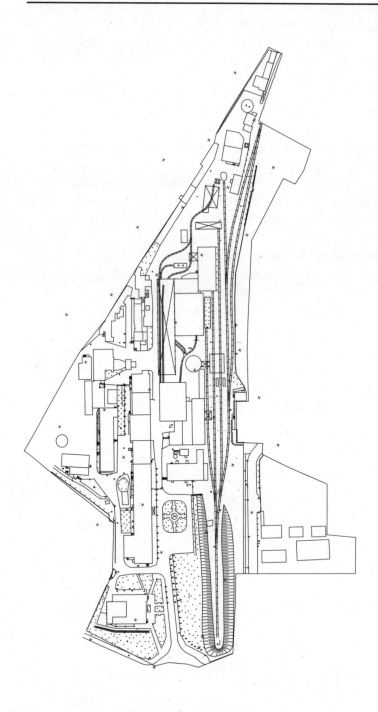

> Without any detectable temporal foreshadowing, the angular black shape of a Ra barque had appeared beside them, its surface glistening with deep-space frozen water. It had probably ported directly from the depths of some ocean, who knows how far distant; or maybe it had been here all along, just a year ago or the day after tomorrow, when a planet might have occupied their current location.
> Wherever it had come from, now it was here, a clear and present danger. It was far from home, but so were they.
> If the Ra were way out here, something of interest must lie nearby. Ki doubted that xe would generate much interest, in xirself: xe had been dark for days, wrapped in a meditative fugue.
> Or could it be that only raw recruits like xir were now left abroad?
> As soon as xe saw it, the barque made its purpose clear.

Rutherford, now intimately connected to the ship, found what now ensued hard to follow. It was unlike any battle he had heard described before. Not a single shot was fired; instead, It was run as a series of possible temporal trajectories, branching futures with different outcomes, each weighted with a set of emotive values. A game of chess where each move is calculated from some starting position, each possible countermove juxtaposed in a pre-emptive sum of gains and losses.

He could see these laid out before him, like a thousand hands of poker played from the same shuffled deck. An algorithm searched for novelty, for a tightrope walk between capability and happenstance, and came up empty.

For Ki, there was no winning hand.

> For a few milliseconds, nothing happened.
>Then the planet appeared, huge and unavoidable, a vertigo-inducing bulk rushing up to meet xir. The momenta dampers went into immediate overload.
> Ki guessed the planet's orbit had intersected their position, and they'd been temporally shunted forward or back several weeks – no doubt the barque had attempted to place them inside the planet itself.
> But it had miscalculated. Maybe its orbit had been perturbed. Maybe their faith wasn't as infallible as the Ra liked to believe. Xe'd never know

for sure, but they now had a slim chance of survival.

> Suddenly there were more of them. They all pointed in xir direction, spinning along their long axes like triangular obsidian arrowheads. They had no windows, no visible means of propulsion; they were just faceted slices of sharp geometry, like shards knapped from a black asteroid.

> Outside a faint emission in the infrared, they were radio-dark. But they could still be seen, as shifting reflected slices of starfield against the stationary background.

> How many were there? One could become several, looped back in time upon itself. X e   p u l l e d   o n e   s e c o n d   i n t o   t e n   i n   o r d e r   t o   p r o c e s s   t h e i r   t r a j e c t o r i e s .

> Three. There were three.

> Ki's vessel bucked. Post-traumatic stress, xe concluded. What had actually happened to its original pilot, in the early waves of the conflict when there was still hope and optimism, xe had never fully unravelled; it was a personal pain, and one xir ship bore with a fortitude xe had never wished to intrude on.

> If this was xer time, xe was going too make sure xe sent as many Ra to their putative afterlife as xe could. A confluence of lines coalesced in xir mind, an optimal solution that would allow xer to intersect without too much compressive torque.

> Xe passed through the first barque at 0.3 light speed, entirely vaporising its forward section. Its rear curved up majestically as the violent depressurisation propelled it away, venting debris. A dozen small forms spun in its wake: flash-frozen Ra bodies.

> The second xe hit front on, leaving nothing but a plasma of free electrons and stripped nuclei. Even from Ki's temporally decelerated viewpoint, xe could sense the enormous energy release buffeting the drone net.

> There was no return fire. The Ra's weapons were not physical.

> Behind, a scatter of high-energy gamma rays sparkled off the debris.

> The remaining barque curved away on a tight arc, clipping the edge of xir extended being. A sense of dissolution shot back into xir nexus, a sub-zero chill of black non-existence. Xir vessel shuddered uncontrollably. Somewhere on that barque the Ra were working their perverse magic.

> Somewhere on that barque the Ra were rewriting the laws of time and

space.

> Ki tried not to picture them, singing their unsettling hymn, holding high the split sun, the symbol of their deadly faith.

> The kinetic absorption buffers began to complain. The green and blue planet was still coming up at speed below. Ki focused again on the telemetry. This did not make sense.

> How had it come so close, so fast?

> The Ra. They had again twisted time. Or space. Or both, it no longer mattered.

> The shielding was a compaction of space-time that choked causative shear. Thrown forward along the direction of travel, it was intended to protect the delicate higher functions of xir being from interstellar particulates which, though tiny, at near-light speed possessed formidable kinetic energy.

> But the buffer was not designed for atmospheric entry, especially at this velocity.

> The ship imposed a grief shunt, rearticulating its point of consciousness away from the impact damage to the dissipating cloud of neutrinos trailing behind in its wake which it could still organise into a elementary synaptic web.

> The last barque was still there, close. It cleaved through the tattered streamers of xir extended being. Ki sensed its resolve.

> It wanted to bend them to be better, perfect them against their will. It was rummaging in the looser extremities of xir thoughts, collating, rewriting. Xe had probably lost a million memories already, but couldn't recall which.

> In quick succession xe brought down into physicality concept after concept from the platonic world of form. Each had a symbolic shape designed to harm not the physical structure of the barque but its purpose: a weaponised morality xe hoped xe could turn against it.

> Each form articulated one of the Consilience's foundational ideals, purged of ornamentals and counterfactuals, sleek, clean, pure.

> Inarguable.

> None had any effect. It was as if xe spoke an entirely different language, one in which even these elementary precepts were unacceptable because they didn't align with the Ra's singular vision. Each conceptual intervention was dismissed without further examination.

There was no way In.

> Xe could sense the juddering of xir vessel's temporal drivers through the semiotic understructure, painstakingly rebuilt only recently. Xe had been this close to a Ra barque only once before. It had not gone well.

> An array of lights winked in xir undervision. There was no possible refolding of the timeline that suggested an escape. Impact was inevitable. Xir vessel began to shake violently.

> Though still too tenuous to vaporise the craft, the atmospheric friction raised the surface temperature to the boiling point of iron. The flight control surfaces along the port side buckled and fell away. Xe was going down.

> Beneath the surface of the planet Ki sensed a churning play of forces – a hot core, a convective mantle pressed inward due to gravity and outward due to radiative heat. A thin crust encased this molten ball, structurally weak but supported on the shifting subsurface flow. Heavier metals had fallen to the centre, the lighter elements sorting themselves into layered strata above. The planet was tectonically active; the crust had folded, faulted, rucked up into mountain ranges that almost pierced the atmosphere. This was a mix of lighter elements: oxygen, nitrogen, other trace elements xe could taste in the back of xir throat. Above, an attenuated mist of ozone suffused into translunar space.

> The clouds parted momentarily to reveal a pre-industrial landscape of vegetation-infested lowlands bordering a grey sea, its surface ridged with the white peaks of waves.

> It was just like so many other planets xe had seen, so many remote and unremarkable agglomerations of silicates and metals on whose surface a green photosynthetic mould had grown.

> Ki instinctively pulled xirself tighter, letting the more ephemeral parts of xir being fall away. Xe was now subject to the brute laws of motion, a blunt instrument on a ballistic atmospheric re-entry, xir trajectory a simple matter of mass and velocity.

> The surface of the planet, a brilliant green canopy of chlorophyll and carbon under which xe could distantly sense the scampering of the simplest of minds, was coming up to meet them.

> Xe drew down a healing field, though there were few hurtmongers who could absorb the trauma xe knew was coming. The hull became a bright display of interlaced linear designs: incantations, sigils of protection.

> They had stolen a few of the Ra's best tricks. In a situation like this, xe wasn't going to let any misplaced ideals of conceptual purity circumvent xir chances of survival.

> There was the acrid smell of combusting oxygen and a supersonic boom. Xe rearranged the remaining forward surfaces to minimise atmospheric friction and thickened and hardened the hull.

> Xe thought of xir broodparents, their bodies forever out of reach on the remains of their poisoned homeworld. They would have no customary interment. For them, the lamentations of nonbeing would never be articulated.

> Atmospheric density increased logarithmically. The adaptive camouflage, even when working, was useless this close to a planetary body, and pulling a subspace fold around

them would distort the local gravity lattice in ways the Ra would easily detect.
> Xe could not hide.
> Proximity alarms began to shriek. The hull was now an incandescent white.
> Xe recited the

seventeen surviving stanzas of the song

of

sile

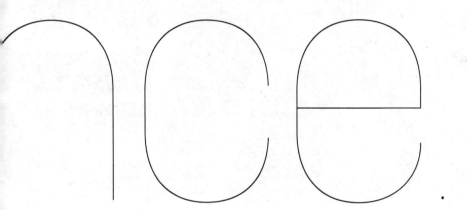

> The force of impact shot back along xir being. Entire sections of xir synaptic web went dark. Consciousness of any kind, machine or biological, was interrupted.

> A plume of dark material, soil and clay and pulped vegetation, shot skyward, held for a second, then fell back to earth, tumbling over itself and spreading out in a roiling cloud.

> A bright electrical discharge, a bolt of lightning caused by ionised gas in the upper atmosphere, followed xir down. A crack of thunder and a wave of concussion pushed out across the landscape from the point of impact, flattening trees for a kilometre around the epicentre.

> Ki's vessel was more than a vehicle; it had become xir own extended body. The ship and the pilot were no longer distinct entities. Both were now in a near-ruined state.

> Autonomous regeneration routines began pulling them together, back towards their original form, by necessity simplifying an essential subsystem here, redesigning a biological articulation there.

> They would do their best.

> They were buried deep in the dirt. The ship's wombbinder had, without Ki's suggestion, pulled xir being into the central core where trauma was less likely. It was instinctual, the least it could do.

> The machine dampened xir life signs. Buried under the earth, shielded by the low-level biosignatures of the indigenous lifeforms, they could hide.

> The barque pirouetted in low orbit, a black javelin pointing down at the surface. It seemed to weigh up the situation; then it vanished, as if it had never been.

The vessel seemed to nuzzle Rutherford's cheek, like a horse trying to get the attention of a thrown rider.

It was concerned, in its own peculiar way.

It wanted him to find out what had happened to Ki.

It wanted its missing owner to come home, and make everything right once again.

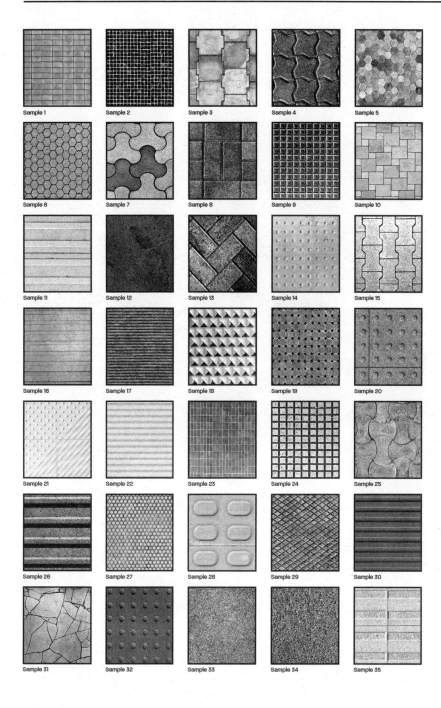

Sample 1

Sample 2

Sample 3

Sample 4

Sample 5

Sample 6

Sample 7

Sample 8

Sample 9

Sample 10

Sample 11

Sample 12

Sample 13

Sample 14

Sample 15

Sample 16

Sample 17

Sample 18

Sample 19

Sample 20

Sample 21

Sample 22

Sample 23

Sample 24

Sample 25

Sample 26

Sample 27

Sample 28

Sample 29

Sample 30

Sample 31

Sample 32

Sample 33

Sample 34

Sample 35

21

291 LEGEND

Ice Prophet, real name Yousef Evans, stood over the shopkeeper, lifting his head from the floor by his necktie. "The cash, and the Hennessy!"

The shopkeeper pointed. His right eye was purpling, he was missing two front teeth, and had positioned his other hand over his groin for protection. He looked up at his assailant in a heightened state of adrenaline-soaked fear.

Ice's roadmen were loading Pringles and Häagen Dazs into a holdall. Ice waved his free hand at them. "Leave that crap. Open the till. Grab the expensive stuff."

"But snacks, Ice!"

"But shit. You can buy all the snacks you want later. We get, we leave. In and out."

He felt a vibration through his puffer jacket. He froze.

No. Not now.

It vibrated a second time.

I've not felt that particular ringtone in years. Not since well before Dad left...

Ice dropped the shopkeeper and drew himself up to his full five feet four inches. His victim fell back, audibly cracking his head on the floor, then rolled into a foetal position to present as small a target as possible.

Ice's attention, however, was now on his phone. Its diamanté cover, which he couldn't decide looked well bling or just gay, sparkled like high-grade crystal under the fluorescent lights.

There was a circular logo on the screen, black and white.

He'd forgotten that app was even installed. He thought of his childhood train set, in a cardboard box on top of a wardrobe at Mum's place in Croydon.

A siren could be heard. The police had been preoccupied with that weird incident in London, and he and his associates had taken the opportunity for a bit of extra-curricular activity.

"Ice, the feds!"

"Bag up, and run. We'll meet later. I got business to attend to." He stepped through the broken door into Acton High Street. Glass crunched under his vintage Nike Air Prestos.

On his screen he could see a red location marker on a map. How close was that? He rotated his phone, tried to get his bearings. Shit. How does this thing even work?

He ran west, towards Ealing Common, then right up Twyford Avenue, his crowbar bouncing in its thong against his leg. A low wall either side of the road told him this was where the railway line passed underneath.

He reached up, caught the top of the wall, looked over. He could see the District and Central lines peel away to the north and south, identifiable by their electrified extra rails. Cables hung from gantries over the mainline tracks, and alongside them he could see a newer line set on a base of fresh concrete. A tangle of points linked them all.

Ah.

How was he going to get down there? His elbows gave out, and he dropped back to the pavement. He took a deep lungful of evening air with an aftertaste of chips in vinegar and jumped up again.

There. He could see a gate just up ahead, at the top of the embankment. He walked over.

It was padlocked. He climbed an electrical box, vaulted the spiked fence and ran down towards the tracks.

In the distance he could see a plume of smoke. The Black Locomotive, or had someone set fire to Ealing Town Hall? It seemed to move closer, though it was hard to tell. He hefted the crowbar, stepped across the ballast and between the rails, then ran up the line.

There were several sets of points, and he was unsure which line the locomotive was actually running on. He looked again at the map on his phone, and tried to correlate it with what he saw in front of him, on the ground.

He used to know this railway shit.
He used to be a Smokeboxer.
He even knew the song. <u>How did it go again?</u>

"Hurrah for the Smokebox Crew!
Book a seat! We'll ride with you.
If you're down, or in distress,
We're the Happiness Express!"

He sang quietly into the faux-fur collar of his hoodie, accompanied by an imagined grime backbeat. There were several other verses, but he couldn't recall the words. Something about a dragon.

"The Smokebox Crew are just the ticket
If you're on a sticky wicket.
Pull the whistle, hear it scree-eam!
The Crew and you can let off steam."

He was letting off steam with his crew when this message came through. Where was the club last year, when the bailiffs came for his Lexus, or the year before, when Mum's new boyfriend had put her in hospital?

> "The signal's green, the line is clear
> Let me hear the Smokebox Cheer! (Huzzah!)
> All aboard! We leave the station,
> Friendship is our destination."

Like fuck.

He found the correct set of points and positioned the crowbar, braced himself and pulled hard. There was a complaining squeal of metal against metal and it began to give.

Why was he out here, switching tracks to help some wasteman he'd never met? What was in it for him?

The points rammed home.

He tossed the crowbar into the bushes and looked up the line. What was the point of this diversion? Wasn't robbery with violence what the real Ice was all about these days?

Life weren't nothing but status, survival and reproduction. One led to the other. Even though he knew this to be true, that everything in his experience told him it was true, he couldn't shake the idea that they were also the primal urges of some base animal.

The column of smoke, like a biblical portent, drew closer. He retreated to the safety of the bank and sat down. On his phone screen he could see a length of railway line, ~~long~~ long uninterrupted sections of which were green, a few red.

Did he want to be respected, or feared?

Both earned you status, of sorts, but he'd recently discovered that one was way easier to achieve than

the other. The second was a shortcut. The first
might require some actual work.

He tapped the section that had been tagged with
his old Smokebox Club username, and it too turned
green.

A message immediately popped up from another
anonymous Club account.

Good work, Snowman!

Another.

Good to know you're still in the Club, sir!

More words of congratulation multiplied down
the screen

Yusuf smiled a wry smile, shook his head.
Fuck this shit.

For the first time in a long time, he felt good.

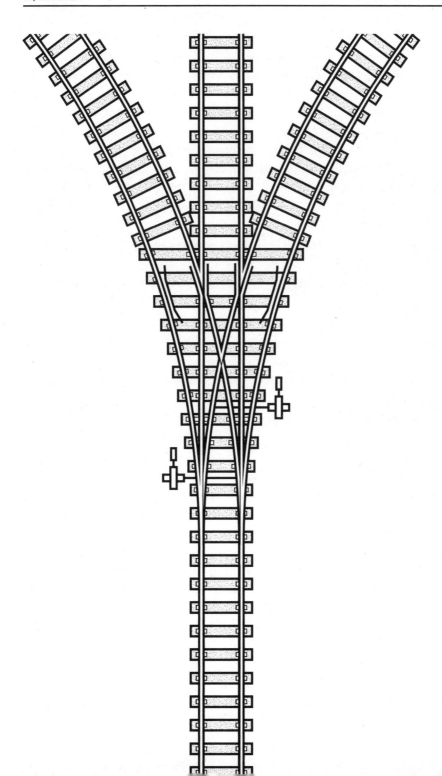

After what seemed like a long journey through open fields punctuated by the occasional built-up area, the landscape was changing. In a matter of minutes they had travelled through the outlying suburbs and were now entering the denser urban sprawl of London itself.

They were fast approaching White City, and the outer edge of the electrical dampening field. The locomotive was attracting some attention – as they passed under footbridges and flyovers, Austin could see larger and larger crowds, waving, taking pictures, pointing. Word must have got around. Maybe they were cheering, too; some had looks of ecstatic joy on their faces, punching the air as they shot by, but if they were he couldn't hear them over the rhythmic *diddi diddi diddi* of six-foot wheels on polished rails.

Roger glanced at his phone. There were sections of the track ahead that were still red.

"It's coming up fast. This is the periphery. We're about to cross the threshold."

The Smokebox Club logo faded. The screen went dark. A second later, the casing began to heat up.

Roger dropped the phone. It hit the steel plating of the floor, where it glowed like a piece of coal that had tumbled from the firebox.

"We've moving at some speed through the EM field." Ray stepped back. "Looks like the current that sets up in its circuits is more than enough to fry it."

Austin kicked it out of the cab.

"We should watch our speed. These urban stretches of rail aren't built for it."

Roger didn't seem to be perturbed. "We're not hauling any rolling stock. We're running light and lean. It's hard not to let her off the leash."

The burning Westfield Centre, then a clutch of brutalist sixties high-rises passed by to the south like a concrete Stonehenge. A looping elevated section of the Westway whipped over their heads then ran alongside them to the north. On it they could see stalled cars with cyclists weaving between them. A bonfire had been lit on the central reservation, around which figures danced, and just beyond that, an upturned coach blocked the road; a Meanwhile Gardens street gang, armed with kitchen knives, was charging a fee for safe passage onwards.

They passed under the Ladbroke Grove road bridge, and Roger pulled the whistle: a long, loud celebratory shout of pure joy.

The navy and red roundels of Westbourne Park underground station flashed by to their right. The tracks multiplied; here there were ten, a dozen running in parallel.

Up ahead, on their line, Austin suddenly saw a stalled Intercity Express. It must have just left Paddington when the power was cut.

"Roger! *Look out!*"

There was nothing they could do. They were moving too fast to stop in time.

Austin braced himself for the inevitable collision.

There was a squeal of wheels against buckling track, and they were brutally thrown to the side as the engine lurched to the left. For several long seconds, Austin judged they must be been riding on only one rail; the cab, the whole engine, was canted to the side.

The wheels along the left flank, finding themselves in mid-air, spun freely, the pistons pumping at twice their design specification. The firebox door swung open, and hot embers rolled across the plate.

Ray stepped to the side to brace himself and accidentally stood on one. His boot shot out from under him. Before Austin could reach out, he'd been thrown clean out of the cab, hands grasping at empty air.

Just as he thought the engine would turn over, it righted itself. Steel connected with steel, and the impact shot up his spine. The engine now lurched drunkenly to the right. Austin had a brief glimpse of a gloved hand holding a handrail, then Ray was back, sliding across the floor of the cab on his back.

The firebox door slammed shut, and he came to rest against it.

The three of them looked at each other, but the expected collision did not come.

The points had been switched.

They had no way of knowing who had done it, or if the points had been set in their favour already. They just knew they were still on the right track.

To their left, large earth-moving equipment and wagons heaped with rubble flashed by.

Abruptly the track began to slope downwards. Concrete walls rose either side. Ahead was a vertical wall in which there were two circular apertures.

Austin had made a calculation. The tunnels were large: six metres in diameter, compared to just under four metres for the deep-level Victoria line. The engines in the Strategic Steam Reserve were all around four metres high at the funnel; even after the rails had been laid, there should still be room to spare.

If his calculations were correct.

They were now on the final approach to Royal Oak portal, and the entrance to the Crossrail tunnel itself.

Sample 1

Sample 2

Sample 3

Sample 4

Sample 5

Sample 6

Sample 7

Sample 8

Sample 9

Sample 10

Sample 11

Sample 12

Sample 13

Sample 14

Sample 15

Sample 16

Sample 17

Sample 18

Sample 19

Sample 20

Sample 21

Sample 22

Sample 23

Sample 24

Sample 25

Sample 26

Sample 27

Sample 28

Sample 29

Sample 30

Sample 31

Sample 32

Sample 33

Sample 34

Sample 35

303 **RECONSTRUCTION**

At the bottom of the ramp Austin could see the two tunnels coming up fast, like the barrels of a giant shotgun. The rails they were riding headed into the right-hand bore. He had just enough time to reassure himself that there really was enough clearance, that the funnel would not collide with the roof, and they were in.

Above, a knot of teenagers in balaclavas paused in their demolishing of an overturned Audi. Leaning over the crash barrier, looking down from the elevated section of the Westway, they saw a sheath of smoke shoot back and out around the engine as it vanished like a loose cork being driven into an oversized bottle. Elegant curlicues formed in the sudden vacuum left behind the tender.

For Ray, Austin and Roger, the evening light was immediately extinguished. The ear-pummelling beat of the engine viciously increased in volume. The sudden enclosure forced air back down the funnel and the firebox door again flew open, scattering more hot coals on the floor.

Ray kicked it shut.

Smoke billowed around the funnel like a low thundercloud; trapped under the curved roof, it had nowhere to go but down and around, enveloping the cab. Sulphurous ash seasoned with sooty smuts buffeted their faces and teared up their eyes. Through gaps in the pall Austin caught flashes of fire leaping from the funnel, flickering strobes of orange lighting the walls like the very fires of hell.

An acrid taste filled their mouths, and the carbon dioxide made their lungs work. Ray pulled his handkerchief from his pocket and tied it around his lower face, bandit style, to provide a mask. Roger was coughing and spluttering like a fourteen-year-old taking his first drag on a cigarette behind the Scout hut. Saturated Stygian steam slicked his hair to his already sweaty scalp.

The stinging heat forced Austin to close his eyes. When he dared open them again the visibility was only around a metre or so. There was a sudden through-draught, a natural recalibration of fresh air pulled down, he presumed, through some ventilation shaft, and the smoke around the roof of the cab whipped back. For a moment, clarity was restored.

The tunnel was usually lit by striplights positioned at intervals along the wall. These, of course, were now non-functional. There was just the sullen glow of the firebox and embers dancing like fireflies in the smoke.

Ray was the first to speak. His voice was hoarse above the din. "The *points?* Were they green all the way? Did you *see?*"

Rodger said nothing.

Austin laid a hand on his old friend's shoulder. "The locomotive knows where to go. The rails will see to that." He sounded more convinced than he felt.

The tunnel was not uniform. To the left and right they could see the occasional dark recess, or open spaces that could be platforms or storage sidings. Some had glass barriers still partially covered in protective sheeting, behind which could be seen stacks of steel beams or pallets of floor tiles.

In the larger spaces were mini-villages: temporary storage huts, prefabricated offices, fences hung with health and safety signs. There was the detritus of work in progress everywhere: stepladders, striped plastic barriers, loops of cable attached to the ceiling, perforated steel sheets, bags of ballast, vacant mountings set into the walls.

All these passed by at speed.

Every major civil engineering project that creates new spaces beneath the capital has to have, at its core, a black budget. There are always unforeseen complications: unexpected archaeological finds, unmapped water mains, plague pits, Roman villas, burial grounds or Victorian sewers – the ground beneath Londoners' feet had been dug and redug so many times surveyors aren't entirely sure where the original ground level might lie.

The stretch of the tunnel that currently terminated at Anomaly 36 branched south from the main Crossrail line between Paddington and Bond Street. This was projected to continue beneath Buckingham Palace and on to Westminster, following the path of the small-bore tunnel that already connected them; thence it would continue on under the Thames, parallel to Westminster Bridge, to terminate at the deep-level section of the old Eurostar terminal beneath Waterloo.

Austin knew the completed portion of the tunnel was empty; after contact with the Anomaly, the tunnelling machine had been pulled back to the last intersection, somewhere beneath Hyde Park, and stowed in the westbound tunnel to allow the archaeologists and their equipment access.

The walls had already been lined by the TBM as part of the tunnelling process, and the floor filled to provide a level surface upon which the sleepers were laid. The completed track reached almost to the Anomaly. Almost – the last hundred metres or so were a temporary fix, laid down to enable the heavy dig equipment to be taken directly to the entrance.

Once they entered the tunnel at Royal Oak Portal, the track would guide them to their final destination – if, and only if, the points that switched from the main east–west line onto the classified southern branch were in the correct position.

They were not on the final straight just yet.

The last time steam trains ran under London, Mark Twain had recorded the experience in unflattering prose. Austin doubted that, after today, it would ever happen again. This was going to be a one-off.

He reached out, held on to the warm brass of a wheel valve. In the stuttering light, the glass faces of the gauges flashed back at him like half-silvered mirrors. He could feel the regular rhythm of wheels on track though his fingers, through his feet, in his ears. Every pulse of his being was one with this magnificent locomotive and its headlong flight through the arteries of London to its very centre, to its heart.

Roger's phone had been melted by the EM field. Ray's and Austin's, if they had survived, would be no use either: electronics did not function within its radius, and even if they did, they were deep underground. They had no way of checking the status of the points, no way to ensure their path was clear.

The signal's green, the line is clear
Let me hear the Smokebox Cheer! (Huzzah!)

Austin felt he should dispense a bit of Smokebox Cheer.

Though the layout of the tunnels was familiar to him, this was all new to Ray and Roger. He thought about the non-disclosure agreements he had signed, the Official Secrets Act, the statutory employment penalties for disclosing this kind of information.

But members of the Smokebox Club were used to keeping secrets.

If those in positions of power didn't value what the Smokebox Club valued, well, it was simply no contest. He knew where his loyalties lay.

They all knew where their loyalties lay.

"It'll be coming up soon. One more junction. One more set of points.

There's a fork south, before we reach Bond Street, that leads to the Buckingham Palace and Westminster branch. Then we're on the home run." He paused. Not that they'd see the points in time if they were set incorrectly. Beautiful machine that it was, they had no way of steering it.

Ray was immune to Austin's forced optimism. He sounded even more insistent. "Roger, did you see? *Was the line green?*"

In the seconds before they had entered the exclusion zone, Roger had managed to take one last glance at the Smokebox app, one last appraisal of the situation ahead.

"The line was green. Green almost all the way."

"*Almost?*"

Roger paused. "Green, but for this last set of points."

That didn't necessarily imply disaster. Many of them had been switched at the last moment. A few had even been in the correct position already.

Would that be the case here?

Had the Smokebox member assigned those last vital set of points, whoever they were, done their job? Not for the first time, Austin wondered who might have access to these tunnels, who else amongst those in the crews he'd dealt with might be a member.

If they had already been here, inside the exclusion zone, chances were they would not have received the message anyway.

But if they had been outside, if they had been somewhere in Greater London, they might just have had time.

If, if, if . . .

The app was secure. All messages were encrypted. That in itself meant that whoever now ran the club was not a novice when it came to secrecy. Were they someone high up in the security service itself?

They all knew these speculations were now immaterial. Green or red, they could not stop the Black Locomotive if they tried.

The note of the engine suddenly dropped a fraction. They had entered a larger section, a junction. Above them the roof shot up several metres, and the smoke lifted.

It had one entrance and two exits.

Austin could just see the fork dead ahead. Events seemed to telescope, a handful of seconds stretch to a minute, more. He could see a signal, but it was dark. There was no way to tell, if it had been lit, what it would have indicated.

Standing below this with their hands on a lever was a figure. On the ground beside them was a kerosene lamp.

A woman. In a suit.

The lever moved a fraction. Whoever they were, they were putting their full weight behind it.

Then it suddenly gave, and swung over completely.

Ray, Roger and Arnold braced themselves. The Lord Hawke lurched to the side as the rails guided them over, towards the right-hand tunnel.

Towards the southern branch, and Anomaly 36.

In the split-second it took to pass the figure, a spark struck from wheel against track lit the tunnel like a photoflash. Austin caught a glimpse of a mane of white hair, seemingly frozen in a majestic halo as the updraught of their passing blew it back from a familiar face.

Georgia Ash.

As if in slow motion her lapel lifted, and underneath the Smokebox Club pin glinted brightly like a miniature sun.

Then they had passed, the tunnel enclosing them tightly once again, and she was lost to darkness.

Austin looked back over the tender. The oasis of pale light thrown by the kerosene lamp was growing smaller behind them, but he could still see her, a silhouette standing astride the track, her hand held down by her side, two fingers out and pointing down in an inverted V.

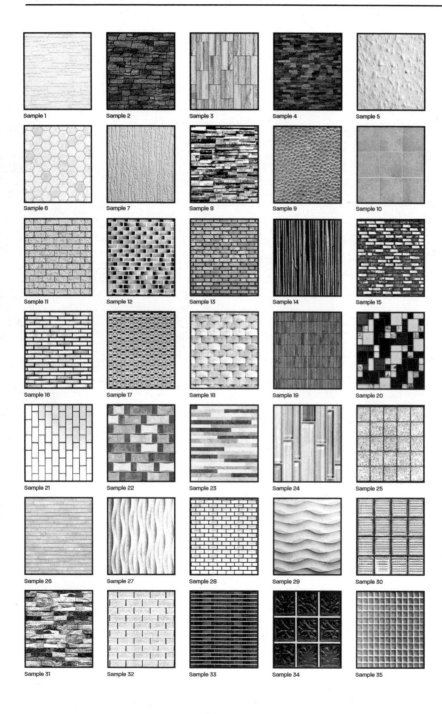

Sample 1 Sample 2 Sample 3 Sample 4 Sample 5

Sample 6 Sample 7 Sample 8 Sample 9 Sample 10

Sample 11 Sample 12 Sample 13 Sample 14 Sample 15

Sample 16 Sample 17 Sample 18 Sample 19 Sample 20

Sample 21 Sample 22 Sample 23 Sample 24 Sample 25

Sample 26 Sample 27 Sample 28 Sample 29 Sample 30

Sample 31 Sample 32 Sample 33 Sample 34 Sample 35

Supplemental 2: **Anomaly 36 (Provisional reconstruction)** CAD 310
Not to scale
Subject to amendment

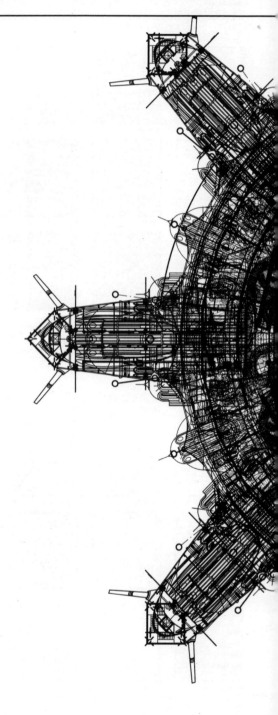

> Ki's ship was lame. Xe needed to find help.

> Xe didn't know how long it might survive without xir, how long xe might be gone, so took a master key. The ship would remember xir, xe was sure, but if xe returned and, for whatever reason, could not enter, this would act as a guarantee. Xe did not want to dwell on what those reasons might be.

> Xe let xirself seep into the ship's systems. The damage was extensive, so xir first act was to mitigate the neuropathic sensitivity in the compromised lower levels.

> Sleep, my friend. If I can't heal you, I can take away your pain.

> Xe stood in the pressure chamber just inside the hatch. Beyond, through the bulkhead, lay this primitive backwater planet with no name, just a number. Xe didn't hold out much hope that help could be found out there; in the moments before impact, xe had only sensed unitary, unevolved minds.

> But xe had to do something. Xir ship was deteriorating, and xe didn't have the resources to keep it alive; if it died, there would be no way off this planet. Xe would be marooned here, forever.

> Though the hull was blackened, it was still reading the exterior atmospheric pressure and composition. Xe adjusted her lung capacity and respiratory function. The terrain xe had glimpsed during the descent had looked primitive — dense vegetation, open moorland, the loop of a river. Through the floor, xe could feel the distant seismic rumble of a volcanic eruption.

> Xir current form — a bipedal gait with articulated arms, a design common on many worlds — would suffice. The gravity was not extreme. Xe became squatter, xir limbs thicker, xir bone density increased. Xe would be able to support her weight easily.

> Xe framed a concept, and the door irised open. There was a fierce flash of low afternoon sunlight, and the saturated greens and ochres of a verdant ecology. Black shapes circled above, caw-cawing, and closer to hand xe picked up the crunch of some large and heavy animal forcing its way through the undergrowth. Over this could be heard a trilling of birdsong and deeper, whooping animal calls.

> The air was heavy with pollen and micro-organisms. Xe adjusted xir biotic filters and prophylactic defences. Xir skin thickened and xir corneas became opaque to ultraviolet.

> Xir ship was at the head of a long scar of cleared earth, a deep trench filled with broken trees and pulped vegetation. It had come to rest at an angle, pushing up a semicircular bank of earth before it. A stream was fast filling the lower part of the trench, and fish flapped in the shallows. A fine aerosol of pulverised biology hung in the air.

> Xe had no destination in mind. Out to the limit of xir senses, there was no technology more advanced than a stick attached to a knapped flint, no animal with a mind preoccupied with anything more than survival, status and reproduction. This place was primitive, and probably stalked by predators that would not distinguish xir from their usual prey.

> A hornet settled on Ki's forearm. Xe stopped to examine it. Xir mind enveloped its tiny consciousness; xe could taste the serotonin and histamine in its sting. Its yellow and black stripes, xe deduced, were a warning. Xe adjusted her own skin tones to match.

> Even if they had not been completely thought out of existence, The Recess would not find xir here. It would be many lifetimes before xe would even be noted as missing, another minor casualty of this un-orthodox war.

> A plume of smoke was visible through the trees; it was as good a direction as any. Xe set off. The uneven ground was a network of roots and burrows, succulent plants and dense undergrowth. Soft tubers gave under xir weight, coating her feet in an orange stickiness; ants climbed up xir bare legs. A tall fern was unfolding itself to xir right, a fan of tight fractal loops. Beyond a stand of elm trees up ahead the space seemed to open up.

> The ground became marshy, the mud pulling on xir feet. Putrescent bubbles came to the surface. Xe broke through the treeline.

> Xe found xirself on the bank of a river. A short distance from shore, among tall reeds, a hippo sat low in the water, its back a glossy green. Further downstream a wooden walkway, crudely constructed from halved logs slung between stakes, extended from the bank out into deeper waters.

> Along this, towards xir, ran a small figure.

> He was clothed in furs, a patchwork of rabbit and elk; his hair was braided, held back from his face with a bone needle. He had a small leather pouch hung over his shoulder. His face was open, friendly, sun-tanned.

> He suddenly caught sight of xir, and stopped. He looked around, behind him, but he was alone. The only route was forwards, towards the bank, where this strange wasp-person stood.

> He cautiously stepped forwards.

> Ki held out xir hands, palms open. Xe reduced her stature still further and let her bright skin coloration fade, adopting a tone more in keeping with this creature. Xe let the frayed extremities of her mind touch his, and saw xirself from his point of view.

> From the walkway, the wasp-person became just a person. She — or he, it was hard to tell — stood there, naked, devoid of any skin markings that would indicate family or tribe. Their head was bald, their features flat and unformed. They were a newcomer to this place.

> But despite this, he or she was just a normal person. Elegant. Beautiful even. No older than his mother. He decided it must be a woman.

> He moved closer. She seemed to be in distress.

> Ki could sense the thread of thought that connected xir to xir ship growing weaker. Had xe walked too far? No, it was impossible.

> Xir ship was shutting down, xe could feel it. System after system was going dark, simultaneous catastrophic failures in too many quarters to repair. Xe looked at the primitive dress of this creature. Xir hopes of finding someone who could help, someone who could coax xir ship back to full heath, evaporated.

> Xe realised that was not to be.

> This planet was pre-industrial. There was no one here who could heal xir ship. What remained of its autonomous intelligence was entering hibernation, a vegetative fugue state in which it could await some future day in which resurrection might be possible.

> Xir new legs buckled beneath xir, and xe found xirself kneeling in the reeds. Water, stained a rich brown with disturbed sediment, billowed around xir, sending eddies downstream.

> Xe looked up.

> The Neolithic boy, no older than fourteen, looked down at her. He had lost all fear, and an expression of concern flitted across his face. He held out his hand to this peculiar stranger. She certainly wasn't from the tribes to the North, who still staged their seasonal raids, or one of the Bearfoot, whose hateful gods were carved from burned oak. Could she be connected to the roaring firebird he had seen fall to earth,

somewhere out there, deeper into the marshes?

> Could she be a fallen angel, a harbinger from the heavens?

> He spoke a greeting in his local dialect, understood by no more than three thousand people. She seemed to smile, though her jaw moved in a disturbingly fluid fashion, as if there were no bones underneath.

> Ki tried to reach out in return, but xir hands lay motionless in xir lap. The symbiotic relationship from which xir and her ship drew their life-force was attenuating. Somewhere, beyond the trees, it was dying, without xir there to tend it.

> Xe could no longer hold xir head up. Xir chin sunk to xir chest, and xir shape began to dissolve. Without the will to sustain xirself, xe shifted sideways like a shapeless bag, a loose amalgamation of skin drawn over a scaffold of ligaments and cartilage.

> As xir last tattered scraps of willpower dissipated xir hands relaxed, xir fingers opening. Pressed into xir palm was the key: a triangle of metal alloy from elsewhere, an arrow pointing towards new technologies that would not be mastered here for a thousand years.

> But they would be: *Homo sapiens* is a curious and creative creature, and eventually mankind would build a city of steel and glass here, in this very place.

> The boy reached out and took it from her open palm.

> The woman, if that is what she was, seemed to slough off the final vestiges of human form and slide like a boneless eel into the river. Vortices of dark, peat-saturated water closed over her, and a constellation of bubbles rose to the surface. For a moment her hand was visible, bloated like a rotten calf. The fingers seemed to reach out, beseech him; and then the current took it, and all that remained was a dissipating swirl of reeds, like the hair of a drowned Beltane witch.

O

O

•

o

·

·

317 **STRUCTURE**

A ustin judged they must have mere minutes before impact.

It was hard to gauge their speed with any accuracy. The tunnel walls were a blur of concrete cladding; the sections had been marked out with stencilled numbers, but they were passing by too fast to read.

Then the rails ran out.

There was a moment of sickening weightlessness, and then the wheels hit bare concrete.

The note of the engine changed, seem to gain an edge of desperation. The familiar rhythm that had accompanied them all the way from Box Hill vanished as the wheel flanges bit into the cladding. The tender slewed to the left, then the right, ran up the curve of the tunnel and back again, fishtailing behind them. The coupling cracked, broke away.

The tender fell behind, ran higher up the wall, hit a cable and flipped over, somersaulting in the confined space. An avalanche of coal, still carried forward by the momentum, reached out for the engine like a black hand.

Austin heard Ray shout. He turned.

The end of the tunnel was in sight, coming up faster than his mind could fully process. He could see the peeled-back petals of the opening to the Anomaly, their final destination.

"Brace, brace! Impact! Imp—"

Then they hit. There was a shriek of metal against metal, steel forged in the furnaces of Sheffield against alloys of unknown but probably extraterrestrial origin, and they were slammed forwards into the instrumentation.

Ahead the funnel was cut cleanly from the engine, the buffers forced back and up into the undercarriage. The smokebox buckled inward; steam pipes fractured and spat hot steam from fissures the length of the boiler. The front axles snapped, the glass in the cab windows fractured, and a gut-churning banshee scream filled the enclosed space.

Gallons of superheated water broke free from its pressurised container and shot up the walls, twin tsunamis forced back and up, meeting at the apex and crashing down on the roof of the cab.

The locomotive only slowed a fraction.

There was a stuttering of rent boilerplate, and the curled nails of the Anomaly dragged themselves along the length of the engine, gouging deep shiny gashes.

Then they were through. Austin's feet left the floor, and the three of them were weightless, falling . . .

In the absolute dark, all he could see was the faint ruddy glow of the firebox door. A chill silence enveloped them.

Austin counted the seconds. *One, two, three—*

Then they hit something soft, something that gave under them, thrusting the front of the engine up with bruising force.

There was another second of weightlessness, and they hit again. A slurry of mud shot up either side, and their speed began to slow.

The complaining squeal of stressed steel and broken engineering reached a crescendo, and they seemed to come to a momentary halt; then the cab tipped over vertiginously, and they were looking down, along the length of the ruined engine, lit by a mess of red-hot pipework and embers, into the darker abyss of the dig site itself.

There was a second or two of precarious equilibrium, but it didn't last; the front of the engine pitched down, the cab lifted under them, and they fell, the ground coming up one final time to meet them.

A soft, white welcoming blankness enfolded Austin, and he gave himself over to unconsciousness.

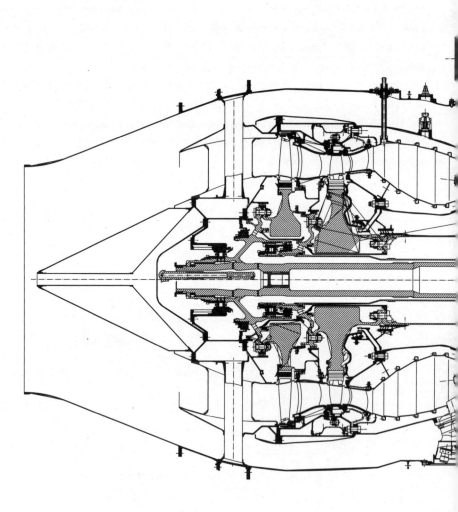

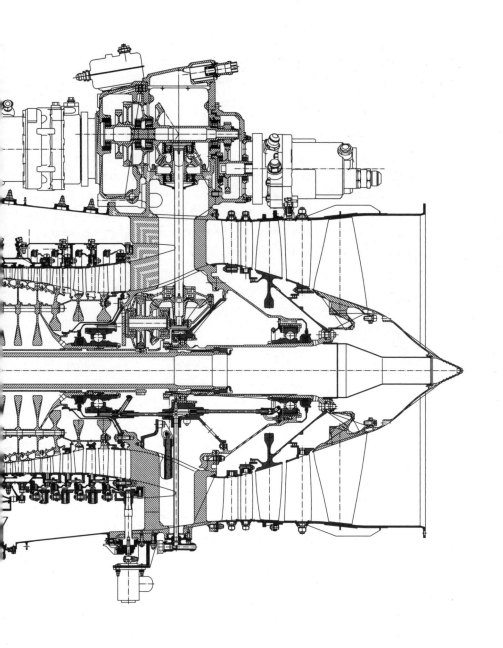

A ustin opened one eye.

It was dark. His ears rang from the unfamiliar silence. His neck ached, his hand had been caught in a railing and twisted back, and the tendons in his lower arm felt as if he'd been lifting weights.

He heard a small scratch, and a match lit. Roger had pushed himself up onto one elbow and was surveying the situation.

Austin's head rested on a big white plastic pillow.

"Airbags? The Strategic Steam Reserve has *airbags?"*

"Health and safety." Roger raised one eyebrow. "The purists hated it."

He reached for an oil lamp that was miraculously still hanging from the interior of the cab, lit it.

"You OK?"

"I'm OK. Shaken and pummelled, but OK." Roger experimentally flexed his fingers, straightened a leg, tried to stand up. The airbag gave slightly under his weight. "Though the Black Locomotive has gone to the scrap dealers in the sky."

The engine, as far as he could see, was canted almost to the vertical. The airbags were between them and the front of the cab. The tender they had left topside, and the back of the cab was now open.

Above them, in the lantern's low light, Austin could see the upper levels of the deserted dig, the carefully excavated terraces, the sections marked out with string, the occasional coloured tag indicating some object of interest.

"Did health and safety have anything to say about kerosene lamps?"

"They did. We ignored them." As he swung the lamp around, dramatic shadows leaped across the stepped banks. In the still air, steam rose up from below in leisurely ribbons, like an evening cigar. They had landed, nose down, with some force.

A sudden realisation made Austin start. "Where's Ray? Can you see Ray?"

Ray was not in the cab.

He looked over the side.

It was as if they were sitting on a white pillow in the turret of a tower; the engine's vertical body had been rammed down into the lower levels of the dig.

Into the hatch.

The hatch itself had vanished under the impact, and the whole surrounding area had been rent inwards, buckling under the force. The engine was now held like a pencil between finger and thumb, and loose sediment from the sides of the dig funnelled through the narrower ends of the long fissure. Above, the lightless floods were now leaning in at a precarious angle, cables looping down around broken ladders. A small mechanical digger was wedged upside down, its scoop deep in the soft silt, just above them.

Roger surveyed the scene. "Well, we've broken through. We're in."

"That we are."

The nearest terrace was just below them, but still some distance out. Austin looked away, across the dig.

There was a strange shape, out at the limits of the lantern light.

"*What*—?"

It was Ray.

He had been thrown free of the cab, and was lying face down on the penultimate level, his left leg bent up and back at an unnatural angle.

Austin judged the jump, stepped back, then took it without hesitation.

He hit the ground, grasped for purchase. The soft earth began to give under him. He reached for an abandoned spade, dug the blade in as forcefully as he could.

It held. He drew himself up.

A moment later he was kneeling beside Ray. He felt at his neck for a pulse, found one. "Over here! *He's alive!*"

A few minutes later Roger was beside him. He hung the lamp on a marker pole and they carefully turned Ray over.

His face was a pulp of blood and dirt. Austin pulled Roger's rag from his belt and wiped his face. "You all right, old buddy? You OK there, Ray, old boy? Speak to me. Tell me you're OK."

Ray opened one eye.

"Hey, hey, hang in there. We're going to get you topside. Don't you worry. Us Smokeboxers, we look after our own."

Ray's face creased into a lopsided smile. His voice was barely audible.

"*If you're down, or in distress*—"A sudden wince of pain shot across his face.

Austin grasped the lamp, swung it around. Across to their right, on the same level of the dig, were two stretchers, left there after the gas incident.

The gas. Austin experimentally sniffed the air. It was cool, with an undertaste of sulphur and iron. His lungs, despite the beating they had taken on the journey here, seemed to be operating normally. It must have dissipated.

Austin pointed. "Roger, help me with that stretcher. We'll take him up to the Crossrail tunnel, try and find help."

Ray had lifted himself onto one elbow and was looking at the engine. *"Sheeeit.* She looks worse than I do."

The three of them paused for a moment.

The Black Locomotive was ruined. Vicious scrapes ran the length of her cylindrical body; her livery had been taken back to the raw metal, which shone in the lamplight like open wounds. Her pistons had burst, her magnificent six-foot-diameter wheels were contorted at unseemly angles, their axles broken, and her connecting rods protruded out from her boiler like broken ribs.

Roger had cared for this magnificent beast for over forty years. He felt a deep shame rise within him, force the breath from his chest. This was not the way she should have gone.

He climbed down to the lowest level and rested one hand on her side, the heat of the metal warming his fingers. Her fire was out; soon she would cool, and in a matter of hours her firebox heart would contain only ashes.

This would be her last resting place. "Thank you, Lord Hawke. You arrived on schedule. You did us proud."

Austin could see that tears were coursing down Roger's cheeks, drawing lines through the soot. Austin climbed down and put a gloved hand on his shoulder.

Roger wiped his face, looked at Austin in awkward embarrassment. He drew a ragged breath and absently smoothed down his moustache, shaking his head.

"Final destination. This train terminates here. All change."

Twenty minutes later Ray had been winched up to the top of the scaffold, just below the entrance. The original top storey had been demolished by their entrance, the hole now four or five times the size.

Austin helped Roger rig a cradle and lift Ray's stretcher up the final metre and a half to the Crossrail tunnel.

"You know I have to go back down. Into the Anomaly. London is in a bad way, and another night without power will be disastrous. I have to fix this."

Roger looked at him. "You sure?"

"Sure I'm sure. It's why we came. The whole purpose of this exercise. This is my responsibility. I shouldn't have let Rutherford out of my sight. Just promise me you'll get Ray topside."

Ray rolled onto his side and lifted himself into a sitting position. "We'll be fine. With Roger's help, I can walk on my good leg. You go."

Ten minutes later, Austin was back at the fissure the locomotive had opened at the bottom of the dig. He held his lamp over the edge. Reaching out, he pressed his hand to the buckled footplate to steady himself. It was held firm, as if in a vice, immobile.

He looked down into the dark space beneath him. The lamp was too dim to reveal anything.

He dropped a stone, heard a small report.

A few metres, tops. Easy. He tied the lamp to his belt and, grasping the buckled footplate, lowered himself down into the hole.

Directly below, a tangle of broken casing and pipework caught at his feet. He swung clear, and hit the ground. Bringing up the lamp, he could see the limits of the chamber he now occupied.

A natural cave? Then why the door?

He quickly discovered the space opened into another chamber, through a peculiar constriction.

Austin knelt, ran a finger along the ground. Rutherford would not be hard to follow. Whatever this subterranean labyrinth was, it had lain undisturbed for millennia; but even sealed from the outside world, a fine precipitation of dust had coated the floor.

Footprints were clearly visible. All he had to do was follow them.

327 PROJECTION

If the first night had mostly been one of impromptu celebration, the second had taken on an edge of desperation.

The mood on the streets was darkening.

All public transport in and out of London was still suspended. Vast parking lots had grown up on the periphery, as close as an idling engine could get. From here, people proceeded by bicycle or on foot. This unplanned pedestrianisation of the capital did have its benefits: the air cleared, and birds could be heard gossiping over Oxford Street.

There was no physical barrier, nothing visible that marked the precise limit of the dampening effect. But at a certain point an approaching car's electrics would fail, the engine would begin to idle, and the steering would lock.

Here, enterprising youths with a nose for a profit stood over racks of hire bicycles, their enforcers in attendance like nightclub bouncers. Other bikes that had not been ridden for decades, their tyres freshly pumped and chains oiled, were changing hands for more than the price of a second-hand Tesla. Trucks ferried supplies to temporary tent villages, where makeshift market stalls had been set up.

Though most of those who ventured into the central zone were essential workers, the nurses, teachers, security forces and engineers, the majority stayed away. Those with more managerial jobs had little to manage – regular commerce, and its attendant support professions, had been suspended by unspoken mutual consent for the duration, however long the duration might be.

Lifts, trams, buses and trains had now all been cleared of passengers by the emergency services. Though no one seemed to suffer ill heath within the zone, a degree of caution was exercised. Those with heart pacemakers or other life-sustaining technology kept well away. Others who had not made it to a phone in time, or who did not have close friends and relatives who were aware of their whereabouts were now, no doubt, lying dead in their homes.

The expected stockpiling of food had not occurred – a good supply had been met by low demand, one easily covered by the entrepreneurs at the periphery.

Tower Bridge, stuck in the open position, had become a skateboarding ramp. Amateur astronomers on Primrose Hill had unobstructed views of the sky, the usual light pollution confined to the suburbs encircling them.

But the previous night's Bank Holiday mood had begun to wane. Like the day after New Year, many were nursing hangovers and contemplating their lives in the lull before the future has had time to get its boots on.

Large groups of people still congregated in the parks, some bringing picnics and drinks, others firearms and bad intentions.

A horizontal banner of smoke vented from the top of the Shard, making it resemble a slim, man-made volcano. Every window along Oxford Street and Bond Street had been smashed, every shop looted. Naked shop dummies lay prone across the pavement, stripped of their designer clothes.

Thugs with visions of bestriding the world like some modern-day Alexander organised their sink-estate militias, every YouTube drill video playing in their heads. Etonian fraternities of barristers in gowns from the Inns of Court prepared to swing their maces, their shirtsleeves rolled up, their skirts tucked into the waists of their sensible opaque tights.

The response from the security forces had been swift; roadblocks had been set up at major intersections, and mounted riot police were out in force.

The looting still spread. Opportunists had tried to steal cars from the showrooms in Knightsbridge, but not being able to start them had set light to them instead. Shops, homes and offices, their alarm systems compromised, had been broken into, but many of the perpetrators, escaping on foot, proved to be easy prey for mounted police.

The BBC sent in reporters equipped with vintage film cameras loaned from the archive, and continued to broadcast from White City, just outside the zone. Offers of help, practical, investigative and financial, came in from around the globe.

Though other cities had braced themselves for something similar, it seemed to be an isolated, one-off event. Several dissident terror groups claimed responsibility, but none of them were taken seriously.

Speculation as to the cause was rife. Was it an electromagnetic pulse attack? Some kind of natural event? If so, it had no precedent. How long was it going to last? The faint tremors recorded when the phenomenon first began had subsided.

Was something happening below ground?

There were only a handful people in the metropolis who knew what the actual cause was.

And their plan to save London was now entering its final stage.

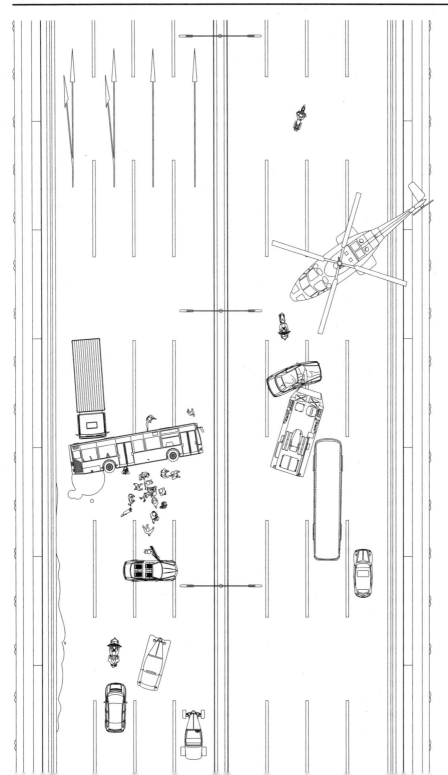

A ustin had spent much of his working life in the subterranean spaces below London, but, as with the torus above, this place defied his expectations.

The air, left undisturbed for who knows how long, was cool and dry; every particle had settled out long ago. There were no currents to disturb the fine powder that took Rutherford's shoe prints like fine flour. He would not be hard to follow, even by the light of the kerosene lamp.

He held it up. Stark shadows wheeled around him, a Vorticist collusion of sharp, bright edges and dark emptiness.

He coughed, and the sound echoed, returned multiplied. He didn't want to alert anyone – or anything – to his presence. Only a few hours ago he had felt jovial and confident, but now he was cautious, out of his depth – this was one machine he didn't understand.

He followed the trail. Sometimes Rutherford seemed to backtrack; other times, there would be evidence of a leap across a chasm, or a suggestion he'd crawled forward on all fours.

He already knew, from the geophysical subsurface radar, that the torus was just a part of a much larger structure, but precisely how extensive it was he had no idea.

There were times where Rutherford's movements were obscure: he'd approach an exit but turn around, a second set of prints leading back out again; or they'd circle an object, as if it was of some special interest to him.

On rare occasions he'd lose his trail completely; then he'd spot a reflective gum wrapper, a little ball of foil, and the footprints would not be far away.

He came upon a circular antechamber, at the centre of which was a series of nested cups, like a fountain.

Then he saw the figure.

It seemed to be asleep, but Austin immediately knew it had been here for a very long time. The body wore a mix of Roman and Celtic clothing, a paper-thin robe of linen, in places no more than a tangle of frayed threads that covered it like a shroud. On its head was a tarnished bronze helmet.

Beside it, as clear as a handprint sprayed on a prehistoric cave wall, was a shape in the dust where something had recently been removed. It had a long shaft, and three prongs mounted at the top, like a trident.

Rutherford's footprints moved around the body, seeming to avoid close contact, but Austin could see scuff marks in the dust around the object's midpoint, where its centre of gravity must have been.

Rutherford had picked up whatever it was – to use as a weapon, perhaps? Why would he need a weapon? This place, as far as Austin could tell, was deserted. Had he had a premonition?

Austin just had his lamp and his fists, for whatever they were worth. Any other equipment he might have pressed into use was back in the dig or the cab of the wrecked locomotive.

He reached out and touched the helmet. It swung around, as if to look at him, and he withdrew his hand in shock.

No, it was just a random movement. It was long dead. He grasped the helmet in both hands and carefully lifted it, letting the head slide out.

It was a woman. Her parchment skin was tight across her cheekbones, her eyes unseeing and opaque, with a frill of an empty iris. Her eyebrows were faint lines, her lips no more than a slit through which he could see a gold tooth. Across her temples and forehead was drawn an elegant floriate tattoo, faded to a pale Prussian blue.

Once upon a time, she had been beautiful.

Who she was he had no idea. Maybe she had managed to gain entry to this maze, and had decided to explore. Maybe she had become lost, and decided to rest a while.

She had lain down here, for the last time, alone, and passed without anyone to comfort her. Perhaps she had had a family who had mourned her disappearance; or maybe no one knew she was gone.

He knew then, without a shadow of a doubt, this would be his fate too; one day he would also lie down for the last time, not here, not on some wild adventure clawing defeat from the jaws of victory, but quietly, without fanfare, at home, alone; maybe a decade from now, maybe three, but he knew it would be another day just like so many others, a day lent a special significance only because it would be his last.

Though he felt as if he might be imposing, he let the backs of his fingers lightly stroke her cheek.

It suddenly came to him that he had not touched another human being with such care and tenderness in decades. Maybe ever.

Austin had, long ago, trained himself not to think too much about physical intimacy, reasoning that if potential lovers never noticed him it was probably for the best if the arrangement was reciprocal. Any contact was on a purely professional level: a handshake, a hand on a shoulder. His close friends were mostly male; this had not been a matter of explicit choice, more a form of self-protection, an unconscious drawing away from the relationships he assumed he'd never have.

If he didn't long for close companionship, for the freely given warmth of someone who loved him, cared for him, who wondered what he might be doing when he wasn't with them, then he wouldn't miss it, and maybe he could be content.

His apartment was just as he left it every evening when he got home: his book open on the bedside table, his vest hanging over the edge of the laundry basket, the half empty cup of coffee in the Starbucks mug still there on the draining board. He could spend his evenings exactly how he wished. He had no living relatives, no siblings, no real responsibilities and no impositions on his freedom, but somehow he still felt trapped, in his mind, in his body, in an existence which he could never see opening up in front of him to contain someone else, someone who would share the intimate spaces of his life.

If he never came back from London Below, who would miss him?

But really, Austin, it would be churlish to complain. He was healthy, for a man his age; he did not want for money. He enjoyed, if in a distracted manner, the rewards of work and the pursuance of his particular hobbies; passions would be too strong a word, as it would have implied a level of emotion he no longer allowed himself to feel.

He found he was crying. Deep, seismic sobs, drawn from the depths of his being.

They were for her, for him, but most of all for the city above that was now in the throes of despair: for London, his first and only love; London, who embraced him and held him tight within her secret inner passages like the wife he would never know.

After a while, he stood.

Austin's thoughts returned to the task at hand. He wondered if he should return to the surface, or at least to the dig site, where there would be water and maybe food. His lamp would last several hours, but it wouldn't last forever.

No, there was no time to turn back.

He moved on. Down here there was no way to gauge the passing of time, and he hadn't thought to wear a wind-up mechanical watch.

He crossed cathedral-sized spaces, where far above there seemed to be not a ceiling but a foam of interpenetrating volumes like frozen bubbles; other antechambers contained rows of curved shapes like giant yellowed teeth pushing up through the floor, or bifurcating growths like the blunted antlers of a rutting antelope.

Even more disconcerting were the gargantuan arenas that seemed to mirror the plazas and squares of some medieval town, a network of roads and alleys dividing blank-faced buildings devoid of windows or doors. These, in their studied half-familiarity, troubled Austin more than he cared to admit; other chambers that contained forms devoid of reference to the world above, without an apparent overlay of symbolism, he found easier to process.

He traversed corridors so narrow he had to turn sideways, holding the lamp up ahead or behind, the walls pressing on his stomach and shoulder blades. Other times, a passage would suddenly open onto a vast, stadium-like space, an empty concert hall maybe, but without seating or stage.

Presently Rutherford's footprints led him into a corridor along the walls of which ran coloured lines. Just ahead was a half-open door.

It looked as if it had been forced open. Austin stepped through. The room beyond was hard to cross – the floor was an uneven network of ridges, like the roots of a tree, not suited to human locomotion. In the centre rose what Austin at first took to be a stump. Moving around the periphery of the room he saw it was a chair: a pilot's seat, a throne perhaps.

At its base was a mummified figure, its disarticulated head placed next to its body.

And in the throne itself sat Rutherford.

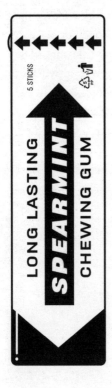

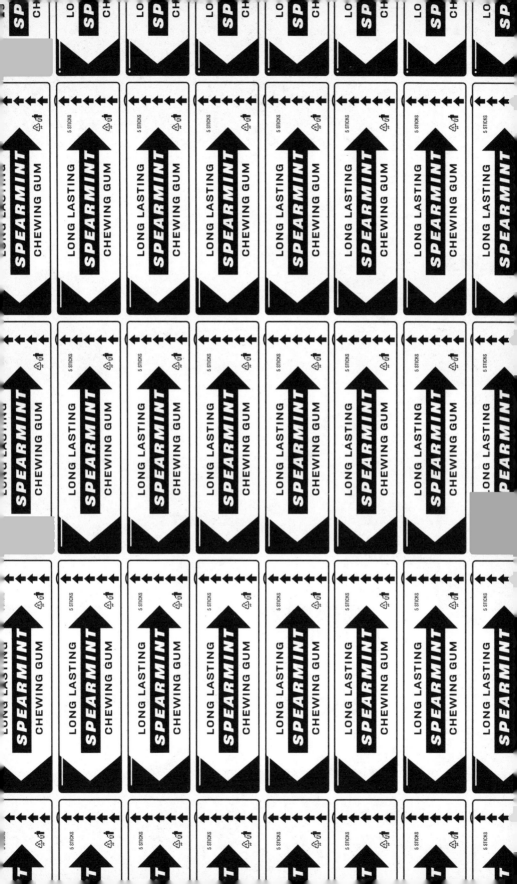

25

339 **ELEVATION**

Inside the throne room, Austin suddenly felt a shift in his inner ear. He braced himself against the wall.

The floor seemed to be tilting – shifting back to the horizontal.

Dust skittered across the ground; one of the Neolithic mummy's detached feet rolled off the dais. The trident, propped against one of the arms of the throne, tipped forward. Instinctively, Austin stepped forwards, reached out and caught it.

Now he was standing closer he could see Rutherford more clearly. The throne had partially encased him, wrapped him in a biomechanical exoskeleton. Articulated booms were arrayed around his upper torso and head, some extruding fine translucent fibres that pierced his skin. He looked like he was being prepped for an operation. His chest was slowly rising and falling. Austin fought down an impulse to run, to get out of this mausoleum.

He held up his lamp with one hand, and with the other pointed the trident at Rutherford's neck.

"Lloyd Rutherford."

Rutherford opened one eye, smiled almost imperceptibly. "Austin."

Austin had no idea what might be happening topside. Here, his only indication that something had changed was the righting of the ubiquitous eight-degree angle. That, in itself, made him very nervous. He pushed the trident forwards, and the central point touched Rutherford's neck.

"Austin. I wouldn't use that if I was you."

"Give me one good reason why I shouldn't separate your head from your body."

Rutherford's eyes closed briefly. He seemed to be supernaturally calm. "Could you really do such a thing?"

"If I can prevent London descending into chaos, maybe I can."

Rutherford regarded him with what seemed to be fondness. "You think I don't care about our city?"

"I have no idea what you care about. You're an enigma, you're . . ."

"A weirdo? A savant? An idiot?"

Austin did not reply.

"I know the streets of London even better than you know the tunnels below. I may not be an engineer, but I think I have some appreciation of what makes a city unique."

"Then stop this. If you can."

"This . . . ship, this machine. I have access to its memories."

Austin wondered if this was a ploy to distract him.

"It's telling me things. Where it came from. How long it's been here. Who originally sat here, in this seat."

"Why should I trust you? Trust it?"

"Because, in a very real way, it is part of our city. It was here before London was even a collection of huts at a crossroads. It has a . . ." Rutherford searched for the right words. "It has a *spirit,* an *energy.* A creative force. It *manifests possibilities*."

It all sounded a bit too New Age to Austin. He was more the practical type. No dreamcatchers. No crystal healing. Just aggregate ratios, load capacities and permissible rock deformation. "And I'm supposed to stand here and allow you to, to interface with this thing? It could be messing with your mind, Lloyd."

"I've never felt more alive than I feel right now, Austin."

"Lucky you. Topside, there are people dying."

Rutherford's expression subtly shifted, and his self-confidence seemed to falter. Had he not been aware of events happening above ground?

"People . . ." Rutherford repeated the word as if it was unfamiliar, as if he was trying it out for the first time.

"People. Like you. Like me. Like, I don't know, Georgia and Sanjay and Yumi and Ray, and eight million more, just like them. London is not just made of concrete and brick and steel. London is made of *people*."

"And who are you in this unfolding drama? Pwyll, the unlikely hero making his epic journey into the underworld? Is this your katabasis? Or do you see yourself as some latter-day Saint George, arriving just in time to save your fair city's honour? Really, Austin, don't you think that trident you're holding to my neck *is* just a tad heavy on the symbolism?"

Austin *had* come in on a monster breathing fire. There was even a George and dragon in 'The Smokebox Song'. But then, if he *was* George, or Arthur, or Pwyll or whoever, wasn't he supposed to *slay* the dragon, not use it as a delivery mechanism?

"At school I dropped English Lit in favour of metalwork. Fuck you and your literary symbolism shit."

"So be it." Rutherford lifted his hand, just a fraction.

In response, the ground shifted under their feet.

Austin pressed the trident's point to Rutherford's neck again. A small drop of blood appeared at the tip. "Whatever you're planning, stop it right now."

Rutherford again smiled that small smile. "I'm just . . . *thinking*, Austin. This magnificent machine was built for thinking. It's a resonator, an amplifier. I think, and lo, my thoughts become actualised."

Austin was of the opinion that reality was not that pliable. There were always the unarguable laws of physics, the brute facts of the matter. Unlike the volatiles of thought, these were not subject to the whim of one man's will, surely?

Now encompassing a sizeable portion of Greater London, the ship's extended field of influence was a sphere; dimpled at the poles, it was described by a three-dimensional set of spacetime equations with its zenith six kilometres above Trafalgar Square. There, if one looked, a pink aurora of charged particles was forming around the inflexion point, a magnetic pinch that was being mirrored deep underground in the beds of Devonian chalk and clay that undergirded the city. The weight was incalculable, but the inertial dampers and localised gravity compensators meant that the city's occupants felt nothing but the slightest tremor, and many of them not even that. Was that a large truck passing outside, a distant thunderstorm, a sonic boom over the Channel, perhaps?

Rutherford closed his eyes, and a furrow of concentration passed over his features. He flexed his new-found muscles. The throne contracted more tightly around him, a carapace of ribbed and articulated alien technology. Bioluminescent flashes cascaded around the periphery of his Kirlean aura.

"Austin, if you knew what I now know, you'd realise there are other, greater dangers to be faced out there. I swear to you I will do my best to see that London – the place *and* its people – will endure."

The ship, and the city that had grown on its back, lifted clear of the ground.

Above, something extraordinary was happening.

For those inside the Anomaly's sphere of influence, there was no perceptible gravitational shift – down was still down, and up was still up.

But other, more subtle changes made the occasional person pause, look around them.

The air became utterly still.

The sun stalled in its progress across the heavens. Early morning shadows halted their advance across the façades of buildings.

This, for the most part, went unnoticed; but then it reversed its direction.

The shadows began to retreat. The first to notice were the flocks of pigeons that rose from the plane trees in Hyde Park and wheeled above, confused and aimless. Seasoned Londoners sensed something was askew, but were unsure precisely what it might be.

Then the sun seemed to increase in intensity.

The volume inside the Anomaly was now fully sealed from the rest of the world, a bubble with its own gravitational vector and angular momentum in which nothing except light of very specific wavelengths could enter or leave.

Inside, a silence absolute now held. The streets were already almost free of traffic; now, the remaining inhabitants stopped whatever they happened to be doing and, alerted by the sun's impossible perambulations, looked up to the sky.

Across the capital, glasses began to hum with sympathetic vibrations; a choir in a sideboard, a symphony hanging above the bar in a Blackfriars pub. The Thames had become perfectly flat, a brown mirror the colour of English breakfast tea.

A complex interlaced harmonic whose epicentre was the Throne Room held it all in place, a field in which the familiar equations of linear Newtonian dynamics had been extruded, flattened, then wrapped around a thirteen-kilometre-diameter sphere.

This sphere, and all it contained, lifted higher.

The haze of the London Basin cleared, and the sky brightened. High above it, a convective updraught sculpted the fine stratocumulus into a beautiful filigree whirlpool.

Freed from inertial mass, the Anomaly now hung a clear half-kilometre above the ground, a cupped hand of earth with an arch of atmosphere above.

It floated above England's fields like a small moon come down to Earth. A polished bauble, made from two perfect hemispheres, the upper transparent, the lower opaque, containing within it an area from White City in the west to Canary Wharf in the east, Highgate in the north to Brixton in the south.

As it slowly rotated, windows in tall buildings caught the low sunlight, sending reflective sparkles across the North Downs like an enormous glitterball.

From below, the subsurface stratigraphy was clearly visible as a series of concentric circles, a layer cake of chalk, clay and limestone, fossilised Carboniferous forests and Jurassic ocean beds. It was a magnificent snowglobe sitting on a base of striated earth, the heart of England contained within a glass bubble.

At the periphery, the transition was sharply defined. Buildings and roads were cut clean through, their internal structures revealed like the cross-section of an architect's elevation; below ground, pipes, Tube tunnels, rivers and sewage systems had all been plugged at the interface, their contents held in a static equilibrium with no place to go.

The Thames was now an isolated stretch of motionless water from Docklands to Putney, a lonely lost dolphin nudging the blocked exit to the North Sea at Island Gardens. Under Putney Bridge a bisected rowing eight sank, the four either side watching their crewmates fall or float away. A bus was halved in Lewisham, a stalled Overground train chopped in two outside Willesden Junction.

There were just under forty fatalities. A jogger lost her legs in Peckham Rye park. A skateboarder at Stockwell Bowl was cut neatly into two in mid-air at the top of a ramp, each half falling away to reveal bone, brain, lungs and stomach, like a prepared medical slide. The Church of St John at Hackney was bisected from the weathervane atop the steeple down through the font. Graves and their occupants were cut clean through at Highgate Cemetery, while the X-ray wing of Charing Cross Hospital in Hammersmith found it was now separated from the main building.

Outside the Anomaly's containing influence, there was nothing to hold back the flow. The Thames poured into the deep crater, in short order emptying its upper reaches as far back as Oxford, where punting undergraduates found themselves stranded on the muddy river bottom. Down through the Thames Estuary came a powerful torrent, the waters carrying shipping over the lip into the abyss from way out beyond Thamesmead. Abandoned cars in the Blackwall Tunnel were flushed out and deposited around the base of the Millennium Dome. The *Cutty Sark*'s enclosure flooded, setting it afloat for the first time since 1954.

In Goldhawk Road, Maud Kingsley stepped out to hang up her washing only to find that her back garden had vanished. Her house now overlooked a six-and-a-half-kilometre-deep pit, into which her ornamental pond had emptied itself, leaving a sole Koi carp flapping uselessly. She could see the pit's smooth-cut face, dark earth pocked with the circular cross-sections of pale roots, and lower down, the familiar diarrhoea ochre of London clay. Away and beyond, thirteen kilometres distant, she could see through a rising mist the towers of Canary Wharf begin to lean. As if in slow motion, like cereal boxes at the end of a conveyor, they were carried over the edge by a torrent of water and alluvial mud, an unstoppable force powered by the sheer weight of the North Sea.

Severed water mains, sewers and tributaries were also sending powerful jets of water out and down, filling the void at a steady rate. A microclimate was forming in which localised showers fell, seabirds circled, and rainbows scintillated in the haze.

Above, London Aloft rotated majestically, precessing like a top, rocking back and forth as it seemed to search for equilibrium. Its mirror-smooth surface reflected the sun, an enormous soap bubble outlined with a golden halo, casting an elliptical shadow back across England's fields to Windsor.

Viewed from inside, the sun appeared to circle as London turned, throwing light into back rooms and alleyways that had only ever been in shadow.

Then it settled, held steady.

In the Throne Room, an inexperienced rider with a blade held to his neck was testing the reins of his new steed. It was unbroken, or at least did not seem to heed his goading; but he was unsure how one might actually control such a machine. It seemed to buck under him, a shifting set of impulses, an entity in its own right that had been adrift without an owner, without a purpose, for four thousand years.

Rutherford sensed a certain joy, perhaps relief, in this interaction; it metaphorically kicked and shook its mane, it lowered its head and sent surges of dopamine cascading into his amygdala.

Austin could see they had reached an impasse. A subsonic hum, felt in the resonant cavity of his chest rather than heard, and an almost imperceptible rocking in his inner ear suggested they were in motion.

If Rutherford was somehow part of this machine, killing him now – even if he could really bring himself to do it – might have . . . unfortunate repercussions.

But could he trust this man?

If what he said was true, he might no longer be in control of his faculties. He could be the agent of an alien technology that did not have our well-being at the top of its agenda, whatever that agenda might be.

The trident wavered. It was heavy, and he could not hold it steady indefinitely.

He was the only other person who knew what was happening. The only person who could put an end to this. It was his responsibility. There was no timetable, no schedule, no works committee above him to which he could defer.

What should he do?

Something buzzed in his pocket.

His phone.

He recognised it immediately – the first two lines of the Smokebox Club song, rendered in a basic MIDI.

Keeping his eyes locked on Rutherford he put down the lamp, hefted the trident to his other hand, and pulled the phone from his pocket. He glanced down.

He had a signal? Down here? How was that possible? Unless . . .

The Smokebox logo was visible. There was a new notification. He unlocked the app and read the message.

He looked up. Rutherford had not moved. His eyes were shut and he seemed to be lost in his own reverie.

Austin knew he might forever regret his decision, but he lowered the trident, letting its tip touch the floor.

If his assessment of the unfolding situation was correct, if this *was* some kind of machine, some kind of engine, they might just need an engine driver.

> He had roused it from its deep fugue, the hibernation it had imposed upon itself in order to heal.
> Over that extended period the local inhabitants of this primitive world had sometimes penetrated its hull, curiously searching around inside it, maybe for arrowheads, maybe for answers. It had watched them with a certain detachment, sensing their simple minds did not have the wherewithal to interface with it directly.
> But maybe it could help.
> Maybe it could inspire them to do better, to pull themselves out of their simple dwellings on the banks of this muddy swamp. Maybe they could build something magnificent, something not just of brick and steel and glass, but of mind: a culture.
> It had lost its owner, but in time maybe it could recruit a new one, chosen from among the creatures that fished and hunted and fornicated above its buried and inert body.
> Maybe it could make a new Ki.

Rutherford tugged at the levers of thought, and felt a response. It was wondering whether to trust him. It could sense he was nervous, inexperienced, but it could also sense he might know how to bring it fully back to life.

It very much wanted to be brought back to life.

He could do it. He could drive this thing. Rutherford pulled back on the symbolic reins, and London rose still higher.

Outside, above, the clouds dropped away and the pure sun of summer, a rare London phenomenon, shone down on the streets unimpeded. Below, there was now a fluffy mattress of clouds.
   The sky darkened to a deep navy, then black.
   And then the stars came out.

Sample 1

Sample 2

Sample 3

Sample 4

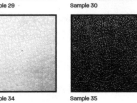

Sample 5

Sample 6

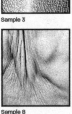

Sample 7

Sample 8

Sample 9

Sample 10

Sample 11

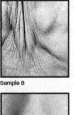

Sample 12

Sample 13

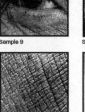

Sample 14

Sample 15

Sample 16

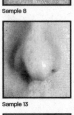

Sample 17

Sample 18

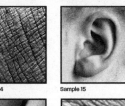

Sample 19

Sample 20

Sample 21

Sample 22

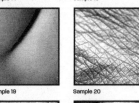

Sample 23

Sample 24

Sample 25

Sample 26

Sample 27

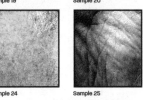

Sample 28

Sample 29

Sample 30

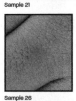

Sample 31

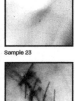

Sample 32

Sample 33

Sample 34

Sample 35

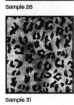

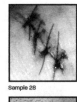

26

351 **BLUEPRINT**

Georgia Ash looked at her phone. The Smokebox Club app was open. New messages were scrolling down the screen in quick succession, one chasing after the other.

The club had existed for over a hundred years, and if the stories were to be believed, many more. In all that time it had operated as a distributed network, one where, with a few exceptions, no one person knew the real name or whereabouts of any other.

For Ash, this had been its USP.

A member could choose a pseudonym, and no one would know whether you were male or female. No one acted as gate-keeper, no one would tell you that you shouldn't be here. You were simply free to share your passion for engineering with like-minded people, without judgement or barriers to entry. In the Smokebox Club, if you had knowledge and curiosity to share, you were always welcome.

Not that societal expectations had ever stopped her. She was somehow immune to the usual teenage pressures to aspire to a specific role or interest or fashion. While her school friends had chased down the latest pair of Reeboks, as worn by whatever hip-hop star they were trying to emulate, she had regarded them as overengineered monstrosities. Why all this non-functional stitching? Why this multilayered sole? Why this particular grip pattern?

They were not elegant solutions to a specific engineering prob-lem – how to build a better shoe – but an exercise in obfuscatory smoke-and-mirrors, designed to justify the high price tag of a status symbol whose only purpose was to position the wearer further up a social hierarchy.

She could see right through it.

In this she had always found herself to be in the minority, so accepted from an early age that that was just how it was going to be. On her civil and environmental engineering degree she had been one of twelve women in an intake of a hundred and ten. Four more years as an aircraft engineer in the Royal Navy and then three as a technical assurance engineer had taught her how to prosper in a boy's world.

She had always found champions and mentors along the way, despite the misgivings of her parents and the attitude of cer-tain managers whose sense of self-importance her competence somehow undermined. Those colleagues had made her feel welcome; they were glad to have a woman on the team.

What they shared with her anonymous Smokebox friends was the pleasure of finding simple, elegant solutions to complex problems. Of these, Crossrail had certainly had more than its allotted share.

There was one promotion, however, she had not sought out.

By all accounts, the Chief Engineer was a position passed down by the incumbent to someone who had risen up through the ranks, who had shown promise and aptitude, someone carefully selected by the previous Engineer.

There was no shortlist of candidates, no open vote.

It was not a democracy.

Like any secret society, its advocates liked to think it counted the great and the good as past members, previous Chief Engineers; like many such societies, she suspected they embellished its history and overestimated its reach and influence.

If the criteria for choosing the next Chief Engineer were arcane or hinged on personal whim, the manner in which the baton was actually passed turned out to be surprisingly simple.

Three and a half years ago she had received a direct message from the Chief Engineer themselves.

> To: Smoke and Ashes
> From: The Chief Engineer
>
> —
>
> It's way past time I retired.
> The scrap-dealer in the sky will call for me soon.
> Will you step up to the plate?

As she read the message the noise in the machine shop seemed to drop away. Her world shrunk to just her and her phone. She looked at the screen for some time, not knowing what the proper form of response might be.

> To: The Chief Engineer
> From: Smoke and Ashes
>
> —
>
> Of course. It'd be an honour.
> Thank you.

There was no fanfare, no ceremonial handover. She was sent an encrypted password that gave her access to the Chief Engineer's account, and that was that.

Respect for the position meant that there were certain protocols to be followed. Smokeboxers could wear the badge, use the hand signal, but other than that all members were still anonymous.

But, as Chief Engineer, she could exercise discretion, especially in extraordinary circumstances. And the situation they now found themselves in *was* quite extraordinary.

If there was an elegant solution to their present problem, the Smokebox Club would find it.

She stood on the roof of 55 Broadway. Here, at the top of the world, above St James's Park Station, above Jacob Epstein's angular sculptures of Portland stone, she looked out over a familiar city rendered unfamiliar.

It was London, the city, *her* city.

Below her the streets were dark, punctuated only with the glow of a burning car or a generator-powered floodlight. She could see flames fluttering in the upper storeys of the Shard like a medieval torch. Distant gunfire echoed through the brick canyons; either that, or the backfiring of a vintage Bentley.

Here, far above the clouds, safe in their bubble of air, London Aloft bore witness to a sight like no other.

They were in low Earth orbit. The sky was thick with stars, a bright scattering of countless points of light. The Milky Way, a curdle of dark clouds against a brighter background, ran from the zenith to the close horizon, just a few kilometres from her position. There, it seemed one could step off the edge of the world into nothingness.

She realised they were still in motion; the sky slowly, gracefully, was rotating around them.

As she watched, a glow formed out beyond Tower Bridge. But this was not the coming dawn, the rising sun shining low through the industrial smog out to the east; this was something else entirely.

The sky lightened further, through a deep purple to heliotrope; then a feathered white arc rose, reaching across her entire field of view. Below the arc, curving away into the haze of distance, were chains of purple mountains, their lowlands a patchwork of deep variegated greens, reaching down to a crenellated shore-line. High cumulonimbus clouds cast long shadows across the landscape.

Beyond, she recognised the Bay of Bengal; Calcutta was a spider's web of light, fading as it approached the terminator between night and day.

It was the Earth.

As it turned beneath her, a second, much smaller crescent rose beyond it. This was a mottled grey, its rough surface unleavened by atmosphere or water.

The Moon.

She had a sudden realisation she was witnessing the workings of a mechanism on a scale she had not contemplated before: the finely tuned balance of gravity, mass and motion that was the solar system itself, the clockwork of the cosmos.

Behind her, the modernist ziggurat that was 55 Broadway's clock tower was silhouetted against the zodiacal light. Its hands had stopped at precisely four thirty, the moment the magnetic disturbance had knocked out the electrical grid.

She lifted her lapel to reveal her Smokebox Club enamel badge hidden beneath. Two lines, like hands on a clock, formed a downward-pointing V in silver on a black ground.

A perfect match.

If she was inclined to divine meaning in such things, she might imagine that there had been a confluence of events that had led her to this time, this place; that everything proceeded with the grace of a well-engineered machine, designed for a clear and specific purpose. But she was an engineer, the Chief Engineer; human ingenuity aside, there was no supernatural watchmaker, and it was the practicalities of their present situation that were now paramount in her mind.

The venue seemed appropriate: though it was currently her office and the centre of operations for the Crossrail project, it had been built in the twenties as the headquarters for the Underground Electric Railways Company of London – the pre-cursor of the London Underground. It had once been the tallest office block in the city, but the city never stood still.

Just below where she now stood, in the oak-panelled drawing room designed a century ago for the chairman and senior exec-utives, she would convene the very first face-to-face meeting of the Smokebox Club.

A column of green dots informed her that there were twenty, twenty-five Smokeboxers currently resident in London Aloft who had answered her call. Would she know any of them?

Would she finally find out who had been riding that black locomotive?

It had passed her at speed, an urgent abstracted force wrapped in a shroud of smoke. Blinded by a spark from the rails, she could not see who was in the cab.

And what, precisely, had taken place below ground?

She guessed she would soon find out.

Churchill, she knew, would be sending her a firm reprimand in his basso voice from the afterlife, but it was time to finally bring the Smokebox Club out of the shed and into the daylight.

As she turned back to the double doors, she began to sing the Smokebox Club song to herself, quietly at first.

"Hurrah for the Smokebox Crew!
Book a seat! We'll ride with you.
If you're down, or in distress,
We're the Happiness Express!"

There was no one else up here. And it might be a lifetime ago, but she still remembered her amateur operatic training. *What the hell.* She sang louder.

"O'er bridge and through the tunnel,
See the smoke shoot from the funnel!
Like the breath of George's dragon,
Roaring on with coach and wagon.

The Smokebox Crew are just the ticket
If you're on a sticky wicket.
Pull the whistle, hear it scree-eam!
The Crew and you can let off steam.

The signal's green, the line is clear
Let me hear the Smokebox Cheer! (Huzzah!)

All aboard! We leave the station,
Friendship is our destination!"

Whoever wrote that could have had no idea they'd end up here.

She guessed the Smokeboxers came from all strata of society. They could be engineers, entrepreneurs and builders; architects, dreamers and politicians, or wasters, scoundrels and whores.

But they would have what she needed: the perspicacity to master old technologies, and the patience to lovingly nurse gargantuan machines back to life.

They'd stoke the firebox, and in no time they'd have built up a fine head of steam. Out here there were no rails to guide them, but rails implied a final destination, and she had no idea where this journey might take them.

An expansive elation lifted her spirit, pushing back a sense of foreboding that had dogged her since the discovery of Anomaly 36. She breathed deep, and the air tasted clean and cool.

If this was just the beginning of a new journey, there was no timetable, nothing had been scheduled. They would have to make it up as they went along.

She turned her back to the view and began to descend the stairs that would take her to the drawing room, and the meeting she had convened.

Through fire and plague, invasion and revolution, the bombs of the Blitz and the belt of the terrorist, London had prevailed.

She had no doubt that the city would survive this current situation – and perhaps even turn it into an opportunity.

The city's strange and creative crew of geniuses and chancers, thugs and saints, always did.

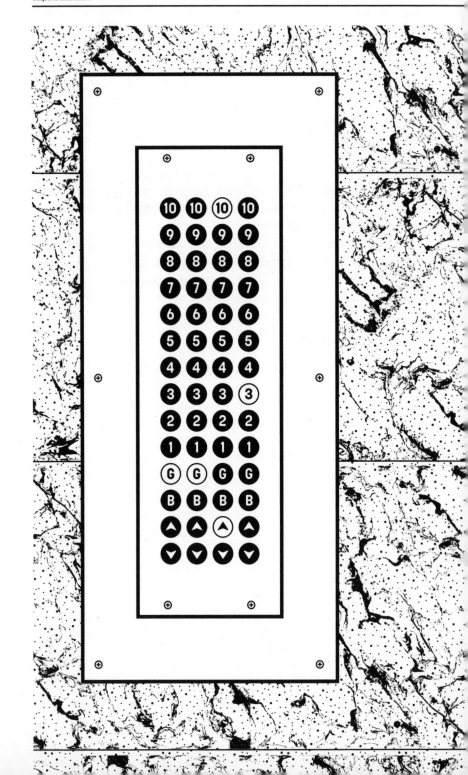

Ten floors below, Austin pushed Ray's wheelchair through the swing doors from the station concourse into the lobby. His leg was in plaster, but he would be up and walking again in six to eight weeks. A step behind was Roger Garcia, his moustache waxed to two fine points, his freshly pressed tweed suit immaculate.

There were a dozen or so other people in the lobby, standing pensively on their own or in pairs around an empty marble desk the colour of dirty vanilla ice cream. Austin regarded them with curiosity. One or two looked familiar, as if he remembered them from television, or had crossed paths with them some time in his career, but he couldn't name any names.

There was a Japanese woman in a sensible office suit, hair drawn back from her face; a couple of kids, no older than fourteen. A young black man in a fur-lined hoodie, head down, who did not meet anyone's gaze.

Other Smokebox members? He'd find out soon enough.

The building's generator must be running: the uplighters were on, and indicators above the lifts suggested they were working too.

Beside each was a round button.

An arrow, pointing up.

Austin pressed it.

ADDENDUM

> Between Mars and Jupiter, hidden amongst the countless small rocks, rubble piles and planetesimals in the asteroid belt, a fourteen-kilometre-long shard of polished obsidian rotated lazily around its long axis.
> It was a Ra barque, and it was pointing directly at Earth.
> A very specific elemental signature had just come to its attention. One it recognised immediately, to a significance of 4.6 Sigma, though many millennia had passed since last it had tasted it. In that time it had circled the sun more than eight hundred times in a state of torpor, each year compressed to an hour and a half from its accelerated viewpoint within a small fold of spacetime. It was nothing if not patient.
> Now it was falling in towards the inner planets, picking up speed as it went. Behind, a collimated beam of tachyons sent news of its discovery back along the fine weft of occlusion space, temporally backshifted so it would reach its destination ahead of time.
> It was an arrow, shot from an invisible bow.
> Its target was London Aloft, and the object that lay beneath it.

Novel analysis 1: **Technical specifications** CAD 367
Not to scale
Subject to amendment

Overview

Title:	The Black Locomotive
Author:	Rian Hughes
ISBN:	978-1-5290-7442-0
Page count:	400
Number of words:	70472
Number of different words:	9911
Number of characters:	401830
Number of sentences:	5049
Maximum sentence length (words):	69
Average sentence length (words):	12.96
Minimum sentence length (words):	1
Number of syllables:	104465
Average syllables per word:	1.62
Complexity factor (Lexical density):	14.5%
Readability (Gunning-Fog Index):	6.9

Word length (characters)	Word count	Frequency
3	15364	22.2%
4	11760	17%
2	10258	14.8%
5	8252	11.9%
6	6747	9.8%
7	5218	7.5%
8	3525	5.1%
9	2414	3.5%
1	2335	3.4%
10	1681	2.4%
11	843	1.2%
12	365	0.5%
13	229	0.3%
14	113	0.2%
15	21	0%
16	19	0%
18	2	0%
17	1	0%

Primary fonts

Lloyd Rutherford	Paralucent Text	Rian Hughes
Austin Arnold	Perpetua	Eric Gill
Georgia Ash	Albiona	Rian Hughes
Yumi Lark	Serenity	Rian Hughes
George, Graham	Goudy Old Style	Frederic W. Goudy
Thelma Sharp	Letter Gothic	Roger Roberson
Fatouma, Charlotte	Urbane Rounded	Rian Hughes
Ice Prophet	Handwriting	Rachel Ainsdale
Ki	Korolev Rounded	Rian Hughes
London	Johnston	Edward Johnston
Title page	Gravesend	Rian Hughes
(revival of type used on original Southern Railway signage)		
Churchill quote	Minion	Robert Slimbach
Song lyrics	Disclosure	Rian Hughes
Chapter dividers	Microgramma	Alessandro Butti

Hardware

iMac

Model Identifier:	iMac13,2
Processor Name:	Intel Core i7
Processor Speed:	3.4 GHz
Number of Processors:	1
Total Number of Cores:	4
L2 Cache (per Core):	256 KB
L3 Cache:	8 MB
Memory:	24 GB

Boot ROM Version:	IM131.0115.B00
SMC Version (system):	2.11f14
Chipset Model:	NVIDIA Geforce GTX
Type:	GPU
Bus:	PCIe
PCIe Lane Width:	x16
VRAM (Dynamic, Max):	1024 MB
Vendor:	NVIDIA (0x10de)
Device ID:	0x11a2
Revision ID:	0x00a2
ROM Revision:	3707
Display Type:	LCD
Resolution:	2560 x 1440
Framebuffer Depth:	24-Bit Color
Main Display:	Yes
Mirror:	Off
Online:	Yes
Rotation:	Supported
Automatically Adjust Brightness:	No
Connection Type:	DisplayPort
Bus:	PCI
Link Width:	x1
BSD name:	en0
Firmware version:	57766a-v1.15
System Sleep Timer (Minutes):	0
Disk Sleep Timer (Minutes):	10
Display Sleep Timer (Minutes):	60
Sleep on Power Button:	Yes
Automatic Restart on Power Loss:	No
Wake on LAN:	No
Auto Power Off Delay:	14400
Auto Power Off Enabled:	1
Current Power Source:	Yes
Dark Wake Background Tasks:	1
Display Sleep Uses Dim:	Yes
Hibernate Mode:	0
Standby Delay:	4200
Standby Enabled:	1
Available Storage:	458.05 GB
Capacity:	1.11 TB
File System:	Journaled HFS+
Size:	1.12 TB

iPad

Storage	16GB
Screen	9.7-inch (diagonal)
Display type:	LED backlit
Resolution	1024 by 768 pixels
Chip	1GHz dual-core Apple A5

Software

Adobe InDesign	vCC 14.0.1
Adobe Illustrator	vCC 23.0.2
Adobe Photoshop	vCC 20.0.4
Notes	4.5
TextEdit	1.13
Glyphs	v2.6.1

Social media

Instagram: rianhughes
Twitter: @rianhughes

Website

rianhughes.com
devicefonts.co.uk

FN Frequency in novel
FS Frequency in comparison sample (English Web 2013)

#	Phrase	FN	FS
1	Hard hat	13	44
2	Dig site	10	21
3	Tunnelling machine	7	1
4	Crash barrier	4	0
5	Drill head	6	0
6	Elevated section	4	0
7	Smoke shoot	4	0
8	Firebox door	4	2
9	Concrete cladding	4	3
10	Sticky wicket	4	0
11	Kerosene lamp	4	10
12	Gas mask	4	28
13	Far wall	4	32
14	Light speed	4	44
15	Correct position	4	62
16	Public outreach	4	70
17	Enamel badge	3	0
18	Tally hut	3	0
19	Split sun	3	0
20	Location marker	3	1
21	Pant pant	3	1
22	Bare concrete	3	2
23	Damp air	3	6
24	Glossy black	3	7
25	Boring machine	3	8
26	Dark material	3	8
27	Dark space	3	9
28	Electromagnetic pulse	3	13
29	Tall tale	3	16
30	Sheer weight	3	23
31	Middle distance	3	27
32	Secret government	3	31
33	Office block	3	38
34	Steam train	3	38
35	Engine oil	3	51
36	Rolling stock	3	83
37	Quick succession	3	96
38	Railway line	3	97
39	Smokebox badge	2	0
40	Motorway crash barrier	2	0
41	Extended being	2	0
42	Q clearance	2	0
43	Motorway crash	2	0
44	Triangular depression	2	0
45	Pneumatic drill	2	0
46	Civic engineering	2	0
47	Fine haze	2	0
48	Subsonic hum	2	0
49	Triangular indentation	2	0
50	Nuts-and-bolts kind	2	0
51	Cage lift	2	0
52	Black livery	2	0
53	Same material	2	0
54	Tour-guide mode	2	0
55	Pant pant pant	2	0
56	Sensory range	2	0
57	Cylindrical shaft	2	0
58	Xir ship	2	0
59	Chicken shop	2	0
60	Supersonic boom	2	0
61	Unlit signal	2	0
62	Bar'roshira Sound	2	0
63	Subterranean space	2	0
64	Complaining squeal	2	0
65	Mock surrender	2	0
66	Metallic tang	2	0
67	Caterpillar track	2	0
68	Geological uplift	2	0
69	Temporary village	2	0
70	Brass wheel	2	0
71	Torch beam	2	1
72	Cylindrical body	2	1
73	Resonant cavity	2	1
74	Scrubby grass	2	1
75	Ticket hall	2	1
76	Half kilometre	2	1
77	Magnificent machine	2	1
78	Peculiar man	2	1
79	Alien origin	2	1
80	Hard radiation	2	1
81	Underground space	2	1
82	Electricity substation	2	1
83	Final destination	4	232
84	Free badge	2	2
85	Atmospheric friction	2	2
86	Black ground	2	2
87	Diesel shunter	2	2
88	Stale urine	2	2
89	Primitive world	2	2
90	Secret handshake	2	3
91	Architectural merit	2	3
92	Arrow point	2	3
93	Short silence	2	3
94	Trestle table	2	3
95	Civic building	2	4
96	Engine driver	2	4
97	Ventilation shaft	2	4
98	Dark stone	2	4
99	Wooden walkway	2	4
100	Coming dawn	2	5
101	Cutting head	2	5
102	Tunnel boring machine	2	5
103	Small platform	2	6
104	Gentle curve	2	7
105	EM field	2	7
106	Wing mirror	2	7
107	Original pilot	2	7
108	Southern branch	2	8
109	Central column	2	8
110	Bare earth	2	8
111	Pale light	2	8
112	Car park	2	8
113	Skeleton staff	2	8
114	Top pocket	2	9
115	Boiler pressure	2	9
116	Hand sign	2	9
117	Low wall	2	9
118	Still air	2	10
119	Black circle	2	10
120	Grey sky	2	11
121	Shopping trolley	2	11
122	Underground car park	2	12
123	Underground network	2	12
124	Domestic space	2	12
125	Perfect city	2	13
126	Catalogue number	2	13
127	Dense vegetation	2	14
128	Harsh light	2	15
129	Hand signal	2	16
130	Diesel generator	2	17
131	Exploratory surgery	2	18
132	Operating theatre	2	18
133	Exclusion zone	2	18
134	Rear wall	2	19
135	Long axis	2	20
136	Natural event	2	21
137	Uneven ground	2	21
138	High overhead	2	21
139	Apartment block	2	22
140	Central pillar	2	22
141	Plate glass	2	23
142	Red glow	2	24
143	Fine mist	2	24
144	Perfect circle	2	25
145	Transistor radio	2	25
146	Due west	2	25
147	Window box	2	26
148	Inner ear	3	154
149	Deep purple	2	27
150	Stunted birch	2	28
151	Laptop screen	2	29
152	Pay grade	2	31
153	Power grid	3	161
154	Jacket pocket	2	32
155	Entire space	2	36
156	Top surface	2	36
157	Wooden frame	2	39
158	Short way	2	39
159	Old technology	2	40
160	Layer cake	2	41
161	Far end	3	184
162	Plastic sheeting	2	48
163	Middle-aged man	2	52
164	Own volition	2	52
165	Top floor	3	192
166	Stuttering breath	2	53
167	Incised border	2	56
168	Dressing gown	2	58
169	Secret agent	2	60
170	Outside world	6	633
171	Entrance hall	2	61
172	Immediate vicinity	2	67
173	White hair	2	72
174	Black smoke	2	72
175	Open position	2	74
176	Rising sun	2	78
177	Short distance	4	384
178	Drawing board	3	240
179	Same material	2	89
180	Back garden	2	93
181	Return journey	2	97
182	Steam engine	2	98
183	Distant past	2	107
184	Degree angle	2	119
185	Social engineering	2	121
186	Symbiotic relationship	2	123
187	Living thing	2	134
188	Middle finger	2	139
189	Shopping centre	2	140
190	Kinetic energy	2	142
191	Civil engineering	2	147
192	Main line	2	147
193	Back cover	2	150
194	Leather jacket	2	160
195	Internal combustion	2	164
196	Right eye	2	164
197	Little interest	2	164
198	Short order	2	167
199	Wedding ring	2	170
200	Cross section	2	183

#	Word	FN	FS
FN	Frequency in novel		
FS	Frequency in comparison sample (English Web 2013)		

#	Word	FN	FS
1	Smokebox	71	37
2	Rutherford	124	27,406
3	Anomaly	34	3,042
4	Lark	29	19,612
5	Austin	251	376,220
6	Yumi	22	8,978
7	Smokeboxer	18	0
8	Ash	58	81,894
9	Trident	17	7,866
10	Barque	12	2,253
11	Crossrail	13	4,942
12	Ra	26	33,909
13	Firebox	14	7,980
14	Black	11	2,448
15	Sanjay	17	18,471
16	Ki	28	46,417
17	Consilience	8	416
18	Subterranean	16	24,530
19	Fatouma	7	45
20	Recess	7	2,936
21	Roger	78	262,063
22	Torch	42	133,312
23	Tunnel	103	359,512
24	Diddi	6	78
25	Arrowhead	9	11,866
26	Georgia	6	0
27	Silt	11	21,552
28	Locomotive	7	6,956
29	Unlit	7	7,002
30	Medieval	7	7,620
31	Pediment	6	3,840
32	Topside	7	8,759
33	Periphery	13	36,856
34	Torchlight	6	5,299
35	Uber	7	9,992
36	Streetlight	7	10,380
37	Fossilise	5	2,022
38	Neville	13	41,708
39	Paddington	7	13,388
40	Huzzah	5	3,712
41	Locomotive	22	94,248
42	Livery	9	26,109
43	Gargantuan	7	15,722
44	Kerosene	8	22,087
45	Ray	92	492,109
46	Updraught	4	131
47	Thames	15	62,140
48	Repurposed	6	12,055
49	Temporally	5	6,625
50	Lloyd	4	1,018
51	Hah	6	13,251
52	Engineer	21	102,465
53	Messageboard	4	1,659
54	Absently	6	13,621
55	Cheer	6	13,723
56	Aloft	4	1,879
57	Rashmi	4	2,124
58	Neolithic	6	14,718
59	Digger	7	21,324
60	Cladding	6	15,356
61	Funnel	18	90,885
62	Stratigraphy	4	2,937
63	Metre	48	281,051
64	Rectilinear	4	3,068
65	Treeline	4	3,086
66	Semiotic	4	3,700
67	Terrazzo	4	3,853
68	Nocturnal	9	37,185
69	Flyover	5	10,841
70	Heft	6	17,668
71	Triangular	10	44,471
72	Indentation	6	18,167
73	Shard	4	4,976
74	Peculiar	23	134,321
75	Oxidise	4	5,105
76	Torus	5	12,307
77	Walkway	14	76,814
78	Fugue	4	6,775
79	Floodlight	5	14,320
80	Chuffer	3	4
81	Consilience	3	36
82	Crowbar	4	7,433
83	Whitewash	6	22,387
84	Kerb	4	7,755
85	Embankment	6	22,850
86	TBM	4	7,925
87	Perambulation	3	774
88	Shunter	3	783
89	Londinium	3	875
90	Cab	24	161,925
91	Heath	6	24,134
92	Sheen	7	33,205
93	Gantry	4	9,769
94	Experimentally	5	18,109
95	Carboniferous	3	2,066
96	Lapel	6	26,415
97	Antechamber	3	2,255
98	Vaporise	3	2,262
99	Dais	4	10,469
100	Crew	12	75,599
101	Detritus	4	10,510
102	Steam	10	59,601
103	Resonant	6	27,047
104	Opalescent	3	2,616
105	Footplate	3	2,654
106	Sleeper	10	60,445
107	Padlock	5	19,759
108	Hatch	22	163,092
109	Undisturbed	6	28,583
110	Amphitheatre	4	11,828
111	Subsonic	3	3,653
112	Cylindrical	6	29,363
113	Memetic	3	3,667
114	Sheeting	4	12,385
115	Girder	4	12,409
116	Roark	3	3,823
117	Hurrah	4	12,502
118	Ziplock	3	4,421
119	Trunking	3	4,445
120	Buckingham	6	31,668
121	Excavate	8	50,036
122	Tunnel	7	41,302
123	Reverie	4	14,199
124	Colonnade	3	5,307
125	Charing	3	5,728
126	Piston	9	61,175
127	Sulphur	5	24,439
128	Trafalgar	4	15,219
129	Mummify	3	5,961
130	Handrail	4	15,330
131	Hub	10	71,764
132	Geometry	15	120,479
133	Spacetime	4	16,068
134	Stalled	3	7,066
135	Stretcher	5	26,446
136	Labyrinth	6	36,190
137	Railway	27	240,508
138	Askew	3	7,279
139	Underpass	3	7,304
140	Interloper	3	7,543
141	Disconcert	5	28,110
142	Filigree	3	8,225
143	Blackness	5	28,401
144	Docklands	3	8,425
145	Forwards	7	49,157
146	Arnold	14	120,800
147	Plinth	3	8,689
148	Badge	19	173,778
149	Audibly	3	9,127
150	Beep	6	40,355
151	Outlast	4	19,763
152	Disassociate	3	9,393
153	Churchill	10	82,729
154	Winch	5	30,639
155	Trestle	3	9,665
156	Footbridge	3	9,760
157	Hydraulics	3	9,864
158	Roaring	3	9,870
159	Ember	4	20,774
160	Hector	6	42,236
161	Tang	4	20,990
162	Punctuate	6	42,593
163	Churning	3	10,365
164	Inoperable	3	10,444
165	Confluence	5	32,182
166	Ochre	3	10,595
167	Bar'roshira	2	0
168	Lactite	2	0
169	Smokeboxers	2	0
170	Backshifted	2	1
171	Hands	2	2
172	Spick	2	77
173	Cabside	2	97
174	Strip light	2	125
175	Throne	17	165,028
176	Annwfn	2	143
177	Doner	2	192
178	Coalesce	4	22,319
179	Slip road	2	240
180	Estuary	3	11,312
181	Relative	2	278
182	Silken	3	11,384
183	Goldhawk	2	347
184	Steeple	3	11,447
185	Circumscribe	2	11,465
186	Crenelate	2	405
187	Clock tower	2	497
188	Lapdance	2	587
189	Disarticulate	2	709
190	Lud	2	732
191	Corsham	2	756
192	Graff	2	766
193	Dexion	2	778
194	Karmann	2	798
195	Tarmac	4	23,518
196	Thamesmead	2	886
197	Iceni	2	998
198	Acton	3	12,421
199	Rust	13	127,163
200	Beeching	2	1,220

Novel analysis 4: **Inorganic structural components**   CAD 370
Not to scale
Subject to amendment

Abutment
Acoustic insulation
Adaptive structure
Adhesives
Admixtures
Air infiltration
Airbrick
Alkali-silica reaction
Aluminium
Anastylosis
Anticlastic structure
Archaeology and construction
Asbestos cement
Ash deafening
Ashlar
Barrier wall system
Base build
Basement excavation
Beam and block
Bedrock
Binding agent
Blinding
Bored piles
Braced frame structure
Brick strip foundation
Brick veneer
Bulk filling materials
Cable net structure
Capping beam
Car park
Carbon fibre
Cast iron
Cellular raft foundation
Chemical injected DPC
Cladding
Clerestory
Coal ash
Cob building
Cold roof
Compartment floor
Compensated foundation
Composites
Computational fluid dynamics
Concrete frame
Concrete slab
Concrete-steel composite structure
Concreting plant
Conoid shell
Construction plant
Construction tolerances
Contextualism
Crosswall construction
Curtain wall system
Curved glass
Demolition
Design for deconstruction
Diamond stitch drilling
Diaphragm wall
Disposable houses
Driven piles
Dry lining
Drywall construction
Ductwork
End racking timber
Excavating plant
Explosives
External work
Fabric structure
Façade retention

Falsework
Fascia
Fast track construction
Ferro-cement
Fibre cement
Fire separation
Flat roof
Floor insulation
Floor loading
Floor slab
Folded plate construction
Formwork
Friction piles
Galvanised steel
Geophysical survey
Geotechnical engineering
Geotextiles
Geothermal pile foundation
Glass block wall
Glass reinforced concrete
Graphene
Gravel
Ground anchor
Ground heave
Gusset plate
Hardcore
Headhouse
Hempcrete
Herringbone strut
High-density floating track slab
Highway drainage
Hydraulic Assisted Bridge
Hyperbolic paraboloid
Intumescent coating
Kerb
Laminated veneer
Lateral load
Lift shaft
Light well
Limecrete
Load-bearing wall
Mesh mould metal
Metal composite panel
Metal fabrication
Micropile
Modular building
Noise barrier
Overbuild
Padstone
Palisade
Pebbledash
Pile cap
Pipework
Pistol brick
Pitched roof
Plaster
Plastic cladding
Polished plaster
Polycarbonate plastic
Polyurethane spray
Power float
Precast concrete cladding
Prefabrication
Prestressed concrete
Quoin
Rafter
Railway engineering
Rapid prototyping
Rebar

Refacing stone
Reinforced concrete
Rendering
Renovation
Resilience
Restoration
Retaining wall
Retrofit
Runway construction
Schematic
Screed
Shear wall
Sheathing
Sheet pile
Shell and core
Shoring
Shotcrete
Site plan
Skeleton frame
Slip form concrete
Socket piles
Soil compaction
Solar shading
Stainless steel
Steel frame
Stepped foundation
Stone dressing
Stratification of concrete
Strip foundation
Structural steelwork
Structural vibration
Structure relocation
Substrate
Survey
Synclastic
Tanking
Tensile structure
Tension cable and rod connector
Tension pile
Terrazzo
Trackout
Translocation
Trench box
Truss
Tunnelling
Underground car park
Underpass
Underpinning
Uplift force
Vertical riser
Vibro-compaction
Wall plate
Welding
Zinc

Novel analysis 5: **Organic structural components**   CAD 371
Not to scale
Subject to amendment

Abdomen
Abducent nerve
Accessory nerve
Acetabulum
Acromioclavicular joint
Anal sphincter
Aorta
Arachnoid membrane
Arm
Arterial circle
Ascending aorta
Atlas vertebra, anterior arch
Atrial appendage (auricle)
Auditory tube
Axillary artery
Basilar artery
Basilic vein
Bile duct
Biliary tract
Bladder
Brain
Bronchi
Bulbo-spongiosus muscle
Cardiac vasculature
Carotid arteries
Carpal tunnel
Carpometacarpal joints
Cavernous sinus
Cephalic vein
Cerebellar peduncles
Cerebral hemisphere, occipital lobe
Cerebral hemisphere, temporal lobe
Cervical spine
Cheek
Chest
Chorda tympani nerve
Chordae tendineae
Ciliary nerves
Clavicle
Cochlea
Colic flexure
Collateral ligaments
Common bile duct
Coronary artery
Corpus callosum
Corpus cavernosum
Corpus spongiosum
Cranial cavity
Cribriform plate
Cricoid cartilage
Crista galli
Descending aorta
Diaphragm
Digital nerves
Ear
Ear ossicle
Ethmoid air cells
Ethmoid bone
Expiration
Eye
Facial bones
Facial muscles
Facial nerve
Female reproductive organs
Femur
Fibula
Fingers
Flexor muscles
Foot

Foramen magnum
Foramen ovale
Forearm
Fossa ovale
Fourth ventricle
Frontal sinus
Great vessels
Greater (long) saphenous vein
Groin
Hamstring muscles
Hamulus
Hand
Hard palate
Head
Heart
Heel
Hindfoot
Hip joint
Humerus
Inguinal canal
Inguinal ligament
Inner ear
Inter-atrial septum
Internal carotid artery
Interventricular septum
Intervertebral foramen
Intestines
Ischium
Jaw
Jugular foramen
Jugular veins
Kidney
Knee joint
Larynx
Lateral ventricles
Left atrium
Left ventricle
Leg
Lingual nerve
Lip
Liver
Long (greater) saphenous vein
Lumbar vertebra
Lungs
Male genital organs
Malleus
Masticatory muscles
Maxillary sinus
Mediastinum
Membranous labyrinth
Muscles
Nasal bone
Nasal cavity
Nasal septum
Nasolacrimal duct
Neck
Nose
Obturator foramen
Occipital bone, basilar part
Occipital lobe (cerebrum)
Odontoid process
Omentum
Optic nerve
Oral cavity
Orbital cavity
Palmar arch
Pancreas
Paranasal sinuses
Pelvic diaphragm

Pelvic muscles
Pelvis
Penis
Perineal body
Perineal membrane
Peritoneum
Phalanges
Popliteal artery
Radiocarpal ligament
Rectum
Rectus sheath
Renal
Reproductive system
Respiration
Sacral
Skull
Spinal cord
Spleen
Stapes
Sternoclavicular joint
Stomach
Sub-arachnoid space
Submandibular gland
Superior orbital fissure
Sympathetic trunk
Tarsus
Tear duct
Temporal bone
Temporal fascia
Temporal lobe (cerebrum)
Temporomandibular joint
Testis
Third ventricle
Thumb
Thyroid artery
Toe
Tongue
Trachea
Transverse ligament of atlas
Trigeminal cave
Ureter
Urethra
Urethral sphincter muscle
Urinary tract
Uterine tube
Uterus
Vagina
Vagus nerve
Vertebrae
Vestibule
Vestibulo-cochlear nerve
Wrist

East entrance

Map 1: **Route taken by the Lord Hawke**
Not to scale
Subject to amendment

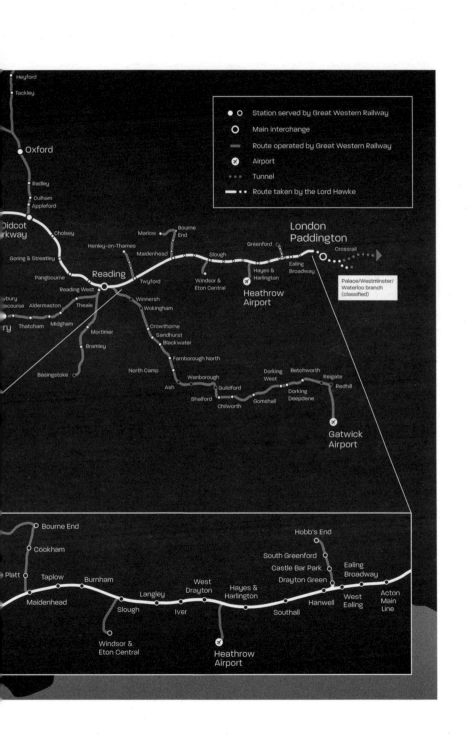

Heyford
Tackley
Oxford
Radley
Culham
Appleford
Didcot Parkway
Cholsey
Goring & Streatley
Pangbourne
Reading
Reading West
Newbury Racecourse
Aldermaston
Theale
Thatcham
Midgham
Mortimer
Bramley
Basingstoke
North Camp
Ash
Marlow
Bourne End
Henley-on-Thames
Maidenhead
Twyford
Winnersh
Wokingham
Crowthorne
Sandhurst
Blackwater
Farnborough North
Wanborough
Guildford
Shalford
Chilworth
Windsor & Eton Central
Slough
Greenford
Hayes & Harlington
Ealing Broadway
Heathrow Airport
London Paddington
Crossrail
Dorking West
Dorking Deepdene
Gomshall
Betchworth
Reigate
Redhill
Gatwick Airport

Palace/Westminster/ Waterloo branch (classified)

● ○ Station served by Great Western Railway
○ Main interchange
— Route operated by Great Western Railway
✈ Airport
• • • Tunnel
—• • Route taken by the Lord Hawke

Bourne End
Cookham
Platt
Maidenhead
Taplow
Burnham
Langley
Slough
Iver
West Drayton
Windsor & Eton Central
Heathrow Airport
Hayes & Harlington
Southall
Hanwell
Hobb's End
South Greenford
Castle Bar Park
Drayton Green
West Ealing
Ealing Broadway
Acton Main Line

Volume 21 number 2, c.1921 *(Earliest extant issue, courtesy of the Churchill Archive)*

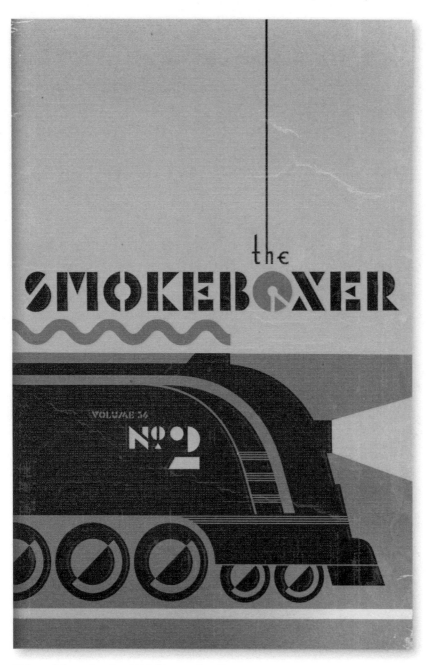

Volume 36 number 2, c.1933 *(issue undated)*

THE

SMOKEBOXER

Nº

CHEMIN DE FER DU MIDI

SOUTHERN RAILWAY
ELECTRIFICATION

"ROYAL SCOT" AND
"FLYING SCOTSMAN" LIVERY

THE CHIEF ENGINEER SPEAKS

STREAMLINERS

·12·

FREE TO MEMBERS

Volume 45 number 12, 1941

Archive 4: *The Smokeboxer* magazine
Not to scale
Subject to amendment

CAD 379

THE

SMOKEBOXER

VOLUME 51, NUMBER 2

NEWS AND VIEWS
SNOWDON MOUNTAIN RAILWAY

STANIER'S BLACK FIVES
THE CHEDDAR VALLEY BRANCH

Volume 51 number 2, 1947

THE
SM●KEBOXER
VOLUME 56, NUMBER 4

This
Issue

TANK
ENGINES

IRISH
RAILWAY
REVIEW

HORNBY'S
'LORD
NELSON'

INDIA'S
RAILWAY
LEGACY

NEWS
AND
VIEWS

3650

Volume 56 number 4, 1953

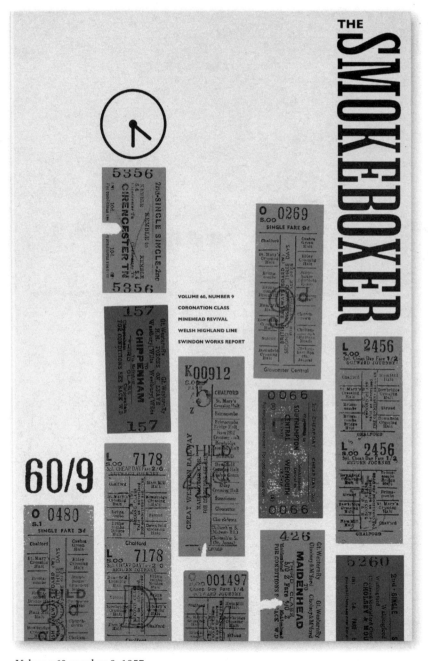

Volume 60 number 9, 1957

SWEDEN'S RAILWAYS
THE CASE FOR THE GAS TURBINE
MONORAILS OF THE FUTURE
THE STEAM RESERVE LEGEND LIVES ON
THE ROYAL TRAIN: A FIRST-HAND REPORT

THE *Smoke* BOXER
EXTRA

VOLUME 62 NUMBER 2

Volume 62 number 2, 1959

Volume 65. *Number* 11

The
⟨ꜛ⟩SMOKE•••
•••BOXER

EARLY MORNING IN THE RAILWAY YARDS

Volume 65 number 11, 1962

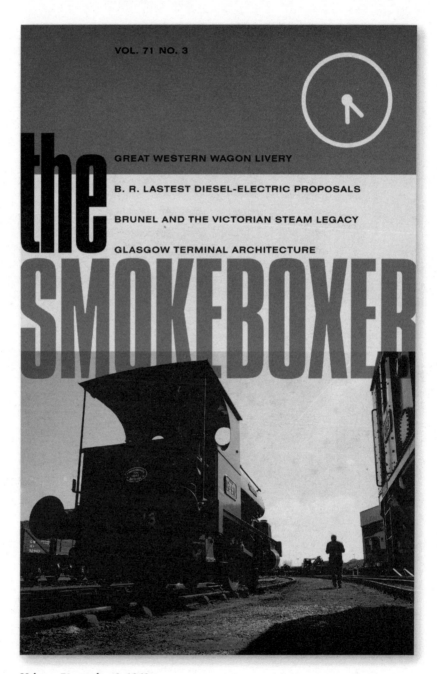

VOL. 71 NO. 3

GREAT WESTERN WAGON LIVERY

B. R. LASTEST DIESEL-ELECTRIC PROPOSALS

BRUNEL AND THE VICTORIAN STEAM LEGACY

GLASGOW TERMINAL ARCHITECTURE

the SMOKEBOXER

Volume 71 number 3, 1968

THE SMOKEBOXER

Free to Smokebox Club members Volume 74, Number 11

Volume 74 number 11, 1971

Archive 11: *The Smokeboxer* magazine
CAD 386
Not to scale
Subject to amendment

Volume 78 number 2, 1975 (*Austin Arnold's personal copy*)

Archive 12: *The Smokeboxer* magazine
Not to scale
Subject to amendment

CAD 387

The

Smokeboxer

Vol.80 No.5

Volume 80 number 5, 1977

Unnumbered 'special edition', 1980

ALL ABOARD!

VOLUME **85**

THE SMOKEBOXER

NUMBER **1**

THE CHIEF ENGINEER —A RAIL LEGACY

FREE TO SMOKEBOX CLUB MEMBERS
SEE PAGE 11: SUBSCRIPTION UPDATE

· 3610 ·

THE BELLES OF NINE ELMS
HOW THE BIG FOUR WENT TO WAR
SOUTHERN STEAM SIGNAGE
THE IRON CURTAIN IRONCLADS

TOOT TOOT!

Volume 85 number 1, 1982

Volume 89 number 4, 1991

Archive 16: *The Smokeboxer* magazine
Not to scale
Subject to amendment

CAD 391

Volume 94 number 8, 1997 *(centenary issue)*

Archive 17: *The Smokeboxer* magazine
Not to scale
Subject to amendment

CAD 392

THE SMOKEBOXER | *Volume 101 Number 1*

Volume 101 number 1, 2004 *(last print issue)*

2015–present

WILL'S'S CIGARETTES

"LORD NELSON" CLASS EXPRESS LOCO. "LORD HAWKE," SOUTHERN RLY.

THIS SURFACE IS ADHESIVE, ASK YOUR TOBACCONIST FOR THE ATTRACTIVE ALBUM (PRICE ONE PENNY) SPECIALLY PREPARED TO HOLD THE COMPLETE SERIES

RAILWAY ENGINES

A SERIES OF 50

10

"LORD NELSON" CLASS EXPRESS LOCO. "LORD HAWKE," *Southern Railway.*

The Southern Railway routes from London, over which the Dover and Folkestone Continental boat trains, such as the "Golden Arrow" Pullman express, are worked, are by no means easy for the locomotives. There are numerous grades and curves, while near London delays are often experienced from the dense suburban traffic. The "Lord Nelson" four-cylinder 4–6–0 express locomotives, named after famous seamen, are used on these workings and also on the "Atlantic Coast" and other expresses to and from Waterloo, Western Section. In working order they each weigh 83¼ tons, and their eight-wheeled tenders 56 tons 14 cwt.

W. D. & H. O. WILLS

ISSUED BY THE IMPERIAL TOBACCO CO. (OF GREAT BRITAIN & IRELAND), LTD.

W. D. & H. O. Wills, *Railway Engines* series number 10, 1936

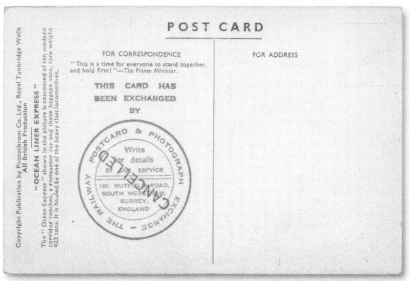

Photochrom Co. Ltd., Lord Hawke on the Ocean Liner Express route, 1930s

Archive 21: **News clipping**
Not to scale
Subject to amendment

CAD 396

Lord Hawke, locomotive number 860, was derailed at St Denys, Hampshire, on 14 August 1940 due to enemy action. A bomb fell on the track ahead of the train, which was unable to stop in time.

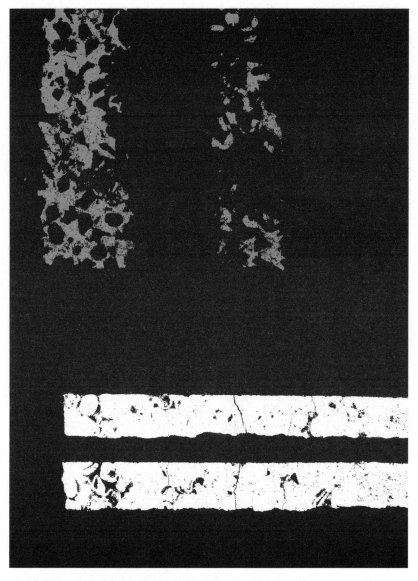

Untitled 50, undated (c.2020), acrylic on Masonite, 174×194cm

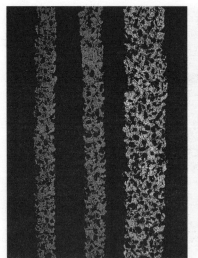

LEFT: *Untitled 31,* undated (c.2016), acrylic on Masonite, 174×194cm
RIGHT: *Untitled 37,* undated (c.2016), acrylic on Masonite, 174×194cm

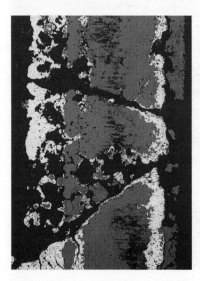

LEFT: *Untitled 8,* undated (c.2010), acrylic on Masonite, 174×194cm
RIGHT: *Untitled 19,* undated (c.2011), acrylic on Masonite, 174×194cm

Artwork 3: **Lloyd Rutherford, *Highway Codes* series** CAD 399
Not to scale
Subject to amendment

Untitled 39, undated (c.2019), acrylic on Masonite, 174×194cm

Naas Library